Also by Jill Shalvis

Colburn Brothers
He Falls First
Free Falling

Falling Into You

JILL SHALVIS

sourcebooks
casablanca

Published by Sourcebooks Casablanca, an imprint of Sourcebooks
1935 Brookdale RD, Naperville, IL 60563-2773
(630) 961-3900
sourcebooks.com

Cataloging-in-Publication Data is on file with the Library of Congress.

Printed and bound in the United States of America.
PAH 10 9 8 7 6 5 4 3 2 1

TO THE BOOK PEOPLE AT 2 A.M. SAYING
"ONE MORE CHAPTER."
THIS IS YOUR FAULT.

PROLOGUE

Tucker

WAS FOURTEEN THE first time I climbed through Hazel Pierce's bedroom window and nearly broke my ass on her nightstand.

Not my smoothest move, but in my defense, it was dark, my ribs hurt, and my plan hadn't extended much past *Get out before Hank wakes up.*

Hazel shot up in bed with a gasp and a swing of her desk lamp like she was about to commit justified homicide. "Jesus, Tucker—"

"Shh!" I hissed, clutching my shin, which I'd just introduced to her nightstand at full speed. "You trying to get me killed?"

"You're the one breaking and entering!"

"Breaking and limping," I muttered.

Her room smelled like vanilla lotion and sawdust from one of her dad's projects, sweet, grounding, and like safety and comfort.

She clicked on her lamp and squinted at me. Her hair was wild, her T-shirt crooked off one shoulder, and she had that sleepy glare that somehow managed to make me feel both scolded and lucky to be alive.

"Your dad?" she whispered, because this was not our first rodeo.

"House was…loud." I was never able to say the words out loud.

Her expression softened. She didn't ask for details, didn't make me talk. She just scooted over on the bed and pulled back the blanket. "You take the bed. I can sleep in the chair—"

"No. The floor's fine," I lied.

"You're not sleeping on the damn floor. There's room for two."

She didn't have to tell me twice. I climbed in next to her like it wasn't the thing I'd been wanting all damn year.

We'd been neighbors since kindergarten, best friends since we were fourteen, and she was the girl I'd been secretly in love with since the first time she punched me in the arm and made me laugh, when normally all I wanted was to disappear.

She turned on her side to look at me, and I saw the second she caught sight of my swollen lip. I was grateful when all she said was "You look exhausted."

"Thanks. Real boost to the ego."

"Anytime," she said, and her smile, that slow, crooked smile that could stop traffic, made my chest feel weird.

We were silent for a few minutes. Me, because my eyes kept drifting closed, my mind finally able to shut down for a few, her because she was thinking, which I knew because she was doing it loudly.

"Was it bad?" she finally asked.

"No." Another lie.

She nudged my socked foot with hers under the blanket. "Kiera asleep?"

"Yeah. She's getting good at pretending everything's fine."

Hazel nodded, eyes shadowed. "Yeah. I know that trick."

That landed like a stone in a still pond. No splash, just deep and true.

She lay back, staring at the ceiling. "One day we're gonna get out of here."

I smiled because she said it like a promise. "You think so?"

"I know so." She turned her head toward me, her eyes catching the moonlight slanting in her window. "We're meant for more than this town."

"Pretty sure my life goals start and end with sleeping eight uninterrupted hours."

"We'll find a place where that's possible."

"'We'?"

She shrugged. "Someone's gotta make sure you eat breakfast and don't die of man flu."

"Sounds serious."

"It's a work in progress."

We both grinned, but the air between us had changed—charged, humming, like something was about to shift if we dared let it.

She yawned but didn't look away. "Your lip's bleeding," she whispered, like she couldn't not say it.

I swiped at it. "Barely."

She sat up, rummaged through her nightstand, and came back with a crumpled tissue. "Hold still."

Her thumb brushed the corner of my mouth, light and careful, but the touch jolted through me like a live wire. Every nerve in my body woke up at once.

Hazel froze too, her breath catching, eyes flicking to my mouth.

We stayed like that, close enough for me to feel her heartbeat in the air between us, close enough that the scent of her shampoo made my chest ache.

Then she cleared her throat and mumbled, "Okay, stop staring at me. I know how wild my hair is, thank you very much."

I loved her hair, but the moment snapped. Too bad my pulse didn't get the memo.

"You can stay till morning. But if my dad finds you, I'm telling him you were here fixing my leaky sink."

"I don't have any tools with me."

"Guess you'd better be quiet, then." Her voice was a whisper as she turned off the light. The room filled with moonlight and the faint tick of the clock on her nightstand.

"Hey, Haze?" I said into the dark.

"Yeah?"

"Thanks."

She didn't answer right away. Then, almost too soft to hear: "Always."

Outside, a coyote called from somewhere past the ridge. Inside, I listened to her breathing, steady and sure, a rhythm that loosened something tight in my chest.

And for the first time in a long time, I didn't feel trapped.

I felt at home.

CHAPTER 1

Hazel

Star Falls—population: still too damn small

ON MY PERSONAL LIST of terrible ideas, moving back to Sonoma County ranked somewhere between cutting my own bangs and texting my ex after midnight. I'd called it a new beginning, like that made it less terrifying. In reality, I'd come back for a do-over I wasn't sure I deserved, complete with small-town drama, unavoidable awkward run-ins, and of course…Tucker Colburn.

Nope. Not going there. Not when the sun was shining and I had a piping-hot breakfast burrito made by my friend Penny at her café, Redwood Roost. I took another bite and moaned. Nobody, and I mean nobody, could make a breakfast burrito like Penny. Served all day, no questions asked.

Take that, McDonald's.

Cruising down Main Street, I had the windows down and music up, and the late-summer air carried the scent of Monterey pines, eucalyptus, and just enough exhaust to keep it real. I stuffed another bite in my mouth and sighed in pleasure at the symphony of fluffy eggs, crispy bacon, and melty cheese on a toasted roll.

Pure bliss.

It should've been smooth sailing. Still, anxiety wormed in like a splinter you couldn't remove. Here I was, on my way to work. I'd become the proud (if slightly frazzled) owner of Pierce Custom Woodworks, fighting to lift it off the ground since my return. Sure, I'd nabbed a few small gigs, but around Star Falls, I was still the infamous teen terror, not exactly the poster child for trust.

I had two contracts at the moment, one of them with Colburn Restorations, which meant every site visit was basically emotional Russian roulette. Would today be the day I ran into *him*?

Tucker.

Not if I saw him first. I mean, looking at his ridiculously hot self whenever I caught sight of him was bad enough. But having to talk? No. I still couldn't even say his name out loud without something sharp pressing behind my ribs.

Tucker was exhibit A for a good guy with an asshat streak. He had presence, the kind that drew attention without even trying. Add in a boatload of annoying charisma. And then there was his smile, the one that made you want to slap it off his face one second and kiss it the next.

Teenage me had wanted to do both.

Teenage me *had* done both…

But I'd left him in my rearview a long time ago.

A car coming the other way on the narrow two-lane highway drifted over the line far enough to have me grinding my teeth as I swerved. My sunglasses slipped and my burrito wobbled.

Sophie's Choice, breakfast edition: my sunglasses or the burrito.

That was easy. My glasses hit the floorboard like a sacrifice to the highway gods. But the burrito? Secure. And still glorious. I took another huge bite as I settled back into my lane and… dribbled hot sauce down the front of my white tee.

I looked like a walking crime scene.

This didn't stop me from taking another bite because this burrito was better than sex. At least from what I remembered. I was thinking about that and wondering if my lady bits still worked when a wasp flew into my work van like it owned the place, legs dangling, wings buzzing, buggy eyes locked on mine.

Someone screamed.

Spoiler: It was me.

I panicked and did the only logical thing. I threw my burrito at it.

The wasp ducked.

Ducked.

Then dove straight for my face, its demon eyes narrowed in battle mode.

My brain slammed the red panic button. Full system shutdown. There was a sharp pain right between my eyes, my tires squealed, and then a gentle but still jarring impact. Almost in slow motion, my van tilted, then lurched, sliding down a slope like a rickety carnival ride and straight into Star Falls Creek.

What if I drown? What if no one even notices?

What if I never get the chance to right my wrongs?

The van thunked to a stop in the center of the creek. I braced for a rush of water, already making a plan: Break the window, crawl out, swim to shore, go straight to the convenience store for chocolate as a reward for surviving.

But…no water poured in. The creek fed into the Russian

River, which in turn dumped into the Pacific Ocean. At any other time of year, the creek would've been raging, but because it was late summer, it was barely a few feet deep.

I wasn't going to drown.

Yet.

My head spun, and I sucked in a breath. Right. I had a big problem, a really big problem, and it wasn't that I'd tried to submerge my van.

I'd been stung right between my eyes, and…I was allergic to wasps. Already, my tongue felt thick, like it belonged to someone else.

I had maybe ten minutes.

I fumbled to release my seat belt, then hesitated. My work tools were in the back. All my custom gear, from molding blades to trim templates to specialty wood bits I couldn't afford to replace. Everything that made my business possible.

If I opened the door and water rushed in, I'd destroy it all. So I grabbed my backpack, climbed out the window, and dropped into the water. It lapped at my calves, cold and real.

Too shaky to make it to shore, I climbed onto the hood, heart racing like a drum solo, vision tunneling.

I was on borrowed time.

I shoved my hand into the front pocket of my backpack for my EpiPen just as I heard the unmistakable *whoop-whoop* of a siren.

Of course. Awesome. An audience. Fine. Whatever. I'd need a ride to the hospital anyway.

I shaded my eyes and took in the road above where flashing lights crested the ridge. A truck with *Star Falls Fire Department* stenciled across the side.

And, oh, hell no.

Tucker freaking Colburn, in his service blues. Even if his face gave absolutely nothing away, his presence hit me square in the chest, a sucker punch of regret and muscle memory I hadn't asked for.

My stomach had hit my toes. *Why him?* Why now?

"Go away," I called out to my biggest regret in the history of ever. My heart pinched, and I had to work to get the words out. "*Just go away.*"

But did he? No. He stepped out slowly, hands raised like I was a wild animal.

I certainly felt like one.

"I'm here to help," he said, his voice annoyingly calm. Steady. It only made everything worse.

We both knew I didn't deserve his help. But that had never stopped him before.

He might be the youngest Colburn brother, but he was the tallest, six four-ish, and leanly muscled in a way that drew attention. I refused to let it draw mine as he pushed his sunglasses up onto his head and gave me that tight-lipped, frustratingly cocky-as-hell look. The one that said he knew exactly how to get under my skin, the gesture so achingly familiar, it gave me a gut and heart check all at once.

When we were teens, he'd been my best friend before he was anything else, the person I trusted with every secret I couldn't tell my dad, pretending we weren't already orbiting the same sun.

And then one night, we stopped pretending.

But that had all been a very long time ago.

"I'm not going anywhere with you," I said, voice annoyingly shaky. I'd been going for heavy sarcasm because it was easier than remembering how it had felt to be seventeen and completely in love with him.

"Wanna bet?" he asked, unruffled as ever, those green-and-gold eyes making me want to cave and spill all my secrets.

Well, except the one.

I opened my mouth to fire back…except my eyes welled up.

No. Not happening. I would *not* shed tears in front of Tucker.

I turned away, pulled the cap off the EpiPen, winced in anticipation, and jabbed it into my thigh. My hand shook so bad, I nearly missed. The sting of the needle was sharp, but it was the rush of relief that nearly buckled me.

From the shore came a low mutter. "*Fuck.* You were stung."

I closed my eyes. It would get better in three to five minutes, I assured myself, but pressed my palm into my chest like I could force the medicine to kick in faster. Anything to get air. Anything to get my sea legs back so I could hightail it out of there.

On my own. Like always.

CHAPTER 2

Tucker

MY HEART STOPPED DEAD in my chest, like someone had yanked the damn plug. Because there was Hazel perched on the hood of her van like some bloodied-up, half-drowned warrior princess, calmly stabbing herself with an EpiPen.

I scrambled down the embankment, dry summer grass crackling under my boots. The sun slanted low behind Hazel like a damn halo. She lifted her gaze, locking those baby blues on me like a heat-seeking missile. Her wavy red hair flew around her face like she'd just walked out of a hurricane. Or maybe *she* was the hurricane… And her expression? It said loud and clear that she blamed me for every single one of her problems.

Which seemed fair. She was, and always had been, my biggest one.

She had a nasty wasp-sting welt on her forehead and blood spattered down her white tee. She was shivering hard enough to rattle her bones, dragging in air like it hurt.

Jesus. "How long since you were stung?" I demanded, splashing through the creek, eyes locked on hers.

"Go away," she croaked, tossing the spent EpiPen aside and pressing a trembling hand to her chest.

For better or worse, I knew this woman. She was riding the edge between throwing up and passing out, white-knuckling it while the epinephrine—pure adrenaline—did its job, constricting her blood vessels, boosting her blood pressure, and, best, forcing her airway open. She could also have internal injuries from the crash. We needed a doctor like ten minutes ago. "Hospital. Now."

"I know that wasn't a command," she wheezed. "Because last I checked, you're not the boss of me. So kindly"—*gasp*—"fuck off."

Right. Should've remembered. Cool and calm was my default setting. *Except* with her. Then I was pure bark and zero chill. But seeing her like this—hurting, wheezing for air, so damn stubborn—nearly broke me.

I couldn't lose anyone else. Especially not her. "You need to—"

"I *know*." She was already sliding down the hood like a spiteful mermaid. I lunged to catch her, but she slapped my hands away. "Don't touch me."

I raised my hands in surrender and followed her as she slogged through the shallow creek. She slipped twice before I swore and scooped her up, my hard look daring her to argue.

She didn't, which told me just how bad off she really was. Her head lolled against my shoulder, eyes drifting shut, but her arms still wrapped around my neck like her body hadn't gotten the memo that she was mad at me.

Like she'd forgotten how to hate me for half a second.

And maybe I'd forgotten too. Maybe I was holding her tighter than I needed to. Maybe I even let myself breathe her in because she was scented with something addicting and innately her and…the worst kind of temptation.

And why did she fit tucked against me, like she'd been born for my arms?

I carried her up the embankment and glanced down at her pale face, ready to hold her until the ambulance arrived, but she slapped her palms to my chest.

"Down."

"Hazel—"

"*Down.*"

"Okay, Tough Girl." I set her down, keeping a grip on her arms when she wobbled. Once she steadied, she shook me off. Heaven forbid she admit to a weakness.

"Déjà vu," I said.

"You've got that backward." She turned and started walking.

I blinked at her back. What the hell did that mean? *She'd* been the one to leave. And now… "*Where are you going?*"

She kept moving, not even close to steady, and my frustration simmered, sharp and familiar.

Lately, it seemed like I was drowning in it—from work, from Hazel, and also from Hank. My dad, who'd once been the biggest hard-ass in three counties, had suffered two strokes last year, followed by a craniotomy. In the mind fuck of the century, he'd come out of the ordeal nonverbal.

And…different.

These days he was golden retriever coded: sweet, unpredictable, and completely unaware of the chaos he left in his wake. Before, when he'd still been a gruff old bastard, he'd managed to get himself kicked out of every assisted living center in the area. Now, my siblings and I were taking turns caring for him. And lucky me, it was my turn. Penny's grandma watched him when I was on shift, but other than that, it was just the two of us and the chaos he'd personally gift wrapped and handed me.

"Hazel."

She didn't turn around. Already halfway down Sweetwater Street, framed by late-summer eucalyptus trees and shiny, touristy storefronts, she gave me a hand-up, palm-out gesture. "Not today, Mr. Bossy McBosserson."

"You used an EpiPen," I called. "You *have* to go to the hospital. You know this."

Nothing. She kept walking.

"I didn't ask for attitude," I muttered.

"Oh, it comes for free," she tossed back, still walking, middle finger high like a royal wave.

Shit. I climbed into the truck and crept along after her, windows down, lights on, siren chirping once. "Hazel."

She jammed in a pair of earbuds with shaking fingers like she was just out for a breezy stroll and not about to hit the pavement. Running when things got tough, like always. She'd been running her whole life, like the summer her dad had smashed her bike and she ghosted me for weeks, or when she'd bolted the night her mom's birthday had hit too hard. Every time life cut close to the bone, she disappeared—mentally, physically, or metaphorically.

Only difference now that we were adults was that I kept waiting for her to stop.

I pulled up next to her. "Get in."

She ignored me, one arm wrapped around her ribs. Blood stained her shirt, and I didn't even know where it was coming from. Too many possible answers, and none of them were something I wanted to find out here on the street.

"Please," I said. "*Please* get in."

She finally deigned to glance over, eyebrows arched. "Did that hurt? Saying 'please'?"

I ground my back teeth. "If I say yes, will you get in the damn truck?"

"Try me."

"*Yes*," I growled. "It physically pains me to say *please* when you're about ready to face-plant on the road. Get in or—"

"Or what?"

Fuck. She wanted to play? Fine. I'd play. "I'll tell all your secrets."

She laughed. Sharp and disbelieving. "You wouldn't dare."

I gaped at her. "You're seriously doing this now? You rolled back into town *months ago* without so much as a *Hi, Tucker, oh good, you're still alive. So sorry I ghosted you for over a decade.* And now you want to mouth off while actively dying?"

She rolled her eyes so hard, I heard them rattle.

Done. I yanked the PA mic from its cradle on my dash and hit the button so that my voice projected down the street. "In eighth grade, after Hazel Pierce was suspended for allegedly plagiarizing her sex-ed paper, she broke into her classroom and turned the whiteboard into a crime scene: fallopian tubes with fangs, sperm in riot gear. Permanent marker. Parental emails for days. She was nearly arrested for vandalism."

"Like that's a secret," Hazel muttered and kept going, even as she wobbled, running on adrenaline and spite alone.

Shit. We passed the convenience store, which had been owned and run by Mrs. Cantu and her son, who'd lived on the second floor for as long as I could remember.

I hit the mic again. "Mrs. Cantu, it was Hazel who ding-dong ditched you every night for years."

If looks could kill, I'd be dead, the murder weapon Hazel's icy baby blues. And I got it; it'd been a low blow. Mrs. Cantu had always had it out for Hazel, certain she was the one shoplifting candy bars from the front display, telling anyone who'd listen.

And since Hazel hadn't actually shoplifted as accused, she'd done her best to get even with the admittedly mean-spirited shopkeeper.

We kept moving, the sun casting long golden streaks across the horizon.

Hazel slowed but didn't stop. It'd be an impressive use of the adrenaline if she weren't about to give me a heart attack. "And let's not forget when she 'renovated' the gazebo overnight," I said into the mic. This also wasn't that big a secret, but I was just pissed off and worried enough not to care. "Built a trapdoor, reversed the benches, and hung three hundred water balloons on the cupola. The whole thing collapsed. That time, she was most definitely hauled down to the police station, but the only thing they could prove was that she'd gotten into her dad's vodka." I knew this was a low blow, that she'd had an unhealthy relationship with alcohol that year, but had by all accounts given up drinking that midnight and had never looked back.

Hazel nearly fell over but righted herself.

God damn it. I went nuclear. It was hard to keep my voice even. "Hey, remember when Adam Weller told everyone you'd slept with him and you egged his dad's dental office in retaliation?"

Hazel stopped short so fast, she nearly fell over. I tossed the PA mic down and was out of the truck in a flash.

She slowly pivoted, and I could have sworn her eyes looked

suspiciously shiny as she stabbed her finger into my chest. "I never slept with him, and you know it."

I did know it. The dick had made up that part, and I'd wanted to kill him for it.

Given how Hazel was looking at me, she also felt murderous. I'd have to sleep with one eye open tonight. I glanced at my watch. Five minutes since the adrenaline had hit. She was going to crash any second, and my worry kicked up ten notches.

So, naturally, Dr. Adam Weller, now the town dentist himself, chose that moment to open his office door, still in his white coat.

"What the hell?" he grumbled.

Hazel shot him a scowl that could've cracked enamel, a warning to stay out of this as she aimed all her fire at me. "*You* egged this place. You never told me why."

I grabbed the hand she still held in midair, entangling our fingers. She was trembling like a leaf. "You know why," I murmured.

"I *don't*," she whispered, tugging. "And I'm still not speaking to you." Her eyes narrowed, but color was leaching from her face.

"Walk or carry?" I demanded, and when she didn't answer, I scooped her up again and carried her to the truck. "And, hey, I didn't even get to tell everyone why the courthouse clock still plays 'Twinkle Twinkle' every hour: You rewired the bell system yourself, leaving a note signed 'Time Bandit.'"

She made a sound low in her throat—could've been a laugh, could've been a sob.

I found myself hugging her tight. "Get in the truck like a good girl, and I won't tell anyone your deepest, *darkest* secret."

She stilled, a flicker of something in her eyes. Vulnerability. Maybe hurt. Definitely hesitation. "You don't know my deepest, darkest secret," she finally said.

I gave her my slow, dangerous smile and used the poker face my mama had given me. "Wanna bet?"

"Please let me down," she whispered.

I did. She stared at me for a long second. Then slowly turned to the passenger door, wavering.

I gave her a second, letting her choose.

She brushed against me as she leaned on the truck, all tremble and fire, and I hated how much I still knew her, that I still knew the exact sound she made when she was on the edge of capitulation.

The way she tipped her chin like a dare. The way she made surrender look like war.

"You're bleeding," I said.

"I'm not."

"Your shirt—"

"It's hot sauce."

"Hot sauce?"

Her eyes narrowed. "If you laugh, I'll find the strength to deck you."

"Haze," I said softly.

At the sound of her nickname, her breath caught.

She dropped her head to my chest.

I felt it then, the full-body sigh she didn't mean to give me. The way her weight shifted, just slightly, like maybe she was tired of fighting.

Screw it. I lifted her into the seat, buckled her in, and slid behind the wheel, purposely not looking at her, not wanting to hear any objections as I took off for the hospital.

And the most terrifying part?

She didn't object. Not a single peep.

CHAPTER 3

Hazel

Lying on a cot in a curtained ER cubicle was bad enough.
Having Tucker pace nearby like a tiger with a grudge?

Torture.

"If you keep that up," I murmured, "you're going to burn through the linoleum and drop straight into the morgue."

He didn't respond, just kept pacing, all broad shoulders and jaw muscles ticking, his shadow stretching beneath the harsh fluorescent lights.

"You know I'm going to live, right?"

He glanced at me—same dark eyes I used to love to stare into, same impossibly sexy mouth—and I was hit with the realization that he'd had twelve years of living without me. Twelve years of experiences and memories.

"Sit. You're making me dizzy."

He folded his tall frame onto the stool beside me. "You scared me today."

"And you annoyed me. So, really, we're square." I smiled to

soften the words, then tried to sit up straighter, wincing because my whole body ached. "I'm going to assume the nonstop PA system humiliation was your twisted way of keeping me from going into shock."

He neither confirmed nor denied, but he didn't have to. Like it or not, I knew him. He could calm down a bear cub in a thunderstorm and also piss one off just as fast, not that I was about to feed his ego and tell him that.

"Look…" He rubbed the back of his neck. "We can't change our past. But we can put it behind us. Especially since it sounds like you'll be around for a while."

"Hopefully not." I was here only until my dad was back to himself after suffering a heart attack not too long ago. But Tucker had a point. "So, what, a truce?"

He gave me one of those crooked smiles that might have melted a bit of my frost. The one I used to think was just for me. "Why not?"

I let out a half laugh. "How long do you think a truce between us will last? We don't agree on anything."

"We could—"

My dad barreled into the cubicle like a Category 5 storm. No knock, no warning, just bluster and concern rolled into a scowl.

"What the fuck happened?" he snapped, turning on Tucker like he'd personally launched the wasp.

Tucker raised his hands. "Wasp got her. She's okay, Bill."

"I want a moment alone with my daughter." Dad was five seven, tops, but the way he held himself—like he could handle himself in any ring—usually had people hurrying to give him what he wanted.

And yet Tucker looked casually to me, a question in his gaze.

He wasn't going anywhere unless I asked him to. So I did. "I'm betting you have to get back to work anyway, right?"

He hesitated, like he wanted to say something, or at the very least finish our conversation, but in the end, he left without another word.

Not surprising. Nor his first time.

Dad plopped onto the now-empty stool, breathing hard.

"Dad, I'm okay. *Breathe.*"

"You breathe," he grumbled, but he stayed seated.

I was propped up with pillows, IV in one arm, hospital smell in my nose—antiseptic, cafeteria coffee, and faint salty air from a cracked window—while my dad hovered like I was six and had scraped my knee. But I wasn't six, and after years of awkward calls and very occasional visits, things felt…off between us.

And I had no idea how to bridge the gap.

"The doctor said to rest," he said. "And relax."

I gestured at myself, prone on the bed. "Check and check."

"I know your mind's going a million miles an hour." His eyes held worry. "Work. Your van… You're lying there worrying."

Fact: I was twelve-out-of-ten worried. Being my own boss came with perks, like always having the final say, and no mandatory team-building in matching shirts. But it also meant the buck stopped with me.

I had a small crew: Tex, a seasoned veteran who acted like he'd invented the hammer, and Annie, a newbie with the enthusiasm of a golden retriever and twice the bounce. They were both great, but I hadn't yet put them on a jobsite without me, and I wasn't ready to do that now either.

Of the two jobs I had going this week, one for the county fairgrounds (which needed its pavilion rebuilt) and the bigger job for Colburn Restorations (which restored historical landmarks and was the best of the best) the latter was almost done. I'd been awarded the emergency finish-carpentry contract after Ricky Herman, the previous subcontractor, had faked having all his tools stolen, committed insurance fraud, and picked more than one fight on-site, causing chaos and instability that threatened the entire job, earning himself a one-way ticket off the project.

I wanted to prove I was the right person for the job, but something felt off about it. Just little things, like small changes to our work that no one could explain. I needed to be there, a clear presence.

My other job was on a tight deadline. Missing that deadline would mean eating a 5 percent penalty. Not the end of the world, but enough to sting.

And here I sat on my ass, no one's fault but my own.

"Tucker handled your van," Dad said.

I sat up so fast, I got dizzy. "What?"

"He didn't tell you?"

"He did not," I said through my teeth. "Why would he do that? It's not his problem." *I* wasn't his problem.

"Well, technically, as an emergency responder, it was his job to make sure it didn't stay in the middle of the creek." He shrugged. "But you've met the boy. No one can tell him what to do. Or not do."

That my dad still called Tucker *the boy* gave me a secret satisfaction. Tucker was many things—big, tough, bossy, maddeningly competent—but *boy* wasn't one of them. He was all man. Muscle, grit, command. The kind who made you forget your own name. Or maybe scream his.

The jerk.

"I didn't ask for his help," I muttered.

"Doesn't matter. Van's already at Mo's Auto. Tucker said there's barely a scratch and that your tools are safe and locked inside."

"I didn't need help."

My dad snorted. "You never do. But maybe, for once, you could let some of us who care about you step up."

Ugh. Emotional ambush. "I'm fine, Dad. You know that, right?"

He shook his head, the lines of stress on his face seeming deeper than they'd been yesterday. "You could have died, kid."

The decades-old pet name hit me square in the chest. "But I didn't."

He shook his head. "You're like a damn cat with nine lives. Who knows how many you've got left?" He pressed a hand to his chest.

Alarm sparked and I shot upright. "Chest pains?"

"No. *Dad* pains. I want to cocoon you in fucking Bubble Wrap."

I liked that he wanted to. That he still wanted to keep me safe, even after everything. Even when I'd made it so damn hard to love me. "I'd just bust out."

He huffed a half laugh, and for a heartbeat, we were in sync in a way we hadn't been since before Mom died my freshman year.

We didn't do deep. We never really had, but especially not since I left Star Falls at eighteen after my dad and I had an epic fight in a long string of epic fights. It hadn't been just that to make me run. Lots of things had contributed to it, and I hated to think about it.

Since I'd been back, we'd kept things surface level. A polite waltz, both of us carefully avoiding old bruises, but I could feel his expectations, his hopes and dreams hovering over me like I could feel the air pressure change with an incoming storm.

He scrubbed a hand down his face. His coppery beard was grayer now but still matched my hair. He was built like a spark plug, Ryder always said. But even spark plugs burned out. After his heart attack, he'd been forced to dial it back. I knew the adjustment hadn't been easy, and I softened.

"You need to think about yourself more." I nodded at the heart monitor he wore around his wrist like a watch. "You're still working too many hours and eating like a teenager."

"Only when you're not looking," he said with a slight smile.

"*Dad.*"

"You might as well ask me to stop breathing." He eyed my IV. "You in pain?"

"Just the pain of being separated from my phone." It was going off in my jeans, hanging on a hook behind him as we spoke. "Can you hand it to me?"

"The nurse said to rest."

"Never mind." I tossed the blanket aside. "I'll get it myself."

He swore beneath his breath and fished my phone from my pocket. "You know where that stubborn streak comes from, right?"

"You."

"Your mother," he corrected. "She's probably up there on a cloud right now, bossing around the angels, especially your guardian angel for letting you get hurt."

That made me laugh, and for another heartbeat, we aligned. Then my phone buzzed for the millionth time.

PENNY:

> You okay?

EMMA:

> Need anything?

KIERA:

> DO NOT check socials unless you want to see yourself looking like a drowned rat in my brother's arms.

The good news? I had friends.

The bad news? Star Falls still gossiped at the speed of light. I shut off my phone and flopped back against the pillow.

My dad frowned at my monitor. "You're stressed."

No kidding.

He studied me. "I know you need more jobs lined up. I'm working on it."

"Dad, I've got it." I'd inherited his love for woodworking. He was a foreman at Colburn Restorations, run by Tucker's older brothers, Ryder and Caleb. Tucker was their project estimator around his firefighter shifts.

My plan was to do such a good job for them that they'd keep sending contracts my way.

"I want you to be happy here," he said stubbornly, complete with a chin jut. "And I've got a plan."

Cue my blood pressure. "Dad. No."

"It's a good one."

"No."

"I'm going to get Ryder to hire you full-time."

"This is not your problem."

"I'm your father; everything about you is my problem. And with the quality of work you put out, you deserve the contracts from Colburn Restorations. Ryder knows this."

"That's not the issue, and you know it."

He grimaced because yeah, he knew. My dad and I clashed on a good day. We tried, but we were each other's kryptonite. Mom had once made Ryder promise to keep us from killing each other and to never, ever let us work together.

Ryder, who had loved my mom, took that promise seriously. But more than this, he'd carefully built an incredible company with an impeccable reputation. He loved me like a sister, but the job he'd given me had been an emergency, or he never would've hired me.

"We're older now," Dad said. "Smarter. Wiser."

Debatable. Especially since we hadn't allowed ourselves to go any deeper than *How was your day?* and *Gee, the weather is nice.* We'd tiptoed around everything else, including the elephant still firmly in the room. "Ryder won't break his promise to Mom just because you're feeling optimistic," I warned.

His face softened. We'd lost her years ago now, but she'd been our glue, the one who'd loved her people more than we'd ever been able to love ourselves. The grief had never faded.

Dad didn't argue my point, just met my eyes. "You let me worry about Ryder."

Oh boy. Ryder was the eldest Colburn sibling and took being in charge seriously. He always said he'd lost years of his life trying to rein in the much wilder Tucker. To this day, Tucker was the only one who could go toe-to-toe with Ryder and keep breathing.

My dad probably sympathized with Ryder in that he'd definitely lost years of his life to my youth.

"Today made me realize we have too much distance between us," Dad said quietly.

"I mean…" I smiled, trying to tease. "You're right here."

He rolled his eyes. "You know what I mean, smart-ass." He hesitated. "Maybe we can start meeting each other in the middle."

"Maybe." It would certainly be new.

"Okay, good." He cleared his throat, smiled awkwardly. "I'd like to hug my daughter now. You have a problem with that?"

We hadn't hugged in years. Maybe a decade. I knew that was on me. I hadn't been a great daughter. Fact was, I'd never been great at *anything*. I'd tried really hard to grow up, but that deep-seated doubt, the one that said I'd never be enough, was still there. "I—"

He pulled me into a solid, warm bear hug.

"Okay…" I patted his back awkwardly. "So we're doing this."

"Don't make it weird."

I snorted and…hugged him back. He smelled like tool oil, and—"Dad. Did you eat *bacon*?"

"No."

"Then why do you smell like bacon?"

"Well, there might have been bacon on my cheeseburger. It's my cheat day."

I pulled back to stare at him. "You're not *allowed* cheat days!"

"*Everyone* needs one. Bacon makes me happy."

His monitor beeped.

I raised my brows.

"Hey, it's because I got to hug my daughter, that's all." He smiled, warm, relaxed, truly happy.

I sighed. "Your phone's been going off too. I'm sure you've got work to get to."

"You kicking me out?"

It was my turn to soften. "I know how we both feel about hospitals. I'm cutting you loose."

"Be good," he said.

"Right back at you."

He kissed the top of my head and walked out, leaving behind the scent of bacon and maybe, just maybe, second chances.

The curtain swished shut behind him, and I leaned back, tired.

But it wasn't the wasp I thought about. Or even my van.

I thought about Tucker.

About how he hadn't said goodbye. About the night twelve years ago. He hadn't said goodbye then either.

It wasn't fair, how much real estate he took up in my mind, still.

We never talked about that night. We didn't talk at all, not the way we needed to.

Probably safer that way.

Because if we ever did talk about it…

I wasn't sure I could survive what he'd say.

CHAPTER 4

Tucker

AFTER RUNNING SEVERAL CALLS at work, I went back to the hospital, pausing in the doorway of Hazel's ER cubicle. Cheeks pale, eyes closed, Hazel looked so damn vulnerable in that hospital bed, but I soaked up the sight of her, exhaling for the first time in hours.

Even as I reminded myself, *You will not fall for this woman again. Not now, not ever.*

Nurse Allie was finishing up checking vitals and gave me a subtle nod. Hazel was going to be okay.

I nodded back, my shoulders easing a fraction.

Allie gave me a second look, this one less subtle, eyebrows raised. Her silent question: *You two a thing?*

I opened my mouth to give an unequivocal no. But the image of Hazel sitting on top of her van, bloodied and fierce, wielding her EpiPen like Badass Barbie, surged through me again. Something deep in my chest stirred, like my heart was saying, *I'll take that one.*

"Wait a minute," Hazel said, voice gravelly. "What was that?"

"What was what?" Allie was fussing with the blanket keeping Hazel warm like it'd offended her.

"The little nod you gave the Human Thundercloud over there."

Allie grinned. "Just telling…*the Human Thundercloud* that your vitals are looking good."

Hazel blinked. "Why?"

"Why?"

"Yeah. You dating him or something?" Hazel gestured to me, as if there were any doubt who the *him* in question was.

Allie burst out laughing. Loud.

I crossed my arms, giving her my best unimpressed-firefighter stare.

She laughed harder. "Lord, no. He's a complication wrapped in sin, sure, but I don't do complicated."

"I'm not *that* complicated," I muttered.

Hazel snorted, her expression saying I was the King of Complicated. Then she laughed, the sound unexpected and beautiful.

I felt my armor crack. "I'm not," I insisted.

"Oh, please," Hazel said, waving the IV-free hand. "You have rules for *everything*."

Rules kept people safe. And the alternative—chaos, loss— tore holes in people that never healed. "It's just good sense."

Allie exchanged a look with Hazel, who almost smiled but caught my gaze and glowered instead.

Felt about right.

Allie patted Hazel's arm. "You know, you're lucky this guy showed up so quickly today. He saved your life."

"She saved herself," I said, and yeah, my voice was gruff with pride. She was brave. Reckless. And still the most beautiful goddamn disaster I'd ever seen.

Allie cocked her head, studying us. "I feel like I'm missing something."

"You're not," Hazel said. "Unless you count him abusing the PA system to publicly shame me into getting in his truck."

"Oh, that." Allie grinned. "That must've been a fun walk down memory lane."

Hazel sighed dramatically.

"Honey," Allie said sympathetically, "what teenager makes good decisions?"

Hazel shrugged, then closed her eyes.

I stepped closer before I could stop myself, worry jamming up my throat.

"Doc'll be in any second," Allie said, patting Hazel's shoulder. "You hanging in there?"

"I get to leave soon, right?"

"Why?" I asked. "You in a hurry to kill another wasp?"

She cracked one eye open. "Is this what we're doing now?"

Allie leaned in and stage-whispered, "He uses sarcasm to deflect from the fact that he cares deeply."

"Thanks, Allie," I muttered.

"Anytime."

"I'm really fine," Hazel said. "Can't you break me outta here?"

Allie shook her head. "Hospital rules. Observation for a few more hours. But I can offer you some lime Jell-O."

"Awesome." Hazel eyed me. "But he can go, right?"

Everyone in the room looked at me.

"Your call," Allie told her.

I took a step back.

"Wait," Hazel said.

It was ridiculous how fast I paused.

"I…um…want to thank you," she said. "For getting my van handled. I really appreciate it." She offered a small smile, and damn if my damn heart didn't seize up like a rusted valve. Her wild hair was barely tamed in a ponytail, that hospital gown not doing much to hide those sweet curves I remembered all too well, and don't get me started on those baby blues, which could ice or warm in a single heartbeat.

"No big deal," I finally said. Lie. I'd called in favors to get it done so fast.

"It's a big deal to me." She lifted her gaze to mine. "You were there when no one else was."

Her voice was quiet, but it hit hard. She didn't have to explain. I'd seen inside her van. It was not new by any means, but other than the muddy exterior from the swim in the creek and the small dent in the front bumper, it was in good shape. It was also her sanctuary. Tools perfectly stored, interior spotless, shelves built with a kind of care that said it mattered. It wasn't just her livelihood. It was her home away from home.

"The interior was untouched," I said. "Only the bumper took a hit, a small one. Mo's already on it."

Relief poured off her like a wave. "Seriously. Thank you."

I should've left it there. But something about her getting emotional over the van instead of for herself, for surviving what could have killed her, flipped a switch. So, sue me, I poked the bear. "Do your thanks include the actual rescue?"

Her eyes flashed. "You mean the public-humiliation part?"

Okay, so I'd definitely taken that too far. But keeping her

angry had kept the adrenaline flowing during the time it'd taken me to convince her to go to the hospital with me. I shrugged. "Or the part where I pulled you out of the water."

"I saved myself."

"Fact," I said simply.

She blinked in surprise as Dr. Ortiz parted the curtain like he was entering a party. "Well, if it isn't two of Star Falls's biggest troublemakers."

Hazel muttered something under breath that sounded like "Next time I'm faking amnesia."

He winked at me. The guy had stitched me up more times than I could count.

"I half expected it to be you on that bed," he said, then looked at Hazel. "Heard you had quite the adventure. Still letting this guy rub off on you, huh?"

Allie snorted.

Hazel rolled her eyes.

Doc laughed. "I don't know who was wilder growing up, you or him."

"Him," Hazel and Allie said in perfect unison.

"Standing right here," I said.

Doc clamped a hand on my shoulder. "And now you're one of the good ones."

"Cue his savior complex," Allie said.

Hazel choked on her water.

Doc grinned as he reviewed the chart. "Vitals look good. We'll keep you a little longer, then send you off with two epinephrine pens. No repeat visits, yeah?"

"How much longer?" Hazel asked.

"In a hurry to escape us?"

She offered him a smile. The kind of warm, genuine smile she hadn't given me in a very, very long time. "Don't take it personally."

He grinned and left.

Hazel held out her arm expectantly.

Allie moved to disconnect her IV. "Glad you're okay. Big guy here was beside himself."

Another fact. My first-responder composure vanished around Hazel. Allie patted my arm, adding a knowing wink, acknowledging the fact that in all the times I'd delivered patients to this hospital, she'd never seen me anything but focused, in control, and levelheaded.

I was exactly none of those today.

"You've got a crowd waiting on you," Allie told Hazel.

Hazel blinked, slow as an owl. "What? Who?"

"Your dad," Allie said. "And your entire family."

"My dad's my only family."

Allie raised a brow. "Ryder and Caleb aren't your brothers? Penny, Kiera, Emma—figments of my imagination? Hank's here too; Kiera picked him up for Tucker from his daycare."

Hazel glanced at me, stunned. That she still had no idea how much she meant to people slayed me.

She bit her bottom lip, taking it in, trying to decide how she felt about being claimed.

I almost laughed. Hazel Pierce, fierce and brave and tough as they came, undone by people caring about her: Ryder, Caleb, and Kiera, for starters, along with Penny and Emma—Ryder's and Caleb's better halves, Hazel's best friends.

"They all tried to pile in here," Allie said. "Front desk kicked them out. So they ordered pizza for the whole staff as a bribe." The nurse grinned. "We love pizza."

Hazel looked like she'd won the lottery, then found out she owed taxes on it.

"I'm going to go work on discharge papers." Allie leaned in. "Try to go easy on him. He's not used to being emotionally attached to the people he rescues."

"He's not emotionally attached." Hazel shook her head. "Not to me."

"I feel emotionally *mugged*," I muttered.

Allie chuckled but paused to look at me. "How's your knuckle-head brother?"

"Which one?"

"Ha." Allie had briefly dated Caleb years ago. He'd ghosted her long before meeting Emma, and these days he walked around like he'd swallowed a Disney soundtrack. "Still a knucklehead then," I said.

"At least he made the most of seeing the three stars fall."

I groaned. "Please don't."

"The legend's real, Tucker."

The Legend of Star Falls was just that: a tale, lore that said if you were lucky enough to see the rare phenomenon of three stars falling in an arch together across the sky, your soulmate would find you. "It's a bedtime story some lovesick teenager made up to avoid their algebra homework."

"Both Ryder and Caleb saw it, then fell in love." Allie smiled. "And rumor is that Ryder and Penny sneaked off last month, flew to Hawaii, got married, honeymooned, and got pregnant all on the same trip."

True story. We were still giving them shit about it.

"And," Allie went on, "Caleb and Emma are planning a big wedding bash for next summer. Coincidence? I think not."

I sighed, and she laughed and left.

Hazel's eyes were closed, face still pale as death, but I could read the sardonic curve of her mouth. She might be down, but she was not out.

Silence reigned, and I realized it was the first time we'd been alone in a room since she'd been back. I needed to make good use of it before she kicked me to the curb and went back to not speaking to me. "You ever going to tell me what really happened?"

Without opening her eyes, she pointed to the welt in the center of her forehead. "Wasp tried to kill me."

"You know that's not what I mean."

She rolled her eyes, then winced and gingerly touched the sting. "Ow."

I took a step toward her, but she shook her head, holding me off.

"Okay," I said, "how about this? I'll answer any question you want if you just tell me why you've been ignoring me since you got back."

The slightest flicker of emotion crossed her face. Then: "Go away."

"No can do," I said.

"Sure you can. Just turn that admittedly very fine ass around and walk out. You've done *it* before."

Her voice wasn't loud, but it landed like a punch. I didn't have a comeback, not one that wouldn't bleed. I exhaled slowly. "I'm not walking away. That's not what people who care about each other do. We stick."

"I'm not surprised you think that. You always assume people care about you."

"People care about you too, you know."

Silence.

"We should talk, Haze. Like *really* talk."

"No, thank you," she said politely.

"Fine." I shook my head. "Bad idea. Forget it."

"Done."

My phone buzzed. Emergency tone. Fire call.

"Saved by the bell," she said. "You gotta go."

Shit. I did. It was the job. Always had been. But this was the first time I didn't *want* to walk away. And that's what scared me most. Because if I didn't walk away, it meant maybe I never really had.

Hours later, after a fire call involving a backyard bonfire, two tipsy teenagers, and a very flammable inflatable Santa, I stared at my phone and gave in to temptation.

ME:

Can I call you?

HAZEL:

You can.

I called and got her voicemail.

ME:

You don't pick up?

HAZEL:

I never said I'd pick up.

ME:

What is wrong with you?

HAZEL:

Unfortunately, too many things to name.

HAZEL:

Hazel has left this chat.

ME:

That's not how that works.

No response. Clearly, she had no interest in what we'd once had. She'd been the one real thing in my life.

Hell of a time for me to realize I still wasn't over her.

CHAPTER 5

Hazel

It was hours before I escaped the ER. Kiera, Emma, and Penny sneaked past the front desk and camped out with me, until Penny launched into a graphic reenactment of the time she and Ryder had gotten caught in his office mid-deed.

By Tucker.

"His face," Penny said, eyes gleaming over the rim of the ginger ale that she was drinking for her morning sickness that lasted all day. "Pure horror. Like he'd walked in on a nuclear disaster. If he'd been wearing pearls, he'd have clutched them."

I laughed so hard, I triggered a mild asthma attack. Which, apparently, gave the nurses an adrenaline jolt, because they swarmed me like I was coding. My friends got booted while I got hovered over like I was flatlining.

Honestly, how many mortifying things could happen to one girl in a single day?

Finally, Allie showed up with my discharge papers. She waited until I was signing to casually say, "So. You and Tucker…"

I nearly dropped her iPad. "W-what?"

She gave me a knowing smile. "The whole town's been talking about you both. Wondering if you're going to chase him again."

I just stared at her. The *again* part had me lifting my chin. "Never."

"I mean," she added, ignoring my comment, "that face of his isn't hard to look at." She winked. "Neither is anything else of his…"

The memory of his *anything else* had been indelibly imprinted in my mind. His jawline. His hands. His firefighter's grip. His ridiculously perfect ass… I sighed as my betrayal-happy brain played a montage reel across the back of my eyelids.

Allie left with a wink, and I sat there, stuck in a hospital gown that seemed determined to flash my butt to the world. My clothes were bagged, still wet and filthy.

Excellent.

Everyone *not* wearing scrubs had been kicked out, which meant it was time to do something I hated more than mansplaining, humidity, guys in flip-flops, and motivational TikToks combined.

I was going to have to do my least favorite thing: ask someone for help.

Then the curtain swung aside and in walked Kiera. As always, she was effortlessly put together: perfect jeans, perfect messy updo, perfect resting judgment face. Caleb always teased her that the reason she had zero patience for BS was that on the day they'd handed out patience, she'd left early when it took too long.

But what I loved about her? On the inside, she was chaos, just like me.

She went through her oversize bag and pulled out jeans, a tee, sneakers, even a bra and undies—all mine.

"How did you—"

"Tucker," she said.

Tucker had picked out my bra and undies… I pretended that didn't give me a secret little thrill.

"He got your van to your dad's too."

That's all. No big deal. Just a guy taking care of things without being asked, like he always had.

I changed quickly, ignoring the prickle in my chest that refused to be called longing, shoving it all deep down, where I kept all my messy emotions. I tied my shoes, stalling, then finally looked up.

Kiera raised an eyebrow.

"What?"

"You know what."

"Not you too," I said, shaking my head. "Nothing's going on. We hardly ever even see each other."

"You live with your dad. Tucker bought our childhood home several years ago, which means he's living right next door to you. How do you"—she used air quotes—"'hardly ever even see each other'?"

"There's gotta be something better to talk about."

"Oh, there is."

I eyed her warily. "Why am I scared?"

"Did you know you and my brother get discussed more than the elusive Star Falls Legend?"

I laughed.

She did not.

"In case I haven't mentioned, it's annoying as hell that everyone remembers my wild youth and expects me to be that same person."

"You sure that's not *you* projecting?"

Kiera always knew where to aim the arrows, but I rolled my eyes. "And anyway, how elusive can the Legend be when not one but *two* Colburn brothers saw it this year?"

Kiera grinned. "Three."

"*What?*"

"*Three* brothers." She leaned in conspiratorially. "Tucker was there both times."

My chest squeezed. My brain called it adrenaline. My heart knew better.

I considered myself a pragmatic, unflappable person. It took a lot to shake me. But my palms were suddenly sweaty, my heart racing.

Clearly just residual adrenaline.

Kiera was watching me closely, with a tiny smile I didn't like one bit. I repeated, "*What?*"

"Oh, nothing." Her smile was all fake innocence.

I deflected like it was my job. "Circumstantial evidence."

She didn't push. That wasn't Kiera's way. Nope, she'd file it away to dig into later.

I was officially on borrowed time. And she had a perfect memory and a long game.

It was fully dark by the time Kiera dropped me off.

"Thanks," I said, and before I could reach for the door, she yanked me into a bone-crushing hug that knocked the wind out of me.

"You do know I was just hospitalized, right?" I joked, gently patting her back.

"It's called a comfort hug. Take it like a grown-up."

"You're the worst," I mumbled and hugged her tight. I hadn't realized how much I'd been craving human contact.

When she finally released me, she met my gaze. "You didn't want to ask for help."

"Who does?"

"Normal people. And you're not alone. Like it or not, you've got us Colburns. Yes, we're bossy—"

"And nosy."

"Accurate," she said. "But get used to it; we're not going anywhere."

I was caught off guard to feel my eyes stinging. "Hadn't noticed." I squeezed her hand. "Thanks for taking time from the twins to help me out." Four-year-old Abi and Alex, aka nature's cutest wrecking balls in action and the wildest dictators I'd ever met.

Kiera hugged me again. "Anytime."

I waited until she drove off, just to make sure she didn't see me climb into the back of my van.

When I was inside, I took a deep breath and looked around, making sure everything truly was okay.

Simple, clean, mine.

I'd built the cabinets along one side and added soft lighting, which gave the interior a golden glow. The mattress, tucked beneath a panel, pulled out smooth and fast.

It was home. Not forever. But for now, it allowed me to pretend I wasn't afraid to want more for myself.

I changed into pj's—a tank that said *Don't Make Me Use My Power Tools* and bright pink sleep shorts—then collapsed onto the bed under my perfectly weighted blanket.

But I couldn't sleep.

My chest felt tight.

Lonely.

And how I hated that word.

Maybe it was being back in a town that knew both too much and not enough about me. Maybe it was the awkwardness with my dad, living here after he'd once kicked me out of the house.

Maybe we were both haunted by the same ghost.

Or maybe…maybe I still had that dream tucked inside me, the one where I grew roots and built something that couldn't be taken away.

Like a life. A family. A real home, one with a front-porch light left on, someone to notice when I was late, no exit plan required.

And…now, great, I needed to pee. Awesome. I didn't have a bathroom, not yet at least, so it was either hold it or head into my dad's house.

I lay there debating, but I really had to go. Option two it was. I threw on a sweatshirt, jammed my feet into my sneakers, and slipped outside.

My childhood home sat at the end of a cul-de-sac. The street parallel to ours was another cul-de-sac, with that end house across from ours.

Tucker's.

All I could see of his place was the side of his garage, which had been handy all these months in aiding me to avoid him. It was a dark night, and I had no idea if he was home or not. I told myself I didn't care either way.

Still had to pee.

Nothing was lit at my dad's house except the porch, so he was probably asleep. This made things easier. Since I'd forgotten my key inside the van, I crept around back, knowing the back door never got locked. After all the times I'd sneaked home past curfew, I could've done this in my sleep. Nostalgia washed over me, annoyingly tender. I wasn't sorry to be here, not really. My dad's heart attack had been an eye-opener. A scary one.

This was a chance to try to be a family again, before it was too late.

Plus, I'd missed the sense of home. I'd missed a lot of things.

Except Tucker. Or at least, that's what I kept telling myself.

On the back porch now, I had my hand on the door handle when it jerked open, startling me.

Then a light snapped on, and I was face-to-face with a baseball bat.

"*Shit*, Hazel." My dad in boxers, still brandishing said bat, glared at me. "You've got to stop lurking like a squirrel with a bladder problem."

I breezed past him and into the downstairs bathroom. When I came out, he was still in the kitchen, now eating a bowl of cereal.

"Seriously?" I asked.

"It's Cheerios, doctor approved. Says right on the box."

"You should be sleeping."

"And you should move into this house so I stop thinking I've got a prowler every five minutes." He shoved in another bite, slurping up milk. "With a bladder the size of a pea."

Move in? I…couldn't. "Dad," I said softly. "You know I'm only here temporarily. Once you're good, I go back to my life."

"So then *temporarily* sleep in your old bed."

I didn't know how to tell him that walking down that photo-laden hallway to my old bedroom meant walking past every frozen memory of Mom. A time capsule. A love story from my past. "I'll think about it."

"Really?"

"If you change the subject."

He sighed. "Fine. I saw the work you did out on the festival grounds off Highway One. The pavilion looks amazing."

"Thanks."

"Why didn't you change out the expensive white oak for the more economical pressure-treated pine?"

I swallowed my knee-jerk defensiveness. "Because I like white oak, and so does my client."

He chewed on that, then nodded.

Wow, that was progress. I smiled. "Did we just…*not* argue?"

"Maybe?" He looked as shocked as I felt.

With a rough laugh, I turned to the door. "I'm heading back to bed. You're okay?"

"That's my question to you."

"I'm fine. I'm not the one who had a heart attack."

"No, you're just the one who went into anaphylactic shock." He let out a breath.

"Sorry to be a trial."

He chuckled. "You've been a trial coming up on thirty years, so why stop now." He glanced out the window at my van. "That Tucker—too damn efficient."

"Dad," I said gently. "I know you've had a long week. You've got to be tired. Go to bed."

He handed me a container from the counter. "Cookies."

My stomach did a happy dance, but my brain held up a stop sign. "You're not supposed to have cookies."

"Sybil made them."

"Sybil?"

"Mrs. O'Brien, from down the street."

"My old math teacher?" I squeaked.

"Yeah." His face reddened a bit. "She says they're healthy. They don't have sugar or fat, and she used shredded carrots and sweet potatoes instead of flour." He shuddered.

The man had never met a vegetable he didn't hate on sight, but with his new diet requirements, he was trying. Only… "Why is my mean old math teacher making you cookies?"

He flushed again, and I felt my brows go up.

"Oh my God. Are you…*dating* her? You remember her, right? She tried to flunk me because I kept getting A's on her tests and she was certain I was cheating, which I was most definitely not."

"That was a long time ago."

"She called me 'demon spawn'!"

"Hazel, have you *seen* the dating pool at my age?"

"Oh my God, you are. You're dating her."

My dad scrubbed a hand down his face. "People change, you know. Would you want to be judged by your teen years?"

"I *am* still judged by my teen years. By *everyone*." I took the container and opened it. The cookies were big and fluffy, and I folded like a cheap suitcase. "Okay, how about this: If these cookies suck, we dump her. If they're good…I'll try really hard to ignore the fact that you're doing my old math teacher."

"I'm not—Jesus." He pointed at me. "If I had to suffer your dating years, you can suffer mine."

"Deal or no deal?"

He eyed the cookies, then shook his head. "No deal."

I gaped. "Ohmigod. You *really* like her." I took a bite and had to fight a moan.

He grinned. "They're good, aren't they."

I popped the entire cookie in my mouth. "Horrible. Terrible. No good."

"You still blink when you lie." He reached for the container.

I clutched it to my chest. "Mine now."

"You can keep them only if you're nice to her."

"I'm not going to see her."

He gave me a long look.

I sighed. "I'm going to see her because *you're* seeing her."

"Now you're getting it." He patted me on top of my head. "Now come on, it's past our bedtime."

"I'm not sleeping here."

"Hey, I'm letting you keep the cookies."

"For which I've already bartered my soul."

His smile slowly faded. "Hazel. I'm sorry."

"For what?"

"You can't sleep here because of me. Because of what happened."

My heart stopped. He didn't know what had happened. No one did.

"You were acting out and getting in trouble, and I didn't understand why. I didn't understand what you were going through after your Mom died. I was…stuck in my own grief. But I want to make this home for you again. I'd give anything to fix this. What can I do to get you to sleep here?"

The house held every memory that I'd long ago tucked into a

box and sealed shut. "It's not you, Dad. It's…" I looked around. "It's exactly as it was when she was alive. It makes me…sad."

He looked around as if seeing it for the first time. "What if we pack up her stuff?"

That he would offer…God, it nearly broke me open. "Maybe," I said softly.

"Maybe," he repeated and nodded. "I'll take that." He opened the back door for me and waved me off.

I was nearly to my van when a car pulled into the cul-de-sac. Rob Hayes stepped out in a suit, as confident and smooth as he'd been in high school.

When he saw me, he crossed the street and smiled. "I'm relieved to see you on your feet. Heard you totaled three vehicles, crashed into the convenience store to steal beer, and wrestled a coyote."

"Seriously?"

He laughed. "Sorry. Couldn't resist. Damn, Hazel, you look good."

"I'm in my pj's."

He just grinned. "I know."

Rob had always been my high school dream guy, the safe option. Still was. And he'd been casually asking me out since I'd come back to Star Falls.

I opened my mouth, then closed it, and he shook his head. "It's okay. You're still not ready."

That's what I'd told him, and it had been the truth. Being home again had brought up a lot of things, and I'd known I needed to take a beat to face them. "I'm sorry."

He smiled easily. "Don't be."

Something stirred inside me. Unfortunately, it wasn't for him.

"I mean, I will say, you don't know what you're missing," he teased.

I laughed in relief. "My loss."

Rob went into his house, and I turned to my van, stilling at the sight of Tucker standing between our houses, hands in his pockets.

Watching me.

That something inside me flared, warm and dangerous. Bad idea. Very bad idea.

And as if Tucker read my mind, he dipped his head in a barely there nod and vanished inside his house, all without a word.

———

The next night, I collapsed onto my van's bench seat. I'd finished the Henderson project for Colburn Restorations. I'd paid Tex and Annie and now just had to finish the pavilion job and…

I'd be out of work.

Freedom.

But also…panic.

I ate the last of Sybil's cookies. Disgusted with myself and my too-tight yoga pants, which had never once attended a yoga class, I set out for a run.

Actually, it was more like a fastish walk because I hated running. Always had, even when Tucker used to drag me out at oh dark thirty with his maddeningly cheerful *You'll feel amazing after*.

Note: I never did.

I wondered if he still liked running. Two miles later, I couldn't imagine why *anyone* liked it. I showered and stared at my face in the mirror. I was…glowing. Damn, I hated when exercise did a body good.

Then I beat my dad at gin, twice, and returned to my van. I sprawled out to read, windows open to the night sounds: wind rustling the oak trees, crickets chirping, an owl hooting.

And then a soft, sad "mew."

I sat up and slid open the van door.

There, blinking at me in the dark, sat a tiny kitten. Gray, scruffy, with sweet golden eyes.

"Hey, kitty," I said, crouching. "You okay?"

She headbutted my palm, then climbed into my lap like she belonged there.

"Okay," I whispered. "Not shy…" And also a female. I looked into her eyes, realizing they were rheumy. There was also a frailness to her, like she was mostly skin and bones. "You're not a kitten, you're…elderly."

She gave me an offended squint, and I smiled gently. "Shouldn't you be inside all nice and cozy?"

She bumped my hand with her forehead again. When I adjusted her, something crinkled.

A note was tied to her collar.

I'd know that handwriting anywhere—Tucker's, all bold slashes and impatient angles.

Once upon a time, those same scrawls had filled the margins of my algebra homework. He handled equations; I faked enthusiasm for grammar. It had been a solid trade—he thought commas were a conspiracy, and I considered long division a hate crime.

Do NOT feed me. I have a home. I'm just a freeloading asshole.

Beneath that was an address.
Tucker's.
Of course. His cat was a grumpy alpha with boundary issues. Why was I even surprised?

CHAPTER 6

Hazel

You've *got to be* kidding me," I said to the cat. "You belong to *him*?"

Why did I feel like I was being *Punk'd?* I whipped my head left, then right. No sign of Tucker. Which didn't mean a damn thing. That man had been the undisputed hide-and-seek champion of our teenage years—and, okay, also adult years apparently. If he didn't want to be found, he wouldn't be.

I called out into the dark night: "If you're out there watching me like some creepy perv, I swear—" I ran out of words. Couldn't think of a punishment cruel enough.

"Mew."

I looked into those sweet, manipulative eyes and sighed. "Maybe you really are his cat and you've just wandered off to use one of your nine lives."

A rumbling purr filled the quiet night.

Crap. She was adorable. So, like a total sucker, I hugged her.

The purring intensified, though it caught in her throat every few beats, like a rusty old engine trying to start in winter.

I sighed. "He's probably worried about you. You need to go home."

Either I was hallucinating, or she batted her eyes at me.

"Look, the note says I can't feed you."

The cat took a few steps. *Limping* steps. My heart cracked.

"Are you hurt?"

"Mew."

That was all it took. I scooped her up and brought her into my van, before opening a tuna packet and dumping it into a bowl so I could check out her leg while she stuffed her face like she hadn't eaten in weeks.

Her leg was perfectly fine. No injury.

When she finished the tuna, she licked her chops and then her lady bits before strutting toward me.

With zero limp.

"You're the cutest little scam artist I've ever met, and I work in construction. I'm beginning to see why you need a note pinned to you."

She purred like a freight train at my feet, blinking up at me with those see-all eyes.

"You just want more tuna."

She blinked again. Then, as if to prove her case, brought back the limp like she was auditioning for a daytime soap.

"Oh, no," I said on a laugh. "Not falling for that again. You've got to go home. He won't want you over here. We don't…get along."

The cat tilted her head.

"I mean, we did once. But it's ancient history, and I'm trying hard not to make waves, okay? So you gotta scoot."

She did not, in fact, scoot.

She meowed.

And I fed her more tuna.

"Sucker."

I turned to find Tucker's brother Caleb standing on the sidewalk, tatted-up arms crossed, mouth serious, but eyes smiling through the glasses he never remembered to clean. Once a hockey god, and still built like one, he'd been the older brother I'd never known I wanted. It'd been cemented back in high school, when he'd once punched a guy for calling me emo, even though it'd been entirely accurate.

"I'm no sucker," I said.

"You fed Tucker's ridiculous cat. The old-lady thing wears a sign for a reason, you know."

"She's so skinny! I thought she was starving!"

He snorted. "She trolls the neighborhood nightly, demanding food. Then she goes home and yaks in Tuck's shoes."

That made me laugh.

Caleb's smile hit his mouth. "You ever going to tell me what your problem is with him?"

"Sure. When hell freezes over."

He crossed the grass and settled onto my dad's porch swing, patting the spot next to him.

I narrowed my eyes but sat. "What are you even doing here?"

He gestured to his sweats. "Was on a run with Tuck." He set us swinging, but I immediately planted my foot to stop the motion.

He snorted. "Forgot you get motion sick if you so much as turn in a fast circle."

"You're an actual menace," I muttered, pressing on my already-tumbling belly.

His laugh was pure older brother.

"You're evil."

"I really did forget," he said.

"No problem, as long as you aren't attached to those shoes…"

He pulled his long legs as far from me as he could get. I should throw up on them anyway.

"You finished the Henderson job for us today."

I nodded, keeping my panic about getting more work to myself. I hadn't been back all that long. Not long enough to build a reputation. Or at least *undo* my teenage reputation.

"So…you doing okay with your dad?"

I was hoping this wasn't a personal question but a business one. Because Caleb was second-in-command at Colburn Restorations, and my dream gig would be to continue contracting with them. They paid well. Treated people right. Expected perfection and gave respect—which for me, a woman in a man's world, meant everything.

"My dad and I are doing fine," I said. "We have an arrangement."

"Which is?"

"We ignore each other as much as possible."

A corner of his mouth tipped up. "How's that working out?"

He was fishing, and I was going to be honest and keep my fingers crossed it didn't bite me in the ass. Did I have to swallow a lot of pride when Dad felt the need to tell me how to do my job every other second? Yes. Was swallowing my pride my favorite hobby? Hell no. But there was only one right answer here. "It's going…great."

He studied me. "So, if you had to work directly with him again on a different job, could you? Especially since you're living with him."

More like I was sleeping twenty feet away like some deranged driveway troll. But I knew what he was asking, and my heart stuttered with a hope I wasn't even sure I believed in. "Yes, I could work with him again." I kept my eyes on his, waiting.

"We've got a new big job starting up."

"The Sonoma project." I nodded. Town had been buzzing about it. The restoration was massive—a two-story brick building from the early 1900s in downtown Star Falls, complete with arched windows, original crown molding, and creaky wood floors that told a thousand stories—and it would all be turned into an artist co-op.

"Yes, the Sonoma project," Caleb said. "You're damn good at what you do. We could use someone with your caliber of skills."

I blinked at the unexpected validation. A warm bloom of pride settled low in my chest. "That means a lot, coming from you."

"Good. You up for the finish-work contract? It's a big one. Time and materials plus a percentage of the profit."

This was a no-brainer for me. Being paid for hours worked ensured I couldn't get screwed if the project went over budget. And a percentage of the profit? I'd died and gone to heaven. "Yes. Absolutely yes."

"And you're sure you can take on a big project like this, from start to finish, and not have problems with Bill?"

That he even had to clarify…it stung. "I won't let you down."

Before I could say more, another voice came from the shadows.

"Her word is gold."

Tucker.

Air stalled in my lungs. Those words. That voice—low and steady, but sharp enough to pierce steel—could still undo me.

Caleb raised an eyebrow. "Eavesdropping?"

Tucker stepped into the puddle of light from the porch and shrugged.

Caleb narrowed his eyes. "You two have been doing your damnedest to make it awkward for the rest of us since she got back."

Accurate. Up until yesterday, I'd been seriously avoiding Tucker. And he'd been letting me, which, honestly, I'd taken as an insult.

"Which one of you two is going to tell me what's going on?" I asked.

"I'm simply reminding you that we take care of our own, always," Tucker said, folding his arms.

Biceps. Forearms. Both corded with strength. Why were forearms even allowed to look like that? They were clearly a threat to my mental health.

"Agreed," Caleb said. Was that amusement in his voice?

I glanced at him and realized he'd caught me staring at his brother. Crap.

He stood. Stretched. "I'll email you the specs," he told me, then bumped shoulders with Tucker on the way out.

I was still spinning over the phrase *we take care of our own, always* when Tucker met my gaze, his own dark, hooded.

I felt unprepared for the sheer overwhelming physical presence of him. He wasn't SF fire personnel at the moment. He wore battered cargos and a Colburn Restorations T-shirt, just regular guy clothes, but he carried himself with the calm authority of a man who could command a room by blinking.

But it wasn't his biceps or jawline that did me in. It was his quiet, focused listening—the kind that made you feel like you were the only thing in the world that mattered.

What we'd had…it defied labels. It'd been a living, breathing, soul-deep *thing* humming between us. We'd been each other's escape hatch, a safe harbor in every storm.

And now?

Now the whole thing still simmered between us like it had never left. And that scared the hell out of me. I didn't know what to do with it. Or the fact that no one had ever made me laugh the way he did. Or think.

Or get mad.

And that it was all still right here when clearly neither of us wanted it? I had no idea what to do about it.

And…I was still holding his cat like she was my emotional-support animal. "I think Caleb just hired me for a new project with Colburn Restorations."

"I know," he said. "We voted on it."

I blinked. The Colburns were all-or-nothing. Two of three wouldn't have won me the job. "If there was a vote, how did I get the job?"

"It was unanimous."

I almost swallowed my tongue. "Well then. That's…" I was stunned. "Thank you."

He shrugged like he hadn't just knocked me off my axis by admitting that not only had he stood up for my character, he'd voted for me.

"So," I said, changing the subject like I always did when I was uncomfortable, which praise always made me, "I had a great chat with your cat."

He eyeballed the thing in my arms. "I see that."

"We discussed that she's sweet, manipulative, and convinced she's royalty."

He choked. "Sweet?"

"Oh, right, you don't know sweet from sour."

He didn't argue that point. "I know you can read, and yet you still fed Her Fluffiness."

"Her *Fluffiness*?"

"Short for Her Royal Highness, Queen Fluffiness the First, Sovereign of the Sunbeam Patch."

I stared at him, and he grimaced, like he was actually embarrassed. Tucker said, "I found her abandoned on a jobsite, injured. Broken ribs, leg. I got her to the vet. She still limps when she begs for food because she knows I can't stand it if she's hurting."

I bit my lip to keep from smiling. "Softie."

"Hey, *you* look into those eyes and try to refuse her."

Touché.

He shifted closer, enough that I could now testify that he still smelled amazing, even after a long day. While I dealt with that knowledge, he stroked the cat's ears, and she closed her eyes in bliss.

"After I paid a fortune to have her fixed up," he said, "I took her to the humane society, who said they'd give her five days before euthanizing her."

My heart pinched. "How long did you last?"

His smile was rueful. "I got to my truck, caught my reflection in the rearview mirror, and went back in. During those three minutes, they'd named her."

"Cute." I smiled. "Did your left eye just twitch?"

He pressed a finger to it. "You called me 'cute.'"

"Don't worry. I didn't mean it."

He almost smiled. I could tell.

"So you kept her. Her Fluffiness. The name alone should've been a red flag."

"I tried to give her to Kiera. She said she already manages enough poop." He slid his hands into his pockets. "The cat insists on being outside at night. Problem is, everyone feeds her, and it messes up her stomach."

"And then she pukes in your shoes."

"It's her love language."

I laughed, a sound that came out lighter than I felt. "Thanks again, by the way. For yesterday. Getting my van back."

"You needed it for work."

"I know I was a jerk. I'm…sorry."

"You were in shock."

And yet he hadn't forced me to go to the hospital. He'd given me a carefully calculated amount of time to get my shit together and come to the realization on my own. "I mean, I could've done without the memory lane."

A small smile curved his lips. "That was the best part."

I rolled my eyes and handed him the cat. Our hands brushed. Our chests brushed. I'm pretty sure our hearts brushed.

We froze.

Something flickered. Old. But also new. Dangerous.

What if you fall for him again? What if he breaks your heart again? What if you don't survive it this time? What if, what if, what if…?

Her Fluffiness twisted in Tucker's arms to gently headbutt me in the cheek.

I melted like a stick of butter on a hot roof.

Tucker's eyes softened very slightly as he cocked his head. "What's going on?"

"Nothing! Absolutely nothing! It's your cat." I pointed at her for emphasis. "She makes me mushy."

"Just the cat, huh?"

"Yes! It's absolutely *not* you. Not even a little." Oh God, I was rambling. I couldn't stop. "Because, obviously, we aren't doing this."

"'This'?"

"Yes!" I waved my arms for emphasis. "I don't repeat mistakes. So you and me? Never again."

He just raised a brow.

Right. He hadn't given me any indication he would even want to. Gah. "You know what? I'm going to stop talking now." But I knew subtitles would still come out of my face.

Back in the day, when one of us was feeling too much, hurting too much, hating everything too much, we'd climb into Tucker's old truck and drive out to the quarry. We'd take a couple of axes and swing at granite and rock until we felt better. "I need something hard to destroy."

He went brows up.

I rolled my eyes. "Like your giant, boulder-thick head."

"Ouch." He laughed. "Are you…flirting with me?"

"You're the one who made it weird."

"Why didn't you go out with Rob?"

I nearly choked. "What?"

He just gave me a long look.

"Wow, would you look at the time—" I whirled to go…

And heard him mutter, "Walking away. Shock."

Dammit, he was right. I was a stage-five runner. My fight-or-flight instincts screamed *flight*. But I made myself turn to face him anyway. "Okay," I said. "Here's the thing. I'm trying to figure myself out. I know people here expect me to be who I was. But I'm not that girl anymore. Problem is, I don't know who I am now. I'm working on it, but…" I paused to swallow a lump in my throat. "I think maybe I'm…brok—"

"Don't you say it." His voice cut through the dark like a blade. "You, Hazel, are not broken."

The words hit like a warm hammer, cracking something brittle inside me I hadn't realized I'd been clutching tight. I didn't know if I believed him. But for the first time in a long while…I wanted to.

I met his gaze, startled by the intensity in his fierce eyes. By his defense of me. His *second* defense of me, if I counted what he'd said to Caleb. That same tightness hit my chest, the one that always came late at night, when I felt like maybe I'd misplaced the best version of myself.

"You asked why I didn't go out with Rob. I see people in love, even people who swore they'd never fall again. But me?" I slowly shook my head. "I can't even imagine it. It's like a color I forgot how to see." I pressed the heels of my hands into my eyes so I wouldn't have to see pity in his. "That's why I said no to Rob. Because he deserves someone who can love him back."

Stunned silence.

Part of me wished I could claw the words back one by one and hide them deep inside where they belonged, but it was too late. They were hanging out there to dry.

I was hanging out there to dry.

Tucker drew a deep breath, and I dropped my hands from my face to find his eyes on me, soft with apology. "I shouldn't have asked you about Rob."

I shook my head. "You couldn't have known what was going on with me."

"No." His voice was almost terrifyingly gentle as he set down

Her Fluffiness and closed the distance between us. "But I'm glad you told me." He shifted, the faint movement as tense as the air between us.

Being the sole focus of his attention was thrilling but unnerving as it also laid me bare before him and yet also grounded me in a way I hadn't realized I'd missed so dearly. I soaked up his steady presence, the way he saw straight through me and didn't look away.

"I haven't felt…*that* way for anyone since I left here," I admitted. "There's been no one I couldn't live without."

"And you think that makes you broken," he said. A statement, not a question.

"Well, I wasn't like this before." We both knew that. "But maybe it was because I knew I had people who cared about me. I felt whole and supported." And loved… "I'm trying to heal so I can handle things better, the trauma of my past, all the anxiety that goes with it, but it's a slow process."

"You don't heal to handle trauma… You heal to handle joy."

I stilled as, moved beyond bearing at his words, I stared at him.

"What?"

"I'm… That was…" I shook my head. "I don't know. Moving. Wise. Unexpected."

"I have my moments." He stepped into me, his usual mask cracking under the weight of the moment. "I know we fell apart, but that doesn't mean I don't care. Because I do. Very much. So you can talk to me. Or, hell, yell at me. I can take it. Whatever you need, I'm here."

Once upon a time, stuck in detention together, I'd told him I didn't believe in soulmates, and he'd drawn a heart on my hand in Sharpie anyway. He'd said, "Then we'll just make our own rules."

And I'd believed him.

Now I blinked back tears. "Thank you. That…means a lot."

He reached for me. Deliberately unhurried, giving me time to back away if I wanted.

I didn't. For once I didn't open my mouth and blow it or, worse, run. Without even thinking, I walked into his arms for a hug I hadn't known I needed. My fingers brushed his jaw; my thumb slid over his cheekbone. His skin was warm. Stubbled.

Real.

I wanted to kiss him. Not because I was lonely to my core. Not because it was a smart idea.

But because he made me feel something I wasn't sure I remembered how to feel. Like hope.

And then there was the terrifying inkling that I might not be broken after all.

His face… My heart raced at the surprise softening of his features, the way his usually sharp composure seemed to come undone.

"Well," he said, setting his cheek on the top of my head, voice rough. "This is…interesting. It's still here."

"What is?"

"Animal magnetism."

No kidding. And since I didn't want to discuss it, I changed the subject. "FYI, same goes about the talking. Yelling. Sitting in total silence. Anything you need."

He lifted his head, and this time his smile was the opposite of soft. It was…wicked. "*Anything* I need?"

I snorted and shoved him back, glad I hadn't given in to my sudden urge to kiss him. "Keep dreaming."

He laughed, but I was pretty sure I heard him quietly say, "I will," as he left.

Two minutes later, I was back in my van.

Not tired. Pulse still elevated.

That had been a close call, and it left me feeling restless. In the past, I'd have solved the problem by heading out to look for trouble and finding it. But tonight? Tonight, I needed something else.

So I grabbed my keys and headed out—on my terms.

I was done running.

I was choosing, even if I still had no idea where I'd end up. At least this time, I'd be the one at the wheel.

CHAPTER 7

Tucker

M Y PHONE RANG AT the ass crack of dawn, and I swore as I struggled to open my eyes. I slapped my hand to my nightstand, searching for the offending phone, dislodging Her Fluffiness, who'd been dead asleep on my chest. She lifted her grumpy face and glared at me like I'd personally offended her.

"Hey, blame whoever's calling me—" I blearily eyed the screen. "It's Ryder. Feel free to crap in his shoes next time he comes by." I hit Answer and growled, "Someone better be dead."

"Next week is my and Penny's anniversary," Ryder said.

I blinked. "Of what? You just got married four months ago."

"You don't want to know."

"Shit." I closed my eyes, too tired to rise to the bait. I was happy for him. Hell, they all deserved what they had—Ryder and Penny, Caleb and Emma. I just hadn't figured out how to deserve something like that myself. "I'm hanging up now. And if your call woke up Hank, I'm delivering him to your door in less than twenty."

"I need you to find that same reclaimed barnwood we used on the Fulton job. It's Penny's favorite, and I want to do an accent wall in our living room."

"You're the contractor."

"And you're the estimator with the connections."

"Fine," I grumbled. "Whatever."

"Thanks. You're my favorite brother."

"This could've been a text."

"Seriously, you're a lifesaver—"

I took petty satisfaction in hanging up on him.

———

Once a week, my chaotic family descended onto one of our places for a meal. We used to meet at the Cork and Barrel, the local bar and grill, but after a few too many conversations-turned-loud arguments, we pivoted to breakfast. Less booze, less brawling.

Mostly.

This week was at Kiera's. No one could drive me up a wall like my sister, but since she took in Dad on the nights I worked around the clock, I let it happen. In return, I took the twins off her hands as often as I could.

She'd lost her husband a few years back. Auggie had been a brother to us. His loss had been impossible to fathom, and we'd nearly lost Kiera to her grief. Watching her crawl her way back to life had changed me in ways I hadn't expected.

I made it to her house on autopilot, yawning the whole way after yet another hellish shift for my crew—Jayden, Tessa, Marcus, and Harlow. We had been out on calls for thirty-six hours straight. A full moon had resulted in two fights and a structure fire. So, you know, classic Star Falls.

Kiera's place sat at the end of a winding oak-lined road that always smelled like woodsmoke and lavender from the neighbor's overzealous garden. Kiera's back porch sagged just enough to creak when you stepped on it, and the welcome mat still read *Go Away.*

Homey in the way only a Colburn house could be—loud, scrappy, and usually in some sort of meltdown mode.

I was dragging my feet by the time I let myself into the house and caught a tiny human blur in midair, then another…

"Unca Tuck, Unca Tuck!" Abi clung to me like a baby koala, arms around my neck and forehead pressed to mine, breathing hot Cheerios breath in my face. "Alex said I'm a girl!"

"'Cause you *are* a girl!" Alex said, indignant.

Abi's lower lip trembled.

"You don't get to decide for her," I told Alex. "She gets to tell you."

Abi beamed. "I'm a Paw Patrol."

"You're a dog?" I asked for clarification.

She nodded, triumphant.

Alex considered that. "Why didn't you just say so?"

The air inside was warm and smelled like maple syrup and whatever plastic toy had been left too close to the radiator. A kids' show blared in the background, and Abi's hair was full of glitter, which had immediately transported itself to me.

Kiera poked her head out of the kitchen with a smile aimed my way, but it faded at whatever she saw on my face. "You okay?"

"Sure." I looked around and didn't see the usual Colburn Circus. "What happened to family breakfast?"

She frowned. "Tuck, it's Saturday. Family breakfast is tomorrow."

Ah, hell.

She came close and gave me a little punch to the arm. Her version of a hug. "What's wrong?"

"Just tired."

"You're taking arson-investigation classes on top of two full-time jobs. Anyone would be tired."

I lifted a shoulder. "I want to do this."

"You know you don't have anything to prove, right?" she asked gently.

"What the hell does that mean?"

"That's a bad word," Abi said. "You gotta pay the jar." She held out her hand.

I searched my pockets and slapped a five into her palm.

Making little crowing noises of victory, she threw herself at me. For some reason, her favorite game was using me as a human climbing gym. She hugged me tight, then ran off.

"You know she's going to put that in her own piggy bank," Kiera said, nudging me to the couch. I barely caught the rest of what she said—something about Caleb being here because he'd picked up her Costco order for her. Then: "Why can't you postpone the classes?"

"I don't want to. Redken is retiring in six months, and I want to take his place."

"Is that all this is, this push to exhaustion?"

"Key." I leaned back and closed my eyes. "I'm too tired for the psychobabble."

She paused, then pushed anyway, because she'd been raised by stubborn, overbearing brothers. "You think I don't know you're a firefighter, one of the best in the county, by the way, because you have a need to save everyone?"

I snorted.

But she didn't smile. "You think you could've saved Mom."

I didn't answer. Couldn't. Some guilt never shut up, no matter how many fires you put out, even if you logically knew the truth—that no one could have stopped her from getting sick.

Kiera wasn't done drilling me. "Auggie died on a ski trip hundreds of miles from here."

Yes, alone. He'd asked me and Ryder to join him. We hadn't. That guilt still hadn't moved on.

"Stop that," she said quietly. "The guilt thing. It's all over your face. After he died, you watched me break down and helped build me back up. You saved me. You also make a living saving perfect strangers. And now, also, maybe, a certain redhead from your past."

I groaned. "I knew you'd go there."

She just smiled. I shook my head and closed my eyes—and the next time I opened them, my feet were in the lap of the woman I'd been dreaming about.

Hazel.

I jolted upright. "What? When?"

She just raised a brow, waiting for my faculties to return. "I was in the kitchen when you arrived."

Confusion befuddled me. "It's not breakfast day. It's Saturday."

Her mouth curved. "Turns out your sister has a life even when you're not around."

"Funny."

Unbothered, she hummed and licked the frosting off an amazing-looking cinnamon roll. Then she sucked some frosting off her thumb, and I forgot my name. God, that mouth. I'd once had a whole mental highlight reel of that mouth living rent-free in my head.

On repeat.

The way it tasted, how it felt on my skin…

She shifted, and my eyes roamed, taking in the way those jeans and snug white tee fit her, turning every neuron I had into a fire hazard. She looked like every good memory I'd ever had, and every bad one too.

Something smacked me in the back of the head, and I glared as Caleb passed by. "What the?"

My annoying-as-hell brother grinned and peeled a piece of paper off my back that read, *Kick me!* "Had to improvise since you're sitting down."

Hazel choked on her cinnamon roll.

When I slid my gaze her way, she fumbled for her phone. "Hey," she said into it. "Thanks for calling me back. I—"

I caught her wrist. Her scent hit me—wood stain, lemon soap, and something warmer underneath, like home, if I were a metaphor kind of guy.

I pulled the phone from her ear and checked her screen.

Blank.

She grimaced.

So *not* in a truce then. Good to know. "Payback's a bitch," I warned her. "This isn't over."

She tilted her head. "Is it ever with us?"

"It was. The night you left."

Just like that, she was gone again. Not far. Just out of reach, where she'd been for years. And senseless me, I kept hoping she'd close the distance.

I spent the next few days kicking my own ass. Why had I said, "It was. The night you left"?

Because maybe Caleb wasn't the clueless one. Maybe I was.

Hazel was relaxed and comfortable with everyone but me. That dug under my skin like a splinter I couldn't get out.

After a long day at Colburn Restorations, estimating and bidding for a stack of upcoming jobs, I picked up Hank from his daytime caregiver.

He was in the same cargo shorts we'd argued over that morning. He'd wanted to wear Grinch pajamas this morning for reasons known only to him.

But his T-shirt was pink, slightly too small, and read *Sassy Is a Full-Time Job.*

Definitely not his.

This had Nell all over it. Nell was Penny's grandma and Hank's caregiver, and Nell…well, she was amazing and marched to her own wild beat. "What happened to your shirt?"

He just smiled.

Awesome. He was feeling playful. And I was too damn tired to keep up. I didn't want to talk. Hell, I didn't want to think, but that was the thing about my dad: It had never mattered what I wanted or needed. Never had.

"Ah," he said, which could mean anything in Hank speak. Probably meant he'd enjoyed whatever chaos had ensued.

He pointed to a guy walking a dozen dogs on a rigged-up belt. "Ah!"

"You want a dog," I translated.

He clapped his hands. Well, he missed on the first two tries, but got it on the third. Occupational therapy was working.

"Sorry, man. We have a cat." I didn't have the brain power or the energy for one more thing in my life.

Hank huffed out a sigh and turned away. His version of a temper tantrum. Once, he would've yelled. Once, he would've shamed me for being a disappointment. Now? A sigh.

I tried to keep my mouth shut, but my mouth wasn't interested. "You do realize I'm able to take care of you because I've convinced myself you're not the same man who raised me, right? You're just someone who needs help. And that's what I do. I help people."

He didn't answer. Or look at me.

Fine by me. I had things to overthink.

Hazel's voice echoed in my mind. *I'm broken.*

She wasn't. But maybe I was.

At home, I helped Hank out of the truck. He grabbed my hand, fingers tangling in mine. Then, with his other hand, he tried to pat me on top of my head. Being six four, I got slapped in the face instead, but I knew what he meant.

It was affection. And possibly an apology, though whether he knew what he was apologizing for was anyone's guess. This from the man who, pre-strokes, had never learned the meaning of the word *sorry*. I stared down at our entwined fingers, squelching the urge to pull free. That wouldn't do any good, because as far as we all knew, he had very little memory of the past. So I sucked it up and held his hand all the way into the damn house.

Her Fluffiness waited in the foyer like a furry time bomb. Two minutes past dinner, and the queen was displeased.

"Ah." Hank patted his own tummy.

Guess the entire kingdom was displeased. "On it."

The house was still warm from the late-afternoon sun, the air faintly laced with coffee from that morning. I walked straight through the kitchen and out the back door to start the barbeque, my dad right on my heels.

The wind rustled through the oaks like it had something to say just as a fluff ball raced past me. Her Fluffiness, on her evening walkabout. "Hey, don't even think about going to Hazel and begging for food again," I called after her.

Like she'd listen. I shook my head at myself and my circus, then went back inside for the food. "Burgers or hot dogs?"

"Ah."

"Both it is." I wasn't sure when I'd begun understanding what the various *ah*s meant. Or, hell, maybe I was just making it up in my head.

My phone had buzzed several times on the way home with incoming texts. Probably Caleb sending me memes I wasn't in the mood for, so I'd ignored it, until Ryder's name lit the screen. "What?"

There was a beat of silence. Most people deferred to Ryder, but we liked to play a little game, the one where he was the most annoying older brother on the planet, and I was the flippant, mocking younger brother who kept him humble.

"You talk to her?" he finally asked.

"Who?"

"Fuck, man, you've *got* to read the family chat."

"Why? You guys do nothing but trade insults all day long. Who has time for that?"

"Listen…Hazel got detained at the state park last night. Cops thought she was vandalizing."

My stomach dropped. "She wouldn't do that."

"They drew on her."

I froze. "*What?*"

"She's got a reputation, earned or not."

I remembered Hazel's face when she'd said people hadn't forgotten. Shame. Embarrassment. "People change," I said tightly, furious for her.

Ryder exhaled. "Yeah, well, check the town IG page."

I pulled the phone away from my face and did just that. Then I stared at a picture of the old gazebo in the state park. It'd been graffiti covered for years, some of it from Hazel herself, but was now gleaming with fresh paint and a new roof.

"She rebuilt it," I said, somehow not surprised, even as something twisted in my chest. Not grief. Not quite pride. Something harder to name.

"Used her own time, materials, everything. But the cops thought she was tagging it. Instead, she was saving it. Now the mayor wants to personally thank her and offer her a commendation."

I closed my eyes. Hazel, the girl everyone had labeled as trouble, had just quietly saved something this town had let rot. "Why would she do that?"

"Ask her yourself," Ryder said. "Oh wait—you can't, because you two are still acting like twelve-year-olds. You ever going to tell me what that's about?"

"No," I said. Because I didn't have the words for the way she still lived under my skin.

"Tuck."

I sighed. "Feelings change. People move on."

"So…you've moved on?" he asked doubtfully.

I knew the answer should be yes. We'd been kids. Time had passed. But saying I'd moved on and *actually* moving on were two different things.

"That's what I thought," Ryder said, then hung up.

I flipped a burger and thought too hard about Hazel. Sweet and sharp and stubborn as hell. Also, she'd kill me dead on the spot if I called her *sweet* to her face.

I was smiling a little as I stood there, grilling for a father who couldn't speak, trying not to read too much into how much my cat loved Hazel, or the way Hazel kept crashing into my life when I least expected it, showing me a woman who was clearly not broken after all.

Just healing.

And maybe, just maybe, I was too.

CHAPTER 8

Tucker

AN HOUR LATER, I'D fed Hank, gotten him into the shower and into his pj's, and left him happily camped on the couch watching *Below Deck*—his latest obsession. He laughed like a stoner at the crew drama and pointed at the screen every few seconds like he knew the cast personally.

To each his own.

I was at the kitchen table in the middle of an online arson-investigation continuing education test, when Her Fluffiness scratched at the door. I let her in and narrowed my eyes. "Why do you smell like rotisserie chicken?"

She sat daintily at my feet and lifted a leg and began to clean herself with haughty indifference.

"Nice."

When she'd finished bathing, I heard a crinkle. She had a note attached to her collar, and not one of mine:

If you don't want me to feed your cute little freeloader, keep

Her Royal Highness on your side of the fence.

Gee, wonder who that could be from? I grabbed a pen and wrote back:

I don't tell my women what to do.

And beneath that:

Nice job on the gazebo…

Because *Are you okay?* felt too dangerous to ask. So did *Do you need me?* But she hadn't needed me in years. Maybe never had.

It was me who'd needed her.

Still did.

I went back to my test. Twenty minutes later, Her Fluffiness came back inside and leaped into my lap. I scratched her favorite spot behind her ears, and—yep. Another note. Same paper:

Or maybe you're just not invested in your relationships.

Oof. That one landed. I set the cat down and grabbed a beer from the fridge, then took it and my laptop outside to finish the test. The sun had dipped behind the oaks and redwoods, bathing the backyard in a soft amber glow. A breeze rolled in from the coast, carrying the scent of eucalyptus and cut grass, and a hint of that late-summer warmth that reminded me fall was just around the corner.

I sat on top of my picnic table, bottle sweating in my hand, watching my cat vanish into the bushes like she had secrets to keep.

A moment later, my dad stepped out onto the porch in a white T-shirt and the blue bunny boxers he'd picked out himself—because apparently personal dignity was overrated. And who was I to judge? We all make our own choices.

For example, I'd go without rather than wear anything with bunnies.

Dad pointed to the sprinter van on the street. "Ah?"

"That's Hazel's," I said. I cocked my head. "You remember her?"

"Ah."

No clue if that meant yes or no. "It ended badly," I added, half to myself.

"That's one way of putting it," said a voice I hadn't heard in nearly a week but had somehow been echoing in my head every damn day.

Hazel.

She peered over the fence, a wild halo of waves framing her face like a warning and a promise all at once.

I lifted my beer in a mock salute.

"Ah," Hank said again and gestured to the foil-wrapped leftovers on the table.

"He wants to know if you're hungry," I translated.

Hazel scaled the fence and landed on my grass with lithe grace as if she did it every day. She wore a cropped sweatshirt, beat-up sneakers, and tiny denim shorts that showed off legs for days—no makeup, just sun-warmed skin and attitude.

Fuck, she looked good—*too* good.

Thinner than when she'd first returned to Star Falls though, and something that felt uncomfortably like worry tightened in my gut. Noticing was one thing. Worrying? That was something else entirely. I told myself not to make it mean anything.

And failed.

She eyed Hank.

He stared back and nudged the food toward her.

When she didn't make a move toward it, I shifted closer and opened the foil. "Your faves."

She looked at me, surprised.

I almost smiled. "Have you forgotten we lived off my cooking during our high school years? Burgers and hot dogs were my specialty." At my side, Hank shifted but didn't make a sound. I ignored him because Hazel's gaze was locked on mine.

"I've never forgotten a thing," she said softly. Her eyes flicked to the food and lingered. "I didn't figure fatty burgers and hot dogs would be on your very grown-up food pyramid."

I did smile now. "They're turkey." I leaned in conspiratorially, with a wink. "Hope you can keep a secret."

The look on her face said she could and had…and I wondered at the secrets she held close to the vest.

"Come on," I cajoled, wafting the food beneath her nose. "Being a vandal burns up a lot of calories."

She eyed a hot dog. "I'm not a vandal."

"I know."

Her eyes flew to mine. She assessed me. I wasn't sure for what, but I did my best to look like something she needed in her life. That might've been too tall an order because she dropped her gaze.

"I know something else too," I said.

Suspicion flared in her gaze. "Like what?"

"The mayor wants to thank you with a commendation."

"Is this the same mayor who wanted to close up the streets at dusk when I got back?"

I laughed and she sighed.

"I don't know what to say."

"You could just accept the commendation with a thank-you."

"That would imply I was over it," she muttered.

I pointed to the food again. The food she was now staring at like she hadn't eaten in a week.

Hank scooted over on the bench to make room for her. When she bit her lower lip, I knew we had her. I ducked inside for a plate and the buns, but by the time I got back, Hazel and Hank were each eating a hot dog with their fingers like long-lost friends.

Hank grinned at me.

Hazel took the plate and began to doctor up a bun. I held out a container.

She stared at it. "Tell me that's your special sauce."

"It's my special sauce. And no, I'm still not telling you what's in it."

She reached for it, but I held it up out of her reach.

"One condition."

"No."

I met her gaze. "You don't even know what it is."

"I don't need to. It'll be a bad idea."

"What the hell do you think I'm going to ask of you?"

Her gaze skittered away.

I wanted to reach for her, but Hank was watching us like it was his favorite soap. "Dad," I said. "Time for your show."

Hank got to his feet and beelined for the door.

"Don't move," I said to Hazel and then moved inside to get Hank settled in his recliner, the remote in his hand and his plate in his lap.

"Ah," he said, which I took to mean *Try not to be a dumbass.*

But I was so good at it.

Back outside, Hazel sat right where I'd left her, those slay-me baby blues sharp and…angsty. Which, gotta admit, hurt.

I sat next to her and nudged the sauce toward her.

"Price?" she asked.

"You stop pretending *I'm* the one ignoring you."

She frowned. "So you're not going to take *any* responsibility?"

Shit. Fine. "I'll accept twenty-five percent."

"Fifty. Final offer." She slathered her burger with sauce and took a bite, closing her eyes like maybe it was the best thing she'd ever tasted.

Once upon a time, *she* was the best thing I'd ever tasted…

"Deal," I said a little hoarsely.

My still-open laptop beeped, and she glanced over at it. "What was that?"

"Online test for arson investigation. Timed out."

She turned to face me. Since I was straddling the bench, this put her in between my legs, but she didn't shy away from the closeness. And it's not like I was going to.

"One of us grew up," she murmured.

"Says the woman who spent all night rebuilding a gazebo in the dark."

She dropped eye contact, and something deep inside me tightened.

"I heard things got a little rough at the state park," I said. "You okay?"

"You keep asking me that, even though you already know the answer. I'm *always* okay."

"You don't have to be. Not with me."

A soft sound escaped her. Half laugh, half tears. "Stop humoring me."

"I'm not," I said. "You're trying to right your wrongs."

She shocked the hell out of me when she dropped her forehead to my chest. "*Trying* being the key word." Her voice was muffled against me, but I didn't miss the thick emotion in it.

I closed my eyes. Anchored by the weight of her, by the shape of her head against my chest like she still fit there. Like nothing had changed and everything had.

I gave her a moment to collect herself. Gave *me* a moment to collect myself because having her this close and touching me of her own free will felt way too good. "Still feel humored?"

A laughing breath huffed out of her. "Shut up."

I couldn't stop my hand from stroking down her hair. "Make me."

She laughed again, and I felt like Superman. "You used to say that to me," she whispered. "'*Make me.*'"

She remembered that? *God help me.* "We used to say a lot of things." Like how we were always going to be in each other's life, no matter what.

She used to sit just like this, between my knees, making me promise we'd take on the world together, forever and ever, to infinity.

She lifted her head. "Why are you being so nice?"

Again, my fingers glided softly down her silky hair. "Thought maybe we could try something new for a change."

She looked at my mouth, her breath hitching again as I slid a hand up her back to the nape of her neck before slowly closing my fingers into a fist around her ponytail, so soft against my callused palms.

Insanity. This was insanity. *We can't go back. We can never go back.*

I knew this better than anyone.

And yet, with a slight tug on her hair, I tilted her head, trying to decide where I wanted my mouth first: her throat or her lips. "Hazel…"

"*Yes,*" she breathed, her eyes drifting shut in permission. She leaned in, her fingers brushing my knee—tentative, then firmer, like she needed the contact as much as I did.

This wasn't nostalgia. This was need—messy, urgent, bone-deep. And I wasn't sure I could walk away from it again. But my heart pounded like a drum, matching the racing pulse at the base of Hazel's throat. Fuck, this wasn't my smartest move, but I didn't care as we breathed each other's air, eyes locked. And then, with heat licking through my veins like an out-of-control wildfire, I kissed her.

The world spun. Hazel melted, wrapping herself around me like a pretzel. The heat of her mouth drove me wild, making me forget everything but the feel of her.

It was like the last decade had never happened. She was the wildfire, and I was already burning, and when she rocked against me, her hands slipping under my shirt and heading south, it took everything I had to catch her fingers in mine and pull back. "Hazel." I wanted her like oxygen. But the last time I'd let myself need her, I'd nearly drowned.

Eyes still closed, she let out a sound of disgruntled disagreement and tugged on my lower lip with her teeth, wrenching a rough groan from me.

It took everything I had to pull back. "*Haze.*"

She sighed, eyes still closed, like she didn't want to come back to reality yet. "I don't even know what that was."

I knew what it wasn't: a declaration.

"I don't want to want you," she whispered.

How well I knew, so I quipped, "Good luck with that." I cupped her face, stroking her jaw with my fingers. "Look at me."

She opened her eyes, and my stomach dropped out. Never in all my life had I seen emotion like that aimed at me. So vulnerable. So hungry. So heated. So…raw.

And real.

Naked desire danced in those eyes—desire for me, so potent that everything else stopped: my breath, my heart, maybe even time itself.

I drew in a deep breath for a calm I did not find and leaned back.

She stared at me. "What are you doing?"

"Walking away," I said, and it nearly killed me. "Before we do something we'll regret." Even saying it out loud felt like ripping something vital out of my chest. I wanted her. I'd always wanted her. But I also remembered what came after the last time I'd let myself believe we could have more. The silence. The empty days. The feeling of helplessness I couldn't fix.

If I lost her again, I wasn't sure I'd come back from it. I knew now how fast hope could turn to wreckage. And I wasn't sure either of us could survive another fallout.

"Regret," she repeated quietly. "Right."

"Haze—"

"No, I get it."

I tried to smile. "Then can you explain it to me?"

She snorted, then went quiet again.

The silence stretched between us, but this time, it wasn't uncomfortable. It was just…heavy. Real. Like we were both trying to figure out if we were even capable of fixing what had been shattered so long ago.

"I don't know what we're doing," I admitted, the words tasting bitter in my mouth. "But I don't want to pretend that this….whatever this is…doesn't matter."

Her gaze softened, and for a moment, I thought I saw something break behind her eyes. Maybe it was the same thing I was feeling: this crack in the foundation of everything we used to be, something that both scared and excited me all at once.

"You're not pretending," she said quietly, the words almost a whisper. "Neither of us is."

I nodded, unsure of what to say next but knowing that there was no easy way forward. No quick fixes. And maybe that was okay.

"*Hazel?*" Bill called out from the other side of the fence. "Where are you?"

I went rigid, like we were fifteen again.

Hazel scrambled behind the table like she'd been caught robbing a bank. "Here!"

Bill rounded the fence and eyed us suspiciously, and I got it. Bill and I had a solid working relationship. But what the two of us did not have was a solid relationship as it pertained to his daughter. Especially the kissing of said daughter…

Long ago, when we'd been teens and had spent a lot of time searching for—and finding—trouble, Bill had put the fear of God in us Colburn brothers, making it clear that if *anyone* with our last name so much as touched Hazel, he would personally take them out like yesterday's trash.

Had I believed him as a hormone-riddled fourteen-year-old? Oh, 100 percent.

Had it stopped me? Nope.

But it stopped me now. Because even though that kiss we'd just shared had been the best thing to happen to me in a damn long time, I tried really hard not to repeat my mistakes.

Bill took in Hazel. "Why do you look like you've just gotten yourself in trouble again?"

She laughed, a little forced. "Haven't you heard? I'm always in trouble. How are you? Did you eat your veggies today?"

"I'm not a child, you know."

"Uh-huh." She held out her hand. "Let me see your food-journal entries for today in your Notes app."

The guy squirmed. Tough, hard-ass, unbendable, obstinate Bill *squirmed*. "I don't have it on me."

Hazel gave him a hard look. "If you're cheating on your diet and putting your health in jeopardy, I *will* find out."

I was…confused. There was tension there, something off. Bill had suffered a heart attack, but he'd told us it'd been so minor, it had barely registered. Mother Hen Ryder had insisted on talking to Bill's doctor before he came back to work and had been assured Bill was doing well, that he was remarkably strong and healthy.

Had something changed? Was that why Hazel seemed so worried? I handed him a burger. "Turkey," I said. "Hot dogs too."

"Which means they're not real," Bill grumbled but started eating. "Huh."

I snorted. "Good, right?"

"Not bad." He took another bite. His phone rang, and he stepped away to answer it.

"It's Sybil," Hazel said. "Our old math teacher. They're dating." She shuddered.

I laughed. "How do you know?"

"The goofy look on his face."

Indeed, Bill was…smiling. With teeth.

Hazel wore a little furrow between her brows, the one she got when she was stressed or feeling something particularly difficult for her.

"What's wrong?" I asked. "This isn't about Sybil."

"No." She paused. "He says he's fine," she murmured. "But he's not. I can feel it."

I didn't know if she was right. But I recognized that look. Hazel wasn't suspicious, she was scared.

My question was this: Had Bill exaggerated his health problems to her? Or played them down for me and my brothers? Bill didn't lie. In fact, his usual MO was brutal honesty.

Bill finished his call and slid his phone away, coming back to us. "So how did the new job go today?" he asked his daughter.

"Good."

Bill nodded. It wasn't always easy to tell since the guy had resting cranky face, but he was most definitely feeling pride as he went on. "This Sonoma project will garner you even more attention than the Henderson job. I emailed you some suggestions for the—"

"Dad."

I looked from one to the other, ending on Hazel. Because if there was one thing I knew about the Pierce family, it was that Hazel was stubborn as hell, but Bill could out-stubborn the devil.

Hazel held my gaze. "It's fine," she said, then looked at her dad. "We are not going to fight. Because my dad is going to respect my job and not try to micromanage every choice I make."

Bill took another bite of his burger.

"*Dad.*"

"Kidding. Absolutely going to let you do your job." He looked through the living room window and saw Hank watching TV. "*Jeopardy!* Nice." He got up and vanished inside my house.

Hazel watched him go before her eyes flicked back to me. "How about you? Think we can manage without doing something ill-advised?"

"It's not you two I'm worried about."

She eyed me for a long moment, and when she caught my meaning, it was like her lungs forgot how to work. "You think that you and I…we're going to do something ill-advised."

"It wouldn't be our first time."

Her eyes hardened. "I gave up doing anything regrettable the night I left Star Falls."

"Same," I said.

And maybe we were both lying through our teeth.

Somewhere behind us, Her Fluffiness let out a long, judgmental yowl, like even she knew we were screwed.

CHAPTER 9

Hazel

THREE MORNINGS LATER, I woke up with my heart pounding and my pillow damp, like my subconscious had decided to throw a sold-out showing of my greatest hits.

My breath came in shallow gasps, and my chest felt like I'd run a mile in my sleep. Sweat slicked the back of my neck.

I hadn't had that dream in years, and the ache felt brand-new.

It had been so vivid, I could still hear the hum of my old car's engine and the slicing wind through the windows as I drove away from everything I'd ever known, including Tucker.

Because he hadn't shown.

And I'd waited.

God, I'd waited.

That night, eighteen and shaking, I was ready to tell him everything—about losing track of my period and then not realizing I'd skipped one until I'd actually skipped two… Then the pregnancy tests, the doctor's visit, the ultrasound.

I'd kept the blurry printout, tucked deep inside an old book I hadn't opened in a decade.

I'd been so scared. I didn't want to leave unless he was with me.

But he hadn't come.

No call, no explanation. Just…nothing. So I did what hurt girls did best—I ran.

And a few weeks later, I'd lost the baby.

Now, twelve years later, I still hadn't told him—not about the pregnancy or the miscarriage.

I hadn't told anyone. And sometimes, I still dreamed about the shape of a life that had never gotten the chance to exist.

I stared at the van's ceiling, blinking against the soft glow of morning. A part of me still wanted to blame him for not showing up, for shattering my carefully laid plans. But in the quiet, uncomfortable place I usually buried under sarcasm or doughnuts, I knew the truth.

Tucker never did anything without a good reason.

I'd just never given him the chance to explain.

I sighed and flopped my arm over my eyes. "Years of therapy, and you're still the reigning queen of emotional constipation."

I needed caffeine and maybe a maple bar. And definitely a plan for how the hell to finally come clean and tell Tucker the truth.

The truth that could blow everything up.

I sat up and took in my day's forecast: slightly exhausted with a 100 percent chance of scattered sarcastic comments throughout the afternoon.

"Mew."

Her Fluffiness, of course. Like clockwork, she came by every day for her snuggles. And tuna. Okay, maybe the snuggles weren't just for her, but at this point, she and I were in a full-blown situationship. She was my most consistent source of physical affection. Even my shower massager was starting to feel taken for granted.

Yawning, I got out of bed and gathered my stuff to head into dad's house and shower. But I must've taken too long, because when I slid open the van door, the cat was already waiting for me on the sidewalk like she owned it, fluffy tail twitching, judgment radiating off her tiny, murderous body, retired-librarian-with-a-grudge vibes.

And honestly? Same.

"Good morning," I said. "Do we have a problem?"

Her eyes narrowed.

Translation: *You know what you did. Feed me.*

I bent to give her some love and spotted the note.

If you're reading this, you've clearly ignored all warnings and fed me. I live with you now. Best of luck.

Oh no, he didn't. It was like the man wanted to get himself throat punched before breakfast.

I jammed my feet into sneakers, scooped her royal pain-in-the-buttness up, and marched across the dewy grass toward Tucker's. I didn't even get a satisfying knock in before the door swung open, stealing my thunder and half my vocabulary.

Tucker stood there, all sleepily mussed, barefoot and shirtless, wearing low-slung sweats that should be illegal. He had a pillow crease high on his left cheek, and his voice was morning rough, not to mention way too sexy. "You bribe her with food. Whatever she did, it's on you, not me."

I scowled as my brain struggled to reboot from the sight of him. He was all hard lines and sleek skin. And muscles. Lots of muscles.

He raised a brow. "Problem?"

Hell, yes, there was a problem. And it was him. Sir Sexiness, loyal knight to Her Fluffiness. "Just wondering what kind of midlife crisis leads a man to write passive-aggressive cat notes."

He grinned.

I crossed my arms. "*What?*"

"You're flustered," he said.

"I'm not flustered! Take that back." I was absolutely flustered. "And if you don't want people feeding your cat—because name me *one* human who can resist her pathetic cry—then keep her on your damn side of the fence!"

Still looking amused, he stepped aside. "I wrote that note last night. Sorry she keeps bugging you, but hell if she listens to me." He gestured that I was welcome to come inside.

I tried not to stare at him as I did. *Don't look. Don't look. Don't—damn.* His body was carved from a daydream. He had a lot of nerve still looking so fit that it made me want to lick him like a lollipop.

I caught sight of a slashing scar low on his belly from the emergency appendectomy he'd had in our freshmen year. The scar on his chin was slightly more recent, from a Colburn-sibling scuffle sophomore year. But there was a new scar on his right pec that I didn't have a story for but refused to ask—

"You could take a picture. It'd last longer."

It took me an embarrassingly long time to find my words. "Shut up." I marched past him. I tried not to look. Really. But the man was a walking temptation wrapped in bad decisions, so I definitely took another peek.

Or a hundred.

Hey, it was natural curiosity. Scientific research. Hormones. Whatever.

I took in the interior of the house. While my dad's drowned me in memories, this one didn't. Given the challenges Tucker had growing up here, we'd spent almost zero time at his place; mostly I'd run wild with the Colburn siblings outside, through the oak-dotted green hills, along the river, and through the high rocky bluffs leading to the Pacific coastline. I'd never spent time inside these walls. Not really. Not like this.

Twelve years ago, this place had been a typical ranch-style home, smallish, run-down. Tucker had completely renovated; it was warm and sun drenched, all farmhouse charm with wide wood-framed windows, shiplap walls, and creaky honey-colored floors that made you want to stay a little too long.

It smelled like sawdust and coffee.

Like comfort.

Like home.

But suddenly I needed a minute. Maybe more than just one. I walked through the living room and straight out the back door.

Whoever had lived here previous to the Colburns had built a tree house at the very back of the property, completely hidden by the woods. If you didn't know it was there, you'd never see it. I headed that way, wondering if it was still there.

"What are you doing?" Tucker's voice came from behind me. He'd shoved his feet into battered athletic shoes. Hadn't grabbed a shirt.

"Go back to whatever you were doing," I said.

"I was sleeping."

The thought of him in his bed, that big body all warm and hard—"Go back to sleep then."

"And miss the fun?"

A few minutes later, we stood deep in the middle of the woods, where the sunlight barely made it through the canopy. We were cocooned by two-hundred-foot-tall trees and silence. It was like time had folded back on itself. To when it'd been just me and him.

"Seriously," Tucker said. "What are we doing out here?"

I pointed upward. "I can see the rope ladder we used to use, but it's caught up too high to reach. Give me a boost."

"You never even used that rope ladder. You used to shimmy up that tree all by yourself—"

"Yeah, and I used to eat Hot Cheetos for breakfast. People evolve."

"You *still* eat Hot Cheetos for breakfast. I've seen the family-sized bag in the front seat of your van."

I turned to face him and caught him checking out my ass.

Unapologetic, he let his gaze peruse and caress its way to my face, taking his sweet time about it too. That's when I remembered I was in a thin sleep tee that fell to mid-thigh, boy-cut undies beneath. No bra. My body reacted predictably. I hated how easy it was to want him. Hated how familiar it felt.

His eyes heated. "You look like a woman who gets what she wants."

I reached for the branch above and missed by a couple of inches. So I jumped.

He smiled like he couldn't help it before grabbing my hips, lifting me like I weighed nothing. And just like that, my body reacted. His hands were steady, warm, and they lingered a half second longer than strictly necessary before I caught a hold of the branch with a secret thrill I refused to acknowledge. "You're going to hurt your back," I said, heart hammering.

He snorted. "Just how old do you think I am?"

"Older than me." By three months, but still… "Don't look up my shirt."

"Why, afraid I'll see your undies?"

"You assume I'm wearing any," I said and had the satisfaction of seeing his eyes darken and his Adam's apple bob. Hiding my grin, I shimmied my way up.

"Fuck, that's hotter than it should be," Tucker muttered below me. "And you're wearing light-blue skintight thin-as-fuck booty shorts."

"That's alarmingly specific," I said.

"God-given talent."

With a breathless laugh, I bypassed the rope ladder and scrambled onto the platform. The wood creaked beneath my feet in greeting, that familiar mix of pine, dust, and sun-warmed wood hitting me like a ghost of my teenage self.

A self who was currently pretending my body wasn't still lit up like a Christmas tree from Tucker's touch.

He was only a few seconds behind me, climbing much more easily than I had, landing beside me with a soft grunt.

The tree house was exactly how I remembered: plywood walls, a makeshift bench against the far wall, a cutout in the plywood above for night viewing—a requirement for a tree house—and last but not least, a metal box we'd found years ago in my dad's garage and then filled with snacks and various treasures. Like the roll of wire we'd strung between our houses. And a flashlight, its batteries long dead and corroded.

If I closed my eyes, I could almost smell the different scents of the seasons that had passed here: woodsmoke and damp leaves in the fall, cold earth and pine in the winter, wildflowers and fresh sawdust in the spring, and honeysuckle and sun-warmed wood in the summer…like now.

Once, this space had been our hideout, our shared little universe. We'd spent entire summers here, pretending the rest of the world didn't exist.

We sat like we used to, side by side, our backs against the familiar plywood wall, staring through the opening at the soft pink and orange spilling across the early morning sky.

The quiet between us stretched long and full, charged with everything we hadn't said. I could feel the heat of him radiating toward me, and I barely resisted scooting closer to absorb some of it for myself. But I knew that if I touched him, I'd forget why we couldn't go back to what we'd been.

Not that anyone could ever go back.

Only forward.

But here in this tree house, time felt like it had curled in on itself. Maybe we hadn't moved forward as much as we thought.

I risked a glance. His thigh brushed mine, warm and solid. His chest rose and fell in a steady rhythm. His jaw was shadowed, and his eyes—those damn hazel eyes—were already on me, pure longing in them as he scanned up my legs, my breasts, before finally reaching my eyes. Given the intensity of the look, I had to assume I was gobbling him up as well. That look—like I was still someone who meant something to him—shattered me a little.

"Why are you still here?" I asked softly.

"I could ask you the same thing."

"No, I mean…you always wanted to leave Star Falls. But I'm the only one who did."

His chest rose and fell with a deep breath. "No one's more surprised than I am, but…" He shrugged. "I'm happy here."

After his childhood, I wasn't sure how that could be possible, but every line in his body told me it was the truth.

"Kiera stayed," he said. "Ryder came back to start Colburn Restorations. Caleb came home after the hockey injury. My family's here. My work at the station, it's the job of my dreams, and I'm working toward the next phase. I'm almost there. My life's here." The corners of his mouth tipped up. "What about you, Haze? What are you still looking for?"

Such a simple question. Easy. But nothing in my life had ever felt either one of those things. The answer cracked something in me. I stood so abruptly, I nearly slipped.

He was up just as fast, hands on my arms, eyes searching mine like he could read the mess happening behind them. "Hey. You okay?"

"No." I laughed, except it wasn't funny. His words were kind. Gentle. But they cut right through me. "Look, I *love* that you know who you are. What you want. It suits you."

"But…" he prompted gently, dipping his head to look into my eyes. "What's going on in that beautiful mind of yours?"

"But…" I lifted my hands. "I don't know who I am here. I thought I'd figured it out, but now…" I shook my head. "Being here feels like slipping into a version of myself I don't recognize." Like I'd stepped back into a life I wasn't sure I deserved anymore. My throat tightened painfully, but if I cried, I was going to be furious at myself. "Being here," I echoed softly, "feels like the past is living under my skin. Every street, every sound, every breath—it's all reminding me of who I used to be. And everything I never became." My voice broke. "I've spent my whole life running. From this place. From you. From myself."

"You could stop." He cupped my face, thumbs brushing beneath my eyes where I'd let a few tears slip. "Just for one second, stop."

I wanted to. God, I wanted to. "It's not that easy. Being back here, I feel a little lost."

Even worse? The feelings I'd buried so deep, they'd fossilized—every single one of them for this man, this impossible man—were back. Loud. Bright. Crashing into me like they'd never left.

Like a storm I'd never really outrun. My chest physically ached from the weight of it, like my heart had outgrown its rib cage and was clawing to get out.

I didn't want him to see that I was still *her*. The girl who ran. Who bolted before anyone could tell her she wasn't worth sticking around for. The one who always chose surviving over staying.

Once, this tree house had been a hideout. Now it felt like a mirror. I pulled back, ducked from under his touch. "Gotta go."

"You promised you wouldn't run off again."

I flinched halfway down the ladder, heart pounding, because yeah, he had every right to throw that at me.

He wasn't wrong.

I'd always been better at moving forward rather than standing still. Easier to keep moving than plant roots I wasn't sure I deserved. And somewhere along the line, I'd decided that if I stayed too long, people would see the cracks and wonder why they'd ever wanted me around in the first place.

I wasn't just running from the emotions.

I was running from *me*—the version of me that had never quite figured out how to stay.

"I'm not vanishing," I called up, voice flat. "It's called *work*." I climbed down too fast, scraping my palms and knees, but I didn't care.

"Sure about that?"

I glanced up to meet his stony, hard gaze, realizing he'd climbed down and stood before me. There was a tension to his gaze now and in every line of his body. "What does that mean?"

"It means that it seems to me, you're staying true to yourself. Keeping one foot out the door."

I nearly staggered as that hit its mark, sharp and unflinching right in my chest, calling out my worst fear, nailed in one casual sentence.

Heat rose in my chest—not anger exactly, but something close. Something raw and tired and just...*done*. "Maybe that's true," I said. "But if it is, it's because no one ever gave me a reason to believe I was worth staying for."

His face shifted into surprise and then regret. And something far deeper flickered behind his eyes. He opened his mouth, but I shook my head.

"I wasn't running from you, Tucker. I was running from the version of me who was never enough for anyone. Not my dad. Not this town. Not even you."

He made a sound like he wanted to take the words back, soften them somehow, but I shook my head again and took a step back.

"Don't."

Silence stretched. Just the two of us in the charged space between the past and everything we still hadn't said.

Then, finally, he blew out a breath, low and shaky. "I never wanted you to go, Hazel. I just didn't know how to ask you to stay—and believe you would."

And that?

That ruined me.

Because I didn't know how to stay either.

Or if I could even learn how.

CHAPTER 10

Hazel

Plated egg-white omelets just as my dad walked into the kitchen. He stopped short and stared at me.

I looked down at myself and back up. "What?"

"You look different. Kinda…peaceful."

I snorted, and he did the same. "Okay, maybe *calm* is a better word. Or *almost calm*."

Huh. I certainly wasn't feeling calm—

No, that wasn't true. Even though I'd taken off on Tucker in a spectacular blaze of emotional glory, something in me had… settled. It hadn't felt good in the moment. But here, with my dad making coffee and the air not thick with tension, I realized maybe walking away had cleared something out.

I understood why he'd stayed in Star Falls. I did. I was envious that I hadn't had the guts to do the same. But I was here now, unsettled or otherwise, and I wasn't going to waste a second chance. "Almost calm, huh?"

"Yeah."

I turned my head and studied my reflection in the microwave's window. "Is it that unusual?"

He hesitated, then went for the coffeepot. "It's been happening more this past week than—"

"In all the time you've known me?" I finished wryly.

"Yes, and I like it," he said quietly. "Maybe you'll even stop living outside like a feral cat."

"I'm not living outside, Dad. My van is perfectly comfortable."

He stared down at the omelet. "What the hell is this green crap?"

"Spinach. Just a little bit. For extra goodness."

He prodded the omelet with his fork like it might bite him. "Anything else?"

"Cheese."

He brightened.

"Dairy-free, fat-free."

"Oh, for fuck's sake."

But he ate it anyway, and I headed out to work.

Twenty minutes later, I pulled up in front of the Sonoma project and used the key Caleb had given me to let myself in.

Early morning light stretched across the gravel parking lot, and fog still clung to the trees beyond. The air smelled like cedar and sawdust, with a faint crispness that hinted fall was coming. I breathed it in like a promise.

The staging area was in the covered pavilion behind the building. I found my delivery right away: massive stacks of gorgeous wood and hardware parts. Heaven. I dove in with my iPad, checking the materials against my order. Running my hands over the wood, I felt a burst of…joy.

I loved this. Being here. Building things. Creating order out of chaos. This part of me had always been real. It still was.

Here, no one eyed me like I was a ghost from the town's past. No pointed glances. Just work. Just me and my tools, and a job I could disappear into.

My smile lasted exactly five minutes, until I realized parts of my order had been swapped out and others were missing entirely. I eyed the packing slip. It matched the delivery.

What the hell?

I called the supplier, who told me they'd sent everything Colburn Restorations had ordered.

But I'd placed the order myself.

I stared at my phone. I knew Tucker was the company estimator, but I didn't want to ask him. I really didn't want him thinking I couldn't handle my job. Caleb would help, but what did it say about me if I had a problem in the first week?

Hell. I so didn't want to do this, but I hit a number and bit back a sigh as I brought the phone up to my ear.

"What's wrong?" my dad barked as a greeting.

"Well, hi to you too."

"You call me only when there's a problem. Spill it. Did you mess something up?"

"Nice. Thanks for the confidence." I drew a deep breath. "And no, I didn't mess anything up. But the delivery isn't what I ordered, and yet the supplier says it is. I've never had this happen."

He listened as I explained in detail. Then he said, "My guess is the supplier substituted for something close. Happens when they're understocked. Don't worry about it."

"They didn't tell me that."

"Not like they'll admit to doing it unless pressed."

"But…" This made no sense. "The materials I paid for cost less than this, which means it's costing *them*."

"It doesn't cost them shit if they saved having to hunt down what you wanted and also got rid of inventory on hand. You can make the job work with what you received, right?"

"Possibly. But the quality—"

"It's still good stuff. Your craftsmanship will make up the difference."

I paused. "Are you not yelling because we promised not to fight on-site?"

"Yes." There was a beat of silence where I imagined him wondering why he'd had a daughter. "I'm also hoping the niceness is contagious."

We hung up. A minute later, I called him back.

"What now?" he asked.

"Just saying hi. Seeing how you're doing."

A pause. Then a genuine belly laugh. "Look at that," he said. "It *is* contagious."

"Ha ha." I put my phone away and got to work. First thing I did was text Annie and Tex and let them know I had work for us starting tomorrow.

Then I went about making sure I had everything I needed and resetting my plan of attack, adjusting to the materials I had.

Hours passed before I noticed the time. My stomach growled, my shoulders ached, and I had sawdust in places sawdust should never venture.

I was digging through my backpack for snacks when Kiera FaceTimed me, Emma, and Penny.

I set my phone on a stack of wood so I could eat my candy bar. "Ladies."

"We're all on a break and decided you should be too," Kiera said. "Well, some of us are on a break. Me, I'm just a girl stuck under a napping child, online shopping with a full bladder and a dying phone, while worrying about what the too-silent awake twin is up to."

"Which one's on the loose?" Penny asked.

"Alex."

"Uh-oh," Penny said.

"Why 'uh-oh'?" I asked.

Kiera sighed. "Because I've got only one kid I could trust to be on their own for a whole weekend, and I know they'd eat veggies, lock the doors, and wash the dishes. And it's not Alex."

We all grimaced.

"I also have to pee," Kiera said. "Distract me. What are you all up to?"

"A customer at the café yelled at my barista," Penny said, "and another managed to spill an entire pitcher of soda down a vent. I'm going to be sticky for weeks, and I've been whispering, 'What, from the bottom of my heart, the fuck?' for hours."

Emma nodded, then said, "I read somewhere that being a woman means whispering *WTF* daily."

"Wait, we're supposed to be whispering it?" I asked.

Penny laughed and rubbed her belly. "My clothes are already getting too tight. I can't wait to be past this."

I looked at my friend, who had everything I'd secretly dreamed about. When I'd been pregnant, I hadn't gotten to maternity jeans, and an unexpected pang hit me right in the chest.

A secret part of me wanted a second chance, and I was afraid I'd never get it.

Kiera tilted her head at me. "Tucker still ignoring you?"

I sighed. "To be honest, it was me ignoring him. But we came to a sort of truce."

"You ever going to tell us what is going on?" Kiera asked.

I wasn't ready to discuss this. "Not anytime soon. Anyway, it's a long story."

"We love long stories," Penny said, then peered closer to her screen, trying to see something behind me. "Oh…holy… hotness."

Emma leaned in close as well, brows raised. "Wow, I knew the Colburn Collective was hot, but it's nice to be reminded. Too bad Tucker isn't here; he just might be the hottest of them all."

On my phone screen, I saw Caleb about twenty feet behind me, with his crew: Danny kept everyone in line. Hawk, whose hairstyle changed more often than my socks. And last but hardly least, Miguel, with his movie-star good looks. He was also the biggest flirt I'd ever met.

And they'd all taken off their shirts. I refused to react. I absolutely did not fan myself like a Victorian widow at a scandalous play. I just…appreciated from a distance.

Miguel came up behind me and flashed his dark eyes and bad-boy smile at my phone. "Ladies."

Emma's and Penny's noses were practically pressed to their screens.

"It's like *Magic Mike: Jobsite Edition*," Emma said.

We were laughing when Caleb caught us.

He gave a barely there shake of his head, like he couldn't believe it. "Seriously?" he said, eyes locked on mine. "We're all hot and sweaty."

"Yeah, you are!" Emma said cheerfully.

Caleb eyed Ryder's pregnant wife. "You too?"

Penny blushed. "It's the baby's fault!"

He muttered something and disappeared.

Not Miguel. His eyes locked on Kiera. "Hey, sweetness."

Kiera grinned. "Guess you've forgotten what Ryder said about flirting with his baby sister."

"You wound me." Miguel clutched his chest. "I'm just checking in on a friend."

"Miguel!" Caleb yelled from another room. "Don't egg them on!"

Miguel grinned at us and sauntered off with a wink.

We all looked at Kiera, brows up. I smiled with them, but it didn't land. I wasn't thinking about Miguel. Or his abs. Or any other shirtless flirt. Just one man who could shut down a room with a single look.

And I'd pushed him away.

Again.

Kiera sighed dreamily, but ever the pragmatist, she also shrugged. "I'm not…ready for anything. But it wouldn't kill me to leave the door open, right? Plus, there's the bonus of pissing off a brother or two." She glanced at me specifically. "Speaking of my pain-in-the-ass brothers, Tucker lost it when he found out you got stopped by the cops."

I froze. "He what?"

"Got them in trouble and everything."

Oh God. Was she talking about that night I'd rebuilt the gazebo? "Again," I said very carefully. "*What?*"

"You know how protective he is. He lost his shit. I mean, the man might as well have peed on you. Good thing you love him. You do still love him, right?"

Emma gasped.

Penny gasped.

I nearly swallowed my tongue. "I gotta go." I disconnected from them, then just stood there blinking.

Love him?

I couldn't afford to. Not when I was hiding so much.

And I knew he didn't love me. So I didn't understand why he'd butted in on the police thing, much less not even told me. It smacked of…what? Control? Possessiveness? Or something worse. Care?

Probably all of the above, but that he'd gone to bat for me now really lit my fuse. I wasn't his business. This wasn't his business. I mean, I'd barely given that night I'd rebuilt the gazebo a second thought. In fact, I'd been out to fix other things since then.

Gah, the man was infuriating, and before I could think things through, I called him and got his voicemail.

"Tucker Colburn. You know what to do," said his deep voice.

My finger hovered over the End button. My chest tightened. Somewhere between my ribs and throat, regret started sharpening its claws.

Because I knew *exactly* what to do. "You got the cops in trouble? You had no right to step in or try to fix things for me. Do you even care how weak it makes me look? Stay out of my business. In fact, stay out of my life."

I disconnected and took a breath as regret slid through me. Shit. I hated how fast I could go from empowered to trivial. From strong to scared. I stared at my phone, wishing I could unsend the message. But not even Google had a fix for me.

Good to know I was still really good at making my problems worse whenever possible.

Okay, so maybe…*maybe*, if he was at the station, he wouldn't have time to check his voicemail. A girl could hope.

My dad appeared. "Hey."

"Hey back," I said, still staring at my phone, still filled with equal parts panic and bad temper. "Aren't you on the North Bend project today?"

"I am." He toed the panel I was about to install. "You're not going to put it in like that, are you?"

I drew a deep breath. "Is that my dad asking? Or a rep from Colburn Restorations?"

He scowled. "One and the same. Grab the goddamn plans; I'll show you how you need to do it."

"Dad. We talked about this. You're not my boss. *I'm* my boss, and I was hired to do things my way."

"Yeah, but I've got decades of experience on you."

Aware of the guys nearby, I dragged him into the oversize front-hall closet that was empty except for two boxes of scrap wood that hadn't been taken out yet. "Did you forget we promised no jobsite fights?"

"Who's fighting?"

"Your level of decibels suggests we are."

He sighed and kicked one of the boxes. "I'm trying to help you."

I took a deep breath. That thing I'd said to Tucker—about no one making me feel worth staying for—maybe it had started right here. "Dad, I know what I'm doing."

"Fine!" He tossed up his hands. "Don't come to me when you fuck it all up."

I flinched like he'd slapped me. "Wow. Nice."

He scrubbed a hand down his face, apology all over his expression. "Hazel—"

"No." I didn't want to hear it. "We're not doing this now, not here. I need a moment."

"But—"

"I need a moment," I said firmly.

He sighed and left just as my phone rang.

Normally I didn't answer calls from unknown numbers. But something in me cracked. Maybe it was the fight I'd just had with my dad, or maybe it was the voicemail I'd foolishly left Tucker—both were burning a hole in my chest. But maybe I was just tired of avoiding everything.

So I picked up.

"Hazel Pierce?"

The voice was crisp, professional, feminine. I straightened instinctively, like she could see me slouched in a half-empty closet surrounded by scrap wood and wounded pride. "Speaking."

"I'm calling from Alder & Stone Restoration in Seattle. We just saw the *San Francisco Chronicle* feature on the Henderson project—stunning. Especially the millwork. We hear that was you. Is that true?"

The breath I hadn't realized I was holding shook loose. "Um…yeah. That was me. And thank you."

"We're looking to expand our custom-woodworks division, and after seeing your handiwork, we'd love to bring you on board. Not as a subcontractor but as staff. Project manager. Full-time. You'd run the entire division."

I blinked as my brain tripped over itself. "Really?"

"Yes. I'm prepared to offer you a contract. It'd be a year commitment, renewable annually. Full benefits. Relocation costs included. I know this might be out of the blue, but we wanted to reach out before someone else did."

My mouth had gone dry. This wasn't just a job. This was *the* job. A career move. The kind of future I used to dream about. The one I'd worked for, fought for, built from nothing. But it meant leaving—again. Starting over—again. But this time, it wouldn't be running. It would be choosing. And that made it so much scarier.

Because by choosing me, I wouldn't be choosing Tucker.

No, I couldn't go there. He didn't factor into this decision. Just the thought of no more scraping together project bids, or wondering if I could afford a new jigsaw blade was… everything.

I sat down hard, knees going wobbly. "That's an…incredible offer."

"Then say yes."

A shocked laugh slipped out of me. "I'm not an immediate-yes girl."

"You need dinner first? We'll fly you up. You're the one we want, and that you're a woman is personally exciting to me. One of the owners is a woman as well, and it's very important to her that the company represent."

I shook my head, still stunned. "I'd like to look over the offer and get back to you."

"Of course," she said smoothly. "We'll email it right away. And once you've had a chance to read through it, let's set up a video call to talk details."

I agreed, and when we hung up, I sat there for a long second, still holding the phone like it might vanish, my heart thudding, wild with disbelief.

This kind of thing didn't happen to people like me.

I let out a breathy, stunned laugh—the kind you give when

the universe throws you a curveball in the best possible way. It turned into a full-body laugh, helpless and a little hysterical.

And that was when I realized the job wasn't the only thing asking me to choose.

The closet door opened.

And there stood the main thing between accepting the job and saying no.

Tucker.

CHAPTER 11

Hazel

Tucker's sharp hazel gaze scanned me, tuned in like only a man with training, muscle memory, and unresolved feelings could be. "Everything okay?"

Was it? I'd left him that horrible message that I could only assume by some miracle he hadn't listened to. If he had, he'd be, at minimum, annoyed.

And then there was the call I'd just taken that had me spinning.

His phone rang, startling me. Tucker silenced it without looking, then scratched the back of his neck, sunlight catching in his hair as he blew out a frustrated breath. "Sorry. It's been busy."

All his days were busy, what with two jobs and caregiving for his father and his sister's twins. And yet, somehow, he made it look easy. Like his life had been built on a solid foundation, while I was still patching holes in mine with duct tape and sarcasm.

I had no idea how he'd pulled it off, built a life here.

Meanwhile, I'd spent a decade half-assing mine on borrowed

courage and caffeine. I hadn't left Star Falls for a fresh start. I'd left because I'd run. Run rather than admit I'd made mistakes and I was mortified and sorry but didn't know how to say it. Run rather than face Dad and settle our issues. Run rather than face my overwhelming feelings for Tucker. I could list my regrets all damn day long.

I'd told myself working as a subcontractor was freedom. That being my own boss meant I was strong. But I hadn't expected to spend more time buried in invoices and supply chain snafus than actually building things.

I hated the business side. I wanted the sawdust and the satisfaction, not the spreadsheet.

The job offer from Seattle? It was more than a promotion. It was a clean slate. A sign I might finally be seen for what I could do, that I could be more than the girl who screwed up everything and then left.

That I could be someone worth keeping.

But it would also mean leaving again, for at least a year. Leaving Penny's breakfast burritos. My dad's reluctant softening. Kiera's chaos. Emma's sass.

The man standing in front of me.

And the terrifying hope that maybe, just maybe, I was home.

"Talk to me," he said gently.

Definitely hadn't listened to my message. "Yes, I'm okay." Technically, this was true. I just wasn't sure how to explain the emotions coursing through me without spiraling. I needed time to think. Plus, we were on the job; it wasn't the time or place.

My stomach knotted at the excuses I was giving myself. Because was this an opportunity? Or an escape?

I knew which Tucker would think it was.

He would think I was running.

I needed to decide on my own if that was true or not before I told him.

"Tex heard yelling," Tucker said.

A sigh escaped me. Tex had excellent hearing and a big, fat mouth. "If you knew my dad and I got into a…*discussion*…why are you asking?"

"Because I was hoping you'd tell me."

Before I could decide if that was sweet or annoying, my dad poked his head back in. He zeroed in on Tucker. "What's going on?"

I opened my mouth, but Tucker beat me to it.

"I was asking about the fight," he said to my dad.

"There was no fight." Dad was attempting to lose his scowl.

I could tell because he drew in a deep breath for calm, like he'd been taught by his PT. He was maybe 40 percent successful.

He pointed at the two boxes behind us. "Need to move those." He grabbed the first one with a grunt. "I'm just gonna—"

"Dad! No heavy lifting! Which part of 'Don't be a stubborn mule' didn't register?"

"I'm fine," he grumbled.

"If you're so fine," Tucker said, nudging him clear of the boxes, "then why is your daughter worried half to death and on your ass about eating and exercising?"

Dad muttered something under his breath before saying, "This is why I work *alone*." He exited stage left, grumbling all the way.

I blew out a sigh, and Tucker gave me a slow look.

"What?"

"You have daddy issues."

"I do not."

He gave me that *if you say so* look.

"I'm serious," I said. "We're trying, but we don't speak the same language. He thinks he always knows better, that he needs to tell me what to do."

"God knows why, since you tend to do the opposite when you're told what to do."

I opened my mouth, closed it again. Dammit. I hated when he was right. "Fine. Maybe I do that. Sometimes."

"'Maybe'?" he echoed, amused. "'Sometimes'?"

"You know what? I don't have time for this." I pushed past him, but he caught my wrist.

"None of us do. So, if you've got a problem on this job, you need to tell me."

"And if my problem is also *off* the job?" I stared pointedly at his hand on my wrist.

He released me but didn't step back. "Then I'd *hope* you'd tell me anyway."

Boundaries. He was trying to give me boundaries.

He meant it as a comfort, as a safety net. But I'd spent years bristling at expectations, even the well-meaning ones, and though I was trying to do better, be better, I was my own worst enemy.

His jaw flexed when I stayed silent. I was frustrating him. Which made two of us.

His eyes unreadable now, he said, "Ryder and Caleb will find us any second. If you've got anything you want to tell me, now's the time."

I swallowed. Everything inside me was chaos.

Still reeling from the job offer.

Still furious with myself for leaving him that voicemail.

Still stinging from my dad's words—*Don't come to me when you fuck it all up*—and unsure whether I was the problem or the solution.

Why I had thought this time with my dad might be any different, I had no idea. That I still wanted—*needed*—his approval drove me nuts. He hadn't apologized, and maybe he wouldn't, but I still wanted him to believe in me. Just once. "No," I said. "I don't have anything I want to tell you."

A lie, but the only one I had.

He studied me. "And here I thought today might be easy."

"I wasn't aware you did easy," I said, voice dry.

He smiled faintly. "Trying a new leaf." He tucked a stray strand of hair behind my ear, a quiet act of intimacy that made my knees stage a protest against gravity. There was no teasing in his eyes now, only that deep, guarded thing he carried. The one that knew how to read people and protect them anyway.

His voice was lower when he spoke. "Haze…what's going on in that head of yours?"

I sucked in a breath at the caring tone and willed the sudden threat of tears away. "I thought you were at the station today."

"No. I was in the Colburn offices all morning, running numbers and estimations." His gaze met mine, all-seeing. "Miss me?"

"In your dreams." But I smiled. He was giving me space, in his own way. Letting me come to him.

I appreciated that more than he could know.

I also needed to somehow make sure he never listened to my horrible message.

He tapped a finger on his iPad. "Okay, so about the materials mishap: We can return the order if you'd like."

"Word travels fast."

"I'd just gotten to work when you called. Your dad was in my office."

Awesome. "Returning it will cost Colburn Restorations."

"It'll cost the suppliers." He shrugged. "But regardless, we fix mistakes. That's the Colburn way. If it works, great. If not, we figure it out and move on."

There was a huge contrast between that and what I'd always felt growing up—constant tightropes, no nets. With the Colburns, whether a week went by or a decade, I never had to earn my place. They just…made room.

"I can make it work," I said quietly.

He didn't question it, just nodded, then produced the box he'd brought in with him. He crouched before it now, sifting through its contents with practiced ease. Graceful. Efficient. Maddeningly attractive.

I tried to focus. I really did.

But he hunkered there in his perfectly worn jeans, all lean muscle and quiet confidence, and my brain shut down.

He said something about finishing edges. I nodded.

Something about timeline. I nodded again.

Something about staring at his ass—

Crap.

He rose and turned toward me, an infuriating glint in his eye. "If you see something you like, Hazel…" He spread his arms. "You have only to ask."

"Ugh!" I shoved him, and the laughing *ass* backed up a step. "So smug."

"You love it."

I grumbled something that would've cost me a dollar to the swear jar and glared at him. "Why are you here?" A sinking feeling hit my gut. "Did you think I messed up?" The question hung between us, heavier than I wanted it to be.

"No."

I took a step back. "I don't believe you. You don't trust—"

He caught me, holding firm. "If I didn't trust you, you wouldn't be here. This has nothing to do with you as our finish carpenter and everything to do with making sure you're safe here."

I blinked. "What?"

"You remember the trouble we had on the Henderson project this past spring—missing tools, sketchy visitors…" His eyes darkened. "When Emma got hurt, and you could have been."

Did I remember? I'd never forget. I'd been there that night. It'd been terrifying, running from an intruder I couldn't see, colliding with Emma in the dark, hovering over her, knowing she was hurt, not knowing if we were safe…

"I can handle myself."

"I know, but on the job, you shouldn't have to." His voice was pure, unbending steel. "How about this job? Have you seen or felt anything off?"

I hesitated and his eyes sharpened.

"Tell me."

"It's just a feeling."

"Your feelings used to be dead-on."

It always threw me when I was faced with the reminder of how well he'd once known me. "It's probably nothing."

"Tell me."

I blew out a breath. "Okay, so a few times, tools or materials have been in a different place than I left them. Like someone moved things around. Only, it couldn't have been, because each time I was either the only one here or the last one on-site."

"And you're just now telling me?" he asked, incredulous.

"I never saw or heard anyone, and nothing has gone missing," I said defensively. "I could just be imagining it."

He took a slow deep breath. "I don't want you to be the last one out here, ever. You understand?"

"Don't worry about me. I've got moves." I shifted my weight to one leg as if I were going to knee him. "Wanna see?"

He smiled, but ever the smart guy, he released me and took a healthy step back. "I know you can handle yourself, Haze. You've had to. But you're a part of us. That means we've got your back. I'm not about to let anything happen to you."

I stood still for a second too long, stunned by the realization I really did matter to him.

Don't ask me why that scared me more than anything else.

Tucker took in my expression, and a slow smile came over his face. His eyes seemed to darken, and he opened his mouth to say something, but his phone buzzed. This time he glanced down and winced. "Give me a sec."

He stepped away to answer, voice low and steady as he spoke into the phone. Even that—his calm in chaos—somehow made my chest ache. I knew that voice. I used to hear it in the dark, whispering dreams against my skin.

Now it was just another reminder that he belonged to this place in a way I didn't. Or maybe I did and just couldn't see it yet.

He returned. "Work call, sorry."

I nodded and grabbed a bottle of water from the cooler nearby, mostly to give my hands something to do that didn't involve yanking Tucker in for a kiss I wasn't sure I'd recover from.

He yawned, broad shoulders rolling in a stretch that lifted the hem of his shirt just enough to flash a sliver of tanned skin and those maddening hip lines that really should be illegal. But it was the exhaustion in his face that held me.

"You look like you haven't slept."

"I haven't." He rubbed his eyes and blinked hard. "We got called out twice last night. Structure fire, then a med call. A guy fell off a ladder putting up Halloween lights."

I winced. "Oof. How bad?"

"Sprained ankle, bruised ego."

I shook my head. "Star Falls: population of creative stubborn idiots."

He gave me a pointed look. "And at least one finish carpenter who looks like she's forgotten how to sleep."

"It happens." I shrugged. "Last night wasn't my best rest."

He nodded like he understood—which, infuriatingly, he probably did. The man always saw more than I wanted him to. And for once, I didn't hate it.

He crouched again, going through the hardware bins. "So what would your best night look like? Hypothetically."

I looked out the windows at the golden sunlight streaking across the work zone, smelling the pine and sawdust in the air. "Best night? I get a solid eight hours, my back doesn't hurt, the coffee's hot, my dad's not yelling at me about my life choices, and the jobsite doesn't have any material delays or raccoons in the Porta Potti."

His mouth twitched. "That happen recently?"

"I'm not at liberty to say."

We shared a smile that felt like…more. But my heart immediately skipped a beat in warning. It wouldn't last. Not once he heard my voicemail.

And then I saw him sit down at the picnic table outside the

trailer, rubbing his eyes like the weight of the day had finally won. Something in me softened, but I forced myself back to work.

An hour later, I walked by the picnic table, shocked to see Tucker still sitting there, his head down, one arm tucked under, the other resting on the table.

His phone peeked out of his back pocket like a beacon.

Or a trap.

I glanced around. The others were working on the far side of the property. I crept closer. "Hey," I whispered. "You awake?"

No answer. His shoulders rose and fell with slow, steady breaths.

My head swiveled again. No one was watching. Tucker seemed to be out, but it was still a gamble to move close. Perching casually against the table, I leaned close, like I was whispering something in his ear, and reached out, fingertips grazing the edge of his phone.

I slowly pulled it free from his pocket and—

A hand clamped around my wrist like a steel trap.

I squeaked.

Tucker lifted his head. "You seriously trying to steal my phone while I'm unconscious?"

"Borrow," I said, breathless. "And I was going to return it."

He stood and tugged me with him. "Let's chat."

"We can chat right here. Right here is great."

But he was already steering me behind the trailer. He let go once we were out of sight, arms crossed over his chest. "Words."

I backed up half a step. Maybe two. Because being around Tucker when he was sleepy, annoyed, and focused on me?

Danger.

He simply moved forward, the space between us shrinking as something charged filled the air, thick and electric.

My back hit the wall. Heat rolled off his body as he leaned in close, his breath brushing my ear. "You're up."

My heart hammered in my throat. "I wasn't going to do anything illegal," I said. "Maybe technically *unethical*, but not *felony* unethical."

He gave me a *go on* gesture.

I sighed. "Okay, so I just wanted to—"

"Erase the message of you yelling at me?"

Well, that was one way to spin it… I sagged in defeat. "You know."

He just looked at me.

Right. He knew everything. "Fine. I wanted to erase it, preemptively. As a favor to your ears. You're welcome."

He gave me a long look.

I squirmed. Apparently, I wasn't going to learn to think first, act second anytime soon. "Look, I'm sorry, okay? I should've come to you."

"Yes. You should have."

"I panicked! It's practically a life skill." Damn, he was close enough that I could smell the cedar in his shirt and the clean skin of his neck. It was sexy and extremely annoying. So I doubled down and jabbed a finger into a hard pec, trying to get the upper hand even though he was so close, I could reach out and put my mouth on that sexy throat of his. Or his strong stubbled jaw. Or those lips I couldn't stop staring at.

"You should have told me."

I jabbed his chest again. "Why, so you could step in and save the day? I handled it myself."

He caught my hand, locking eyes with me. "You were harassed for trying to do something good. I couldn't just let that go."

"I'm not your problem, Tucker!"

His jaw ticked. "Caleb's a dead man walking."

"Caleb didn't tell me."

"Then Ryder."

"Nope."

"Kiera?"

I smiled faintly. "Bingo."

"Fuck." He let out a low, rough laugh. "That traitor. I'm going to buy the twins a drum set and electric guitar."

"So is *she* the dead man walking?"

"No." He gave a low, rough laugh. "Hell no."

I stared at him, then snorted. "You're scared of your baby sister."

"Terrified."

I grinned, and he ran a hand over his face.

"It's cute that you think I'm kidding."

That made me laugh, but then I realized how close we were. Still wrapped in tension. I could feel it vibrating between us like a live wire.

"You're not a problem," he said softly, tipping my head up to his. "You're part of my life. There's a difference."

My heart fluttered with a rash hope I didn't know what to do with. Not because I didn't believe him—I did. And that made it worse. He meant it. And I wasn't sure I deserved it. "I really am sorry," I said softly.

"I know." He nodded. "But next time? Just come to me."

"And tell you, what? I got mad and left you a message I don't want you to listen to?"

"Yes."

God, I wanted so badly to lean in, to believe this fragile

thing between us could be strong again. That we could be the grown-up version of us, built on something more than lust and good intentions.

I remembered being sixteen and furious with my dad over something so little that I couldn't remember it now. Tucker hadn't said a word. Just handed me a hammer, a bucket of nails, and a length of cedar plank, then sat beside me while I built something just to hear the sound of destruction. He didn't fix it. He just stayed.

That had always been the difference between us—he showed up. He stayed.

But there was still too much between us.

I had no idea if it was his reluctant smile or the way he looked in work clothes, ready and willing to face anything. Hell, maybe it was the entire package, but my brain aligned with what my body wanted from him.

Everything. My body wanted everything. Dangerous, dangerous waters. "Don't laugh, but I think we really might need some rules."

He gave a slow smile that changed the rhythm of my heart, dammit. "You can't trust yourself with me without rules."

"Rule one," I said, ignoring that because he was right. I gestured vaguely between us. "Maintain a safe distance at all times."

A corner of his mouth quirked. "Should I move to the other side of the country?"

"Ha ha. But I think…" I let my gaze skim over him slowly. "Nine inches should be enough."

He laughed out loud, and damn. "Nine inches, huh?"

"Don't say it," I warned.

So he said it with his eyebrows instead.

On the outside, I rolled my eyes. On the inside, I went soft and pliant. "Rule two," I said, then faltered.

"Rule two: no more running."

The world tipped for a half a second, and we stared at each other.

The air thickened. My throat ached. "Rule three," I whispered. "We leave the past in the past."

"Starting over?"

I nodded. "Exactly. Hi. I'm Hazel Pierce. Nice to meet you." I held out my hand.

He slowly took it. "Tucker Colburn. And if you break the rules, you face the penalty."

"What, you gonna send me to time-out?"

"No." He leaned in, lips brushing my ear, giving me a full-body shiver. "You face the past."

Oh boy. "I was hoping for something easier. Like streaking through the town square."

He laughed, full and low and deep.

I started to smile, picturing *him* streaking down the street, and had a hot flash instead.

That won me another smirk. "You seem pretty fixated on seeing me naked."

"Been there, done that," I said as nonchalantly as I could. "Your naked body's burned in my mind."

He gave me a slow, smug smile. "It's even better now."

I shoved him, even as something deep inside me quivered. "So humble."

He gave a warm, rumbling chuckle, and for one shining second, everything in me quieted.

I wanted more of this.

More of him.

And then it hit me like a truck—I still hadn't told him.

Seattle.

The offer.

And I'd just agreed to a clean slate. The potential move might ruin this truce before it even had a chance to bloom.

I stepped back.

He noticed. Of course he noticed.

"What?"

I shook my head. "Nothing. I just…should get back to work."

He let me go. But he watched me walk away, the weight of his gaze staying with me all the way across the jobsite.

I turned to walk in the other direction and plowed into my dad.

"What?" I asked, startled.

He frowned at me. "You okay?"

I stood there, heart thudding, the ridiculous urge to bolt completely gone. Even scarier? I wanted more moments like that with Tucker.

More of him.

The sunlight slanted golden across the building, catching on the fine sawdust that danced in the air. Voices echoed from the jobsite—someone calling for a level, someone laughing. Life humming forward.

"Hazel?" my dad asked.

"I'm fine."

He didn't believe me. But he didn't push.

I turned back just once. Tucker was already inside the trailer, fingers moving on his laptop. Already gone.

It was like I *wanted* to destroy everything we'd just started to rebuild.

CHAPTER 12

Tucker

HAZEL PIERCE HAD A black belt in avoidance. If emotional running were an Olympic sport, she'd have more medals than Michael Phelps.

There'd been a time when fixing things for her had been easy. Back when we were just two teens trying to out-stubborn the world, sitting on her porch roof and making escape plans we were both too young to understand. She used to laugh when I swore I'd build her a house someday, one with a lock I actually felt safe behind.

She'd been my first best friend beyond my siblings.

And she'd also been so, so much more.

But somewhere along the way, we'd stopped speaking the same language. Now she ran, and I let her, because chasing her hurt worse than watching her go.

Two nights after our talk, I dreamed about Hazel in those faded threadbare jeans she wore on the jobsite. The tees that were a modest cut but hugged her body as if they knew exactly what they were doing to me, a tool belt slung low on her hips.

No one had ever looked as good in a tool belt as Hazel Pierce, a tape measure on one hip, hammer on the other, a walking, cursing, perfectly built hurricane in battered boots. All legs and opinions. Confident in a man's world, not because someone gave her permission, but because she took up space and didn't apologize for it.

She worked with an unconscious grace, like she'd been born with a nail gun in hand. Concentration furrowing her brow, tongue caught between her teeth—and every time she stretched, every time her shirt rode up just a little, it made me hard enough to forget my own name.

I jerked awake to my phone having a seizure on my nightstand.

It was 3:00 a.m. and *Most Important Brother* flashed on the caller ID. Caleb had changed his contact name in my phone forever ago, and since it annoyed Ryder, I'd left it.

I answered with "Someone better be dead."

My back ached like hell.

I'd just finished a brutal forty-eight-hour shift, and this one had left scars. Most first responders learned how to help without absorbing the pain. I thought I was good at that. But today? Today had bled straight through the armor, leaving me, along with Jayden, Tessa, Marcus, and Harlow, shell-shocked.

Our last call had been a head-on collision. Four teenagers, playing chicken. Two were in the ICU, barely hanging on. The other two were about to have their lives rewritten by charges and guilt.

I'd been running on fumes. Now I was running on dread.

"She's at it again," Caleb said in my ear. My brain was still fogged from the dream, but his tone cleared it fast.

I rubbed my eyes. "Who?"

"Hazel. Who the hell else? Guess where she is right now."

That snapped me fully awake.

He didn't wait. "Same warehouse she got arrested at in high school. Only now it's a women's shelter. And someone spotted her up on a ladder."

I remembered. Seventeen, painting a mural. Had overheard dogfights and called the cops anonymously. Stayed until they showed. Had gotten arrested with the rest of them—paint on her hands, fury in her bones.

Hazel had always run straight toward the fire.

"Fuck," I muttered, already out of bed.

"You gonna go get her before she gets herself arrested again, or should I?"

"I've got her." I was already half dressed, yanking jeans over my hips.

From the foot of the bed, Her Fluffiness lifted her head and gave me a judgmental blink.

"Don't wait up."

Ten minutes later, I rolled into the alley behind the shelter, headlights off. The back of the building glowed in the work light Hazel had strung up on a rafter. Just off the building was a concrete pad, weeds growing through the cracks. Two picnic tables were the only furniture.

And then there was Hazel.

On a ladder.

Of course.

She was painting the fresh wood of a new overhang above a pair of picnic tables. Cherry red, from the look of the dripping brush. The siding back there had clearly been replaced. The overhang was new. And the flower pots flanking the back door? No way those were standard-issue.

Hazel stood there like she owned the night, her hair wild in the breeze. Fierce. Focused. Vulnerable in ways she didn't let most people see.

Even from here, I could tell something was eating at her. The tight set of her shoulders. The crease in her brow. She didn't move like someone looking for permission. She moved like someone who knew this world had tried to break her and she'd made art out of the cracks.

I walked into the pool of light and stopped beneath her. "What are you doing?"

She startled, swore, and dropped the brush—right onto my head.

"Oh my God!" She scrambled down, eyes wide. "You scared the crap out of me!"

I swiped red paint off my forehead. "And now I look like a murder victim. We're even."

She bit back a laugh and handed me a rag. "I'm sorry, but seriously, why are you here?"

"Someone reported vandalism."

She blinked, shook her head, then muttered, "Of course they did." She crossed her arms. "I don't care."

Lie. I could see it in her posture. That stiff, bracing-for-impact stance she always tried to pretend wasn't armor. I knew that expression. She cared *too* much and didn't know where to put it.

I looked around. New siding. Clean overhang. Fresh flowers in the middle of the night.

"It looks good," I said.

She hesitated as if surprised. "Yeah?"

"Yeah. *Really* good."

She stared at me, and then her gaze flicked to my mouth. "I feel like I should make a public service announcement that I try really hard not to do stupid stuff anymore."

I felt a stupid smile cross my face. "Same." I stepped closer. "But I don't have regrets."

She laughed low. "Me neither." She reached up and swiped at the paint still in my hair. "Gave you red highlights."

"At the risk of repeating myself—payback's…"

"So you've said." Her voice dropped. "I could hose you down."

I didn't want a hose. I wanted her. But not just physically. I wanted to pull her in and ask what she was running from tonight. And then promise that she didn't have to run anymore.

"Tucker?"

Her eyes were locked on my mouth, and my hands found a home on her hips. "Hazel."

She drew in a shaking breath. "What would you say if I told you I had an urge to do something…wildly ill-advised?"

Every blood cell in my body saluted, then rerouted south. This woman was going to ruin me in the best possible way. "If it involves you, me, and a reckless disregard for common sense, I'm fully on board."

The night was still. A dog barked in the distance. Wind rustled the trees and my paint-soaked hair as she nudged me up against the new siding.

Heat and hunger swamped my bones. "You going to be gentle?"

"Not a chance." Her arms wrapped around my neck, and her mouth found mine, slow, deep, hot as sin.

One taste was all it took. I reversed our positions, pressing her against the wall now, pinning her wrists above her head. She moaned into me, wrapping her legs around me like we were built for this. When she sank her teeth into my bottom lip and tugged, I growled.

She laughed low in her throat. "Love that sound."

"Your turn." I freed my hands to explore, smiling against the hollow of her throat when she whimpered as I worked my way south.

Her hands slid beneath my shirt to touch my bare skin, and my control slipped.

"Cheating," I murmured against her throat.

"I don't play fair."

God, I loved her not playing fair. When I teasingly closed my teeth around a peaked nipple over the thin material of her shirt, she gasped and clutched me hard. "*Tucker.*"

"Anything. Name it."

"I need—"

Headlights blinded us as a car rolled into the alley. High beams. Shit.

Police.

"Don't move!" Officer Joey Morgan jumped out, eyes wide on me. "Jesus, Colburn, is that blood?"

Hazel and I looked at each other. We did have red paint… everywhere, including a handprint across her chest that was so perfect, they could've gotten my prints off it.

"It's paint!" she called out to Joey.

He blinked, then laughed. "Holy hell. I cannot wait to tell this story."

Hazel slid down my body and glared at him. "You 'bout done?"

Joey scratched his head. "I don't know. You causing any trouble? I mean, other than with your tongue?"

"Go away, Joey," I said.

Still chuckling, he backed out and drove off.

Hazel crossed her arms. "Maybe you should go too."

Even with paint in my hair and Joey's amusement ringing in my ears, my body hadn't caught up with the fact that the kiss was over. My heart definitely hadn't. "Or I could help you finish up here."

An hour and a half later, we packed everything into her van, the back of which was organized down to the last inch. She slammed the doors shut, nearly catching my nose.

"We need to clean up," she said, staring at her handprints all over me like maybe it meant something she wasn't ready to say out loud.

"Why do you do this in the middle of the night?" I asked softly.

Her almost smile slipped away like mist. Wind tugged her hair, and her mouth trembled just enough for me to notice. Then there were the smudges of exhaustion beneath her eyes…

"Because you can't sleep," I guessed.

She looked away. So yes.

"Is that because you're sleeping in your childhood home where…?"

"Where my mom died. Where I found her," she whispered, looking away.

The words cracked something wide open in me. I studied her profile, aching to reach for her. "I didn't understand then what that must've felt like," I said. "Not truly, but I do now."

Her eyes came back to mine, full of ghosts. "Because of your job?"

I nodded. "My first call ever was a doozy. Still haunts me."

"Tell me," she said.

"It was maybe a year after you left. I was still volunteering with the fire squad. We got called to a house fire—a foster mom and eight kids. We saved everyone except the youngest. A two-year-old. He'd hidden."

The breath shuttered out of her lungs as her hand found mine. "You didn't find him in time."

"I found him, but definitely not in time."

"Oh, Tucker." Her fingers tightened around mine. "And you still carry it."

I still carried all of it—my own mom, that boy…especially Hazel.

I stared down at our entwined fingers. "Are we back to a truce?"

"Maybe," she whispered. "A temporary one."

I'd take it. I pressed her back against the van, flattened a hand on the door next to her face, and leaned in, dropping my gaze from her eyes to her mouth. "I'm going to kiss you now."

"Yes."

Sliding an arm around her waist, I pulled her flush and brought my other hand up to cradle the back of her head. Our lips were a fraction of an inch apart as we stared at each other.

"You know you have to actually make contact to call it a kiss, right?"

"Smart-ass," I said and touched my lips to hers.

The kiss was nothing like the first. It wasn't wild or reckless. It was slow. Sure.

Unshakable.

Pleasure jolted through my heart, and then again when she moaned and clutched at me like I'd tilted her world on its axis.

Tilting her head, I kissed her again, deeper. And again…

When we ran out of air, we pulled back and stared at each other, and apparently she was equally at a loss for words as me because she backed up a step. "You are…"

"Sexy? Charming? Something you can't live without?"

"*Dangerous.*"

And with that, she got into her van and drove off.

I stood there, heart still threatening to break free of my chest, watching her taillights disappear, wondering if I'd just gotten closer to her, or lost her all over again.

The alley went quiet. The streetlight flickered. A breeze kicked up the scent of paint and pine, and somewhere inside me, hope and fear went to war, and neither was willing to back down.

CHAPTER 13

Hazel

Trying to predict the weather in Sonoma County in late summer was like gambling blindfolded. Did I need a jacket or a bikini? Flip a coin.

Today, though, was a perfect eighty degrees and sunny. I sweat my way through work, but with Tex and Annie at my side, we made real progress on the Sonoma project.

It'd be done before I knew it.

The Seattle offer waiting in my inbox kept poking at the back of my brain like a nosy little sister. I'd started a pros and cons list. So far, the pro column was stacked:

1. Steady work.
2. Steady paycheck.
3. Not seeing Tucker every day would keep me from doing something very, *very* stupid.

The con list had only one thing on it:

1.   Not seeing Tucker every day.

God, I was down bad.

At lunch, Caleb had pulled me aside. "Why does Tucker have a red tinge to his hair?"

I bit back a smile. "Ask him."

"I did. He told me to ask you."

"Oh, well, then I guess I can tell you—he got a bad highlight job." I smiled sweetly. "I told him he should ask for a refund."

Caleb stared at me, a slow, wicked smile across his face. "You're evil. Love it."

I was driving home when I got a text.

TUCKER:

Truce definitely over.

I snorted and laughed all the way to my dad's house.

He was at the front door, saying goodbye to Sybil.

With his lips.

I squelched a grimace as they broke apart, Sybil smiling up at him with soft eyes, patting his cheek like he'd hung the moon.

"Have a good evening, sweetheart," she called out to me as she passed me on her way to her car.

I stared after her, then turned to my dad. He was watching her go, a ridiculously mushy smile on his face that I hadn't seen in…years. "I need to bleach my brain," I muttered. "And maybe my retinas. But I'm glad you're happy, Dad."

"I'd be happier if you let me fleece you in poker over a loaded pizza."

We sometimes played cards at night. It allowed us to hang out and connect without having to actually talk. Avoidance with structure—my specialty.

"Yes to poker," I said. "No to loaded pizza. We can play cards over the chicken salads I'm going to make." I waved the bag of groceries I'd stopped for on the way home.

He sighed like I'd canceled Christmas. Then sighed again when I won fifty bucks off him in Texas Hold'em.

After I'd showered and made exactly zero progress on the Seattle situation, I wandered the hallway. Every photo lining the walls had been taken before my mom had died. Like life was now frozen in place. I stopped in front of one—me at ten, holding up a birdhouse I'd built, beaming.

Mom had snapped the photo.

Grief came in waves, I'd discovered. One day I was fine, and the next I stood in the frozen aisle at the grocery store, tearing up at the sight of my mom's favorite ice cream.

I needed something. Air. Quiet. Escape.

I didn't think. I just moved and was on my way to the tree house via the path behind Tucker's backyard before I realized what I was doing.

His gate was open, like an invitation. I hesitated, just for a second, then stepped through before I could talk myself out of it.

And came to a dead stop.

Tucker had set up a kiddie pool on the grass. Kiera's twins ran full tilt around it, covered head to toe in mud. Tucker was mid-chase, laughing and losing.

He scooped up Abi, who squealed in delight and immediately

smeared mud all over him as she hugged him tight. The red tinge in his hair caught the sun.

Oops.

He plunked Abi into the pool, then lunged for a giggling Alex, who dodged him like a pro.

I snorted, and Tucker's head whipped to mine. "Hey," he called out. "You laughing at me?"

"I am."

"You try this—they're slick as little piglets."

I laughed. "Aw, is the big, bad firefighter being bested by two little four-year-olds?"

"*Yes*—" He finally caught Alex mid-sprint and held him like a squirming football.

Abi, now rinsed, promptly escaped and made a beeline back to the mud.

At one point, she wrapped herself around his leg like a koala and wouldn't let go. He nearly went down like a redwood.

Near the fence, Hank sat in a lounge chair with a bowl of popcorn, clapping with glee.

"You've got the right idea," I said, settling in beside him to enjoy the Tucker Colburn Bested by Toddlers show. "This is better than Netflix."

Every time Tucker got one kid clean, the other one was back in the muck. The yard was a swamp. Her Fluffiness observed the scene from a safe distance on the back stoop with a lifted chin and deep feline judgment.

Then Abi dragged a step stool toward the kiddie pool.

"Hey," I called to Tucker. "Pro tip: When a toddler walks past you lugging a step stool, nothing good is about to happen. Look alive."

He gave me a look that could've melted paint off a wall.

I just grinned as my worries faded away and my heart lightened. That ache in my chest eased for a moment. It was the kind of light that comes from watching someone you care about being happy, even if you aren't ready to admit how much that matters.

A shadow suddenly blocked out the sun.

Tucker, standing at the foot of the lounger where I sat.

I tried not to notice the black board shorts with little white smiley faces on them, or that his previously white shirt was now filthy and clinging to his torso like he was trying to win a wet T-shirt contest, or how his hair stuck up in muddy clumps.

"You going to help?" he asked. "Or just sit there and admire the view?"

"Definitely door number two."

He shook his head, still smiling.

I loved watching him with the kids. He never raised his voice. He was endlessly patient, and every time he caught one, he hugged them close like they were the best thing that had ever happened to him.

I'd once thought he'd look good as a dad. I hadn't been wrong.

And the twins melted into him like they knew it. Like their little hearts recognized safety when they felt it.

My throat tightened. There was something about watching him like this—unguarded, playful, full of joy—that cracked me right open. Like the past hadn't taken everything after all.

My hands slid to my belly. What if I hadn't lost the baby? What if he'd shown up that night? What if we'd become a family, stayed each other's home base?

What if, what if, what if…?

A slice of grief slid through me that we hadn't gotten our

chance. But, oh, how I understood why Abi and Alex melted for him. I knew just how warm and strong his arms were, how they made it feel like nothing could penetrate and hurt you. And I mentally added another con to leaving: not getting to see Tucker like this. Happy. Unburdened. So damn good with kids, it made my heart hurt.

I decided to take mercy on Tucker and stood to help. "Kiddos. Come."

They galloped over, eyes bright.

"How do you two feel about a hose?"

Cheers all around.

I rinsed them off, got them dry, and tucked them in beside Hank, who made a satisfied "ah," which was universal for *These kids are awesome.*

Kiera emerged from the house and surveyed the carnage. "Did I miss a cyclone?"

Tucker, drenched and still battling mud, sent her a look. "Your kids are the sweetest little menaces I've ever met. They tag teamed me."

"I'd say they'd never, but then they go ahead and never like they've never nevered before." She whistled, and the twins immediately ran to her.

She shot Tucker a proud look and ushered her crew inside, Hank included.

Tucker faced me, dripping, shirt clinging, looking somewhere between exasperated and impressed. "You're still good under pressure."

"That wasn't even close to pressure."

He smiled. "You're liking it here. In spite of yourself."

He wasn't wrong. And that scared the hell out of me. I couldn't afford to feel this settled. Or this seen. Not when everything was temporary. Not when I still hadn't told him so much.

So…I lifted the hose and nailed him in the chest.

I'd really hoped for an unmanly yelp. But he just laughed, running his hands down his torso, pushing off chunks of mud like it was a spa day.

"You forgot something," he said casually.

"What's that?"

"Payback."

The image of him hosing me down, then following that up with those big, skilled hands sent a shiver down my spine. "Don't. You. Dare."

His eyes gleamed. "Yeah, you're definitely starting to like it here." Then he stepped in close, wrapped a hand around mine on the hose…

And turned it on me.

I squealed and laughed, spinning away in a shower of cold spray—but inside I was bracing.

Not for the cold water.

But for the fall.

I already knew what it felt like to lose him.

And I was terrified of finding out what it felt like to let him in again.

CHAPTER 14

Tucker

Hazel shrieked and twisted as the cold water sprayed down her back. "You're still wet," she gasped.

"Sure am," I said, stepping closer.

She spun the hose around and aimed straight for my chest. We danced around the yard like two saps in a romantic comedy. I ducked; she missed. She lunged; I caught her wrist and turned the water back on her, only to trip over a kid's sand pail and almost eat shit in the grass.

She laughed so hard, she nearly lost control of the hose entirely, but her competitive streak was strong. She wrestled me for it like we were fighting for a WWE championship belt.

We rolled across the grass, laughing, limbs tangled, slipping on wet turf. Then her icy fingers slid under my shirt, found my ribs, and dug in.

I yelped. "Hey!"

Me being ticklish was a secret—and a bitch.

Triumphant, she cackled and straddled me like she'd just

conquered Everest. She was soaked, flushed, laughing, and hands down the most beautiful thing I'd ever seen.

Then her eyes narrowed at my smile. "You let me win."

I grinned and trailed my fingers just barely under the hem of her shorts, brushing the soft skin of her upper thigh. "Did I?"

She caught my wrists, heat flaring in her eyes. "You're cheating."

"Have to keep up with you somehow, don't I?"

She leaned over me, and some of her hair curtained around us, making the moment seem even more intimate.

"Just so you know," she whispered in my ear, "I had one more move up my sleeve."

"Yeah? What?"

"I was going to stick the hose down the front of your pants."

I laughed until my abs hurt. Nobody made me laugh like Hazel. But she was cold. Not that the wet-shirt look wasn't working for me, because holy hell, it was. That soaked white tee was plastered to her skin, sheer enough to reveal a white lace bra that I wanted to remove with my teeth. That image alone was going to live rent-free in my brain until the end of time.

But her teeth were starting to chatter, so I rose to my feet, pulled her up with me, and snagged a towel from the picnic table to dry her off.

"I'm not cold," she insisted.

The pride on this woman. "Okay," I said easily, still wrapping her up.

"Calling me a liar?"

"Right to your face." When I had her as dry as I could get her, I grabbed my sweatshirt from the table.

"I'll get it all wet," she said, backing up and bumping into the picnic bench.

"Suck it up, Tough Girl."

"I know you mean that nickname as an insult, but it has the opposite effect on me."

I looked at her. "Opposite as in…" I waggled my brows.

"No!" She laughed. "It makes me feel…I don't know. Proud? Because I *am* tough."

"That was never in doubt," I told her. "And I've *never* meant it as an insult."

Her lips parted, then closed again. Like the words hit someplace deep that she wasn't ready to admit existed. She'd said it like she still had something to prove—to the world, to herself. But she didn't. I'd seen her hold her dad together, rebuild a life out of scraps, and *still* find time to tease the hell out of me. That wasn't just tough. That was battlefield-grade resilience dressed up in sarcasm and tool belts.

And it was sexy as hell.

We stared at each other for a long beat. She swallowed, and I did too as I dropped my sweatshirt over her head. It fell to mid-thigh. She grumbled but snuggled into it, burying her nose in the collar and inhaling like she loved the scent of me.

That alone nearly did me in. My heart kicked like it was trying to break out of my chest.

"Is this how you melt your women?" she asked. "You share your clothes?"

I felt a smile curve my mouth. "You melted?"

She rolled her eyes so violently, I expected them to pop out and roll into the grass.

I tugged gently on a wet strand of hair clinging to her throat. "Cute."

She slapped my hand away with a scowl. "What did I say about calling me *cute*?"

I smiled. "I've shared my clothes with…*zero* women. Pilfering my Giants jersey doesn't count."

Her eyes widened, disbelieving. "You knew it was me?"

I smiled. "Who else?"

"Hey, it was surprisingly soft. And cozy. And…I might still sleep in it sometimes."

The image of her in my jersey, falling off a shoulder because it was so big, her bare legs tangled in sheets, the hem riding up high enough to—

"You can't have it back," she said. "Not even if one of your dates wants it."

"You're fishing." And I liked it more than I should've. "First, melted. Now fishing."

"You take that back."

I didn't. I just said, "I haven't dated anyone in a long time."

"How can that be true? Have you seen yourself?"

I let out a rough laugh. "Hazel, the only woman I'm seeing is you."

We were still holding eye contact when Kiera stuck her head out. "Oh good," she said. "Everyone's wet and emotionally compromised."

"Can we help you?" I asked.

"You're out of mac and cheese."

"Thanks for the update."

Kiera winked at Hazel. "Call me later. I want to hear everything."

Hazel turned red. "There's nothing to—"

"Oh, please." Kiera looked between us. "You two are one accidental grope away from a Hallmark movie. I need help getting the twins in the car."

I didn't break eye contact with Hazel. "Be right there!"

Hazel stepped back. "I should go."

"This'll take only a minute. Wait for me. I've got cookies. *Not* made by Sybil."

"No way," she said. "You think processed sugar is the devil. You're that person who, when someone's having a sugar craving, you suggest an apple."

"Apples are delicious."

"Sure, but they're not cookies." She paused. "Do you really have cookies?"

I grinned and jogged toward the house.

Kiera met me at the door with a look of exhaustion that could curdle milk.

"You look tired," I said.

"Have you looked in a mirror? Because so do you." She handed me three backpacks and Alex. "Rough week?" she asked, scanning my face.

I shrugged. "Call after call last night. I think we got maybe an hour of sleep."

"Yeah, well, I got woken by 'Mommy, my fart's on the floor.'"

I blinked and shuddered. "You win."

I walked her and the kids out front.

"So…" she said casually. "When are you going to tell me what's going on between you and Hazel?"

"Never."

"Wrong answer."

My sister could get intel out of a locked vault. The CIA had nothing on her skills.

At my silence, she just smiled smugly. "You'll break eventually. They all do."

I didn't say a word. She might be the nosy police, but I could hold a secret like Caleb could hold a grudge—forever and with receipts. "I'm not going to break."

"Don't worry. I can be patient."

I laughed. "Since when?"

"Hey, I've already waited over a decade. You just take your time." She yawned so wide, her jaw cracked.

I hated to see her so tired. "What can I do to help?"

"I mean, I wouldn't turn down a genie wanting to grant me three wishes."

I slid her a look. "Give me a real way to help."

"Okay, okay…" She thought about it. "I'd sell my soul for five minutes to myself to drink my coffee while it's still hot. Or to pee in peace. Or to take a bath all by myself."

I rubbed the back of my neck. "Okay, so…what color genie would you like?"

She cracked up, then hugged me—only to quickly recoil. "You're still wet!"

"Sure am." And I hugged her anyway, laughing while she slapped at me, trying to free herself.

She pointed to her eyes, then mine. "I *will* get you back."

When Kiera made a threat, she carried through. I'd have to sleep with one eye open, because like an elephant's, Kiera's memory was long.

When she drove off, I found Hazel lounging in a chair, face

tipped up to the sun like she was solar powered. I stopped at her feet, blocking her light.

She cracked open one eye. "Where are the cookies?"

"Inside."

That got both eyes open, and she cocked her head at me, gaze warm and curious now. "You think you can coax me inside with cookies?"

"Can't I?" I taunted. "And don't forget, I know you. Your toxic trait is watching the *Great British Baking Show* religiously while *not* being able to bake."

"No, my toxic trait is assuming people have common sense and getting mad when they don't."

I snorted. "Okay, I stand corrected. You have two toxic traits."

She huffed out a laugh. "Why did you ask me to stay?"

I sprawled out on the lounger next to her and shrugged. "Maybe I wanted to talk."

"Great," she said far too easily. "You first. Why don't you do relationships?"

I hesitated. How had this turned on me? "I have. They just don't…age well. Apparently, I don't commit."

She gave me a long, thoughtful look. "You're one of the most committed guys I've ever met. That's not it."

I exhaled, looking out over the yard. "Then what?"

"Well, for starters, you grew up watching your parents fight like hell, and your mom never left," she said gently. "Anyone who'd lived through that would be naturally wary of love."

I closed my eyes, tipped my face to the sun. "I used to beg her to leave him, but she never did," I heard myself say. I'd never talked about this. Not ever. "And I think somewhere along the line, I decided I wouldn't risk putting anyone through that. So I keep it casual. Safe."

She reached out and took my hand, her expression softer than I could take. "Tucker…"

"I'm good. I like casual. It's…safe." Why the fuck was I still talking? But there was something in her gaze that compelled me to finish, to make sure she understood, because hurting her would kill me. "Don't feel sorry for me. I go out plenty. I just prefer an expiration date." I tipped my head back and closed my eyes. "I don't have to worry about making someone miserable for the rest of their lives or failing them in some way."

I waited for the obligatory *You'd never hurt anyone* or *You shouldn't shut yourself off that way*, but all she did was squeeze my hand.

"I don't do serious either," she admitted. "Too many bad endings."

I had no idea why my heart was pounding or why I wanted her back in my life so goddamn bad that I actually ached with it, but I did. I wanted to figure out a way to have her, have *this*, and not fail.

Terrifying in its own right.

"Aren't we the pair," I managed to say. "Want to talk about it?"

She shrugged. "I wasn't interested in seeing anyone for a long time after I left here. Guy number one dumped me after four years for still grieving the loss of my mom. Said I was emotionally unavailable—and he was right. Guy number two told me I was *the one*, then ghosted me after we slept together. Should I go on?"

My chest burned.

She smiled tightly. "Long story short? I'm never enough."

Damn, I wanted to punch something. A freshly

eighteen-year-old Hazel had been kicked out by her dad for making mistakes, then left behind by me, then abandoned by every guy who followed. *Of course*, she believed she wasn't enough. She'd learned it the hard way. I wanted to go back in time and throttle every man who'd ever made her feel like she had to earn love.

"So…" She stood. "I'm on a man moratorium."

I stood up as well. "You gave up sex?"

She snorted. "Sex and relationships aren't the same thing, you know."

We stood toe-to-toe. Her eyes locked with mine, heat radiating from the ground, the truth sitting between us like a loaded weapon.

"I'm not ready for the likes of you," she whispered.

"Ditto."

But we didn't move. Didn't blink.

Finally, she laughed low, shook her head, and walked away.

———

Later that night, I woke to Her Fluffiness sitting on my chest, glaring. It was still oh dark thirty in people time. But in cat time? Breakfast.

Grumbling at being owned by a cat, I padded to the kitchen, with her trotting along behind me, letting out a pleased chirp when I filled her kibble bowl.

And then I realized she had a note on her collar.

Last night I howled outside your neighbor's window for thirty minutes. You owe her sleep and a full refund on her peace and quiet.

I stared at Her Fluffiness. "Seriously? We've talked about this."

The feline turned her back on me and lifted a back leg to clean her lady town.

I flipped the note over and wrote.

Never been able to convince a woman to do anything she didn't want to. But I always pay my debts.

"Mew."

I slid her a look. "If you wake up Hank, you're sleeping with him and his nocturnal emissions."

She sniffed and stalked to the couch.

"Wise choice—" I froze, my gaze caught on something outside. I leaned in to see better.

Someone was crouched at the Pierce back door, eyeballing the lock, and my stomach clenched.

Hazel was inside that house, sleeping.

Shit.

I sprinted out, heart in my throat as I realized the asshole had given up on the door and was attempting to climb through the small open window in the door.

I moved closer but didn't say a word, watching as she—yes, *she*—got stuck halfway through.

Since I knew exactly whose sweet ass I was looking at, I relaxed—not that I was going to let Hazel know that. "You've got two seconds to crawl back out of that window," I barked, hard steel. "I've already called the police."

"Liar," she said, completely unfazed. "You're a control freak who handles everything himself. You'd never delegate a takedown." She wriggled, then cursed.

Yep, stuck.

Enjoying myself now, I leaned against the siding. She was wearing what I assumed were pj's, albeit the smallest, silkiest pair of pj's I'd ever seen. Every time she wriggled, trying to drop into the kitchen, those itty-bitty shorts got shorter.

And my view got better.

"Why are you breaking into your own house?" I asked idly.

"My dad bolted the door. *Are you going to help me or what?*"

"Trying to decide."

"Oh my God, decide faster!"

I grabbed her hips, and here's exactly how small her little silky shorts were—they didn't cover nearly as much of her as my hands did.

"You going to stand there all day staring at my ass, or are you going to save said ass?"

I tugged but couldn't get any leverage. Wrapping my arms around her, I tried again, and she shot out so fast, it was like we'd greased her up with butter. I fell backward, and we landed in a heap.

Best three seconds of my life.

This close, I saw that her pj's had little hammers all over them. Across her chest read, *I Nail Things*. I snorted, and she wiggled like she had no idea she was killing me.

Only Hazel could weaponize pajamas.

I gripped her hips and held her still. "What were you doing? Because I'm guessing you aren't out here looking for the Legend of Star Falls."

She gave a single harsh laugh. "If those stars saw me coming, they'd blink out of existence."

I hated that she believed that, but I was still in mission mode and needed answers.

"Fine." She crossed her arms over her chest, which only plumped her breasts up and nearly out of the cami. My mouth went dry.

"If you must know," she said, in a tone that I would bet a million dollars Her Fluffiness would use if she were human, "I have to pee."

I blinked. "And you're not using the front door because…?"

"I told you. My dad locked it," she said in a *duh* tone. "And I don't have a key for the bolt."

My mind was not working. I blamed her pj's. "Your dad locked you out?"

"Well, not on purpose. He accidentally hit the bolt. Or at least I think it was accidental. I mean, we both know it wouldn't be the first time he kicked me out, but I didn't get arrested or do anything to tick him off this time, so…"

I hated being confused. "Why are you outside if you have to go to the bathroom?" I turned and eyed her sprinter van, realizing the side door was open and I could see a mattress made up with bedding, rumpled…as if someone had just gotten out of it.

A toolbox sat beside the bed, half-open. A tiny framed photo of her mom balanced on the shelf above.

She was…living in her van. Alone. Hiding in plain sight. My gut tightened as an unhappy thought crossed my mind. "Don't you dare tell me you've been living in your fucking van."

"Okay, I won't tell you."

Sharp, biting humor got her out of a lot of situations, and she was a pro at it, but not this time. "You couldn't come to me?"

"You'd have asked questions."

"Damn right I would've asked questions! Like why aren't you living inside with your dad?"

"It's complicated. And it's not forever."

"You've been living twenty feet from my house."

"I know."

"I would've…" I shook my head. "I don't even know what I would've done."

"You would've tried to fix it. That's who you are. But I don't need fixing."

I stared at her. "You could've told me. You should've told me."

"I was scared."

I hated that. "Of me?"

"Of what it meant to be back. Of what it meant to want to stay."

That stopped me.

We were both quiet. Then she squirmed again. "*Bathroom.*"

I helped her up. "You can use mine. Then cookies."

She hesitated, gaze catching mine like I'd offered her something too fragile to trust. "You always do this," she said quietly.

"Do what?"

"Make me feel like I'm not alone."

"You're not," I said. "You haven't been. Not for a long time."

She was quiet for a beat. "What if I told you stuff about me that would change your mind?"

What the hell was she holding inside? "Haze, there's nothing you could say that would make me walk away."

Her eyes went suspiciously shiny for a beat. She swallowed hard and looked away.

"Hey," I said, my chest tight at the pain I'd seen in her gaze. Those beautiful eyes held secrets. Secrets I was guessing she didn't want to keep anymore. "Whenever you're ready," I said quietly.

She looked away a moment, gathering herself. "I'd like to pee now, then eat cookies."

"Priorities," I said.

Her fingers tightened in mine as we stepped into the warmth of my house, like she didn't want to let go.

Like maybe she was starting to believe it too.

And for the first time in a long time, I let myself believe this thing between us might not end in disaster. But hope is a tricky thing when you've been burned before. And I was already on fire.

CHAPTER 15

Hazel

A FEW MINUTES LATER, I tiptoed out of Tucker's bathroom in full stealth mode, but Her Fluffiness had other plans. The cat let out a dramatic yowl loud enough to wake the dead.

The hallway light clicked on. Tucker stood there, arms crossed, leaning against the wall. Calm. Cool. Completely unreadable.

Also still shirtless, because of course he was.

"Let me guess," I said, heart thudding. "You want to talk about my life choices. And probably also my failed B and E at my dad's house."

"It's your house too. And I'm guessing you've got a very good reason for not wanting to sleep there. Like…your mom."

A sharp ache bloomed in my chest. "Everything in that house is a reminder of her. And it hurts." I paused. "I know you understand that."

He gave a single nod. "I do. I gutted this place down to the studs because of memories. But that's not what I wanted to talk to you about."

Something quivered inside me, and I began to move. "If there aren't any cookies, I'm pretty tired, so…" I slipped past him, but he gently caught my ponytail, keeping me in place.

"Hold up," he murmured, his lips ghosting my ear.

My knees promptly forgot how to function. "Very manly," I said, heavy on the sarcasm. "Alpha vibes are out of fashion, by the way."

"You're not going to sleep in your van. It's not safe."

"I've got defense moves. If you're okay with never having kids, I'll show them to you."

"Hazel." His voice dropped an octave and rumbled from his chest into mine, scattering my thoughts like confetti. His hands slid down my arms, turning me to face him. His eyes held mine with calm certainty, and just like that, my resolve started to erode.

"Talk to me," he said.

"It's late."

He rubbed his jaw, the sound of stubble against his fingers a low rasp that made my skin tighten, doing something to my insides that I refused to acknowledge. And the fact he wore nothing but those sleep pants, slung so low on his hips they defied decency, didn't help.

I wasn't stuck now, and my eyes were having technical difficulty staying on his and not on those abs and that glorious V of muscles that doubled as an arrow to the motherland. It was impossible to keep my gaze where it belonged.

I exhaled shakily and rubbed my chest without thinking.

Clocking the gesture, he gently reeled me in, his hand sliding to cradle the back of my neck. "You still get nightmares?"

After losing my mom, I'd had them constantly. Sharp, brutal, unforgiving things. They'd faded away over time, but Star Falls had brought them back like a freight train. "I can still see her," I whispered. "On the floor, and…" My voice cracked. "We'd just had a big fight. I'd told her I hated her."

"Hazel." Voice low, pained. "She knew you didn't mean it."

Did she? I'd never know. "I need to go to bed."

I made it to the front door, but he beat me to it.

"You're not sleeping in your van tonight."

"Actually," I said, "since I'd rather walk through a minefield in clown shoes than sleep at my dad's, that's exactly what I'm going to do. Or maybe I'll sleep in the tree house."

"Not funny." His stupidly perfectly square jaw tightened. So did his eyes. He was displeased.

He could join my club.

"Sleep here," he said in a firm voice that probably worked for him with most people.

But not me. "Did hell freeze over?" I asked sweetly.

He didn't budge. He wasn't playing. "I've got four bedrooms. I'm in the primary; my dad's in the one off the living room. You can have your choice of the other two."

"I don't like your tone."

He sighed like I was exhausting.

Fair.

"It's not like we haven't slept in the same house before," he said.

Oof. That landed like a sucker punch wrapped in nostalgia. Back in high school, every time Kiera stayed over at a friend's— which was often, because teenage girls love sleepovers and Tucker had hated his house—he'd crawl through my bedroom window like it was the most natural thing in the world.

I kept a sleeping bag on my floor for him. He never tried to sleep in the bed with me. And I'd never invited him.

Until I did.

One night. One reckless, couldn't-take-it-back night, when the rules changed and we let the truth slip between the sheets and gave in to everything we'd been holding back.

And then that one night turned into another. And another. Each better than the last. And, God, the things I'd felt for him, things I'd never felt again or since.

I'd known things would never be the same. They would be better. Us against the world.

I'd never been more wrong.

The next day, I was stupid enough to tag the side of the courthouse building on a dare and got caught. My dad's and my fighting kicked up a notch over the next few weeks until one night when he said I should get out. He'd said it before, an empty threat, really, because we always managed to get over it, at least enough to cohabitate. I don't know what it'd been about, that last fight, that last *my rules or the highway* that had me wanting to run. For real.

It was in my blood not to stick. When my mom had died, I'd retreated from everything. Sports. Friends. School. Boys…

The only thing, the one person I'd never walked away from had been Tucker. And technically, I still hadn't. Nope, he'd been the one to walk away from me.

And so I did my thing. I ran. Leaving Star Falls in my rearview. Tucker included.

So much time had gone by, but here we were, back in that space—one of us offering the other safety, both pretending we didn't unravel each other by just breathing.

"I can't sleep here," I whispered. Translation: I couldn't be this close to him and not fall again.

Because staying meant wanting, and wanting meant risk. It meant remembering what it felt like to be wanted in return. And I wasn't sure I could survive losing that again.

He stared into my eyes, his own hooded. Then pulled something from the front pocket of his sleep pants.

My van keys.

"I got them when you were in the bathroom," he said.

"You mean you stole them so I wouldn't vanish."

"Toe-may-toh, tah-mah-to."

I reached for them, but he held his arm up over me.

"You want these?"

"You know I do."

"Then take them."

I considered climbing him like a jungle gym, but if I did, I'd probably forget about the keys entirely. "Give them back."

With a daring smirk, he slid them into his front pocket. "Come and get 'em."

I hesitated, but probably not for the reason he thought. I wanted those keys. I also wanted to cop a feel—and more. But that would be bad, stupid, and *bad*. "You're infuriating."

"So I've been told." He led me down the hall. "Pick a room," he repeated. "One has bunk beds. The other, Kiera uses sometimes and would be more comfortable for you."

"Thanks."

He didn't respond, just led me down the hall, pointing to the first door. "Hank's." He then opened another door.

The room was big, with dark masculine wood furniture, everything clean and neat, including the massive bed with navy bedding that was scented like him and made me want to plop onto the mattress and just breathe it in. Clearly Tucker's. "Do you always make your bed with perfect corners like that?"

He chuckled. "I wouldn't if you were in it."

The rich laugh? It was a touch. A kiss. It reached places I hadn't even realized were still tender.

When he read the emotions rolling across my face, his grin vanished, and I locked my traitorously wobbly knees and reminded myself to ignore his sexy, easy charisma. It was a trap, one I would not get caught in.

The next room had soft-green walls, a faded quilt, and a sunbaked oak scent that made my chest ache.

"Sheets are fresh," he said.

"It's lovely."

He shrugged. "That's all Kiera. Sometimes she joins me and the twins when we're having a sleepover." He caught my hand as I started to move inside.

"We good?" he asked.

I nodded.

"And you." He peered down into my face. "*You* good?"

I let out a rough laugh. "That's a bigger ask."

He nodded like he understood. "You're breathing. You're here. You're safe. If you're good, in the morning I'll make you pancakes that will change your life."

I snorted. "For a second, I thought you were going to offer something else."

His eyes darkened, his voice low. "Didn't think that was on the table."

My heart thudded at the urge to run like someone had just yelled *feelings* in a crowded run. "Me neither."

He took another of those deep breaths and stepped back. "This isn't me making a move on you. It's me trying to keep you safe and comfortable. Your job is labor-intensive, and you need sleep so you're sharp. That's all."

I gestured to his outfit. Or lack thereof. "You sure about that?"

A corner of his mouth quirked. "Why? See something you like?"

"Who wouldn't?"

He stared at me. "Right back at ya."

My entire body buzzed with awareness, hopeful and trembling. He didn't miss that either, raking his gaze over me slowly, appreciatively.

"Deal on the pancakes," I managed. "But fair warning—I'm using your shower, plus your sexy-smelling soap and shampoo, and I'll probably steal some clothes."

"I'd expect no less. Water pressure's shit," he warned. "I shower Hank at night, but I use it at five thirty a.m." His eyes flashed. "Go before, after, or better yet, join me. Just don't use the water while I'm in there, or you'll freeze me out."

Then he was gone.

And even though he wasn't in the room, I didn't feel alone anymore.

I woke at 5:30, stunned I'd slept through the night but also mildly offended to be up so early. As I padded into the kitchen— followed by Her Fluffiness, who undoubtedly expected to be fed—I heard the pipes rattle.

Tucker was in the shower.

I filled the coffeepot with hot water and smirked when a very loud, very manly squeal echoed from down the hall. Look at that: Mornings *could* be fun.

I was still grinning when I turned to the coffee maker, which, frankly, looked like something NASA might pilot to Mars. So many buttons. So few brain cells this early. I could no more figure out this machine than fly to the moon.

And then he appeared.

Barefoot. Wet. Rumpled. Not shaved. Wearing nothing but black knit boxers that revealed miles of mouthwateringly lean muscles on the kind of body that should come with a warning label.

He was all sleepy heat, quiet danger, those hazel eyes promising me retribution—which, for reasons I refused to analyze before caffeine, made my nipples stand at attention.

He could seduce me by breathing.

Meanwhile, I probably looked like a cross between a sleep-deprived raccoon and a confused sloth. I'd piled sweats on top of my pj's, no doubt giving off an impression of stylish depression. My hair had most certainly rioted, and I was 90 percent sure I was drooling.

Sexy, I was not.

And yet, despite it being way too early for sexual tension, here we were, the air crackling around us like it had a vendetta.

"Feeling playful today, are we, Tough Girl?" he asked in a voice that changed my body chemistry.

I lifted my chin. "Don't know what you're talking about."

His smile was pure trouble, his eyes calculating, as if he were cycling through a few scenarios: Seduce me, kill me, toss me out, or—my personal favorite—bend me over the kitchen table and make me forget my name.

Without a word, he nudged me aside and took charge, working the overly complicated rocket ship with ease, getting coffee going in seconds like it was his love language, all while looking like sin on a mission.

Then he fed Her Fluffiness, who thanked him by rubbing up against his legs while aggressively purring.

The hussy.

We didn't speak. We just stood there, leaning back against opposite counters, empty mugs in hand.

Staring. Watching. Simmering.

I knew Tucker wasn't a morning person, and yet he somehow made silence seem sexy. Same with the stubble, the hair, the hooded eyes. I was one prolonged look away from sponta-neously combusting, when my stomach betrayed me and let out a dramatic growl that echoed off the walls like an air horn.

Her Fluffiness glared at me, then turned and walked out of the room.

In horror, I slapped my hand to my belly.

Tucker just snorted and opened the fridge. And then proceeded to make pancakes and hand delivered a loaded plate.

"Are they any good?"

He smiled, took the fork from me, cut himself a bite, and brought it to his mouth.

With eye contact.

His lips closed around the fork. His tongue flicked to catch a stray smear of syrup like it was a live demonstration of foreplay, and I had no one to blame but myself. I was the one who'd brought hot water to a firefight.

Then he licked the fork.

Slowly.

My brain crashed like a Windows 95 desktop, and my soul left my body. I stuffed a bite into my mouth and moaned sinfully.

His eyes darkened as he turned away to fill our mugs with coffee. His back flexed in all the right places.

And I forgot how to use words.

With a knowing look, he added cream and sugar to my mug and handed it to me. Nudging it to my mouth.

I rolled my eyes but complied like a woman with no self-preservation instinct. Sipped. And then blinked in surprise.

The coffee was heaven.

Damn it.

I took another long gulp of caffeine, then dug into the pancakes like they owed me money.

Tucker stayed quiet, leaning against the counter, watching me eat. By the time he finished his coffee, I'd inhaled every bite on my plate and was seriously considering licking it clean.

He smiled. "Go ahead. I won't tell anyone you actually liked something good for you."

"Good for me?"

"They're protein pancakes, and the syrup is sugar-free."

"Shut up. Really? It's like dessert."

"It's fuel. You won't crash in an hour or reach for a candy bar at ten a.m."

"I don't do that *every* day…" I rinsed the plate and set it in his dishwasher. "Thanks. That was nice of you."

"Contrary to popular belief, I'm a nice guy."

I took in the sight of Morning Tucker in all his mussed-hair, shadowed-jaw, coffee-making glory.

He'd housed me.

He'd fed me.

I had no idea what he wanted in return.

His brows went up when he caught me staring. "What?"

I shook my head to clear it. "You remember how I like my coffee."

His eyes held mine. "I remember how you like everything."

Cue quiver in inappropriate places…

He grinned.

This man needed a hazard warning. I took a sip, looking for the upper hand. "How was your shower?" I asked sweetly.

"Great." He slid me a look that both thrilled and terrified me. "Though you should sleep with one eye open."

I rolled said eyes. "*Please.* I've lived with power tools more dangerous than you." Lies. All lies. "Oh, and before I forget, your back porch's railing?" I gestured to the back door with my mug. "You'll be lucky if someone doesn't fall and sue."

"Is that someone going to be you?"

"Ha ha. I can fix it if you want. I'll even offer a friendly discount."

"Define 'friendly.'"

"The kind where I don't report you to OSHA," I said breezily.

When I left for work a little later, I was grinning. Was I worried about Tucker's promise of retribution for the short shower? Yes. Was I also looking forward to it?

Also yes.

CHAPTER 16

Hazel

THANKS TO TEX AND Annie, the day flew by. We made serious progress on the cabinetry, and once the altered materials were stained, everything looked seamless.

When Ryder brought the clients by for approval, they were thrilled.

At the end of the day, I was cleaning up and in my thoughts when someone came up behind me.

"Heard you had a win."

I turned and smiled at Tucker before I could control myself. "Hey."

He was in his station wear, looking hot, sweaty, and deeply over it.

I was doomed. "Long day?"

"Too much action," he said. "And not the fun kind."

That one hit me right in the soft spot. When I had a bad day, it usually meant someone didn't like their cabinet hardware.

When Tucker had a bad day, it meant someone might not have made it home.

"I'm sorry," I said softly. "Shouldn't you be face-first on a couch somewhere, drooling into a throw pillow?"

He gave me a look that said, *Probably*, but here he was anyway.

"Delivering this." He handed me a house key. "Caleb and Emma are taking Hank to bingo tonight, and I'll still be at the station, so the house will be all yours."

I stared at it, throat tight. The Seattle job offer had felt like a way out. But lately, I didn't want out. I wanted this. "Caleb went willingly to bingo?"

Tucker grinned through his obvious exhaustion. "Oh, he hates bingo. But Emma loves it, and he loves her, so…"

"Sweet."

"Don't let Caleb hear you say that."

"All you Colburns have your moments."

He scowled. "Take that back."

"Nope."

My dad passed by, grumbling about the schedule and overages. He glared at us. "We standing around now? Because in case no one noticed, we're staring down the deadline, and if we don't finish on time, we'll get hit with a daily overage charge. Ryder'll take that outta my ass, so don't think I won't take it outta yours."

"Hi, Dad," I said with extra cheer. "I'm having a great day, thanks for asking." I turned to Tucker. "You?"

"Amazing," he said, dry as dust.

"The owners were just here," I added, hoping to break the tension *and* change the subject.

Dad crossed his arms.

I realized I'd just done the same thing. Like father, like daughter… Nothing like looking into the DNA pool and seeing your own reflection glaring back. I immediately dropped my arms.

I was pretty sure Tucker smirked, then moved away to give us privacy.

"And?" Dad asked.

"They loved it. Not a single change order."

His face brightened with a rare grin. "Of course they did. Your work's impeccable." He ruffled my hair like I was five. Normally, that would've made me bristle. But this time, it just made me feel seen.

Across the room, Tucker was watching me—not like I was a hot mess to fix. Not like a puzzle missing too many pieces. He looked at me like I was important to him. And I—finally, undeniably—soaked it up.

I walked over to him, looking up into his eyes, which had warmed at my approach. "Maybe…" I whispered, "maybe it doesn't have to be complicated."

He cocked his head, making me realize that I'd had an entire conversation in my head and he had no idea what I was talking about.

"Us," I said. "I'm making it too hard."

A corner of his mouth quirked, and I sighed. "I'm being serious."

"Then, by all means, continue."

"Us," I said. "No past. No future. Just now."

He looked at me for a moment. "No promises, no strings."

"Yes. Worth a try?"

Another long beat. "You're always worth a try, Haze." He let out a half laugh. "I mean, what could possibly go wrong?"

———

That night, alone at Tucker's, I fixed his back porch's railing, which was oddly satisfying. I'd never imagined I'd find my worth in my work, but I had.

It was late when I slid into bed, wearing one of his T-shirts. I curled under the covers. Just another night in another borrowed space I didn't quite belong in.

Even if a secret little part of me wanted to.

I drifted, but as it often did now, the dream found me.

Vicious. Cruel. Unrelenting.

Because I knew no matter how fast I moved, I'd still fail.

I was fifteen again. Grounded for sneaking in after curfew.

I hate you, Mom! I'd screamed it at her…

Darkness. Panic. Tangible distress dragging me down the hallway. And then—

Her body on the floor.

No pulse.

No movement.

Her bright, joyful eyes closed. Her mouth twisted in pain.

Skin blue. Lifeless.

Then her eyes opened. "Hi, my beautiful girl. Don't cry. I love you to the moon and back…"

Mom, don't go. Please.

I have to, baby…

I woke up sobbing. Shaking. Drenched in sweat. A scream trapped in my throat and panic clawing down my spine like it had teeth. I fumbled for air, for blankets, for reality, my breath coming in gasps, shallow and ragged.

I heard the door open.

Tucker.

No words. No questions. Just him and all that controlled, silent grace. He sat on the edge of the bed and wrapped his hand around mine with just enough pressure to ground me.

He didn't say, *You're okay*. He didn't say, *Let it go*. He simply leaned back against the headboard and opened one arm.

And I moved.

I crawled into that space he made for me without thought. Curled into his side like the part of me that was locked in the past knew he had me, and I could let go.

My cheek against his bare chest. His heart steady. Warm. Strong.

One arm wrapped around me, and the other hand threaded into my hair. Slow, rhythmic motion. Thumb tracing over my cheek like he could soothe the nightmare out of me.

Still no words. He didn't need them.

I had no idea how long we stayed like that. Ten minutes. An hour. A lifetime.

But slowly, the dream loosened its grip. The shaking stopped. I could breathe.

His arms never wavered.

And for the first time since that awful night…

I let go.

Of the guilt.

Of the fear.

I love you to the moon and back…

Finally…finally…my tense muscles relaxed one by one. I

hadn't let anyone in like this, not in years. But something in me trusted him with all my broken pieces, even the ones I hadn't touched since that night.

And I slept. Because maybe this was how you started to belong—you built one solid thing, then let someone hold the rest.

When I woke up, Her Fluffiness sat on my chest, a note in her collar:

Dinner tonight? Dessert included.

Like I was going to say no to dessert.

Or Tucker…

CHAPTER 17

Hazel

BY SEVEN THAT NIGHT, I wasn't sure whether to be insulted or worried. Tucker hadn't come home at the end of his shift. Or called. Or texted.

I tried to go with insulted. Easier on the pride. I took a shower, stole another of his perfectly soft T-shirts from the load in the dryer that he still hadn't folded, and since I hadn't done laundry, also grabbed a pair of light-blue boxer briefs. I had no shame, and he had great taste.

But something felt off. Tucker didn't flake. Or forget. Was he frustratingly direct and brutally honest, with a moral compass you could set your watch to?

Yes.

So, if he'd changed his mind and didn't want to do dinner, he'd say so.

Worried it was then.

I knew he was just waiting for me to run, like I tended to do. Not because I was afraid of work or people—it was the only way

I ever knew how to breathe when things got too heavy. I'd been running since I was a kid, long before Tucker Colburn ever tried to save me. Leaving wasn't about not caring.

It was about surviving.

I didn't know why, but something pulled me outside and through the woods. When I caught a faint telltale glow of a lantern up high in the trees, my chest squeezed tight.

No sound, no movement, but I felt him.

It felt odd déjà vu from the times I'd come out here to hide from the world. I ached at how bad his day must've sucked to send him out here, alone.

I stopped beneath the canopy of the tree. "Hey," I called up. "You good?"

Silence.

I looked around. No rope ladder.

Seriously?

"Real mature." I muttered something about splinters and bad life choices and started climbing. Clearly, he was in a mood. Rare, for him—Ryder was the Colburn with the sulks.

At the top, I found Tucker sitting against the back wall, head back, legs sprawled out in front of him, palming an expensive-looking, nearly full whiskey tumbler in his fist, the bottle at his side.

He wore an ancient T-shirt that hugged his chest and arms. Jeans so faded and threadbare, they clung in all the spectacularly wrong places for my self-control. Old running shoes. Hair damp, messy, like he'd showered but couldn't be bothered with anything beyond fingers and frustration.

Her Fluffiness was curled in his lap, still, staring up at Tucker with a concerned look on her little furry face.

My heart gave a sick lurch. Something was wrong. Bad wrong. And Tucker, being the brick wall he was when he didn't want to feel, looked carved from stone.

So I went with what worked best for us: sarcasm. "Hi, Haze," I said in a mock baritone that didn't come close to his low, rough, stupidly sexy one. "I'm good. What's up with you?"

"Hazel." He barely breathed my name, and with it, a warning. But nothing more.

His face was carefully blank. The kind of forced, hollow nothing that meant everything.

Reticent, stoic alpha-male mode activated. I tried not to sweep my gaze over his whole tall, gorgeous, emotionally constipated self and failed spectacularly.

His eyes were already on me. Dark. Scorching.

Yep. He was most definitely feeling some sort of way.

"Thanks for pulling up the rope ladder; that was helpful," I said.

A dark chuckle escaped him. "Maybe I wanted to be alone."

"I'm going to choose not to take that personally."

"You should assume more things are personal, Hazel."

I stopped directly in front of him and nudged his shoe with mine. "I could've died. I'm out of practice climbing trees."

He flinched. Actually *flinched*.

Shit.

Something awful had happened on one of his calls.

With no idea how to help, I lowered beside him and nudged his shoulder. "I'm not going to ask if you're okay," I murmured, knowing damn well he wouldn't open up about whatever it was until he was good and ready. "And it's clear you don't want to talk, so…" I pulled a deck of cards from my pocket. "I'll even give you a leg up since I just fleeced my dad."

Nothing.

"All right." I tried a teasing tone. "Strip poker. Final offer."

His head turned slowly, some base masculine part of him reacting to my offered distraction.

"Tucker," I breathed. "What's wrong?"

He lifted a broad-as-a-mountain shoulder. "Shitty day. House fire out in the sticks. It was bad."

"How bad?"

"A woman's in the ICU, burns over most of her body. Not expected to make it through the night." He closed his eyes. "Single mom. Two kids, who right now are sitting with a distant relative, waiting to see if their mom's going to make it."

My heart cracked wide. I could only imagine what this had stirred up inside him. Because there'd been a time when Tucker was the person sitting in the ICU with *his* siblings, waiting to see if their mom was going to make it.

He dragged in a breath. "We found her curled over her youngest. Shielding her with her body. Like she knew. If we'd been two minutes sooner, we could have gotten her out before seventy-five percent of her body burned."

I pressed a hand to his arm. "You did the best you could."

"How do you know?"

"Because I know you."

He stared at me for a long beat. One corner of his mouth quirked slightly. "You think so, huh?"

"I know so." I drew a deep breath. "You can't focus on the ones you lose, Tucker. You have to focus on all the ones you save."

He tipped his head back to stare at the towering canopy of valley oaks overhead and the night sky that peeked through. "My biggest fear is that I can save all these strangers, but when it comes to the people I love, I…can't."

"Hey." I slipped my fingers into his, anchoring us both. "You were young when your mom got sick. That wasn't on you. No one could've saved her."

He shrugged. "Fears aren't rational."

Boy, didn't I know it. "You know what my biggest fear is?"

He turned his head to look at me.

"That you'll eat all my Hot Cheetos."

He snorted. Shook his head. Almost smiled.

That nearly undid me.

His fingers brushed my thigh, lingering just long enough to make me forget how to breathe.

"I'm afraid I'll always be judged by my past," I added, quieter now. "That I'll have to change to be loved, and I'm not sure I know how."

Tucker

I laced my fingers tighter around hers. I knew I was in bad shape. I hadn't wanted to see anyone; I didn't want to talk. Fuck, I barely wanted to breathe.

Luckily, my dad was spending the night at Kiera's, which made her my favorite sibling at the moment. While I normally didn't mind wrangling Hank, I was grateful not to have to argue with the man who could express a full TED Talk with just one syllable: *Ah.* As in, *Ah, why do I have to wear underwear?* And *Ah, why isn't a party-size bag of chips considered a balanced meal?*

All I wanted was a cold beer, edible food, and eight uninterrupted horizontal hours with no questions from Team Ah.

And something to take this bone-deep ache from my chest before I had the promised dinner with Hazel, something to make me feel human again.

But she'd come looking for me. And had found me. I met her gaze, my own intense. "Nobody who matters will ever judge you."

She gave me a *get real* look, which on a different day would've made me smile. She might be down, but she was not out.

Silence settled over us. Comfortable. Familiar.

And the pain reverberating inside me dialed down a notch.

One thing about Hazel, she understood space. How to give it, how to sit inside it without making it feel like pressure. She just…was. Sitting beside me, wearing one of my vintage firehouse T-shirts that was slipping off a creamy shoulder, bare legs folded beneath her, looking criminally sexy.

Her Fluffiness, having ditched me for Hazel, sat smugly purring in her lap like she was the world's most judgmental chaperone.

My cat shot me a look. *You're welcome. I preheated her for you.*

"Did you steal more of my clothes?" I asked.

"Since they've been in the dryer for days, I figured they were abandoned and needed a new home." She ran a hand down the shirt. "Hope you don't mind."

My mouth went dry and my brain short-circuited. She looked like home. My past, my mistakes, and the one thing I'd never stopped wanting—all wrapped up in one.

I offered her my glass. Anything to give my hands a job besides touching her.

"That shirt's a collector's item," I said casually.

"Oh yeah?" She ran a hand down the front again, fingers brushing where my name sat faded across her chest. "What makes it collectible? The ratty collar? The ancient logo?"

"My name across your breasts."

She stilled like a deer in the headlights. "You're…better at flirting than I am."

All thoughts of food and sleep vanished. Just looking at her, I felt…lighter. And wide awake. I smiled. "Is that what we're doing? Flirting?"

She took a sip from the tumbler, grimaced. "Maybe."

"You fixed my railing. And the back steps too." The repair was flawless, but that was Hazel. Selective with what she cared about, but when she picked something, she gave it everything. "You planning to bill me?"

"Oh, you'll pay. You do realize you need new casing on the east side of the house?"

"Yeah. We had a hell of a winter. A tree came down and did some damage. And you should be careful. You keep fixing things, people are gonna start thinking you like it here."

Her expression flickered, just for a beat. A crack in the armor. "I wouldn't want to ruin my brand." She shifted, and the shirt rose up her thighs.

Suddenly, there was only one thought in my brain, a question. "What are you wearing underneath my shirt?" *Please say* nothing…

She flashed me a quick peek of a pair of my boxer briefs riding low on her hips, and my brain flatlined.

"You okay?"

"Just trying to survive the sight of you in my clothes." The air between us shifted—thicker now, hotter. The hunger she stirred up in me hadn't gone anywhere, and now it had teeth.

She stretched her legs out in front of her, took another sip of the whiskey. "You ever think about what you would've done? If you'd gone with me that night?" She said it softly. Carefully. Like she knew the question might crack something inside me.

It did.

I took the glass from her and set it down. Then came up on my knees.

Between her thighs.

"I think about it all the time," I said.

Her gaze locked on mine, open and raw.

"It haunts me," I went on, running a finger down her throat and along her shoulder, bare where the shirt slipped down to her elbow.

She gave a husky, mirthless laugh. "Yeah. Same." Then shook her head. "Ignore me. I shouldn't have asked. It's the storm. Static electricity." She twirled a hand near her ear. "It does something to my brain. Makes me say stuff I shouldn't."

I caught her hand. "Don't talk about the woman I'm crushing on like that."

Her mouth fell open in surprise.

With a grim smile, I shifted, sitting with my back to the wall, tugging her into my lap so that she was straddling me. I wrapped her up tight, holding on to her, not sure I could let go even if the world were on fire. Then I buried my face in her beautiful, silky, wild hair. "I've got this ridiculous, insatiable need to be near you," I murmured. "Always have."

She didn't pull away.

Neither did I.

CHAPTER 18

Hazel

AT HIS WORDS, I whimpered, soft and stunned, while he slowly kissed his way up my throat. I cupped his face to hold him close, heart pounding, thrilled at the rough stubble beneath my palms.

Tucker lifted his head, eyes dark, looking hard and dangerous.

But I wasn't afraid of him. Never had been. Never would be. "I've got you," I whispered so softly that I wasn't sure he heard me.

But he made a low, rough noise deep in his throat and pressed his forehead to mine. "Fuck, Haze… Tell me to keep my hands to myself."

I gave him a single headshake. "I can't do that."

His grip tightened on my hips like he was fighting restraint. "We said never again."

"We did." But I hadn't meant it. *Never again?* Who was I kidding? I couldn't keep my hands off him even if I wanted to. "When we said never again, we were on your porch…"

He pulled back, those hazel eyes burning into mine. "And…" An almost smile hit his mouth. "We're not on my porch."

"We are not."

He drew a deep breath. "I'm going to need you to spell this out for me. What are we doing?"

"Ideally? Each other." I bit my lip. "Just a onetime pass, and that's it. No more."

"A onetime pass," he echoed, possibly fighting a smile.

"I mean, we've both probably got new moves to show off…" *Look at me, body in control, mouth fully hijacked.*

His arms tightened. "Do you want to show me yours right now?"

"I do." I slid my hand down his chest to the hard length straining beneath denim.

His eyes went molten as he caught my wrist. "Here?"

"Here." I quivered at the way he looked at me—like he was starving. "Can you turn down the lantern?"

"Not a chance." That slow heated look as he took me in from head to toe and back again made me ache in places that hadn't ached in years.

"I'm not going to miss a single second of this," he said so low, it was almost a growl.

I breathed him in like oxygen, a citrusy, sandalwood scent clinging to his skin, making me want to eat him up. "Kiss me, Tucker. *Please.*"

"Hmm, love the 'please.'" His fingers tangled in my hair, angling my head the way he wanted. He kissed me then. Deep. Soul stealing. He tasted like whiskey and heat and something heartbreakingly familiar, and I clung to him. Losing myself.

He slid a warm callused palm to the nape of my neck as our eyes locked, a question lingering in his: *You still with me?*

I melted into a puddle.

His slow smile was cocky as hell. So I nipped his bottom lip, tugging just enough to make him groan.

That sound? Dirty as hell. I desperately needed him inside me, but we were still fully dressed. "*Tucker,*" I moaned. It was all I had.

He stood in one smooth move, lifting me, then dropped into the beanbag chair with me sprawled on top of him. He didn't speak. Just pushed my hair from my face, looking at me like he needed to memorize every detail.

"Don't even think about stopping," I whispered.

His eyes darkened. "I won't." His voice dropped to smoke and gravel, and suddenly breathing felt like too much effort.

He nipped my earlobe, giving it a little tug, and I shuddered, grinding down on him. His hands clamped onto my hips, not to hold them still, but helping me keep a rhythm that had us both gasping.

"You're fucking dangerous," he murmured.

Already breathless, I trembled in his arms. "You love that about me."

"I do." He yanked me down for another kiss that left me feeling wild and desperate when he pulled back. He stared up at me like he was memorizing every inch, like he couldn't quite believe we were here, like this.

"More." I tugged at his shirt, and he grabbed the hem of mine and slowly lifted it up and over my head. The heat in his gaze as he took in the sight of me in nothing but boxer shorts rolled low could've powered the grid for all of Sonoma County.

"Fuck, Hazel…" He shook his head. "You're the most gorgeous thing I've ever seen."

"*Mew.*"

We both froze.

Her Fluffiness sat watching us like we'd interrupted her during an episode of *Love Island*.

"Close your eyes," Tucker told the cat, gaze locked on mine.

I laughed and rocked my hips again. He groaned, his eyes nearly rolling back in his head.

"You're overdressed," I pointed out, reaching for the button on his jeans.

He stripped down to skin in a blink, and I made a sound of deep pleasure, reaching out to wrap my fingers around his.

He caught my hand mid-motion, then reversed our positions like it was nothing.

"What—"

He nipped at my bottom lip. "I'm slowing this down," he murmured. "You deserve that."

I could feel *exactly* how ready I was and rocked up into him to prove it.

"You're not going to rush me. Not on this."

"But I was about to have my way with you," I complained.

One knee pressed into the beanbag at my hip, forearms braced around my head, he gripped my wrists. "Hold that thought."

His mouth made its way down my throat, across my collarbone…

Breathing became optional. My eyes drifted shut.

"Open your eyes," he said softly.

I did because he was right—I didn't want to miss a thing. I also wriggled my wrists.

He just tightened his grip on them as he slid down my body, those big hands everywhere at once, dragging helpless moans and *yes please* sighs from my throat. Kissing, nibbling, and sucking every single inch of skin he passed, he slowed to tease my nipples into hard pebbled peaks.

Eventually, the sounds I couldn't contain spurred him into more southern territory, a hot kiss pressed to my stomach, hip…

He nudged my legs apart, wide enough for his stupidly broad shoulders, and when I tried to shift, he nipped my inner thigh.

I almost came.

"Be still."

"I need—"

"I've got you, Hazel." He nuzzled my lower belly, finally letting go of my wrists to grip my hips.

"Tucker, I swear—"

His mouth found my center, and I stopped talking. Stopped breathing. Stopped every single thing except feeling his mouth on me.

"God, look at you," he murmured and teased me with decadently lazy swirls of his tongue, adding his fingers into the mix, indeed taking his time until I was writhing beneath him, fingers fisted in his hair, mindlessly grinding against his face as he slowly, thoroughly took me apart.

And then put me back together again.

When I opened my eyes, he was braced above me, eyes dark with something dangerously close to reverence. His body—God, his body—was taut with tension.

"Hazel."

"I swear to God, if you've changed your mind—"

"I don't have a condom."

Oh. *Oh…* I bit my lip and stared up at him. "Um…"

"I'm so sorry," he murmured, pressing a kiss to my temple. "I shouldn't have taken it this far—"

"I'm on the pill," I whispered. "And safe."

"Me too. The safe part, not the pill part." He smiled, slow and sweet. "So…" He nudged the hardest part of him against the softest part of me. "This is okay?"

"It's so okay, I will cry all over you if you don't—"

He slid into me, and we both gasped in sublime pleasure.

"Eyes on me, Haze," he said softly.

When had I closed them? I managed to drag them open and nearly came at the look in his.

"You feel so…fucking…good, Haze."

"Right back at you," I whispered. "Now, please. Please, please, please, *please* can you do me?"

With a husky laugh, he began to move—slow, deep, driving me right to the brink and holding me there, not letting me fall.

"*Tucker*, I… I need—"

"I know." He lowered himself so that I could feel every inch of his body against mine and moved faster, his mouth ghosting mine as he whispered, "God, Haze… I can't get enough of you. I'll never get enough of you…"

Just words, I tried to tell myself. Words spoken in the heat of the moment. But I wasn't buying that story. Something had flared to life between us, a well of emotion I'd never, not once, felt before.

I cupped his face, sliding my fingers into his hair as we came together, the world splintering around us in a rush of heat and something that felt dangerously close to more.

We lay breathless and tangled, thundering hearts struggling

to slow as dusk surrendered to night. Neither of us moved. Neither of us spoke.

Something had cracked wide open between us, and pretending otherwise suddenly felt impossible.

An owl hooted.

A coyote howled.

Tucker shifted. Life coming back online.

We slowly sat up.

Her Fluffiness still sat in the middle of the floor, tail curled, head high, eyes slitted.

Unimpressed.

"Told you not to look," Tucker muttered. He brushed my damp hair from my cheek and stared into my eyes. "That's one way to make some new memories."

"We certainly defiled the old ones." I smiled. "Good thing that was just a onetime thing…" I'd never survive a repeat.

"Good thing," he echoed.

And I wondered if either of us believed it.

———

Tucker

I woke up sprawled across the tree house floor, my cat draped across my ribs like a judgmental paperweight.

The lantern was out. The air had cooled, and a blanket had been pulled up to my stomach. Hazel had covered me.

And then left.

Her Fluffiness lifted her head and gave me a look that could cut steel. *She's scared. You scared her. Now fix it, or I'll be pooping in your shoes for the rest of my life.*

She would too.

I sat up, everything aching, my brain still playing a highlight reel of the night before. My despair, then her showing up. Our insatiable hunger. How we'd turned to each other again and again.

She'd looked at me like I was more than just comfort or nostalgia.

Like I was home.

Which made the empty space where she'd been feel cavernous. No way was she running. I knew that much.

But she was retreating.

And I knew exactly why.

A onetime pass, my ass. Last night hadn't been just sex, and we both damn well knew it.

Because it had meant something.

My phone buzzed. Kiera. Shit. I'd promised to get the twins and Hank to daycare. Real life waited for no man. Not even one who'd just had the best night of his life and wasn't sure how to function now.

Twenty minutes later, Abi bounced into her booster seat in the back of my truck with a juice box and a story already loading.

"Unca Tuck Tuck!" she announced. "Guess what?"

"What?" I asked, yawning wide. How much sleep had I gotten? Maybe two hours, max. Even after Hazel and I had worn each other out, neither of us had been able to stop touching. Kissing. Laughing. Tasting. Wash, rinse, repeat.

And I still wanted more.

Abi kept bouncing. "Teacher Miley said, 'Griffin, put your booty away!'"

I blinked. "His what now?"

"His bum-bum," Abi confirmed solemnly. "It was out. I saw the whole crack and everything."

I choked on air.

Hank, riding shotgun, snorted. I blinked and then eyed him. He gave me an innocent look.

Sometimes, like right now, I felt completely ill-equipped to deal with my life. Some mornings you woke up with a cat on your chest, your pants on the floor, and a hangover of the soul. Other mornings, your niece casually dropped a butt crack story before breakfast. Sometimes, it was the same morning.

I laughed. What else could I do?

"Why are you laughing?" Alex wanted to know.

"Just tired, baby, that's all."

He squinted at me like he didn't believe a word. "Maybe you need a nap."

I needed more than a nap.

I needed Hazel.

And the guts to tell her that last night hadn't been a mistake. That it had been everything.

CHAPTER 19

Hazel

TRIED TO LOSE myself in work, but knowing I'd slipped out on Tucker like a thief in the night made that difficult. Even though it hadn't been night, not really, but just before dawn. I'd lain there wrapped in his arms, watching him sleep as if I could brand the moment in my brain so I'd have it forever.

And then my phone had softly beeped, letting me know Tex and Annie were on their way to the jobsite.

So really, it wasn't an escape. I'd had to get to work. Period.

But through the day, as my team and I installed restored crown molding from the early 1900s, I fought a totally mysterious, definitely normal goofy smile.

Annie, crouched before her toolbox, reloading her nail gun, glanced up at me. "You ever going to tell us what that smile is about?"

"I'm not smiling." Wait, was I? I tilted my head to catch my reflection in a window.

Cue goofy smile.

I narrowed my eyes at myself and internally ordered, *Stop that!*

Myself didn't listen, and the goofy smile stayed. "I'm just happy," I said, trying to deflect. "We're doing great work, and we're ahead of schedule."

Annie looked at Tex, and they exchanged a smile.

"What?"

"Nothing," Annie said, a little smugly. "I just won a bet with Tex, that's all."

Tex pulled out a twenty and slapped it into Annie's hand.

I narrowed my eyes. "What bet?" They exchanged another look, and I went hands on hips. "*Hello?*"

Annie grinned. "Whether or not you're doing the last single male Colburn."

I choked on my own tongue.

"Sorry," Annie said, not looking in the least bit sorry. "But everyone knows he's seen the Legend of Star Falls with his brothers, who were knocked off the market in fairly quick succession." Her eyes were flat-out merry. "Oh, and thanks for the easy twenty."

I jabbed a finger at them both, but no words came out. I was speechless.

"She'll figure out something to say eventually," Tex murmured to Annie, amused.

Ugh. I turned my back on them and continued working while also mentally replaying every slow, delicious, sweat-slicked thing Tucker and I had done to each other the night before.

I was in so deep, it was sink or swim.

I should have woken him up when I left, instead of covering him with that blanket, brushing a barely there kiss over his jaw, and escaping.

I needed to remind us both it'd been amazing, but our onetime pass had been used, no renewals available.

But what I wished I'd done was…stay.

Dammit.

———

I didn't see Tucker for the next two days. He was on shift, but let's be honest; I wouldn't have had the guts to seek him out anyway. Not when I knew I'd probably beg for an encore.

Then I found myself dragged to the local rec league's touch-football game by my self-appointed unlicensed emotional-support squad with boundary issues: Kiera, Penny, and Emma.

It was the fire station team versus Colburn Restorations' finest. But calling it a game was generous. It was more like a WWE cage match on a glorified weed patch.

Tucker, playing for the fire station against his brothers, was taking a gleeful beating. Ryder and Caleb kept tackling him like they were settling childhood vendettas. Judging by the shit-eating grins on their faces, they were having the time of their lives.

Tucker, who could outrun, outthrow, and outmuscle both of them, didn't seem to mind letting them think they had a chance. I couldn't decide if that made him cocky or generous, but either way, it was working for me.

Honestly, the only thing more entertaining than the game itself was watching Tucker try to keep his composure. His usual unruffled expression had sharpened with fierce competition, and the mud streaking across his face and arms only made him look hotter. Every time he wiped dirt away in that casual too-sexy-to-care way, I had to concentrate not to drool into my hot dog.

After the game, I found him sitting on the tailgate of his truck, sweaty and grimy like a postapocalyptic gladiator, peeling off his T-shirt, which was stubbornly clinging to every infuriating muscle.

There'd been a time not long ago when I couldn't have felt settled or grounded to save my life. And yet somehow, this guy—bloody, muddy, and grinning like a menace—made me feel more grounded than anything ever had.

"You okay?" I asked, about two seconds from offering to get into a shower with him to help him for "medical purposes."

He shot me that quick sideways grin, the one that said he knew *exactly* what I was thinking. "We won, didn't we? I'm great."

I eyed his bloody elbow and raw, scraped knee. "Want a Band-Aid? Or do tough guys just rub dirt in their wounds?"

He chuckled, his smile turning wicked. "Want to play doctor?"

I rolled my eyes but couldn't hold back the laugh. "I think we've done enough damage."

He watched me walk away like he wasn't done with me yet. And that look? That lazy, confident grin? It stuck with me all the way home.

Fifteen minutes later, I pulled up in front of my dad's house to check in, feed him, and see if maybe he wanted to lose at cards again.

Big mistake.

I pushed open the door and immediately slapped both hands over my eyes. "OH MY GOD!"

Dad and Sybil. Couch. Possibly fornicating.

"*Why is no one wearing appropriate amounts of clothing?*" I yelled.

"We were watching a movie!" Dad shouted, followed by frantic scrambling and fabric rustling.

I was trying very hard not to throw up in my mouth when my dad finally found his words.

"It's okay now!" he yelled, even though I was only a few feet away.

I peeked through my fingers and instantly regretted it. They were flushed, rumpled, guilty...and smiling. "This is cosmic punishment for how much I hated high school algebra, isn't it?"

My dad cleared his throat. "Sweetheart—"

"No. Nope. Don't 'sweetheart' me. I just walked in on you and my tenth-grade math teacher doing...*things*! On the couch I sit on!"

"We weren't doing things," Sybil said primly.

"No? Tell that to your lipstick, which is currently married to my dad's chin," I shot back.

Without missing a beat, Sybil licked her thumb and wiped his chin like a woman who'd once assigned seventy-five equations over winter break and had no shame about it. "Hazel, hon, you do realize that your father and I are consenting adults."

"Totally," I said, backing away like the room was on fire. "I just don't need to witness the...consenting. I'm going to bleach my brain now. Possibly call a therapist. 'K, bye."

"We'll, uh, be more careful next time," Dad called after me.

Groaning at the thought of a next time, I paused at the door. Hypocrite. I was a giant hypocrite. I sighed. "Sorry, I should've knocked. Carry on."

I autopiloted to Tucker's house. He wasn't home, and I had no idea what time he'd show up, but I let myself in with my new key. I showered and located clean pj's—aka stole another shirt of

Tucker's. I thought about getting into the bed that had claimed me as its own, but my feet ached from long days of work. You know what? I deserved some self-care.

Five minutes later, I was perched on the edge of the bathtub in the hallway bathroom with a pilfered family-size bag of chips, soaking my feet in deliciously hot water and Epsom salts, while wailing "You Need to Calm Down" at the top of my lungs.

I munched on Cheetos and doomscrolled for a bit, then sucked orange crumbs off my fingers and checked my email. I had an offer for a penis enhancement, a car-insurance bill, and… gulp, Alder & Stone Restoration in Seattle wanted to know if I'd had time to consider their offer.

The offer that came with a six-figure contract, health insurance, a city skyline view, and a fancy title.

Everything I'd once thought would prove I was worth something.

Professionally, this was everything I'd worked for.

But emotionally? It felt like running.

Why hadn't I told anyone yet? Was I still waiting for the perfect moment? Or was I just scared to admit I didn't know what I wanted anymore?

Her Fluffiness appeared out of nowhere and sat on the bath mat, tail curled tightly to her body, her sweet face studying mine like a furry little therapist.

"What do *you* think I should do?" I asked.

She yawned, licked her paw, and turned her back to me.

"Cool. Avoidance and denial it is."

She flicked her tail, annoyed.

"Fine." I ran a hand down her soft fur. "I know avoidance and denial isn't the right path, but it's just that I'm so good at it."

Another flick of her tail.

"And it's not that I don't want it," I said. "The big, new, fancy job. I just don't know if I still want it the same way."

Her purr kicked in, steady and strong, like she could feel the tightness in my chest and wanted to keep me grounded. Like she was saying, *I'm here, but I got nothing.*

"Yeah," I murmured. "Me neither."

It actually wasn't the job I was afraid of. It was staying. Choosing something—someone—and possibly having it all fall apart again.

I heard the front door open and froze.

"Hazel?"

Even if I hadn't recognized Tucker's low voice, my nipples absolutely did. Why hadn't I shut the bathroom door and locked it? I remained still as stone, looking at Her Fluffiness as I put my finger to my lips. I'm pretty sure she rolled her eyes.

"I know you're here. I can hear you panic breathing."

Then it was my turn to roll my eyes.

"I've got something for you."

On the chance it was the previously promised cookies, I sat straight up. "In here."

Tucker appeared in the doorway, propping it open with his shoulder as he took in the scene before him. His eyes locked on mine, and every cell in my body betrayed me.

One look and it all flooded back again—him moving over me, inside me, muscles straining, mouth claiming mine like I was the only thing he needed.

Damn. I was so far gone, I needed a search and rescue team.

CHAPTER 20

Tucker

HAZEL SAT ON THE edge of my tub, soaking her feet, my cat on the mat, the two females eyeing me like I was the one who didn't belong. Hazel's hair was fifty shades of wild, her T-shirt—actually, *my* T-shirt—doubling as a parachute while her pj's bottoms put the *short* in *shorts*, and somehow she still managed to knock the damn breath clean out of me.

Still the most beautiful thing I'd ever seen.

Damn. I was toast. Burnt toast.

I hadn't come to terms with that. I'd never imagined being in this position again, trying to resist her cluelessly sexy charms.

And yet here I was, shoving my hands in my pockets to keep them from reaching for her.

I wasn't just burnt toast; I was a fucking fool.

I was also bone-tired, strung out on two hours of sleep and a whole bunch of regret for not having sought her out since the tree house, but the second I'd seen her, everything inside me had kicked back to life like I'd taken jumper cables to the chest.

The image of her from our night in the tree house—lit up beneath me, fingernails digging into my ass, breathless and wild-eyed, panting my name like it was the only word in her head—crashed over me like a wave.

She stared at me, not saying a word.

"What are you doing?"

"Exactly what it looks like."

Okay, no small talk. Noted…

She waved a hand in front of my face. "Did you just fall asleep standing up?"

I blinked. Yawned. "Very possibly."

She tilted her head, concern creeping in. "You're swaying on your feet. You need rest."

"I can rest when I'm dead."

"Not funny."

Debatable. "Maybe we should talk."

"No, thank you."

"Haze."

She sighed. "Fine. But only if you're joining self-care night."

I eyed the tub. "I wouldn't appreciate it. But I will share those Cheetos."

She clutched the bag to her chest. "No soak, no Cheetos. It's called *self-care*."

Our gazes locked and held.

"What do you have against being nice to yourself?" she asked.

"I'd rather sleep." I gestured to her attire. "You stole another shirt, one that could fit Sasquatch."

She lifted her chin. "Also self-care." She paused. "And a strategic block against you getting ideas."

A laugh tumbled out of me, and it felt dangerous. What was

happening right now? I was feeling things I had never in a million years thought I'd be feeling again, and certainly not for this woman, the one who'd hurt me more than I'd thought possible.

Which made me a damned fool but didn't remove the smile from my face. "You're lying about not wanting me to get ideas. You're wearing that shirt to keep *you* from getting ideas."

She neither confirmed nor denied, but we both knew it was true.

And something else true? A few weeks of talking to her again, plus one night of world-stopping sex that had felt like a lot more than just getting off, and I was gone for this woman.

Tough, scrappy, biting Hazel, who wielded her words and the jut of her chin like knives. Loyal Hazel, who'd braved returning to a town that hadn't always been kind simply because her dad needed her. Giving, caring Hazel, who went around in the middle of the night fixing things because she thought she owed the past. Quiet, unexpected Hazel, who fed my grumpy cat, sought out my company, and kissed me like I mattered to her as much as air.

Brave, fierce, loyal, temperamental Hazel, who'd once upon a time turned me upside down and inside out. Tenderhearted Hazel, whose smile could lower my blood pressure and make me feel way too much. Even now, as I stood there, my heart didn't just want her—it flat-out needed her.

Terrifying, since anything that mattered this much would not end well.

"So…" she said, eyeing me. "Where are the cookies you keep promising?"

"I've got something better."

She fought a smile and lost. "I've already seen it."

I grinned like a mad man. "And?"

"And it's spectacular, as you damn well know. But cookies are better."

I laughed. "I was actually talking about dinner. Real food that won't come with a sugar crash."

"Is it pizza at least?"

"Technically, yes."

Suspicion colored her words. "With extra cheese and sausage?"

"Veggie and grilled chicken. On flatbread."

She narrowed her eyes.

"If you don't love it, I'll order you a sausage pizza," I promised.

"With extra cheese."

"Deal," I said. "Come with me to the kitchen."

"Sure, but there's one little thing you need to do first…"

Three minutes later, I was also sitting on the edge of the tub, sans socks and boots, pants rolled up…feet soaking in water hot enough to peel barnacles. "This better count toward hazard pay."

Hank, who'd heard us talking and didn't like to miss anything, sat on the other side of Hazel in boxers and a T-shirt that read, *STILL GOT IT (BARELY)*, happily swinging his feet in the tub.

When Caleb and Emma showed up, Hazel improvised, directing them to sit on the counter on either side of the sink, which she filled with hot water and Epsom salts. So now they too were…soaking their feet.

Caleb's knees hit his ears so high, he nearly gave himself two black eyes. When Emma moaned in pleasure, he perked up, solemnly promising to get her to make those sounds again later.

"Good luck measuring up," Emma said, making me and Hazel laugh.

We were still laughing and throwing around insults when Ryder and Penny found us.

Everyone froze.

Well, everyone but Hank, who farted.

"Ah," he said and pointed to Her Fluffiness still sitting on the mat.

Her Fluffiness, who objected to the accusation with a *how dare you* look, padded out of the room, head high, tail swishing like a metronome of superiority.

"She's going to poop in your shoes," I told him, then turned to Ryder, who was laughing at us and taking pics "for proof."

Shaking his head, he put his phone away. "Wait until the guys see two badass Colburns primping at spa night."

"Yuk it up, Chuckles. You're next." I looked at Penny. "You too."

"Don't threaten me with a good time." She was already kicking off her shoes and glancing around. The small bathroom was standing room only, zero vacancy on tub or sink real estate.

"I've got it!" Hazel announced, then ran out of the bathroom, her wet feet slapping on the floor like an escaping duck. She came back a minute later, breathless, carrying two empty five-gallon buckets.

"I'm not putting my feet in a bucket," Ryder said.

"You are if you want to get lucky tonight," Penny said, then happily sat on the hamper, her feet in the bucket Hazel had set up for her.

Ryder stared at Penny.

Penny smiled sweetly.

Ryder sighed and kicked off his shoes. He lifted one foot and lowered it into the bucket. "Ouch. My toes are too crunched."

"That's what you get for having a size-thirteen foot," Penny said.

Ryder smirked. "Well, we all know that exceptionally large feet mean—"

"I've got it!" Hazel once again ran out of the room. This time she returned with a cardboard moving box she'd gotten from the garage and a big black trash bag.

Two minutes later, Ryder sat on the floor against the wall, his feet in the bag, which was in the box and filled with Epsom salts and hot water.

"Don't even think about farting now," Ryder warned Hank. "We'll asphyxiate."

Bill chose that exact moment to appear. He froze in the doorway, eyes taking in the scene: six full-size adults, feet in buckets. "What the actual circus hell is this?"

"It's self-care," Ryder said. "You're up."

"The hell I am. I don't go for this girlie crap."

Hazel looked him right in the eyes. "If you don't, I'll tell everyone that you and Sybil scarred me for life."

"Shit."

Hazel set up her dad with the bucket Ryder had rejected.

All of us—fully grown, allegedly competent people—sat there like putty in Hazel's hands.

Bill pointed at everyone in the room. "If any of you says a word about this, you're dead to me."

He was a hard man. Always had been. But ever since Hazel had come back, he'd been trying—still gruff, still grumpy, but softer with her. Kinder. He wanted her to stay.

He wasn't the only one.

Bill's phone buzzed. He read the text, smiled to himself, then stood, sloshing a little water over the side of the bucket. "Gotta go. Uh…work emergency." He looked at Ryder. "Nothing I can't handle."

"Work emergency?" Hazel asked.

"Yep."

"A work emergency named Sybil," Hazel muttered.

But Bill had already hightailed it out the back door like his ass was on fire.

I slid Hazel an amused glance. "You didn't tell him he forgot his shoes and his dignity."

"Nope," she said cheerfully.

I laughed, and Hazel stood in the tub, sloshing around Hank's feet to get to me, stepping between my legs. My hands went to her hips as she bent to kiss me—soft, warm, and full of mischief. Then, looking pleased with herself, she sat on my lap, straddling me.

I immediately tightened my grip on her so she couldn't get away. Because yes, I lived here now, right between her thighs.

"Is this okay?" she asked. "Am I too heavy? Can you breathe?"

Could I? Yes.

Was I? Not even a little.

My mind was consumed with the memory of the last time I'd been between her thighs. My hands were on her hips, the pads of my thumbs brushing the bare skin between the hem of her T-shirt and her sleep shorts.

From the bathroom sink's counter, Caleb stage-whispered, "Do you think they remember we're here?"

"Shh," Emma said. "How often do you get to see two love dorks in the wild?"

Ryder high-fived her.

First chance I got, I was going to high-five Ryder, right upside the back of his head. Sibling bonding: It's important.

"I've got a question," Caleb said. "A two-part question. One, is either of you ever going to tell us what the hell happened all those years ago that made you two not speak for over a decade? And two, what's happening now? Oh! And are you two doing it yet? Because there's a pool at the office, and I intend to win."

Correction: I was going to have to kill *both* brothers. "That's three questions."

Hazel's timer went off, and she jumped up. "Saved by the bell!" She eyed her phone. "And would you look at that? I've got stuff to do. Lots of stuff! Okay, well, buh-bye now——"

I caught her wrist. "Out," I said to everyone else in the room, tightening my grip when she made to leave. "Not you."

"Uh-oh," Caleb said. "Mom and Dad are going to fight." He took Emma by the hand and led her out of the bathroom.

Ryder and Penny laughed and followed, taking Hank with them.

And then it was just us, staring at each other.

I sloshed my way out of the tub while still holding on to her. I was trying to figure out what to say when her stomach growled loudly, making me laugh. "Guess the Cheetos weren't enough."

We padded to the kitchen, still quiet as I pulled the foil off the flatbread. Steam hit us like fresh-baked mercy. Finally, I said, "The trick is to ignore them," I said.

"I'm not ignoring your family."

"They're *your* family too."

Her eyes softened as I resettled my hands on her hips and gave a light squeeze.

"Haze?"

"Hmm?" She drifted a little closer, those baby blues drawing me into their sweet depths.

I'd happily drown in them.

"You were going to say something," she whispered. "Probably that you want to kiss me."

"I *always* want to kiss you."

She looked at my mouth. "I'm a firm believer in following your instincts. Would you say this is an instinct? Like…an *unbearably* irresistible instinct?"

God, this woman. "Most definitely irresistible."

Her smile came slowly. Hot as hell. Helpless to resist, I yanked her into me, her laugh ringing like I'd just gotten away with something as she slid her hands up my chest and settled over my heart, which drummed loud enough to drown out rational thought.

I cupped her face. "I care about you." *Way more than I intended to say out loud.*

She squirmed, cheeks flushing. "I…um…same."

I grinned. "Still crushing the whole emotional-vulnerability thing, I see."

She rolled her beautiful eyes. "Yeah, well…" She scowled. "You have plenty of things that aren't your strong suit, like…" She fell silent, coming up empty.

"Say it," I teased. "Say I'm not bad at anything."

"It's not funny when it's true!" She shoved me back and set her hands on her hips.

I grinned. "Come on. You know damn well I'm bad at plenty."

"Name one thing."

My smile faded. "Apparently, making sure you know I'm on your side."

She seemed stunned, and my chest clenched.

"Haze, tell me you know this."

She drew in a breath. "I do. But it's nice to hear out loud."

Then she rose onto her toes, sliding her hands up my chest and around my neck, giving a little tug.

I bent my head to meet her halfway, and she kissed me. Soft, warm, and alive. I hauled her in, anchoring us together like I never wanted to let go.

"Is this okay?" she whispered.

"It's the best thing that's happened to me today."

She smiled against my mouth and then kissed me again, deeper this time, like the world was on fire and we were only a few feet above the flames. Messy. Desperate. Everything.

We came up for air, staring at each other. I had no idea what she was thinking, but I was wondering how fast I could get her behind a closed door with a lock and no brothers anywhere within a five-mile radius.

But first...I pulled back a fraction of an inch. "You want this?"

"I want this," she whispered. "I want *you*. And I'm tired of pretending I don't."

"No more pretending—"

The words weren't even out of my mouth before she launched herself at me. I caught her, turned, and headed for my bed without passing Go, hoping like hell Hank was snoring like the dead.

"Do you think this is just nostalgia?" she asked breathlessly.

I stopped in the living room to pin her to the wall with my body. "Our chemistry? It's not nostalgia." I held her gaze. "It's real."

She searched my eyes as if she wanted to believe me more

than anything. She drew a breath. "You keep showing up, and I keep waiting for you to realize I'm nothing but trouble and not worth it."

"You are."

"Which? Trouble or worth it?"

"Both." I pressed her into the wall hard enough to free up my hands to cup her face. "You're worth it, Haze. You've always been worth it. Even when you're setting my world on fire, you're worth every damn second."

Her mouth opened and closed. Twice. "No one's ever said anything like that to me before."

"Then they didn't deserve you."

She wrapped her arms around my neck as I gathered her in close and gently sank my teeth into her earlobe, pulling a full-body shiver from her.

"Tucker," she gasped, breathy and shaky.

At least I wasn't the only one losing myself here. I skimmed my mouth along her slim throat and smiled as she fought to hold in a moan and failed.

"How do you do this to me?" she whispered, turning her head to give me better access. "I don't even know what to do with it all."

"Just don't run." I lowered my mouth to hers, and what was meant to be something sweet turned into something else entirely as she climbed me like a tree.

"Love it when you do that," I murmured into her ear. "Clutch at me like you can't live without me."

"You wish."

"I do."

She rocked against me. "You seem like a man on a mission."

I laughed roughly. "You have no idea. I've given a lot of thought to this. There's a list of things I want to do to you." My hands squeezed her sweet ass. "A detailed, comprehensive list."

Hazel's hands fisted in my hair as she rocked her heated center over the fly of my jeans until I nearly embarrassed myself. I drank in her moans while I moved us down the hall, then froze when someone knocked at the front door.

"Tuck," Ryder said through the door. "We forgot to ask you about the Moreno estimate."

Excellent. Murder, it is.

Hazel's wide-eyed gaze was on mine. We were still plastered up against each other, so close that I could see the pulse at the base of her neck fluttering wildly.

She didn't have to say the words for me to know she wasn't ready to loop everyone in on the fact she was staying with me. Not when neither of us even knew what we wanted this to be. No, that wasn't true. I knew exactly what I wanted it to be. But damned if I'd rush her.

The front door's handle turned but didn't open because I'd locked it on our pass to the kitchen. "Go the fuck away."

"Let us in." Great. Caleb too.

I bit back a sigh. "I thought you left."

"We were talking in your driveway. Got a question."

I dropped my forehead to Hazel's. "*Go away.*" I brushed my mouth against her ear. Then whispered, "I'm sorry."

She shook her head as if to say, *No apology necessary*, and then she kissed me, reigniting the wildfire in my chest.

I had no idea how she could make me lose my mind at a single look, a single touch, but I couldn't stop, couldn't think.

There was only the sensation of Hazel matching my intensity, tongue stroke for tongue stroke, ragged moan for ragged moan, that fire in my chest rushing south as her hips ground against mine—

"Huh," Ryder said behind us. "Interesting."

I let go of Hazel's legs so she could slide down, holding on to her for an extra beat while she found her equilibrium.

I turned to my brothers, who'd let themselves in through the unlocked back door. "I hope you enjoyed that," I said tightly, "because I'm changing the locks tomorrow."

They just grinned, and I knew it was because they cared about us both, that they wanted me happy, but fuck, their timing *sucked.*

"How are your feet?" Hazel asked.

"Smooth as a baby's ass," Caleb said.

I pointed to the door. "Out."

Caleb's brows were so high, they vanished into his hair. "You really expect us to pretend we didn't just walk in here to find two of my very favorite people trying to swallow each other's tonsils?"

I rubbed the headache forming at my temples.

Ryder looked at Hazel. "I hope you know what you're doing, because this guy"—he hooked a thumb in my direction—"doesn't."

"Standing right here," I muttered.

"Where's the lie?" Ryder asked.

Hate that he's got me there.

Heavy footsteps down the hall, sounding like a two-hundred-pound duck slapping its webbed feet on the hardwood floor. Hank came around the corner still in his T-shirt and boxer shorts, smiling brightly when he saw us. "Ah," he said, then pointed to his belly.

He was hungry.

Proving she was a better person than me, Hazel nodded at my dad. "Come on, let's get your tank filled."

And just like that, spa night pivoted to snack night—romance surviving against impossible odds, like us.

He grinned happily and headed toward the kitchen, following after her like a puppy.

I banged my head a few times against the wall.

"Star Falls Legend, hard at work" Ryder said.

Shit. I'd forgotten about the Legend. Also, I wanted to punch my brother's gleeful face. "More like Star Falls *Curse*."

"Walk us out," Caleb suggested, and the two of them dragged me out the door.

On the porch, I planted my feet and crossed my arms. There'd been many times in my life when they'd tag teamed me, and not a single one of them had ever been good. "What?" I asked flatly.

"You tell us," Caleb said. Smug bastard.

"I'm not telling either of you fucking busybodies anything."

"Insulting," Ryder said.

"Extremely," Caleb said.

They both gave me long looks, and beneath their fucking superiority, I could see the genuine concern, which took me down a notch. "Look, we're not talking about this. I'm trying not to even think about it." Or feel it. Because it was Hazel. And if I let myself fall again, it might kill me.

"When Penny came into my life, you made me talk about it," Ryder said.

Caleb nodded. "Same for me with Emma."

"Yeah, well, you were both way more fucked-up than me." I started to walk back inside, but Ryder tripped me. The porch swing broke my fall. With my face. The swing's momentum sent it slamming into the siding.

We stared at the dent.

"You're fixing it this time," I said.

"Yeah? And who's going to fix your hard head?" Ryder retorted.

We really had left most of our brawling behind us years ago, but we had no problem having a go at each other to blow off steam as needed. "Didn't we just do this at football?"

"Two against one," Caleb noted casually to Ryder, ignoring me.

I shrugged. "The last time it was two against one, it was *your* head to the wall. Your hallway's still got a hole in it because you only painted over it. You didn't replace the drywall. Now what the hell do you two *really* want?"

Caleb looked at Ryder.

Ryder shrugged. "We want to know what's going on with you and Hazel."

"Why, so you can be a dick and order me to stay away from her like you did to Caleb when he fell for Emma?"

Regret crossed Ryder's face. "Look, I've admitted I was wrong about that, all right? This isn't about me or Caleb. It's about us wanting you to be…open."

"Open. About what?"

"Something good."

I rolled my eyes. "Penny made you go back to book club again, didn't she?"

"Be an asshole all you want, but which one of the three of us *isn't* getting laid every day?"

Okay, so at least they didn't know about the tree house. "Does Penny know how fucking interfering you are?"

"Yes, and she loves me anyway. Look, you guys busted my balls about being open to a relationship with her for months. Why can't I do the same for you? You and Hazel used to be tight. Then something happened, and you didn't speak for years. Now you're suddenly sneaking around, hiding a relationship? Why?"

"It's *not* a relationship," I clarified. *Yet.*

Caleb sighed. "Two smart people. So stubborn. So stupid."

I snorted. "Motivational speaker now, are we?"

"You're collecting strings, Tuck. Maybe she's the one."

"Just out of curiosity," I said, "how do you know when you've found the one?"

Ryder shrugged. "It's sort of a mixture of *Damn I can't imagine my life without her in it* and *This woman's gonna be the death of me.*" He grimaced. "Don't tell Penny I said that."

"Do you want the truth?" I asked. "I don't know what's going on with me and Hazel." I knew only what I *wanted* to be going on.

"Bullshit," Caleb said. "You *always* know what's going on. It's your superpower."

I stayed quiet. Not because I didn't have something to say, but because saying it out loud would unravel me. Plus, I refused to break. Hazel didn't deserve the fallout if I opened my mouth and confessed all.

But my brothers could sniff out a lie from a hundred paces. So I gave a truth. "We're friends."

Ryder and Caleb looked at each other.

"So you and Hazel are really just friends," Ryder repeated as footsteps came down the hall.

I hadn't said *just*, but I wasn't going to correct him. "That's it. That's all—"

My brothers sucked in a breath.

I turned.

Hazel stood there, expression unreadable. Cool. Flat.

Fuck.

I broke out into a cold sweat of sheer dread. "Haze—"

"Good to know." She backed toward the door like I'd burned her. "Guess I misread things again."

And she was gone.

I stood there like it was my job, ribs splintering around the truth. I'd told myself I was protecting her, but based on the look in her eyes? I hadn't protected her at all.

I'd hurt her.

CHAPTER 21

Hazel

I WASN'T REMOTELY IN the mood for a girls' night. I wasn't in the mood for anything except being deep under my covers, hiding from the world. But if there was a woman alive who could dodge the unholy trinity of Penny, Kiera, and Emma, it sure as hell wasn't me.

So here I was, squeezed around a high-top table at the Cork and Barrel. Emma and Kiera were a bottle deep into wine, while Penny and I were on our second mocktails—her because she was pregnant, me because I'd given up alcohol that long-ago day when I'd left Star Falls. That it had been painfully difficult to do only helped my resolve to never go back to it.

I hadn't eaten lunch, so the sugar buzz should've been numbing everything. Instead, I just felt more…exposed.

Kiera pointed at Penny and Emma. "You two have a glow. I hate you both. This is my longest streak of no glow since I met Auggie in high school." She glanced my way, and her eyes widened. "Hold the phone. I just found a third glow."

Penny's and Emma's heads swiveled my way in unison.

"No glow," I said. "I got some sun today at work."

The three women looked at one another with amusement.

"I did!" I said. "I bet my no-glow streak was longer than all of yours put together."

"A glow comes from the inside," Kiera said.

"Hey." I covered my hot cheeks with my hands. "It could totally be a sunburn."

Everyone cracked up—except Penny. She just tilted her head like she'd had a birdie whisper something in her ear. "*Was*," she murmured.

"What?"

"You said your streak *was* longer than all of ours added up together. As in past tense."

I stared into my drink, making sure it wasn't alcohol. I couldn't find any other excuse for why I was so stupid. And grumpy. And still furious.

And sad…

It'd been two days since the "just friends" incident, and I'd become a master at slipping in and out of Tucker's place at the right times to avoid him.

I had missed calls. I had not read texts.

And I knew this was just another form of running from a problem, sticking my head in the sand, but I was nothing but a cracked heart taped together with sarcasm and french fries.

With not a single intention of acknowledging *any* of it.

How could I have been so reckless with myself? He'd been beyond fun and sexy, and wildly uninhibited, which in turn had allowed me to be the same.

But he'd never promised a thing. Which meant I'd done this to myself. Me. Myself. And I.

"Something you want to share with the class?" Kiera asked me.

"Nope." I mimed zipping my lips and throwing away the key.

Penny raised her brows. "So Ryder *didn't* catch you and Tucker in a full-on lip-lock up against a wall?"

I groaned and sank in my seat. "I can't believe he told you."

"If it helps," she said with a grin, "I had to make all sorts of promises I have no intentions of keeping in order to get him to spill."

"Spill what?" Emma demanded.

Penny looked at me.

I sighed in defeat. "Tucker and I—"

"*Did the deed?*" Emma gasped, clutching her heart. "Finally!"

I opened my mouth to lie but couldn't do it. I sighed and dropped my head to the table and thunked it a few times. Without lifting it, I muttered, "It was a shit show."

Emma choked on her drink. We all reached over to thump her on the back while she cough-laughed herself to tears.

"Damn, I'd have thought looking how he looks, he'd be good at it," she wheezed, swiping under her eyes.

"Well, he's not," I said, lying with the enthusiasm of a woman seeking vengeance.

They all howled.

I crossed my arms and glared. There was no way in hell I'd admit Tucker had taken me apart and put me back together again in spectacular fashion and then dumped a bucket of *just friends* over my head. "Listen, mistakes were made, okay? We can't go back. And anyway, I don't see what's so interesting about all this." I looked around for our server. "I need fries. Right now."

"You don't see what's '*so interesting about all this*'? Really?" Emma leaned in, wide-eyed. "You're living the dream! Every woman in Star Falls has wanted a Colburn brother at some point, even if they're not single. Or born in the right decade. I mean, people still talk about what those three got up to when they were younger, more than they talk about the Legend of Star Falls! And *you* snagged the last single male Colburn."

Jealousy flared, sharp as glass.

Because I hadn't snagged him at all.

"I'm hoping some women in this town have more sense than to lust after a Colburn."

"I mean, I don't," Emma quipped. "But I get your point."

"Ditto," Penny said. "Though I wouldn't mind a whole bunch *fewer* women wanting my man."

"But you're in love. That's different. Tucker isn't in love."

At the beat of surprised silence, I realized I'd given my own feelings away. So much for stealth. Dammit.

Kiera's expression softened. "Look, the Colburn men? They can be assholes. Tucker included." She reached across the table and squeezed my hand. "Want me to make him pay? No one can make a man suffer like his sister."

"Thanks, but no. And I really don't want to talk about it anymore, if that's okay." The sadness was fading, replaced by something far more productive: anger. I was furious with myself. And deeply bruised. Once again, I'd put my heart on the line and had gotten burned. But I was done bleeding. "All that matters is that there's nothing going on between me and him. Not like that."

I knew I was just fooling myself by pretending that with a few days' distance and a bunch of overthinking, I'd be completely over him.

But pride? Pride was a hell of a lot easier to carry than hope.

Kiera gave me another squeeze. "You sure? He can be hard to read. I speak fluent Colburn. I could translate."

"Strawberry shortcake," I said, then slurped the last of my drink while groans sounded all around. Because *strawberry shortcake* was our safe word. Words. It meant no more questions.

"I'm going to the restroom," I said, getting up. "It'll give you a minute to gossip about me."

I weaved through the crowd and into the dim hallway. I was heading toward the glowing LADIES sign when a hand clamped down on my shoulder.

I turned with a half smile, assuming it was one of the girls.

It wasn't.

The guy was built like a battering ram with something to prove, his face twisted with recognition, and not the good kind.

"I know you," he said.

Unfortunately, I knew him too. Ricky Herman. Fired months ago from Colburn Restorations after trying to take a swing at Caleb and sabotaging the Henderson job. Subtle as a sledgehammer, then and now.

And by his expression, that hadn't changed.

"Ricky." I kept my tone even, fingers curled around my phone like muscle memory, prepared to call for help.

"*You* got me fired."

"Actually…" I swiped on my phone to bring up the Phone app. "You did that all on your own."

"I went to *jail*. I had to pay fines out the ass. I got dumped by my wife *and* my insurance company *and* sued for fraud. *You ruined me.*"

"Again, not me." I craned my neck to check down the hallway—empty, of course. I managed a polite smile, gesturing that I wanted to get past him. "If you'll excuse me—"

He sidestepped, blocking my way, close enough that I could smell the alcohol and resentment on his breath. "I want my job back."

I gave a mirthless laugh. "You know that's not up to me."

He stepped in even closer, his eyes lit with something sharp and ugly. "I don't know which Colburn you slept with to land that gig, but it's bullshit. You all fucked with my livelihood. Now I'm going to fuck with yours."

"Is that a threat?"

"A fact."

His eyes were clearer now that he'd let out some tension. I was going to chalk this up to too much alcohol plus an excess of bluster. "Back up, Ricky."

"*You* back up." He shoulder checked me hard enough that I stumbled into the wall. By the time I caught my balance, he was gone.

I exhaled slowly, the tension still buzzing under my skin as I walked back to the bar.

Emma was saying, "Someone talk me off a ledge so I don't murder a coworker. And by 'coworker,' I mean Caleb."

"Murder's a lot of paperwork," Kiera said.

She nodded. "That'll do it." She tilted her head at Kiera. "You seem off, babe. What's going on with you?"

Kiera drew a deep breath as I slid back onto my seat. "Yesterday would've been my sixth wedding anniversary," she said softly.

All our hearts stopped for her. She'd lost Auggie three years ago, and I couldn't imagine the grief.

"Oh, honey." Emma reached out for Kiera's hand.

Kiera shook her head. "I actually almost forgot, which is what got to me. Abi found me crying in the pantry with a bag of chips. She wrapped her little arms around me and whispered, 'Is it because of your hair?' So then I was crying for two reasons."

Penny sniffled loudly, and I handed her a napkin. "Pregnancy hormones?"

"Yes!" Penny wailed.

I slid an arm around her and looked at Kiera. "For what it's worth, I *love* your hair."

Kiera gave a soggy smile. "I ten-out-of-ten recommend having a daughter so you can argue with an even sassier and more stubborn version of yourself, all before eight a.m."

We stayed for another hour, laughing more than I'd thought I could. Which felt like a miracle, given the emotional minefield we'd all been dancing through and my run-in with Ricky.

Finally, Kiera had to get home to relieve her babysitter, and Penny and Emma Ubered together.

Penny rolled down the window and yelled at me: "Don't do anything I wouldn't do!"

Since she and Ryder still dragged each other into dark rooms and corners to make out, I didn't take this too seriously.

"Hazel?"

I turned. Kiera was behind me, mist curling around us.

"I love you like a sister," she said.

"Are we about to drunken hug?" I asked. "Because I'm a little hot and sweaty right now."

Kiera stepped into me and hugged me hard.

"Okay." I sighed and hugged her back.

She squeezed me again, then added a little shake. "You have every right to feel however you want. I'll back you up. Always."

"Thank you, though I sense a *but* coming my way."

"*But*…I have to say this. Tucker is a solid guy. The *best* of the best of the solid guys."

I sighed again. "I know."

She nodded. "But what you might *not* know is that while he risks everything on the job without a single thought for his own safety, in his personal life, he's much more guarded. Oh, he's good at hiding behind that affable smile and quick wit, but there's a solid brick wall around his heart. He hasn't lowered it for anyone."

She didn't have to say it. I'd come up against that wall with two little words: *just friends*.

"Except," Kiera said, "possibly you."

"I don't intend to hurt him, if that's what you're getting to."

"Hazel, no." She reached for my hand. "That's not what I'm getting at. I know my brother, and the thing is, he's great at being a good time. But I'm not sure he's ever learned what love actually is. Until recently, he hasn't had a lot of good examples."

I felt a twinge of sadness. I'd been there. I knew what his life had been like growing up.

"What I'm trying to say," Kiera went on, "is that I'm worried about *him* hurting *you*."

Too late… But as I looked into her bossy, know-it-all, caring eyes, my throat tightened. I'd been back for months, and yet I still wasn't used to having people know me, care about me—the kind of care that came from decades of knowing someone. For as much as I'd loved the experiences and adventures I'd had over the past ten years, I'd missed this.

Missed them, all of them. Even Tucker. Maybe especially Tucker. My dear "just friend" Tucker.

How terrifying was that?

CHAPTER 22

Hazel

M Y UBER DROPPED ME off at my van. I loved the van. I did. But that didn't mean I wanted to sleep in it. Not when there was still an amazing bed less than a football field away. Why should I suffer just because Tucker wouldn't unlock the gate to his heart?

I started heading over there, then spotted my dad on the porch doing…jumping jacks?

"One sixty-three," he panted. "One sixty-four…"

"Dad." The man hated all forms of exercise except lifting—as in lifting chips into your mouth. "What are you doing?"

"What does it look like?" He huffed like a steam engine. "I'm supposed to be moving more. One sixty-five—"

His monitor beeped.

"Stop!" I ran up the porch. "Dad. Seriously? Sit down right now."

He dropped onto the swing, breathing hard.

We hadn't talked much since the worksite "discussion" in the closet, unless *At least it's not going to rain today* or *I'll grab some groceries on my way home* counted. Either way, things seemed lighter between us, and I'd be lying if I didn't acknowledge how much that meant to me.

But at the sight of him sweaty and a little shaky, suddenly his getting bossy with me on the jobsite no longer mattered.

"Deep, slow breaths," I said, my own heart hammering as well. I did as I preached, in through my nose and out my mouth, nodding when he did the same. The alarm quieted, and I narrowed my eyes. "What is going on?"

"I'm taking my recovery seriously."

I studied him. "You've been fighting this for months. Why are you all of a sudden working out? Is there news from your doctor?"

He looked away.

"*Dad.* You're scaring me."

"I don't have any news." He sighed. "I wanted you to see me trying."

"So…you're doing this for me?"

"Hazel, *everything* I do is for you."

I didn't know what to say to this. "Like kicking me out of the house the night I graduated from high school?" Huh, guess I knew exactly what I wanted to say.

A wince came and went across his features. "That was…very wrong of me."

I raised a brow. Whenever we'd danced around this subject in the past, it'd turned into a fight.

But this time, he kept his voice quiet. Earnest. His smile was wry as he said quietly, "Hi. My name is Bill Pierce, and I was fifty-nine years old when I apologized for the first time ever."

"You're sixty. And I didn't hear an apology."

He rolled his eyes. No shock where I'd gotten that skill. "I was wrong," he said again. "And I'm truly sorry. I've regretted it every day since, but I didn't know how to take it all back. I didn't even mean half the things I said. I was just…"

"Furious because I was a wild, untethered, angry teen," I supplied helpfully.

"Yes," he said. "It made me angry to watch my beautiful, smart, amazing daughter throw her life away." His voice cracked as he scrubbed a hand down his face, which suddenly looked older than I wanted it to. "But as your father…there should've been nothing you could do or say to make me tell you to get out." He met my gaze, his own bleak. "I hate that I said those things to you. Because I was wrong, Hazel. And I've wasted so much time. That's on me. But I'm done living with all this regret. I don't deserve it, but I want a second chance with you." He cleared his throat and shifted to get up, probably assuming I was done discussing this.

Instead, I caught his hand and bumped my shoulder to his. "I was almost thirty years old when I learned how to apologize," I said quietly. "I'm sorry too, Dad."

He stared at me, then gave me a small smile before shaking his head. "Don't give me the out, Hazel. I was the grown-up. If your mom had been around, she'd have kicked my ass, and I'd have deserved it."

My throat felt tight because he was right. My mom had been a fierce mama bear when it came to me, her cub, and God, I missed her so fucking much. "After we lost her, I put you through hell," I said, voice quavery as I gave a watery laugh. "I mean, I could find trouble with my eyes closed, and I almost always brought that trouble to your door. I was angry and horrible, and for what it's worth, I truly am sorry."

He gripped my hand tight. "Neither of us knew how to grieve. And then you left. I thought I'd never get you back."

I set my head on his shoulder. "I'm sorry it took you having a heart attack to get me here. But—"

"No, don't say it, don't say you're leaving so soon." He shook his head, eyes pleading. "Let me have tonight, okay? You're here, and for now, that's enough." He put our linked hands against his chest, over his heart. "Having you here these past few months, it's been…" He swallowed hard. "*Everything*. I hope you know that."

I nodded, and he gave a small smile. "I've heard the stories, you know. You've been going around town late at night fixing and renovating and rebuilding things. Helping people. I went to see for myself. The shelter work was my favorite. Emma said the women cried when they saw it finished. And you fixed the jungle gym at the park."

I'd done that last week, then watched as a little girl climbed all over it, her mom smiling up from a bench nearby. I'd watched for a long moment, a lump in my throat.

This. This was what staying would look like.

"The work you've done has people talking about you—in a good way."

"Righting my wrongs," I corrected. Which felt like ripping out a page I never should've written in the first place.

Pride lit up his face, so bright that it hurt to look at. "Do you want to sleep here tonight?"

I looked at the house and gave a small headshake.

"I apologized," he said, wounded. "I thought we came to some semblance of peace."

"It's not you, Dad. It's the house. I told you before. It's hard when this place is still a shrine to Mom. Just walking through…" I pressed a hand to my chest and shook my head.

He stared at me. "I didn't follow through with my word to make some changes, but I can fix that. I'll get it cleared out. I promise."

"That feels too easy."

"I might need some help." A flash of guilt crossed his features. "I should've done it years ago." He hesitated, then murmured so quietly, I almost couldn't hear him: "There're a lot of things I should've done differently."

Something in his voice had my stomach going tight with an odd feeling—mistrust—and I didn't like it. "Dad, what aren't you telling me?"

He drew a deep breath. "I could've taken this monitor off last month." He fiddled with it rather than meet my gaze. "My doctor was satisfied with my condition at my check-in, but I asked to keep wearing it."

My brain tried to reject this intel. "For…peace of mind?"

He hesitated again.

"*Dad.*"

"So you'd see me taking care of myself. And stay."

I had to take a deep breath. "So…you've been manipulating me?"

"I didn't want you to go." He closed his eyes. "And is that so wrong? You were gone for fucking *years*. Nothing I ever said brought you any closer. And then *this* happened." He gestured to his chest. "And suddenly you wanted to be here, watching over me. Can you blame me if I don't want it to end?"

Maybe it was my lingering anger with Tucker. Or the two glasses of mocktails that had over-sugared me up. Or sitting on this porch finding out that my dad had manipulated—and still was manipulating—me. Emotions churned in my belly, none of them good. I stood. "It's late. I need sleep." I stopped and looked at him. "I need something from you."

"Anything." He jumped to his feet and nodded. "Name it."

"Honesty going forward, even if I'm not going to like it. One hundred percent, or I'm out."

He gave a slow nod. "I understand."

Not the same thing as promising me, but I didn't exactly have a leg to stand on. Not when I was holding out on telling him so much. Not just about me and Tucker, but also the Seattle job offer, which I still didn't know what to do with.

My fear was that this time, it'd hurt more to stay than go…

And the secrets were weighing on me. I knew I couldn't continue to keep them. Not without risking everything.

"I meant what I said about cleaning out the house," Dad said quietly. "That's what you wanted, right? To box up your mom's stuff?"

"I'm not trying to erase her, Dad. I don't ever want to forget a single thing about her. But it's not healthy for the house to be exactly as she left it. For anyone."

"Sybil told me the same thing."

At her name, I wanted to make a face, but I couldn't deny she seemed to make him happy. And she was, albeit unknowingly, on my side regarding the house. "I can help."

His smile was small but genuine. "I'd like that."

I nodded. "Night, Dad."

I watched him go inside, then found myself standing on the grass equidistantly between dad's house, my van, and…Tucker's house.

I knew where I wanted to go, but was it the smart thing to do while feeling far too emotionally vulnerable and mentally unmoored?

Definitely not.

I tipped my face up to the night sky. The mist had cleared, revealing a blanket of black velvet littered with stars glittering like diamonds. I stood there, beneath it all, feeling small, so small, and then—

Impossibly, three stars streaked in unison across the sky as if they were tethered by invisible string, seemingly coming right at me.

I gasped and blinked, and when I looked again, they were gone.

Heart pounding, I desperately searched the sky. Was I so desperate to be loved that I'd imagined seeing the Star Falls Legend?

My phone rang. Tucker. I connected the call, and he spoke before I could.

"You're *not* sleeping in your van."

I spun around, completely out of breath, but didn't see him. "Are you stalking me?"

The front door of his house opened, and he stepped out, phone still at his ear.

"Flu took out half of today's crew, so I'm filling in but forgot my laptop." He stopped in front of me, sliding his phone away. He studied me for a half a beat before going on alert, scanning the area around us. "What happened?"

I shook my head. "I thought I saw—never mind. It's nothing."

"Your face says it's not nothing."

"I'm not scared."

His brow lifted. "Liar."

"Fine, that was a big, fat lie. But legends aren't real, right? They're just as their name claims—legends."

His eyes widened, and he tipped his head back to stare up at the night sky. "You saw the stars—"

"Shh!" I covered his mouth and looked around—for what, I had no idea. "You can't say it *out loud*," I hissed.

"Why not?" he asked, words muffled.

"Because then it'll come true!"

He nipped at my fingers, and I jerked them away, flustered at the shock of chemistry that bolted through me.

His grin was wicked, but his eyes were steady. "You totally saw the Legend. And now you're freaked out because you know what happened when my brothers did."

"I'm happy for them," I said. And I really was. "But I believe if you get it right once, when it breaks apart—and it always will, since everything does—you don't get it back."

He grimaced as if in pain. "You're talking about your mom."

Her death destroyed my family, and it still wasn't the same. I nodded. "And when you didn't show up that night to go with me." I certainly hadn't planned on saying *that* out loud, but I wouldn't take it back. We'd been best friends. More than best friends. We'd become something I hadn't had a name for back then, but he'd made it clear it wasn't reciprocated. It had shattered me.

He had wrecked me.

"Hazel." His voice was terrifyingly quiet and full of so much emotion, I choked up at just the sound of it. "I was packed."

I stilled in shock, staring at him. "You were?"

He nodded.

"Then why didn't you—"

"Show up?" He rubbed the back of his neck. "I couldn't leave Kiera. I was the last barrier between her and Hank."

The words penetrated, and it was like opening the shades to let the light in. All the blame I'd shoved on him—the anger, the grief—flipped on its head. Of course he couldn't leave Kiera. She was fifteen. And I hadn't put the pieces together. How selfish I'd been to even ask him to run away with me in the first place. I rubbed at the physical ache in my chest. "God, I'm so sorry," I whispered hoarsely. "So damn sorry, Tucker. I didn't think—"

"You needed out. I got that."

"But I didn't even ask why you couldn't come. I just assumed it meant I wasn't enough."

"You were always enough."

"Why didn't you tell me?"

"Because you would've stayed. Or worse, you would have tried—and probably succeeded—in talking me into going, and I…I'd have hated myself. As much as I cared about you, I couldn't leave Kiera. And I figured if you knew that, you'd hate me. So I said nothing, like a coward."

"You're the opposite of a coward, Tucker." The weight of his words settled over the night like a warm blanket, heavy but comforting in its truth. A light wind rustled the trees, filling the silence, which was no longer oppressive but a space to breathe, to absorb what had been said. "You really thought telling me the truth would change what we were?"

He let out a dry, humorless laugh, a storm of conflict in his hazel eyes. "What was I supposed to say? *Please don't go*? I knew you couldn't stay any more than I could come with. Plus…" He hesitated, his gaze flicking away. "I don't have a history of good things staying good."

God, I ached at the rawness in his voice, and I nodded. Because *same*. I had zero history of good things staying good.

But he was right about something else: "I would've stayed."

With so much emotion in that hazel gaze, he nodded and cupped my face. "We were kids, Haze. And Kiera, she was only fifteen. She needed me. I couldn't leave her. Not even for you."

"That nearly killed me, but I understand now."

"I know it must feel like I put Kiera in front of you, but I had no choice. I needed her to be okay. I was bound by ties and promises, but you weren't, and I—I needed you to have a shot at something better than Star Falls. I should've found a way to be there that night," he said. "But Kiera was messing around in the kitchen and broke the coffeepot. I took the blame, and Hank wouldn't let me leave."

I ached for Past Tucker. I ached for Past Hazel. But we couldn't change the past. "We were so young," I finally said. "The odds were against us anyway." I shrugged, a much lighter gesture than I felt. "And we both know, once something's broken, it can't be repaired."

He looked at me for a long moment. "I used to think that was true. But look at Ryder and Caleb. They found the real thing."

"So…you believe in love now?"

He didn't hesitate. "Yes."

"Because you saw three stars?"

"Because I saw you again."

The words hit me like a wave. I couldn't breathe.

"Hank's with Caleb," he said. "You're cold. Go inside; you'll be safe and warm."

"You just don't want me to sleep in my van."

"I don't want you to go sleep in your van."

There'd been a time I'd defended the van like it was my fortress. My freedom. But maybe it'd really been a hiding place. A mobile apology for taking up space. And I was getting tired of apologizing.

I met his gaze. "'Just friends' don't go feral for each other's safety."

He winced as if I'd hit him. "Fuck, I *knew* that would bite me in the ass," he said flatly. "And I get that I asked for this when I let my brothers get under my skin the other night. But you need to know, I didn't mean it. Any of it. I've been trying to tell you—"

"Maybe it's better this way," I said, but it came out thin. Unconvincing. Like I didn't believe it at all.

"Haze—"

"Night, Tucker."

And then I did what it turns out I did best: I walked away and didn't look back.

CHAPTER 23

I T WAS PAST MIDNIGHT when I got home. I already knew—because yes, I'd been obsessively checking my damn security cameras—that Hazel had *not* gone inside my house. And I'd lay down money, or my own life if it came to it, that she hadn't gone inside her childhood home either.

I might have figured she was out in Star Falls somewhere, restoring something with fury in her fingers, but her van was parked on the street. Lights off. Silent. Empty.

Worry gathered in my gut like storm clouds, thick and pressurized. Guilt came right behind it, relentless and cold.

I stood in the middle of my front yard, right where Hazel had stood a few hours ago, and closed my eyes, trying to feel her.

She'd been brave enough to come here. Brave enough to face down the memories, the loss, the rumors. She hadn't flinched, hadn't run. It seemed she'd truly wanted to face it all, to look that past straight in the eyes and say, *I can do better.*

But me? I'd considered myself someone who would do the

same, face my shit head-on as well. Coming from the kind of childhood I'd buried, I hadn't had the luxury of avoidance.

Except that's exactly what I'd done. I'd buried the hard stuff so deep that when Hazel stood in front of me, practically holding her heart out in both hands, I'd…dodged.

I hated what that said about me. Hated more the idea that I might lose her because of it.

Where would she go?

Just the question hit me with a memory—of the days when it was me looking for a place to disappear, to catch my breath. To seek comfort.

She'd always been that place.

And just like that, I knew where she was.

It took five minutes to walk through the inky-dark woods, where little starlight reached past the three-hundred-foot-tall trees swaying like ghosts. The air was thick with pine and eucalyptus. The night surrounded me, and I squinted into it, letting my eyes adjust.

I stopped beneath the tree house. *Our* tree house.

"Hazel." My voice sounded loud in the hush of the trees, the words bouncing off the branches, hanging in the air between us like a fragile thread.

As I had not too long ago, she'd pulled up the ladder. A sign she wanted to be alone. But she hadn't let me get lost in what had been haunting me, and I wasn't about to let her either.

I drew a deep breath and climbed the tree. At the top, I pulled the penlight from my pocket and swept the beam over the cavernous dark, over the old crates, the big beanbag, and the various supplies that had long ago been left behind, until I caught—

A pair of eyes staring back at me.

She was tucked in a corner between a crate and the beanbag, curled up tight, arms around her knees, eyes a little too shiny.

My heart nearly lurched out of my chest. "Hey, Tough Girl. You hiding out from anything in particular?"

Her eyes flashed, the first real spark of life in them since I'd entered. "I'm not hiding. I'm thinking."

"About me?" I quipped, hoping to tease her into telling me what was wrong.

"Oh, I'm definitely thinking about you. For instance, I'm thinking about tossing you out of this tree house."

"Fair." I crossed the creaky floor and squatted in front of her. Assessing her was second nature. She looked pale, tired, guarded.

But she also looked at me like I was unshakable. If only she knew how hard I worked to pretend. "So what are you doing here instead of sleeping?" I asked softly.

"Eating your expired snacks." She held up a sad bag of trail mix. "I'm pretending the dust is flavoring. I'm also cultivating a bad attitude. Don't you worry. It's going great."

"Aw, cute, you've got a new hobby."

She let out a rough laugh as I sat down opposite her, my back against the rickety wall.

"I'd like to join your club," I said. "Dues up front, or can I pay in sarcasm?"

"It's a closed club."

I nodded. Gave some thought to what I wanted to say. "I left out something I was thinking when I stupidly told my brother we're just friends."

She looked at me warily.

"First, we've never been just friends. Not once. Not even when we were teens. And second, I know if I admit out loud that we're so much more than that, then I also have to admit I might not get to keep any of this. You. Us."

She flinched, her eyes full of heartbreak and fire. "You could've just said that. I'm not seventeen anymore. You don't have to protect me from my own feelings, or from anything. I told my dad that too."

"You talked to your dad? Like really talked?"

"Yeah, and it turns out he's chosen to leave out some facts about his health. Such as that he doesn't have to wear the heart monitor anymore, but he chose to keep it so I'd see him trying to take care of himself after his medical scare."

To remind her of what he'd been through. To up her guilt factor so she'd stay longer… *Shit.* "And you said…?"

"That from here on out, he has to be honest with me. Same goes for you. And if it can't be done, I'm gone."

"So, what, you'll run again?"

She shot to her feet. "We made rules, remember? One"—she put up a finger, and not the one I deserved—"maintain a safe distance. Two"—another finger—"no running. Three, leave the past in the past." She had her hands on her hips now. "And I've honored that. I'm tired of paying for my teenage sins, Tucker. No one ever lets me forget them, even though I've done the work. I've shown up. I've stayed."

She paused just long enough to pull on her boots. Then she stomped past me and shoved the ladder out the opening. "And for the record, this isn't me running," she called over her shoulder. "It's called going to sleep. *Alone.*"

I looked up at the stars, searching for something… Hope, maybe? Whatever it was, I didn't find it. But I made a wish anyway, even if it was too late. Even if she didn't believe. Because I did.

I always had.

Hazel

By the time I reached the edge of the woods, my anger had burned off, leaving something rawer in its place—hurt, bone-deep and humiliatingly familiar.

I didn't bother with a door at my dad's house. I went straight for the window of my childhood bedroom and climbed in like a raccoon with trust issues.

Which was fitting, as I felt feral. Unraveled. Unmoored.

I threw myself down onto the ancient twin bed, sheets still smelling like lavender and old grief. After slipping Tucker's pilfered hoodie from my backpack, I slipped it on and pulled the covers over my head. I'd faced down a graveyard of old ghosts tonight. But this—letting him in—might still be the scariest thing.

A soft knock on the window made me sit up.

Tucker's dark gaze met my own through the glass. He cocked his head, silently asking if I was going to let him in.

I hesitated for a single beat—not because I didn't want to, but because I was terrified by how much I did.

When I didn't answer, he slid the window open and eased inside. Quiet. Careful, like he was giving me plenty of time to hurl something at his head or call the police.

I heard the soft thump of feet on the hardwood floor. Then: "Can I come in?"

"You're already in."

He stayed by the window, hands loose at his sides. He'd

moved so quietly, the way he always did when sleep had been scarce and his head was loud.

"I'm not talking about just this bedroom," he said. He looked at me like he meant it. "I'm talking about everything else."

Something in me cracked open as the memories of our past collided with the present. All those times he'd climbed in this very window… I grabbed my spare pillow and then the extra blanket folded at the foot of my bed, before tossing both to him.

The pillow hit him in the face.

There was a beat of quiet shared laughter—because how many times had I done that to him to lighten the mood?—and then, as he had so many, many times before, he made a nest on the floor beside the bed.

But this time he wasn't bruised, or bleeding, or barely holding on.

And neither was I. My heart caught at the memories, and I blinked them away.

He was safe. I was safe.

Nothing else mattered.

No running. I'd said it like a dare. Now I had to mean it.

"I missed this," he said softly.

I closed my eyes at the rough timbre of his voice, at the memories battering at my defenses like this was a game of *Minecraft*. Except the stakes were way higher.

"Did you bring snacks?" I asked.

"Too busy chasing my own idiocy."

That made me smile in spite of myself. "You used to be able to multitask. Since when can't you spiral and snack at the same time?"

A quiet laugh. "I realized something on the walk here."

"That I still haven't returned your sweatshirt and it's mine now?"

"No." There was amusement in that one word, but it faded when he said, "I've been hoarding feelings like they're mine alone to carry. But you…you wear yours like armor. Even when it hurts. You're always clear on where you are emotionally, even when it's you wanting to throttle me." He smiled at my soft laugh. "You've always been braver than me, Haze."

Something twisted in my gut. Guilt. "You're wrong about that." My voice shook. "There are things…things that happened all those years ago that you don't know. Things I've kept buried so deep, I wasn't sure I'd ever say them out loud."

I heard him shift and knew he'd turned on his side, head propped with his hand, looking at me in the dark. His voice was soft when he said, "When you're ready to share, I'd love to hear them."

And just like that, the pressure eased. My eyes burned as I nodded, even though I wasn't sure he could see me. But this was what I *always* got with Tucker. Acceptance. Patience…

I hadn't done a very good job of returning the favor. But I would. He deserved better.

I don't know how long we lay there with the sounds of the night as our only company.

"Haze?"

I peered over the edge of the bed.

"In the name of honesty…" His voice, low and rumbling, resonated with truth. "What I said about us being friends, it wasn't just for my brothers. In my head, I needed to believe it, because otherwise I'm falling for someone who might leave again."

The words hit me like a defibrillator.

I didn't answer. Not out loud. But my hand dropped off the side of the bed and found his.

He entwined our fingers and gave a gentle squeeze, and I knew that for now, this was enough.

CHAPTER 24

Hazel

THE REST OF THE week blurred. My days were filled with work, helping dad clean out the house, spending time with my friends, and slipping away now and then to knock another fix-it-because-you-broke-it task off my list.

And then there was Tucker.

Making late-night snacks had become a ritual. We didn't plan it. We didn't talk about it. But somehow, we kept ending up in his kitchen, the world muted, the quiet between us warm, intimate…and electric enough to burn the edges off my restraint.

The other night, when we'd walked down the hall to go to bed, we'd stopped right between his door and mine, then stared at each other. He slid a hand to the nape of my neck and kissed me good night on the forehead.

I tipped my face up, and our mouths ended up a fraction of an inch apart. We stared some more, and then he whispered my name.

I whispered, "Yes," and he took my hand…

And then we went to his bed, where we lost hours in each other. He touched me like he was learning every part of me, kissed me like he was trying to memorize the shape of my soul. We took each other apart and put the pieces back together, aching and hungry, and still starved for more. We moved in rhythm like muscle memory, like a prayer, slow, reverent, and greedy. Every gasp and graze rewrote the past, and nothing else existed.

We didn't talk about it. We talked about everything under the sun except…it.

Maybe because it felt too fragile.

Or maybe it was a way to protect our hearts.

Every morning when I woke, wrapped up in Tucker's big, warm body, I wondered how long we could keep pretending. Because this couldn't last, right? And when it ended, could I stay in Star Falls without breaking wide open?

Or would the Seattle job save me by giving me a new place, a clean slate, and a job I knew I'd love?

Did I want a fresh start? Or did I want *this*—this life, these people, this man—to work?

Deep down, I knew what I wanted. I just didn't believe I could have it.

Then, one night, I'd gotten home just as Tucker finished grilling chicken and veggies. The scent alone made my mouth water. Or maybe that was the sight of Tucker cooking with a casual efficiency that seemed ridiculously sexy.

Everyone showed up. Hank, Caleb and Emma, Kiera and the twins, my dad. And…Sybil.

The woman made my dad's plate, smiling sweetly—*sweetly!*— when he asked for butter on his veggies but didn't give him any.

Dad looked down at the plate she'd set before him and sighed.

And I actually found myself laughing with the woman who'd made my high school life a special kind of hell.

"You had potential, you know," Sybil said, settling in beside me. "In class. That's why I was always hard on you. You gave zero effort, but you could've taught the class."

I blinked, unsure whether to be flattered or confused. Had hell frozen over?

She nodded, smiling at the look on my face. "I'm happy to see you making something of yourself. I've heard about your woodworking. Seen the new gazebo. The women's shelter. And I have a feeling the cantilever shade structure at the bus stop downtown has your fingerprints on it too."

I hadn't told a soul about that one. "How did you—"

"Just a feeling." She smiled, tapped her water bottle to mine, and turned to tease my dad about his untouched zucchini.

I was still blinking in surprise when Tucker set a plate in front of me. I stared at the mouthwatering chicken and veggies, then realized he'd either pulled out the zucchini or eaten them for me, and I stared at him.

"What?" he asked.

"You remember I hate zucchini."

"You hate any green foods," he said, his tone conveying *duh*.

I made a sound that was supposed to be a laugh but missed. "You know stuff about me that no one knows."

"Yes," he said, then leaned in and kissed me. Soft but sure. Like it was the most natural thing in the world.

Around us, you could've heard a pin drop, and I froze. Oh my God, that's how stupid he made me—I forgot everything when he looked at me like that.

Caleb was first to speak, because of course he was. "Does this mean you're more than…just friends?"

Kiera smacked him upside the back of his head.

"We are friends," Tucker said easily, not taking his eyes from mine. "We're a lot of things. All of them none of your business."

There were a few laughs, and conversations restarted. Everyone moved on, and Tucker gave me a slow smile. The kind that felt like a promise. My insides went mushy as I struggled to pretend my world hadn't just tipped off its axis.

Tucker went on shift for two days, burning the candle at both ends like he always did.

Me too. And today had been…a special kind of terrible.

The air was cooler than usual, dusk settling in with streaks of orange and purple across the horizon. I sat in the grass outside my childhood home, knees pulled to my chest, staring at the house.

Once, it'd been full of life and laughter. Once, it'd been where I went for acceptance and love. But then I'd lost my mom.

Today was her birthday.

Around me, the air felt thick with grief and the kind of homesickness you feel only for someone who's gone. For the first time since being back, I *wanted* to go inside. I wanted to lose myself in her memories but felt stuck, trapped in a swirl of emotions I didn't know how to untangle. I actually wanted to go inside, but I was afraid. I couldn't feel her anymore. I closed my eyes, trying to summon her voice, her laugh, the warmth of her embrace, but it was all gone.

"Hey."

My heart stuttered at the sound of Tucker's voice behind me, and I hurriedly swiped my eyes as I straightened. Slowly, I turned to find him standing at the edge of the yard, a bag in hand.

"I'm not going to ask if you're okay," he said, mirroring my long-ago words back to him. "But do you want company?"

I closed my eyes. How did he always know what I needed, even when I didn't?

And why couldn't I open my mouth and say yes?

Somehow understanding me as always, Tucker didn't wait for a verbal response. That armload of emotional intuition was already walking toward me, slow and deliberate, like he was checking for land mines. He crouched at my side, meeting my eyes, searching my face, undoubtedly catching the remnants of the tears I'd shed.

He handed me the bag.

I opened it and peered in to find a cupcake. Vanilla with thick pink frosting and a single unlit candle. I stared at it, stunned.

"Her favorite," he said, quiet.

My throat burned. He'd remembered. Of course he had. He always remembered. I looked at him, and for a second, I couldn't breathe.

He sat next to me, long legs out, leaning back on his hands. Neither of us spoke for a long time, just sitting with the soft sounds of the neighborhood carrying faintly on the breeze.

"Thank you," I finally whispered, the only words I could get out.

He nodded and let the silence be a comfort. After a few minutes, he said, "So…Her Fluffiness is officially on kibble strike. I'm feeding her tuna now."

I couldn't help it. The smallest laugh bubbled up from my chest.

"You like her," he teased, the corner of his lips lifting into a small smile. "Admit it. You like her *and* me."

"I might." I pulled the cupcake from the bag.

Tucker pulled matches from his pocket and lit the candle. I stared at the flame, made a wish, and blew. "Happy birthday, Mom."

I bit into the cupcake. Heaven. I turned and offered it to Tucker, but instead of taking it from my hands, he simply leaned in for his bite.

When it was gone, he looked at me. "Still can't go inside?"

I eyed the house again. "I've gone in a lot this week. We've been packing up her things." I let out a breath. "But today, my feet don't want to take me inside."

He nodded. He knew firsthand.

"All day, I've been thinking about the fight she and I had right before she died. The last thing I said to her." I swallowed hard. "I don't know how to go inside today."

"You go in with someone you trust."

I met his eyes. He meant it. He meant *him*. I could use him as an unfailing, unwavering support. A tether.

I hesitated, but he stood and held out his hand, not letting go as we walked up to the house.

Inside, I paused, taking it in, the air so thick with memories.

"Your bedroom?" he asked.

"Yes."

As he'd no doubt already noticed from the night he'd crawled in the window to sleep on the floor, my dad and I hadn't gotten this far yet, so the room was virtually untouched and had been for years. In fact, it was exactly as I'd left it. I ran my fingers over dust-covered books and long-forgotten teenage knickknacks, such as the lamp my mom had given me when I was fourteen. It was all still here.

The version of me I'd thought I'd outgrown, but maybe hadn't.

The past was alive and well.

Tucker stood at my side, waiting for my cue, silent. Solid.

We started with the bookshelf, packing up the photo albums but got distracted for a moment, sitting on the bed, on my old comforter, flipping through pieces of a life that didn't feel like mine anymore.

"She'd be so proud of you, Haze."

I lifted my head to meet his gaze. "You think so?"

"I know so."

And maybe I believed it. Just a little. Because Tucker did. And sometimes, that was enough.

I set the photo albums aside. I'd keep these. Turning to the closet next, I drew a deep breath and opened it up. I'd taken my clothing with me, so what little I'd left, we now packed. Same with the dresser.

I kept my focus tight, one item at a time. Until, kneeling in front of my dresser, the bottom drawer open, I pulled out the small stuffed bear Tucker had given me for my sixteenth birthday. It'd come with a birthstone necklace—emerald.

"I wore the necklace every day," I said softly. My hand drifted to my throat instinctively, to the place it used to rest. "I was so sad when I lost it years ago." I shook my head. "Why did I let only the negative memories of my teenage years stick? There are good memories, really good memories."

Kneeling beside me, close enough that I could feel his warmth, he stroked a thumb over my throat, right where the stone had once nestled, and kissed me gently. Pulling back, he stared into my eyes and gave a small smile. "I'm glad you remember."

I smiled, and my eyes landed on an old iPhone in the back of the drawer. I searched around and found a charger for it and plugged it in, knowing exactly what I was looking for.

I navigated to the voicemail and hit the message I'd never deleted.

And just like that, the years vanished as my mom's voice filled the room. "Hey, hon, don't snack when you get home. I'm making your favorite—lasagna. Love you."

I didn't realize I was crying until Tucker gently turned me to face him.

"She'd love seeing you now," he said, brushing my tears away. "Strong. Smart. Unstoppable. Beyond talented."

He thought I was strong. And I wanted to be. So I drew in a deep breath and opened the next drawer, knowing what I would find before I saw it.

A book with the sonogram tucked inside. The one I'd never shown to anyone, including Tucker.

My breath stuttered with sudden nerves, but I didn't hide it. I wanted to be honest—I *needed* to be honest. For a beat, I stared at it, heart drumming. I felt the air in the room turn thick, like the walls were closing in on me.

Not my first time feeling this way. That day all those years ago when I'd realized I'd missed a period, the walls had closed in on me too. I bought a home test, even as I convinced myself it was a fluke.

After all, I'd slept with only one person, and we'd been so

careful. At least, as careful as two stupid, hormonal teenagers could be.

I took the test, then stared at it in shock. Earlier that day, I'd done something stupid. I'd been caught tagging the gazebo and had ended up with a ride to the police station. When my dad had shown up to take me home, he'd sat me down at the kitchen table and told me he couldn't do this anymore, that I needed to change, get my shit together, or…get out.

Even knowing my dad hadn't meant it, as always, my teenage pride had taken the worst possible choice.

As I remembered the loneliness and anger and hurt now, all of it crashed down on me, just as it had when, later that night, Tucker hadn't shown up at our rendezvous spot.

Now he was watching me, quiet. Patient.

"I need to tell you something." My voice felt raw, thick with the years of silence. "Something I've wanted to tell you for a long time. Something I've never told anyone."

I could see the wariness in his eyes, but he nodded. Even gave me a small encouraging smile, tugging me closer, cuddling me into him. "You can tell me anything, Haze. You know that."

Closing my eyes, I gave myself a few seconds to burrow in. No one hugged like Tucker—no one. He gave every inch of himself over, wrapping me up in those arms, kissing my temple, holding me tight.

But as I knew all too well, all good things came to an end. I backed out of the hug and handed him the sonogram.

He stared at it in confusion, taking in the date at the top, before his eyes widened in realization. "Is this a—"

"Fetus masquerading as a tiny bean? Yeah." I tried to calm my pounding heart. "I miscarried a few days after the ultrasound."

He made a wounded sound. "You were pregnant."

"Yes," I whispered, guilt crashing over me in waves.

He inhaled sharply, gaze flying to mine. "Mine?"

When I nodded, he stared at the ultrasound in shock. He backed up a step and sat heavily on the bed, like his legs had gone weak. His hands gripped the edge of the mattress, white-knuckled. His sudden tension, the weight of his disbelief and confusion, rolled over me like a tsunami. Finally, he drew in a deep breath and lifted his head, eyes unreadable now. "Tell me everything."

So I did. I told him how I'd found out, how I'd left, how I'd gotten two states away before the cramping had started, then the horror of realizing what it had meant. I let it all spill out, my voice trembling, breath hitching as I relived the memories of being in a faraway hospital with strangers, feeling more alone than I ever had in my life.

Tucker listened intently. He didn't interrupt, but I could feel guilt and regret emanating from him as I finished.

When I had, for a moment, the only sounds in the room were my breath and the soft hum of the world outside.

"I really need you to say something now," I finally whispered, hands tightly clasped in my lap where I sat at his side, not touching.

He reached out and put one of his big, warm hands over mine. "You should have told me."

The words hit me like a slap. "Oh, I'm sorry. Did this happen to you?"

His expression tightened. "No. But it happened to *you*, and you were everything to me."

Were.

The past tense sliced through me.

He reached for the sonogram again, staring at it like it had the power to shatter him. "This was our baby." He lifted his gaze. "Did anyone know?"

I shook my head.

He did the same, the betrayal in his voice cutting deeper than any knife when he said, "Why? Why didn't you tell me? Did you think I wouldn't be there for you?"

"I…" How to explain? "I was going to tell you that night, but—"

"I didn't show up." He flinched, then drew a slow breath, as if his legendary composure had slipped. "I get it. Your default always was—and is—to assume the worst of people. That they look at you and see the worst of you. That they'll fail you because of it."

Hard to be insulted with the truth.

He closed his eyes, a hand pressed to his chest like it'd caved in, like he couldn't deal with the thought of what had happened to me.

This, more than anything, slid right beneath my defenses and shook me to the core. He cared. He cared deeply, and he was right. I should have tried talking to him before I left. "I'm sorry—"

"No." He looked stricken. "Don't apologize. You aren't to blame for the miscarriage. Or your reaction to it. Or my reaction, for that matter. I just…" He shook his head. "You were scared and alone, and I wasn't there. I didn't show up. But, Hazel—God, if I'd known, I would've. You shouldn't have been alone."

Our eyes met and held, and I wondered if mine reflected the same devastation in his. "You think I needed saving."

"No." His voice cracked. "But I know you, Haze. You don't

let people in. You don't trust. And you don't believe you can be loved as is."

The harsh truth spelled out for me hit swift and hard, stealing my breath. Because this, *this* was my deepest, darkest secret, and to have it thrown at me so easily like he'd always known…

I stood, shame and panic and old reflexes kicking in hard, clouding my decision-making. "I take back what I said about wanting you to speak."

His smile was grim and short-lived as he stood as well. "You want to know why you didn't call me? Because you didn't believe I'd choose you. You never really believed I would."

I crossed my arms. "I'd like to be alone now."

He nodded. "That tracks."

Temper felt a whole lot better than the sadness and grief. "It was you who didn't show that night. And I know you had your reasons and they're valid, but you broke my heart, and it's still in pieces. Even if I wanted to give it away again, which I don't, I *can't*. I won't." I opened my old bedroom door.

To my shock, he headed for it, before stopping to say one last thing.

"If I'd known, I'd have torn the world apart to get to you, Hazel," he said, quiet but fierce. "Even if you didn't want me there, I'd have sat outside that hospital to be with you in spirit so you wouldn't be alone."

CHAPTER 25

Tucker

THE TRAIL WAS STILL cloaked in mist when my brothers and I set out for our pre-family-breakfast ritual—our unofficial, no-one-admitted-we-liked-it run along the river.

It was early. Too early for me, given the past few nights I'd had, tossing and turning.

Alone in my bed.

Hazel had gone back to the spare bedroom.

But at least she hadn't left.

Caleb was already five steps ahead, jogging backward, grinning like a man who knew he was about to be insufferable.

"You keep frowning like that and your face is gonna freeze that way," he called. "Even Hazel won't be able to pretend you're the best-looking one anymore."

"*I'm* the best-looking one," Ryder deadpanned.

"Not even close," Caleb said confidently.

I didn't respond. Mostly because I was too busy trying to hold myself together. Every step hit the dirt path like it was personal.

The salty fog drifted in off the river, hanging low and thick, cling-ing to the moss-covered branches like it didn't know how to let go.

Neither did I. Not when she'd handed me that sonogram like it was a piece of herself she never thought she'd share. Not when I'd seen the way her hands shook and heard the way her voice splintered and realized that she still somehow thought walking away had been the right thing.

From here we could hear the ocean booming softly, that slow rhythmic heartbeat of the coast I'd grown up with. It usually grounded me.

Not today.

Because all I could hear was Hazel's voice in my head—the way it'd broken when she'd handed me that sonogram, raw and shaking and honest in a way that still had my chest caving in two days later.

She'd truly believed she had to go through it alone.

Apparently my silence was suspicious, because Ryder slowed his pace and shot me a look. "You good?"

"Peachy."

"What a totally normal way to say that," he said. "Very convincing."

Caleb doubled back, still jogging in reverse like a man with zero regard for personal space or emotional land mines. "Yeah, and why haven't you lectured us yet about how this isn't real cardio?"

"What's wrong with saying 'peachy'?"

"Nothing," Ryder said. "If you're eighty."

I grunted.

Caleb glanced at Ryder. "Did he hit his head again?"

"Not this week, that I know of."

I didn't crack a smile. Couldn't. My brain was still stuck on the look on her face when I'd said the wrong thing. Again. And then the sound of her voice when she'd said, *I'd like to be alone now.*

Because she believed that's what she deserved.

And what had I done? I'd left, like the biggest asshole on the planet. I hadn't tried. I hadn't even told her I loved her.

My brothers flanked me like overly aggressive mall cops, subtle as bricks, loud as toddlers with drums, and just as relentless.

"You didn't send me the renovation estimate for the Baxter place," Ryder said. "You said I'd have it today."

"And you will." My legs burned. The chilled air seared my lungs. Or maybe that was just the ache in my chest taking up too much space.

Caleb gave Ryder a look, and they both slowed to a walk.

I kept running.

So Caleb tripped me.

I tucked and rolled on instinct, then lay on my back in the damp grass, staring up at my soon-to-be-dead brother, calculating how long I might spend in jail for burying his body out here.

"Talk," Caleb said, planting a running shoe on my chest so I couldn't get up.

I grabbed him by the calf and yanked, satisfied when he hit the grass on his back with an *oomph*.

"Rude," he gasped.

"I don't want to talk."

"Tough shit," Ryder said. "Because whenever I don't want to talk about something, you still make me."

I stared up at the pink-and-gold sunrise. "Yeah, well, you can't make me."

They sat on either side of me. Caleb nudged my shoulder.

"Is it Hazel? Did something happen? Did she shrink-wrap your truck again?"

"She pull another Houdini?" Ryder asked.

"Did she take out another tree along Main Street?"

I let out a low laugh at the list of some of Hazel's adventures, but there was no weight behind it.

Ryder sobered. "Talk."

I scrubbed my hands over my face. "She told me something. Something she never got the chance to say back then. All I knew was that Bill had told her to straighten up and fly right, or leave. He'd said that before, many times, but she took this one at face value."

Both of them stilled.

"There's more," Ryder said.

"Yeah." I stared up at the sky like it was my job. It was going to be a warm day, eventually. "She was pregnant when she left. She miscarried. Alone."

Caleb went still, his expression sliding from curious to gutted. "Yours?" he asked quietly.

I nodded.

"I take it you didn't know."

I shook my head. "She was going to tell me the night she left. But I didn't show. Hank had been on a tear and had refused to let me go anywhere. I could've sneaked out, as I had many, many times before, but I couldn't leave Kiera. I just…couldn't. And before either of you says anything, you wouldn't have either. I knew that, just as I knew you'd protected me from Hank for years. And I knew I was going to do the same for Kiera."

Ryder cursed low.

Caleb let out a breath like he'd been punched in the chest.

I could still see that damn kitchen clock ticking past midnight, knowing Kiera was asleep in her bed, counting on me to make sure she stayed safe. Me standing guard over Hank, who'd passed out drunk in his chair.

I'd thought I was doing the right thing. Thought Hazel would understand.

Above me, the wind rustled the pines, birds squawked, and the ache sitting heavy in my chest got heavier.

Because now I knew what I'd missed.

A whole life. A heartbeat I never got to hear.

And I hadn't even known to grieve it.

"Hazel carried that on her own. For twelve goddamn years."

And she still did. Even now, she tucked her pain behind sarcastic smiles and *I've got it handled.* Like it was a habit she couldn't break.

Caleb blew out a breath. "Shit, Tuck."

"Yeah."

"I always wondered why she left like that," Ryder said. "It never made sense. So, you two were…?"

"Yeah," I said. "We were."

Caleb dragged a hand through his hair. "You're lucky Bill didn't bury you behind Al's Diner."

"He still might, depending on what Hazel tells him. If she tells him."

Ryder tilted his head. "Where do you and Hazel stand now?"

I gave a joyless laugh.

"How are you going to fix this?"

I looked at Ryder. "I can't. She's shut me out, back to shouldering everything on her own."

"You mad at her?" Caleb asked quietly.

"No. I'm not. I would never be mad at her for this. I hate that she didn't tell me, but I hate more that she had to go through it alone."

I hated that I'd failed her. Then and now. That when it had counted most, I hadn't been there.

"You love her," Caleb said, simple and sure.

The sun broke through the treetops, slanting across the clearing. "Yeah. I do."

Ryder didn't even blink. "Then you figure out what comes next."

"We've got your back," Caleb added. "Even when you're an idiot."

I nodded, because for the first time in days, the silence settled—not just around me, but inside me too. Not like dead air, but like space.

Room to breathe.

Room to move forward.

Maybe it was the beginning.

Maybe now I could start figuring it out. Not just how to say the right thing. But how to show her she mattered. That she always had.

Maybe I'd find a way to prove to Hazel that she wasn't alone anymore.

CHAPTER 26

Tucker

THE REDWOOD ROOST WAS packed, the usual chaos humming—mugs clinking, kids squealing, and the kind of conversation you'd get only in a place that had perfected breakfast.

Which Penny had. She was a breakfast wizard. The scent of fresh coffee, sizzling bacon, and eggs so amazing they could be considered art filled the air, thick enough to make you gain five pounds just by breathing. It brought a false sense of normalcy that I could almost believe…

I spotted my family instantly—Hank in his usual spot near the window, slurping coffee like it was a bowl of soup, Caleb with Emma tucked close beside him, Ryder stealing sausage off Penny's plate, and Penny stealing his toast.

So the usual.

I dropped a kiss to the top of Kiera's head.

"I ordered for you," she said. "But you should hurry and claim it before the heathens do. They're eyeing your bacon."

"Thanks." I slid into the open seat beside Hank, accepting the full plate that Kiera handed me. I eyed her. "Why is there only one piece of bacon?"

"You snooze, you lose."

Everyone around me was having fun, catching up—even if both Ryder and Caleb kept giving me quietly concerned looks, which I ignored—while my sister, ever the ringmaster of this circus, directed the chaos.

The twins were going all Hunger Games over the pancakes. And then Abi ate Alex's bacon, and the world came to a sudden shrieking halt.

I gave Alex my last piece of bacon, which he promptly crammed in his mouth like he hadn't eaten in days. That bought thirty seconds of quiet.

"You're a lifesaver," Kiera said around her own mountain of bacon, with zero guilt whatsoever.

"You could've given him *yours*, you know."

"I already gave them my sleep, my boobs, and what was left of my bladder control." She bit into another perfectly crunchy piece of bacon. "This bacon is sacred."

Fair enough.

She gave me a second look and tilted her head. "What's wrong?"

"Just tired."

"Yeah," Ryder said beneath his breath. "And the Easter Bunny just walked in."

Abi and Alex jumped to their feet on the bench seat in our booth, heads whipping every which way. "Where? Where? *Where?*"

Ryder made a show of searching the café around us. "Sorry, I thought I saw him for a second, but I was wrong."

Caleb reached to steal a piece of my sourdough toast, and I stabbed his hand with my fork.

"Seriously?" Caleb shook his head and glared at me. "That hurt."

"No blood, no foul."

Caleb rolled his eyes. "Just go talk to her, man."

"Talk to who?" Kiera asked, eyes narrowing. "Hazel? Why?"

"Drop it," I said tersely.

"Fine, jeez," Kiera said. "You don't have to be such a—" She broke off, glanced at her kids, then whispered, "D-I-C-K."

Abi bounced up and down. "I know what that spells!"

Kiera looked horrified. "You do?"

"Yep! Dog! That's what the letter *d* is for. Dog. Ms. Granger says so."

Kiera had to work at keeping a straight face. "You're right, baby. *D* is for *dog*."

"But Unca Tucker isn't a dog. He's a firefighter."

Kiera reached into her purse. "Sticker books!" she called out, waving them. "Who wants?"

The kids snatched them up, and blissful silence reigned. Not that it would last.

Kiera focused her laser eyes on me again. "Does this have anything to do with Hazel and your stupid 'just friends' thing? I mean, despite the kiss I saw you lay on her, you also put your foot so far into your mouth, I bet you're still flossing with your own shoelaces."

Caleb choked on his orange juice. "Damn." He swiped his mouth. "Sometimes I forget how mean you can be."

Ryder was still eyeballing me closely.

I hadn't felt this exposed since sophomore year, when Sadie

Roberts told everyone I'd used too much tongue under the bleachers during homecoming week. Total lie, by the way. We hadn't kissed. We'd done a *lot* of other things, but no kissing… And hell if I was going to explain whatever Hazel and I were to each other. Mostly because I had no idea. We'd been sleeping in the same bed—at least until the sonogram discovery.

"Seriously, what did you do?" Kiera asked me, pulling out her phone. "I'm going to call and make sure she's all right—"

I snatched her phone and tossed it to Ryder. Because I was over this. Then I nabbed Caleb's three pieces of bacon and shoved them into my mouth at once. The crunch was glorious. So was the look on his face.

Caleb turned and eyed Emma's plate, which still had bacon on it.

"Love you," Emma said sweetly as she moved her plate away from him. "But don't even think about it."

The café door opened and in walked Hazel as if I'd conjured her myself, heading straight for the take-out counter. She was in jeans, work boots, and a dark green T-shirt I hadn't seen before. Damp red waves were twisted into a loose knot, a few long silky strands escaping, flying around her makeup-free face. She looked as though she'd barely slept either.

And just like that, everything in me kicked to life—heart, lungs, want. It hit me so fast, I nearly dropped my coffee.

God, I missed her.

"Invite her over here," Kiera demanded.

"I think she needs space."

"Or maybe she needs *you*, dumbass."

Hank gave me a thumbs-up. Which might've meant he agreed. Or that he just liked the pancakes Emma was cutting for him.

Hazel spoke to the woman at the counter, then stepped aside to wait. She scanned the room for a moment, and bam, her eyes locked onto mine like she'd felt me thinking about her.

Her expression shifted. Not a smile. Not quite. But not nothing either.

Time hiccuped even as my pulse kicked. For that single heartbeat, it was just me and her. The rest of the world faded away, the noise of the café, my family, everything. Just me and Hazel, frozen in place.

A server handed her a coffee to go. She looked like she might bolt. But…she didn't.

"Hazel!" Caleb called out to her, waving cheerfully. "Over here!"

Ryder immediately started shuffling people around to make space.

Fucking nosy busybodies, all of them. I never should've told them the truth.

Hazel hesitated, knuckles white around the to-go cup like it was an emotional shield. The weight of her gaze, heavy and unsure, settled in my chest like a stone.

So much unsaid between us. So many barriers.

I gave her a small but genuine smile and nodded that I wanted her here. With us.

Something in her shoulders eased. Only a little. But it was enough. She drew a deep breath and made her way toward our booth.

Penny got to her first. "Hazel! That light you fixed out front? I don't trip over that damn sidewalk anymore. My knees thank you."

She shrugged, trying to play it off, but I could tell Penny's words meant something to her.

Kiera patted the empty space at her side.

Hazel sat, accepting hugs from Abi and Alex, who happily scrambled into her lap. "Hey, cuties," she murmured.

The sight of her cuddling the twins like she'd been doing it for years, like she really belonged here, was a part of us, knocked the breath out of me.

"How are you doing?" Hazel asked them, voice soft, smile genuine. "I'm sure you've been precious angels, haven't you?"

"Oh, they've been something all right," Kiera said. "We owe Penny a massive tip for keeping a straight face when Abi tried to order the 'vagina' for breakfast instead of *lasagna*."

Hazel laughed, the sound warm and real, and I felt some of my tension release.

Conversation flowed easily around us. Ryder thanked her again for stepping in when we'd needed her skill set after losing Ricky, complimenting the job she'd done re-creating complicated century-old crown moldings, calling her the best finisher we'd had in years.

All true. She'd done an incredible job, as always throwing herself wholeheartedly into everything she did.

At Ryder's assessment of her work, something flickered across her face—surprise, maybe—as she shifted on the bench, like praise wasn't something she was used to hearing.

But I knew how hard she'd worked to get here. How much effort she'd put into proving herself. "It's true," I said. "Your work is incredible."

Our eyes met. "Thanks. I couldn't have done it without Tex and Annie, and all of you. Working jobs is easy when you've got a solid team behind you. Haven't had that in a hot minute."

It was the first time she'd opened up about her time away, and her words hung in the air, all of us aware she was talking about more than just construction sites.

"You've always had us," I said. "But as for work, we should've hired you sooner."

Kiera reached for Hazel's hand and gave it a squeeze. "What Tucker said."

Ryder leaned forward, voice serious. "He's right. I was wrong not to hire you the minute you stepped back into Star Falls. You deserved better from me. I'm sorry."

"Whoa." Caleb pulled out his phone. "Say that again."

Ryder subtly rubbed his nose with his middle finger, then looked at Hazel, eyes regretful. It was impressive, because Ryder rarely if ever did regretful. "Tucker wanted me to hire you from the jump," he said. "I hesitated, but I think your mom would've wanted this."

We were all stunned. First admitting regret, and now admitting to being wrong. I looked over at Hazel for her reaction. Her lips had parted in shock. She gave me a small smile, and I realized it wasn't Ryder's apology that had shocked her.

It was learning that I'd stood up for her.

"It's okay," she said softly. "I'm happy it's working out now."

"I'm not going to hesitate again," Ryder said. "From here on out, all our finish-carpentry contracts will be offered to you first. You don't have to take them, of course; I just want you to know that."

At the stunned but marveled look on Hazel's face, I felt my throat go thick. I'd known Ryder was going to offer that to her; we'd talked about it. It wasn't a favor—we wanted the best of the best, and that was Hazel.

Around us, the café was getting crowded. Some of my crew

came in the front door in their turnout gear; Jayden, Tessa, Marcus, and Harlow, clearly seeking breakfast. When they saw me, they veered in my direction.

Jayden, six foot six and built like a battering ram, grinned wide and tossed something on the table like a grenade.

Fuuuck. It was the annual firefighter's calendar, and there I was, the cover boy: holding a hose, wearing nothing but turnout cargoes low-slung on my hips, a helmet perched on my head, and a puppy tucked under my arm.

I looked fucking ridiculous.

A collective *delighted* gasp sounded from the table. Caleb cackled. Kiera shrieked. Ryder looked torn between laughing and grimacing. Emma and Penny pounced like it was Black Friday at Macy's.

I should never have gotten out of bed this morning.

I risked a glance at Hazel. She waggled her brows.

Silent sarcasm. Beautiful.

Kiera glanced through the pages. "I'm torn. You're my brother, so…ew. But someone's been working out."

"Right? Gimme." Emma grabbed the calendar and thumbed through the pages, oohing and aahing. "You've been holding out on us, Tucker."

"Sitting right here," Caleb muttered, scowling. "And *anyone* looks good holding a puppy."

Emma grinned. "Did you hear that? Caleb's getting me a puppy!"

"We already have two massive dogs."

"And soon, a new puppy as well," Emma said on a laugh.

Penny got the calendar next. "*Holy cow.*"

"Holy cow *squared*." Emma said.

Awesome. They found the centerfold—also me.

My crew was now laughing so hard, no noises were coming out.

Smart-asses.

"Look at those abs," Penny said, then pretended to swipe for drool.

"Hey, *I've* got a six-pack too," Ryder said.

"Yes, but Tucker's is an *eight* pack."

Glaring at Jayden and the others, I snatched the calendar back. "It's for *charity*. Ask them." I pointed to the jackasses I worked with.

My entire squad just laughed at me and headed for the coffee bar.

"Did you oil yourself, or did they have a person for that?" Emma asked.

Caleb gave her a raised brow.

"What?" she said. "I'm just saying, whoever has that job must be a happy person all the time."

"*Charity,*" I repeated, then set my forehead to the table and banged it a few times, hoping I'd wake up in bed instead of here. When I didn't, I lifted my head. "It's for *charity.*"

Hazel's eyes were flat-out laughing at me. I ignored this and pointed at all of them. "None of you know anything about anything." I looked at the twins. "Except for you two." My gaze slid to Hazel. "And you. The rest of you can…" I was going to say *fuck off*, but Abi and Alex were sponges. "Bite me."

Alex shook his head. "Biting is a no-no. Even if Tommy took my cupcake at lunch without asking."

I was still giving a hard look to the adults—minus Haze. "I mean it," I said.

Penny leaned in and stage-whispered, "Is it just me, or does he suddenly sound all commanding like Ryder?"

"Okay, that's enough," I growled, reaching out to snag the calendar, only for Hazel to beat me to it.

She held it above her head, much as I'd done to her when she'd wanted my phone.

"If you want it," she said in a singsong voice, "come and get it."

Everyone laughed, and I growled. "I hate all of you."

"Your abs say otherwise," Emma said.

Hazel's eyes danced, and she hugged the calendar to her chest like it was Christmas morning, smiling—and even though it was at my expense, I didn't give a shit; I smiled helplessly back. For a split second, there was no history, no unresolved tension. Just us.

But, of course, Ryder had to ruin that too.

"You two ever going to get your sh—" Ryder eyed the twins. "Er, shizzle together?"

Everyone's heads swiveled in unison to me and Hazel, eager for an answer.

Hazel saved me, just not in the way I wanted.

"We're not…" She grimaced, her face scrunching up in that familiar endearing way that made me want to kiss her. "We're not whatever you all think we are."

Ouch.

Caleb leaned in. "You tell that to the chemistry between the two of you?"

Hazel snorted, and I could feel the tension between us crack just a little more. "It's antagonism, not chemistry."

"No way," Caleb said. "Have you seen him mooning after you? He can't keep his eyes off you."

Emma put a hand on Caleb's arm. "If your vagina doesn't get

a heartbeat when you see him—especially on that cover—he's not the one anyway."

Hazel choked on her coffee.

I stood. "Okay, we're done here." I glared at my siblings. "You all need to grow up."

They were unrepentant. I grabbed Hazel's hand. She let me.

On the sidewalk out front, she said, "I'm not giving this back." And with that, she slid the calendar beneath her sweatshirt. Wait a minute, that was another of *mine*.

"The calendar or the sweatshirt?"

She lifted her chin. "Both."

"Keep them." My sweatshirt. My heart. My jugular. My everything. Hers.

She must've seen something in my face because her smile faded.

So did mine.

Something flickered in her eyes as we stood there, toe-to-toe, close and yet not close enough.

"I'm sorry about them," I said.

She shook her head. "They love you."

"They love you too."

She shoulder bumped me, and I caught her hand again, not wanting the moment to end.

"Hey, um, about the other day. I…"

"Yeah." She nodded, voice soft as she gently squeezed my fingers.

I pulled her in for a hug. She melted into me, arms tight. I closed my eyes and just breathed her in. "Maybe we could talk."

She nodded, a strand of her hair catching on the stubble on my jaw. A small moment, but it felt incredibly intimate.

"I'm working today," she said, pulling back. "Meet you at the house later?"

I nodded, and pretending she hadn't told my family we weren't what they thought—what had that meant?—I kissed her goodbye, not light, not soft, but a real kiss: direct, meaningful, real.

Just in case she needed reminding.

I didn't know what would come next. But for the first time in days, I felt like maybe, just maybe, we had a shot.

CHAPTER 27

Hazel

THERE WAS SOMETHING ABOUT finishing a job that felt like a victory lap. The Sonoma project was nearly there: clean lines, fresh trim, and enough sweat equity in the walls to bind us for life.

Still, it hadn't been the highlight of my day.

That honor went to breakfast.

I could still feel the soft warmth of Penny's café clinging to my skin like sunlight after a storm. Coffee, pancakes, my name being shouted across the café like a battle cry, and Tucker pretending not to smile when I teased him about the calendar. At first, he'd kept on his game face, like maybe nothing had happened.

Like we hadn't unraveled in my childhood bedroom, layer by layer, confession by confession, until I was raw and exposed and wide open in a way I hadn't been in years.

I was proud of myself for talking about the past, and even though some of what he'd said had hurt, I was proud of him too.

This didn't mean I had any idea of where we stood.

But this morning, I'd caught him looking at me like I mattered. Like I wasn't a mistake he'd dodged, or a girl who'd once broken his heart, but someone who still took up space in it.

And in an hour or two, we were going to talk.

And not in the flirty, ignoring-our-past way. A *real* conversation.

My palms were already sweating just thinking about it.

Part of me wanted him to tell me again how he'd meant to come that night. That he'd regretted not showing up ever since. And not, as I'd feared all these years, that he'd felt like he'd dodged a bullet.

Which, let's face it, he had.

But he'd already bared his soul. And the real truth was I held equal blame. I hadn't reached out while I'd been gone. Not because I didn't forgive him but because I didn't think I deserved him.

I was holding out hope that we weren't just two people who'd almost made it. Maybe we still had a shot. And maybe that kind of optimism was dangerous.

Hope had a sneaky way of slipping under my skin, making promises it had no business making. And it wasn't just about Tucker. I'd had calls from people who lived in Star Falls, people who wanted me to do work for them, renovate their house, their office. With or without the Seattle offer, I had more work than I could dream of.

If I wanted it.

So, instead of spiraling into the what-ifs like usual, I threw myself into work. Because work made sense. Tools didn't lie. Nails held their promise. Wood split and sanded and bent if you applied the right kind of pressure.

Unlike people.

I wiped my hands on my jeans, leaving behind a constellation of sawdust. The day was already warm, sun slanting through the skeletal frame of what would one day be a wraparound porch. My crew had cleared out for lunch, leaving the jobsite blessedly quiet, until a familiar SUV crunched to a stop on the gravel drive.

Kiera hopped out, a canvas tote slung over her shoulder and a suspiciously cheery smile on her face. "I come bearing snacks and sibling-related gossip."

I gave her a look. "And…?"

"Wow, suspicious much?"

"You don't normally drive out to the edge of town just to bring me snacks."

Kiera held up two iced coffees like a peace offering. "Bribery first. Interrogation second."

"Fair." I took the coffee.

We sat on the edge of the porch foundation, legs dangling, boots covered in dust. Kiera opened her tote and pulled out a bag of cookies.

I dove right in, then moaned in delight. "I'd marry this cookie and have its babies."

"They're from Penny. She says being pregnant makes her want to bake."

"She also says being pregnant makes her horny, sad, and homicidal, all at the same time."

Kiera smiled. "She's become a true Colburn."

"You going to tell me what you want to know, or just feed me into submission?" I asked in amusement.

"Fine. I do have a question."

"Okay," I said. "But if I don't like it, I get the rest of the cookies to myself."

"Deal." Kiera stared at me a beat. "Listen. I know my brothers can be clueless, but I also know how much you mean to Tucker. Then and now. He's always been the most private of all of us. I think he simply wanted to keep it private, between the two of you."

"I know."

"You do?"

"Yes," I said. "But also, that wasn't a question."

Her eyes softened. "You don't have to tell me anything. Ever. But if you ever need to unload, I'm here. They might be clueless, but I'm not. You're my sister, in every way that counts."

My throat tightened around a mouthful. "Thank you, and right back at you. But I still haven't heard a question."

Kiera snorted. "Fine. I'll get to it. At breakfast, Tucker looked like he'd been kicked in the soul. Didn't even touch his pancakes. And that man could eat an entire stack during a five-alarm fire."

I looked down at my cookie. "You want to know if he's okay."

"Yes," she said gently. "He wouldn't tell me anything."

I exhaled slowly. "It's complicated. It's also my fault."

Kiera didn't push. Just pressed her shoulder to mine in solidarity.

"He—I told him something," I said. "Something I should've told him a long time ago."

Kiera nodded but stayed quiet.

I swallowed the cookie that had turned to dry cement in my mouth. "I was pregnant when I left Star Falls. I miscarried a few days later." I hadn't planned on saying it. Not yet. But the words had clawed their way out of me, raw and too loud, and now they just…hung there. My hands trembled, so I pressed them to my thighs to make them stop.

Kiera's breath caught. Her hand curled around mine, tight.

I tried to smile, but it wobbled. "So yeah. That happened, and I kept it to myself."

"Oh, honey. *Why?*"

I shrugged. "I guess because I didn't know how to talk about it without falling apart."

"You were so young." She held on to my hand, probably in case I turned into a flight risk. "I know it's not the same, our losses, but I understand."

My eyes welled. Kiera had lost the love of her life. "Loss is loss," I whispered. It was disorientating how quickly joy could turn into memory, and memory into pain. But I wasn't running, not this time.

Kiera slapped at her pockets and came up with a few tissues. She handed me one and blew her nose with the other. "How did Tucker handle it?"

"He was…" I tried to find the words. "Tucker. Stoic and calm. He was worried about me, concerned that I'd gone through it alone." I hesitated. "I didn't want to tell him. I knew, even all these years later, it would hurt him."

"You did the right thing," Kiera said fiercely. "He deserved to know. You weren't protecting him by keeping it in. You were just carrying the weight alone. And that's one thing he never wanted for you. He's the strongest of all of us. He'll shoulder this gladly, because he'll see it as a lessening of the burden on you. He'd rather carry that pain than let you carry it alone." She met my gaze. "He'd do anything for you, Hazel. I hope you believe that."

I let out a breath. "I'm starting to. I just don't know what to do with it. Even thinking about opening my heart…" I shook my head.

She nodded. "I understand that too."

And she did, down to her bones.

Miguel and Hawk walked by, each carrying sheets of drywall, biceps straining. Hawk nodded in greeting and kept moving.

Miguel set down the drywall. "Hazel." He smiled in my direction, but when he looked at Kiera, he turned the charisma up a thousand watts. "Hey, Key. You're a sight for sore eyes."

Kiera smiled, all flirty.

I nearly choked on my cookie. Was I hallucinating?

"Risking your life again?" she asked him.

Miguel grinned. "Now's our chance. Run away with me, gorgeous."

She made a show of checking her calendar. "Sorry, I have a hair appointment this afternoon."

He laughed. "Then dinner. Have dinner with me."

Kiera bit her lower lip like she was actually thinking about it. Then she said, "What about your bossy boss and his no-fraternization rules?"

Miguel shrugged. "He'll get over it. You and me? We're the real deal."

Kiera's cool demeanor slipped slightly, but she recovered quickly. "You know I've got two wild wolf pups at home, which means it's never just me. *No one* wants to have dinner with my circus."

His smile softened. "Then I'll bring dinner to you and the pups. Circus and all."

Kiera eyed him for a long moment.

He withstood the scrutiny with his usual laid-back smile.

Finally, she shook her head. "I'm sure I'm going to regret this, but I'm calling your bluff. You're on. Don't forget dessert."

Miguel, always confident, always with the swagger and an

easy grin, blinked like she'd just short-circuited his brain. But he recovered quickly, a slow smile spreading. "I never forget dessert." He hoisted the drywall back onto his shoulder with ease, nodded at me, then sauntered off like a man who'd just won the lotto.

I turned slowly, eyebrows halfway to my hairline. "Was that you…flirting?"

"Please. If I were flirting, there'd be fireworks and fainting goats."

"Uh-huh." I bumped her shoulder with mine. "You realize you just said yes to a date, right?"

"Oh shit." She exhaled a shaky breath and watched Miguel's retreating back. "I did." She drew a deep breath. "Apparently I'm ready."

I smiled. "Ready looks good on you."

We munched on cookies, feeling the breeze flowing through the wide-open framing. "Do you want me to babysit tonight?" I asked.

"You seriously want to babysit the small humans who think farts are a second language?"

I grinned. "They're adorable."

"Thank you." She smiled in agreement. "But for this one, I want to make sure I'm not wasting my time."

"You mean you want him to see your real world and not bolt for the hills."

"Maybe. Yes." With a laugh, she laid her head on my shoulder. "I missed you being around so much. No one else appreciates my sarcasm or tells my brothers to shove it with so much finesse. Do you know you're wearing two different kinds of socks?"

"It's laundry day. I'm also not wearing undies."

It was Kiera's turn to choke as she left.

Much later, I startled at Tex's voice booming across the large room. "You look like you're down a quart, boss." He tossed me a bottle of water and an apple.

He laughed when I looked at the apple, a little crestfallen.

"Sorry, you ate my last candy bar yesterday."

I bit into the apple. "You're a god among men."

"Got that right."

I laughed and chugged the water while he unbuckled his tool belt and squatted before our huge toolbox, slotting screw guns into their chargers.

"Where you off to?" I asked.

"He's got a hot date tonight," Annie said, sauntering in and peeling off her dusty sweatshirt. She fluffed her hair and smiled. "With me, in case that wasn't clear. He doesn't want to be late. There are penalties if he is."

"Penalties?"

Annie smiled. "Trust me, you don't wanna know."

Catching a glimpse of the time, I gasped. "Oh shit, it's six. How did that happen?"

Tex smiled. "Well, when the a.m. and p.m. love each other very much, sometimes they get together and—"

"Go—get outta here before you have to pay the penalty."

"I mean, I kinda want to pay the penalty because it means she'll—"

"No!" I covered my ears. "Don't you dare finish that sentence! Now leave. I'll be right behind you. I'm late."

"Seems boss has a date too," Tex teased. "He can thank me later for *not* delivering you hangry."

"Ha ha." My stomach jangled with nerves because I was pretty sure it wouldn't be that kind of date. We were going to *talk*. One of my least favorite things. But I owed him this. I'd spent half my life running from things I loved because staying had always hurt worse. "Go."

"Nah, we'll wait. Everyone else already cleared out. I don't like the idea of leaving you alone this far out from town."

"I'll be right behind you," I promised, while texting Tucker: Sorry, running half hour behind. Save me a bite of something.

A few minutes later, I heard Tex and Annie peel out, blasting nineties country and arguing about what counted as vintage.

Left in their wake was a whole lot of blessed quiet and a calm, golden twilight, the kind that made the oak-dotted green rolling hills feel soft around the edges. I checked that the windows were shut and locked, and—

Heard a sound I couldn't place.

I froze. Listened. There it was again—metal against metal. Close. Too close.

Out back, where I was parked.

Shit.

I crept around the building. The air was filled with silence, but not the peaceful kind. The charged, skin-prickling kind. I wasn't alone, and every hair on my body stood up.

Another metal *clang*. I knew that sound—someone was in my toolbox. I peeked around the corner—and there he was.

Ricky, the walking cautionary tale himself.

He'd climbed into my trailer and was hunched over my toolbox—my closed, locked, and very clearly labeled toolbox— swearing and tugging at the lock like it owed him money.

His beat-up truck idled nearby, tailgate open and waiting.

"Seriously?" I muttered.

"Fuck! I'll just tow the sucker." He spun to the back of his truck, rage twisting his features when he saw me. "*You*," he snarled.

"You're not welcome here, Ricky. Get the hell out."

"You and your dad ruined me. I'm returning the favor. Stay outta my way, bitch."

Wow. Straight to misogyny. Bold strategy. "Again, you did this to yourself," I said evenly.

He reached into the trailer and came out with a hammer—mine—and gripped it like a weapon.

"Don't do it, Ricky."

He laughed harshly and threw my hammer at my head.

I ducked, and it hit the siding behind me with a heavy *thunk*. Slowly, I straightened, heart trying to punch through my lungs. "You really want to make this a felony?" I mean, it was *already* a felony—not that he was smart enough to know that. "Think about this."

"Pass." And he threw a heavy metal tape measure, also at my head.

I ducked again, and the window behind me shattered.

"You destroyed my reputation!" he yelled.

"This is your version of a redemption arc?"

He hoisted a nail gun next—my new one!—and hit the trigger.

It had no nails in it.

"Fuck!" He chucked it at me and hit the back door, making a big dent. "You think you're so clever! Trying to make me look like the bad guy. Well, it worked. My wife took our kid to Florida to live with her mother. You have any idea what it's like to lose a kid?"

My heart stumbled. Yeah, I knew. I hadn't been able to take

care of my baby either. I took a deep breath, steeled myself, and held up my hands, thankful his were now empty. "I'm sorry about your kid," I said quietly. "Really. But you know I didn't do this to you."

He didn't listen. Rage made him fast. He lunged, and one hand closed around my arm like a vise. In the other, he held his phone.

"Say it!" he shouted, shaking me. "Say you people set me up!"

I saw stars. My teeth rattled. My knee gave out, and I went down hard, rolling my ankle.

Ricky loomed over me, camera in my face. "Say it!"

"You're literally recording yourself assaulting me, genius," I said, breathing heavily.

When he hesitated, I kicked him square in the knee. I didn't get his balls, but the crack of my boot into his leg was the most satisfying sound I'd heard all day.

He howled and went down like a felled tree.

I didn't stick around. I scrambled up, ankle screaming, and bolted. Pain lanced through my ankle with every step, but adrenaline kept me going. *Just a little farther. Just make it around the corner. Just hide.*

I limped around the side of the property before ducking behind a tree, breath coming in panicked gasps as I yanked out my phone. My fingers shook as I hit 9-1-1. "I need help," I whispered. "Sonoma job site—Ricky Horowitz just attacked me. I'm hiding. He's trying to steal my trailer."

I hung up and called Tucker.

"Can you come to the job?" I whispered, barely breathing, keeping an eye peeled for Ricky.

On Tucker's end, I heard a rustle of clothing and his keys

jangling. Then his engine starting. I nearly burst into tears. He used to say I always ran. He wasn't wrong. But this time, when I ran, it was straight to him.

"On my way," he said, voice terrifyingly calm. "Talk to me."

"Ricky. He grabbed me. He's—he's pissed. And—"

"Are you hurt?"

"No, just, please hurry."

"He still there?"

"I don't know."

"Hide, Haze. Hide like you used to when you won the Colburn hide-and-seek tournament. Don't hang up—I'm putting you on hold to call the cops."

"I already did."

"Good girl. Six minutes out—"

Static.

Beep.

Nothing.

My phone was dead. Of course it was.

Tucker

The line cut out. "Fuck!" I hit Redial—straight to voicemail.

She'd sounded shaky. Frantic. And just like that, everything inside me clicked into place.

Mission mode.

I'd trained for this, starting from when I'd been a child and it'd been up to me to hide Kiera when my dad was on a tear, continuing into adulthood by choosing a profession of saving people, requiring calm under pressure, sharp leadership skills, and the ability to separate myself from the problem in front of me.

That last one was where I faltered now.

Saving people wasn't just what I did. It was my contribution. It was my self-worth.

But when it was Hazel?

All bets were off.

My phone lit up. Caleb.

"Cameras picked up Ricky at the Sonoma site," he said.

I gritted my teeth. "He assaulted Hazel. I'm en route. Call Ryder and Bill."

"Already did. We're en route too."

I hung up, then got my hands locked tight on the wheel.

Hazel was tough.

And she wasn't alone anymore.

Not ever again.

CHAPTER 28

Tucker

TOOK THE LAST turn onto the jobsite gravel, my headlights sweeping across the clearing like searchlights. Knowing Hazel was out here, alone, after being assaulted by a guy I knew was unstable, was enough to short-circuit every survival instinct I'd honed over years in the fire service.

For one sickening second, I saw nothing.

Then—movement.

A figure emerged from the trees, limping, and my heart clenched.

Hazel.

I'd know her anywhere, even in the dark.

I threw my truck into Park before the tires stopped rolling, flung open the door, and hit the ground running. My boots pounded the dirt as she staggered forward.

I caught her. "Hazel," I breathed, pulling her into me, wrapping my arms around her like a human shield. She was shaking like a leaf in a wind tunnel, sucking in air like she'd been running, skin cold and clammy, despite the warm night.

My arms tightened as I pulled us into the shadows, scanning the perimeter. Nothing but darkness. No motion lights. No sound but the pounding in my ears and the panicked rhythm of Hazel's breath.

Caleb had said the cameras picked him up, but where the hell were the exterior motion sensors? Why the fuck hadn't they kicked on?

"You're safe now. I've got you," I murmured into her hair, pressing my lips to her temple. "Where is he?"

"I lost him."

"But he's still here?"

"I haven't heard his truck start up."

I slipped an arm around her waist, taking on most of her weight as we moved toward my truck. Once I got her behind the wheel, I handed her my flashlight. "Lock yourself in." I pressed my keys to her hand and cupped her face. "Stay low. Don't open that door for anyone but a Colburn."

She opened her mouth to protest, so I kissed her. Hard. "Please," I said against her lips. "I can't think when you're in danger. I'll be back, I promise."

"He's armed himself with tools," she said. "He'd make a shit pro pitcher, but still, be careful."

That was my girl. I shut the door. "Hit the lock."

I waited until she did, then turned and went hunting.

I found Ricky behind the building, trying—and failing—to start his truck.

"You motherfucking fucker," he yelled, slamming his fist on the steering wheel.

I yanked the door open and hauled him out.

"What the fuck—"

I shoved him against the truck, one hand around his throat. Not tight. Yet.

His eyes went wide. "Hey," he said when he recognized me, lifting his hands. "I don't want any trouble."

"Too late. You put your hands on Hazel."

"I did not! Did she say that? Where's that bitch—"

I squeezed his throat just enough to cut off that word.

"Christ, you're all feral, you know that?" he rasped. "I'm going to sue the shit out of you! Take you for everything you're worth."

Sirens wailed in the distance. Seconds later, red and blue lights swept over the trees. I backed up a step but kept my eyes on Ricky.

He started to come at me, but when I straightened, he thought better of it and sagged back against his truck.

"She had it coming," he said. "You all had it coming."

Ryder and Caleb rounded the corner.

"Tucker!" Caleb barked.

"I didn't do nothin'!" Ricky shouted.

"You put your hands on Hazel," I ground out again, fury burning through every syllable.

"Prove it."

Cops surrounded us in a flurry of flashlights and commands. Once they saw it was me, I explained fast while Ricky yelled about conspiracies and collusion.

I didn't stick around. I ran straight back to my truck—and Hazel.

Penny and Emma were with her.

The second Hazel saw me, she launched herself out of the truck and into my arms.

"They got him," I said.

She nodded and then unraveled. She buried her face in my chest, her entire body shaking.

Emma and Penny stepped back, giving us space.

"I'm sorry," Hazel gasped. "I don't know why—"

"Adrenaline letdown." I cradled the back of her head in one hand, the other gripping her waist, shifting her against me so she didn't put weight on the leg she was favoring. "Just keep breathing."

"D-don't let go."

"I'm not going anywhere."

She shuddered, like she wasn't getting air. Which she wasn't, because she was holding her breath.

"Deeper, Haze," I said, inhaling with her. I waited as she matched me, breath for breath, until her body finally started to calm down.

"D-does this happen to y-you?"

"Used to. My body's better at processing it now. Keep going. I've got you."

Eventually, her breaths steadied. I peeled off my sweatshirt and wrapped it around her. She lifted her head, her blue eyes locked on mine.

"You did good," I whispered, my lips near her temple. "I'm so damn proud of you."

"He said I ruined his life. That I took his kid from him."

"You didn't. Don't take that on. That's his guilt talking, not the truth."

"I just wanted to build something that didn't fall apart," she said softly.

I cupped her cheek. "You are. Hazel, you're the strongest person I know. You show up. You fix things. You fight for what matters. Even when it's hard."

Police lights stuttered over her face. On the other side of the house, Ricky was still railing at the world.

Hazel held on to me like I was the only thing anchoring her. "I didn't want to call you," she said. "Didn't want to need you."

A rueful smile tugged at my lips, even if my gut was a mess of anger and fear. "Thing is, you've got me. Whether you want me or not."

Then I kissed her.

Not rushed. Not needy. Just steady. Grounding. The kind of kiss that said, *You're not alone anymore.*

"Think this is going to stick this time?" Penny asked.

"It better," Emma said.

Behind them, Ricky was being loaded into a cruiser, still yelling nonsense about collusions and schemes.

Caleb stepped in and stole Hazel from me, hugging her tight, bending a little to look into her eyes. "You okay?"

"I'm great," she rasped.

An ambulance arrived, and I took Hazel from my brother. "Let's get you checked out."

"I'm fine."

"Of course you are."

"It's just my ankle."

"Then let's get just your ankle looked at." I set her at the back of the ambulance, watching as her ankle was wrapped and she gave her statement to the officers, never letting her get more than two feet from me.

Caleb leaned in. "Unless you want the whole town talking

about how the Star Falls Legend just worked its magic on a third Colburn, you might wanna fix your face."

I turned my head and pinned him with a glare.

He smiled. "That's the one."

The officers found photo evidence on Ricky's phone, enough to charge him with B and E and attempted burglary, on top of assault.

They drove him away. Hazel watched, guilt flickering across her face.

"Don't do that," I said quietly. "Don't feel bad for Ricky."

"I don't." She shook her head. "Did you know he lost his wife and kid?"

My heart pinched at the regret on her face. "I didn't."

She was silent for a beat. "I know my miscarriage was different. But it doesn't change the fact that we've both lost something."

The difference was, only one of them had turned that pain into a weapon.

Ryder was talking to a cop, looking ready to chew nails and spit fire, but the second he saw Hazel, his expression softened as he moved in for a one-armed hug, handing her a water bottle. "You good?"

"Sure," she said, all bravado. "Just another day in the life, right?"

He gave her a grim smile. "Next time you want to prove how badass you are, maybe just show off the scar from when you beat Caleb in that framing contest freshman year, even after you accidentally shot your hand with your nail gun."

Hazel smiled, and it was everything.

Ryder hugged her again, then looked at me.

I nodded. I was good too, because other than a twisted ankle that she needed to keep her weight off for a few days, she really was okay.

A miracle.

Especially when I thought about all the things that could have happened to her tonight.

Bill showed up, and without a word, he hugged Hazel like he might never let her go. "This was on me," he muttered. "I didn't see it coming. I'm so fucking sorry."

Hazel pulled back, frowning. "How was this possibly your fault?"

He shook his head, eyeing our surroundings as if searching for more danger. "When you fire people, shit happens. Even when they deserve it." He ran a hand down his face, looking tired and haggard.

But Hazel was done, drained, and I wanted to get her out of there. "Come on, Tough Girl." I took her hand.

"Where we going?"

"Home."

CHAPTER 29

Hazel

SAT ON TUCKER'S kitchen counter, one foot swinging slightly, the other propped on a pillow with ice on my ankle, eating ice cream straight from the tub. I was wrapped in one of his oversize hoodies that fell to mid-thigh and smelled like his shampoo. His skin. *Him.*

Hell, maybe it was me since I'd helped myself to his shower— while he joined me, hovering like a bouncer moonlighting as a nurse.

Now he leaned against the counter across from me in sweats and a faded Star Falls Fire shirt, his hair damp and wild, his eyes soft but worried.

There was a wrench on the counter—mine. My purse was flopped on the table like it'd fainted, and one of my sneakers had rolled under a chair as if it were trying to escape. "I think my stuff's reproducing. Sorry for the mess."

He shook his head. "I love that you're comfortable here."

"I should pay rent for me and my stuff," I said.

His eyes held mine as he crossed to me and handed over a mug of tea. "I don't need rent from you or your things."

Which raised the question: "What do you need?"

He turned away, busying himself with pulling out the makings for grilled cheese. "Whole sandwich or half?"

Thrown off by his unusual dodging of the question, I answered automatically: "Half."

He nodded and got to work assembling the sandwich like it was a high-stakes operation. Was he really not going to answer?

But maybe that *was* my answer. Nothing. He needed nothing from me.

And of course he didn't. He had his whole life together—his dream job at the fire station, working toward being an arson investigator on top of that, his family, friends, squad mates, and a town that adored him. And though he'd told me he wasn't into commitments, he'd been no monk.

Me? I was just a girl he used to know. One who brought heartache and trouble. I shrank into myself a bit. "You know what? I think I'll just go—"

"Don't."

I stared at his squared shoulders. "You can't even look at me, much less answer my question."

"I know the answer to your question. I'm just not sure you're ready to hear it."

"Try me," I said, tighter than I meant.

He paused to slice the cheese and assemble the sandwich with surgical precision. "It's a two-part answer. I'll give you the first, but then I have a question."

"Okay," I said, voice stronger than I felt.

"What I need from you is…you." He paused, still working

on the sandwich. "And now for *my* question: How much do you feel like running right about now?"

I narrowed my eyes at his back. "*That's* your question?"

"Yes."

Unbendable alpha male. "Well, it *was* a one out of ten. But it's a good solid eight right now." Look at that—my voice didn't shake, even though I was on the last dregs of trust. "Why can't you just say what you want to say?" And damn, I was feeling shakier than I had while facing down Ricky.

With a flick of his wrist, Tucker turned off the stove and moved the pan to a cool burner. He turned to face me, the heat in his eyes enough to cook the sandwich right there on the counter.

What he wanted…was me.

"Oh," I breathed.

"Ask me again, Hazel," he murmured, staying where he was.

"What do you need?" I whispered.

His eyes darkened, and every nerve in my body stood at attention.

"I need…" He came closer, until he bumped my knees. Lifting his hands, he cupped my face. "I need you to be okay."

"I am."

"I ache for you, Hazel, down to my bones."

My heart rolled over in my chest, but as usual, my mouth had to try to joke the goodness away. "One *bone* in particular, right?"

That earned me an almost smile. "Always. But I'm serious, Hazel. I told you that relationships didn't work out for me in the past because I couldn't commit. But what I didn't tell you was that I couldn't commit because they weren't you." He gripped the edge of the counter on either side of my hips, trapping me in the most deliciously sexy way.

"And there's another thing I should've told you all those years ago," he said. "You're the most important thing in my life, and I want this. You. Us. I'm hoping you choose to stay. Everyone wants you to, but no one more than me."

The words cracked something wide open inside me, and in that moment, I knew I wasn't going to take the Seattle job. I was also glad I'd never mentioned it, because I didn't want him to think I could walk away. I wanted this, nothing but this, him, for the rest of my life.

"Tucker?" I breathed.

"Yeah?"

"*Touch me.*"

With a low masculine growl of pleasure, he slid his hands up my bare thighs, grounding me physically and emotionally in one perfect stroke.

There was something new in his eyes tonight—lingering adrenaline, sure, but something deeper too. Need. Hunger. Fear of losing what we'd barely found again…

He reached for the hem of the sweatshirt I wore. "I love you in my clothes." He toyed playfully with the hem, teasing me with warm fingers sliding just beneath it. His voice dropped, husky. "What are you wearing underneath it?"

I smiled.

"Mmmm." He pressed a kiss to my shoulder while the backs of his knuckles dragged up my thighs, unhurried, sensual as they made their way beneath the material.

When he found only skin, he groaned. "Killing me." He kissed me then, pulling the sweatshirt up, up, up…exposing me to his dark gaze an inch at a time, breaking the kiss to guide it over my head, slowly, so slowly, taking his sweet time, so that when the sweatshirt finally hit the floor, I was practically vibrating.

He backed up a step to take it all in. Me on his counter, wearing nothing but a smile.

"Fucking gorgeous." He stepped between my legs. "You wreck me, you know that? In the very best of ways."

Something about the way he said it, raw and reverent, made my pulse stutter. My entire body tightened in response, suddenly desperate for more of him. I tugged at his shirt. "And you're overdressed."

He laughed and peeled it off. It joined the sweatshirt on the floor behind him.

I greedily slid my hand inside his sweats. Filled it with him. One stroke of my hand, and he stilled, head falling back with a rough groan, his entire body tense. He held himself still for one suspended moment, like it took effort not to lose control. And that effort made me want him even more.

"Wound up?" I asked.

"You have no idea."

He scooped me off the counter and strode through the kitchen, carrying me down the hall past an annoyed Her Fluffiness, and into his room, kicking the door shut behind him.

He tossed me onto the bed, and I bounced with a laugh, but it backed up in my throat when he stripped out of the rest of his clothes like he had a vendetta against fabric. My amusement caught fire somewhere in my chest and turned molten low in my belly.

"You're quick," I teased, letting my gaze drag over him.

"Not exactly what a guy wants to hear when he's naked." But his smirk said he wasn't too worried.

I was still grinning when he tugged me to the edge of the bed with a delicious lack of restraint. Then he crawled up my body, eyes full of mischief and heat, and with a wicked smile that sent lightning dancing down my spine, he pinned my wrists above my head and kissed me like it was his life's purpose.

He gazed down at me and pressed his forehead to mine for a beat. "I used to dream of this. You in my bed. Looking up at me like I'm your world."

He'd held me like this before, but it felt different tonight. It felt like we were building something true, something everlasting. I shifted and my ankle twinged, a reminder of just how badly I hadn't wanted to call Tucker for a rescue.

And how grateful I was that I had.

His lips ran gently along my jaw, and then he nipped at my bottom lip. I arched into him, a distinctly needy sound escaping from my throat before I could stop it. He kissed me then, long and deep and hot, until I was rocking up into him, desperate and needy. "*Tucker.*"

"I got you." His mouth found my neck, leaving a trail of kisses to my ear, which he nipped. "Close your eyes, Haze. Let me take care of you."

I wanted to freeze time, to press Pause on this feeling of being cared for. Happiness this big felt dangerous.

His talented mouth made its way down my body, distracting me, making it impossible to think as his broad-as-a-mountain shoulders spread my legs to make room for himself. He drank in the view of me like I was his personal feast and he hadn't eaten in days.

"Here's what's going to happen…" His words were hypnotic as his warm palms ran up my thighs, his fingers stroking teasingly over my center, the rough pads of a callused thumb circling in a way that brought me to the edge in shockingly little time. "You're going to come for me," he said in that *don't argue with me* voice.

After half a second of debate with myself, I decided to give in to his demands. He'd had a rough day after all. Who was I to deny him anything?

So I did as he demanded. I came, first with his fingers between my slick legs. And then on his tongue. Finally, I tugged at him.

He looked up, hazel eyes bright, pupils blown. "What do you need, Haze?"

I was tired of hiding my feelings for him, tired of running, of the walls around my heart. So I gave him the truth. "You. I need you. All of you. And I need it now. *Please*, Tucker."

"Fuck me," he breathed.

"I'm trying!"

With a rough laugh and a groan, he buried himself inside me in one slow roll of his hips. I wrapped my legs around his waist, my heels pressing against his lower back, urging him on. Faster, harder, deeper.

He shuddered and lifted his face from where he'd buried it against my hair. Watching me, he slowed himself down, taking care to stroke and touch every inch of me he could reach.

My muscles clenched and tightened around him, and he stilled, head falling back for a moment, lost in the myriad of sensations.

God, he was beautiful.

When he finally began to move, I gasped his name. He linked his fingers with mine and raised them above my head, his body sliding over mine like warm silk, every inch of him caressing me as the ripples of another release twisted and curled deep in my abdomen.

He stared down at me. "Fuck, Haze, I can't hold back with you."

"So don't."

He rose up, sitting back on his heels, pulling me with him, sinking into me so deep, I gasped and clutched at him. At this angle, I was already trembling, my body taut enough to shatter, and he…

Went utterly still.

"No! Don't stop. Please don't stop!"

"I won't," he vowed, then began to move again, not stopping, not even when lights burst behind my eyelids, the pleasure almost too much. I cried out his name, and he came hard and gorgeously, shuddering in my arms.

Even as we fell to the bed, he kept a hold of me, his arms wrapped tight like a cast holding together what had once been broken.

When our bodies had cooled down and pulses recovered from the near stroke level they'd been at, I came up on an elbow and took in the amazing, mouthwatering view of the sprawled-out and lazily sated man next to me. "Do you know you look the same now as you did at seventeen?"

He grinned. "I was scrawny as hell. And *way* smaller." He sent me a wicked grin. "*Everywhere.*"

I choked out a laugh.

"So you agree."

I rolled my eyes. "Not feeding your ego. It's big enough." But it was true; he looked…amazing.

His grin widened.

"Cocky bastard," I said with much more affection than I meant to. I chalked it up to the fact that my legs were jelly.

Because wow. That was…

Tucker stroked a finger along my temple. "Still with me?"

"Yes." I smiled, but this time it somehow felt deeper—no pun intended—and more meaningful than anything we'd ever shared.

I didn't know what to do with that.

It's okay to let someone in. It's okay to need…

Emma's words played on repeat in my head.

"Hungry?" he asked.

"Starving."

Back in the kitchen, he resumed the grilled-cheese duty. Her Fluffiness padded sleepily into the kitchen, complaining with a yawn and a tired "mew" as she settled at Tucker's feet.

He fed her a little piece of cheese.

I hopped onto the counter, smiling. "Isn't that against the rules?"

"Apparently none of the women in my life care about rules or listen to me."

"Maybe we listen; maybe we just don't always agree."

He brought me a perfectly browned grilled cheese. "Story of my life." He leaned in and kissed me. "Eat. I have plans for you later."

I snorted and took a bite, then moaned.

He smiled. "I know that sound."

I felt myself flush.

He pulled himself up to sit next to me on the countertop, playfully nipping my earlobe. "In fact, I *love* that sound. I plan to get you to make it a whole bunch more times tonight."

The parts of my body that I'd thought were tired suddenly perked up and came back to life. Maybe we had trouble figuring out where we stood, but in the bedroom, we seemed to have no such problem.

And just like that, my warm, fuzzy feeling turned quiet. Weightier. Was he even half as scared as I was that we'd mess this up as we had before?

He nudged me gently. "You okay?"

"Pretty sure you know just how okay I am…"

The Tucker I remembered would've responded with a joke, deflecting with charm and teasing. This Tucker reached out, tucking wayward hair back from my face. Eyes warm and curious, he gave me a small smile. "We were supposed to talk tonight."

"Yes, luckily, I was assaulted and dodged a bullet," I quipped with a smile.

He didn't return it.

"Too soon?"

"*Way* too soon." He studied me for a beat, contemplative. "Can you tell me about it?"

"Ricky?"

He gave me a long look. "The years you were gone."

"Oh. Right." I drew a deep breath. "What do you want to know?"

"Everything."

There was pain in his eyes, and I realized while I'd come to terms with what had happened back then, it was all brand-new information for him. "I'm sorry I didn't—"

He touched a finger to my lips. "No more apologies. No more guilt. You were in survival mode, and frankly so was I. I don't mean to bring up bad memories for you, but I…I need to understand. How did you manage? What was your life like? Did you stay away to punish yourself? Punish *me*?" His voice was low, careful. "How did you live? Were you okay?"

The plate in my hands trembled slightly. He took it and gently set it aside, putting a hand over mine.

I gave him a weak smile. "Whew. I think I'm nervous."

"You don't have to tell me. I just…" He drew a long, ragged breath. "I've been imagining the worst, and it's killing me."

"I'm not sure where to start. I made a lot of mistakes."

"You don't have a patent on that." The brown and green of his eyes swirled together, rimmed in gold. Warm. Patient. "No judgment."

I nodded. "I stayed in a women's shelter after the hospital. The director's brother was a contractor. When I felt better, he hired me as a day laborer. I soaked up the work, loved it," I told him when he sucked in a breath at the idea of me working as a day laborer. "When he found out that I'd worked for my dad in construction since I could hold a hammer, he taught me more about finish work. When I eventually moved on, I kept learning." I shrugged. "Built a life that worked for me at the time." The worry on his face… "I survived, Tucker. Even enjoyed myself."

He listened like I was telling him something sacred.

"I missed everyone," I admitted. "I missed *you*."

"But you stayed away because…"

I swallowed. Grimaced. "I didn't want to fall back into the girl who couldn't see past her own mess. Every time I thought about it, I got so anxious, I could hardly breathe."

He looked gutted at that. "Anxious of what?"

"Not being worthy of coming back."

His face fell. "Haze—"

"You wanted the truth."

"I did. So you're back because of your dad's health."

Something in his tone gave him away. I wasn't the only one nursing a hurt. "Yeah. At first," I agreed and held his gaze, watching my words affect him. "But somewhere along the line, it became more. Like…my feelings for you." I gave a short laugh. "Wow. That sounded really cheesy."

He cracked a smile. "I love cheesy."

"I'm still working on myself," I warned. "Still working things out. I don't know how to be someone's…person. Hell, I'm still figuring out how to be my own person, how to not turn tail and run when I feel too deeply."

He cocked his head. "You're scared."

"Yes." I tossed up my hands. "Join me, won't you?"

A small smile curved his mouth and warmed everything inside me.

"*Why* are you smiling?" I asked, helplessly smiling back.

He yanked me into him. "Because you're one of the fiercest women I know. You didn't used to do scared."

"Maybe *cautious* is a better term," I decided, running my hands up his chest. Damn, I loved the feel of him. "Let's be cautious."

His smile went wicked. "Where's the fun in that?"

I drew a breath. I wanted to say, *What if I go all in and you don't?* It was only my stupid pride that kept me from voicing it. "You know what I think we should do right now?"

"Does it involve continuing this conversation?"

"Yes." I stepped into his arms and nipped his bottom lip. "But let's converse in the way you and I do best."

He had one hand in my hair, the other on my ass. "You might be on to something."

Outside, the world kept turning. But inside this quiet kitchen, wrapped in his warmth and this tender, aching honesty, I felt it: hope. Not perfect. Not painless.

But real.

Maybe, just maybe, for tonight, it was enough. And maybe, just maybe, we could start building something real. One nail, one wall, one guarded heartbeat at a time.

The next morning, after a long shower—the kind that involved more soapy hands than actual rinsing, resulting in a second round, half of it with no hot water because we'd run out—I was digging through a drawer for something to wear.

"I like what you've got on," Tucker said from the bed, head propped on one arm like he had all the time in the world.

"That's because I'm wearing your T-shirt and nothing else."

His grin was slow and satisfied, the kind that made my nipples perk up like they hadn't already gotten the memo.

My phone dinged. "It's Kiera," I said. "She wants to borrow a sundress of mine. Said if I drop it off, she'll feed me."

"She's gonna want to grill you about yesterday."

"Maybe she wants to grill me about last night. Maybe even to tell me I could do better than you," I teased.

His smile turned smug. "After those sounds you made last night, I'm pretty confident in where I stand."

I snorted, then caught the gleam in his eyes and the way his fingers were absently brushing the inside of my wrist like he didn't want to let me go just yet. Like maybe he was memorizing me.

The joke caught in my throat, tangled with something that felt dangerously like longing.

He leaned in, resting his forehead to mine. "You scare the hell out of me, Haze. But I want every second."

My chest squeezed. "Even the chaotic ones?"

"Especially those."

I brushed my lips over his, soft and slow, like a promise. Then, with a rough sound of hunger, he pulled me in and deepened the kiss.

I moaned and threw my arms around his neck and held on tight.

"You gotta go," he said against my lips.

Damn. I did.

"Tell Kiera hi," he murmured, pulling back just enough to see me. "And if she grills you, tell her she can come over to see how much info she can get from me."

My heart did a ridiculous, hopeful little lurch. "You never break."

"Exactly."

I walked out of his house with sore muscles, a lighter soul, and the terrifying suspicion that I'd fallen, and fallen hard.

CHAPTER 30

Hazel

THIRTY MINUTES LATER, I walked into the chaos of Kiera's kitchen in a hoodie, damp hair, and a grin I couldn't get rid of after one of the best nights of my life. The kind of night that left you more exposed than naked, and somehow steadier because of it.

The first thing I noticed when I stepped into Kiera's kitchen was the scent of bacon, coffee, and—be still my heart—syrup, which always meant something good.

The second was that Kiera looked like a woman who had either committed a crime or was about to.

Sunlight slanted through the big window over the sink, catching steam curling off the stovetop. The tile was cool beneath my bare feet. A rare moment of peace in the general Colburn bedlam.

Kiera yanked open the oven and waved a spatula like a white flag. "Hey, I'm going to warn you—it's already been a day."

"It's eight in the morning."

The twins barreled into the kitchen, raced around the island, and vanished again.

"They're fast," I said.

Kiera held up a finger. "Wait for it—"

Aaaaaand they were back in three seconds.

"They've been making laps since five a.m.," Kiera said. "Do you know what I'd like to do? *Not* see five a.m. on my clock. Five a.m. should be illegal. What were *you* doing at five a.m.?"

I was pretty sure she didn't want to hear *your brother,* but it was the truth. At 5:00 a.m., I'd been riding Tucker like Zorro on a mission, taking him apart piece by piece just to see him lose his famed control. I'd loved every single second of it.

In fact, 5:00 a.m. just might be my new favorite time of the day.

Ryder popped his head in the back door, and I did my best not to look like I was fantasizing about his baby brother.

He smiled at me and then looked at Kiera. "The heathens ready?"

"You're late."

His smile turned into a grin. "Penny had a surprise for me this morning."

Kiera covered her ears. "Ew!"

"Not that." But Ryder laughed in a way that told us it had been exactly that. "She made me breakfast in bed."

"Good for you." Kiera rolled her eyes and yelled, "Uncle Ryder's *finally* here to take you to the zoo!"

The house shook with the stampede of two pint-size elephants squealing in delight as they ran in and headed straight for him.

He caught one under each arm and slung them over his

shoulders like twin sacks of potatoes, gripping their ankles like the seasoned uncle he was.

More happy squealing.

"Kisses!" Kiera ordered.

Ryder pivoted so she could press kisses to their giggling foreheads.

"Be good. Don't ask for presents." Then she eyed Ryder. "Remember, when they tell you they have to pee, it's already too late. Run like your life depends on it to the bathroom. Let's not forget the Home Depot incident."

He grimaced. "In my defense, I didn't know Abi had a bladder the size of a pea. And when she soaked my shoes, I didn't even make you deal with them. Or my dignity. Or my therapy bills."

"Bring me back a churro," she said.

Once the Colburn tornadoes cleared out, peace returned.

Kiera poured us mimosas, and I finally got a good look at her. Her hair was tousled, her cheeks flushed. And… "Your tee's inside out."

She looked down at herself. "Well, shit."

I added up the clues and grinned. "You've been holding out on me."

Kiera turned away. "I don't know what you're talking about."

"Uh-huh." I crossed my arms. "Spill."

She dropped a banana into the blender and turned it on.

"Subtle," I shouted over the roar.

She clicked it off and lifted her chin. "I have no idea what you're talking about."

"Sure, you don't. Your mouth says innocence, but your hair and inside-out shirt say, *I just got wall banged against the laundry room door.*"

Her head snapped toward me, expression horrified, mortified…and maybe a hint of smug. "*Shh!*"

I grinned. "No one here but us." I leaned in. "Admit it. You got some."

Kiera gave me a classic Colburn look that could've melted granite.

It made me snort.

She crossed her arms in that intimidating Colburn way. Good, but not Tucker level.

"Dammit," she muttered. "I always forget how tough you are. You don't cave."

"Exactly. So spill."

But before she could, the back door opened, and in sauntered…

Miguel.

Six feet of sleep-ruffled, postcoital hair, cargo shorts, a faded T-shirt advertising a dive bar in the Maldives, and a grin that didn't say, *I just came over to borrow sugar.*

Holding two coffees, he froze mid-step.

I grinned.

Kiera groaned.

Miguel handed Kiera her coffee. Then he smiled at me and offered me the other.

"I'm good, but thank you. You probably need the sustenance."

The tips of Kiera's ears flushed pink.

Miguel moved to her and dropped a kiss to the top of her head. "I can go—"

She caught his hand. "Don't even think about it. The kids are gone for hours. *Hours*, Miguel."

His smile deepened as he tipped her face up for a quick, soft kiss. "In that case, I'll be answering emails in the living room. Take your time."

We both watched him walk away, but only one of us had her eyes locked on his ass, and it wasn't me.

The second he was gone, I turned to Kiera with a glee I hadn't felt in days. "So. You and Miguel."

Kiera pointed the spatula at me like a weapon. "Not a word."

"Not even one?"

"Hazel."

"Okay, five. Five words, but that's my final offer." I paused for effect. "I'm so happy for you."

She glared at me, but beneath it, her skin glowed with unmistakable joy.

And I wanted to bottle it up for her. But you didn't coddle Kiera, unless you were willing to lose a finger. "Come on, you can't throw that juicy a bone and not expect me to go full *National Enquirer*."

"It's nothing."

I tilted my head. "The hickey on your neck says otherwise."

Kiera slapped a hand to her neck, which was very much hidden under her hair. Realizing I'd tricked her, she groaned. "Dammit."

I raised a brow.

"Okay, fine," she said. "It's maybe something. But it's also complicated. Ryder would kill him."

"So you're hiding your very attractive, very capable, very forbidden boyfriend like a Victorian widow with a scandal in the attic?"

"He's not my boyfriend."

"Uh-huh. And I'm not using this conversation to avoid another one."

She gave me a long look. "Don't think I won't circle back." She hesitated. "I'm not sneaking around because I'm ashamed. I just…this is mine, you know? Just for me. I want to figure out what it is before the whole Colburn family declares it in a town hall meeting."

The thing about Kiera was she wasn't scared of much. But the more she liked Miguel, the more careful she'd become. And maybe I was doing the same thing—holding on to something good by pretending not to want more.

I smiled and hugged her hard. "That's the most relatable thing you've ever said."

Kiera sighed into her coffee, still watching the door Miguel had gone through.

I laughed as I turned to the back door. "I think my work here is done. Don't forget to stay hydrated. Maybe stretch first. And for the love of God, tell Ryder before he finds out and commits a homicide."

"Oh my God." Kiera's ears flushed again. "Why do I keep you around?"

"Because I have a cute sundress you want to borrow." I nodded to where I'd set it over a chair when I'd come in. "Plus, I know where all your skeletons are buried."

She laughed. Then—"Wait!"

I turned back. "You want to tell me all the dirty details? Because I will not stop you."

"No, this is about *you*," she said.

"Me?"

"I spilled. Now it's your turn. Secret for a secret. Unless you'd prefer a blood oath."

I reached jokingly for a knife in the block on the counter.

"Ha ha," Kiera said. "Look, just give me one little secret, and I won't have to kill you for knowing mine."

I pretended to look at the time. "Gee, I'm pretty busy. I've got to reorganize my junk drawer by emotional-damage level, and then there are all those questionable life choices to make… Oh! And I'm overdue on an existential crisis, plus my latest Taylor Swift playlist isn't going to make itself, so—"

"Oh, no, you don't." Kiera slid between me and the back door, blocking my exit by holding her arms out for dramatic effect. "You don't get to stand there with your sassy-ass self, knowing eyeballs, and sparkling sneaks, judging my choices without coughing up some tea of your own."

"Okay, first of all…" I lifted my worn-out blue sneaker. "These are vintage." And they'd been my mom's. I'd swiped them when boxing up some of her stuff the other night… "And second, I don't have a scandal." I paused. "Exactly."

She pointed at me. "Tell me or…"

I crossed my arms and waited. "Or…?"

"Or…" She smiled. "I'll cry."

"You know I hate it when you cry."

"Sucks for you. *Talk.*"

"This is emotional blackmail," I said.

"And?"

I could lie. I wanted to. But Kiera's expression—part fiercely loving sister, part nosy bloodhound—said she wouldn't let me leave without something true. Plus, if I was being honest with myself, I knew my friends, Tucker included, would be hurt that I hadn't told them. "I have a job offer. It's in Seattle."

Kiera froze mid-sip.

"It's a yearlong contract for a big restoration company. Full creative control. The kind of pay that makes you question your entire path."

She stared at me. "What does Tucker think about it?"

Now I wished I'd taken Miguel's coffee. "You're the first person I've told."

Kiera crossed her arms. "Are you planning to tell him?"

"I wanted to make up my mind before adding other people's opinions to the mix." A white lie…another version of running. I knew this.

Kiera's eyes narrowed. "How long have you known?"

"A few weeks."

"Hazel!"

I grimaced as guilt crawled up my spine. I should have told him. Should have told everyone. I knew this. I did. But I was afraid. Because what if he told me I should go? I tipped my head back and stared at the ceiling, hating that my throat had gone tight and my eyes were burning. "I don't know how to do this, Key," I whispered. "I mean, what if I tell him and he says I should go for it? Or what if…?"

"What if he fights for you?" Kiera asked.

I sniffed and shook my head.

Kiera frowned. "You really think he wouldn't try? After everything?"

I tossed up my hands. "I'm afraid to risk it. This thing between us…it feels good. And I'm scared if I push too hard, it'll all come toppling down."

She softened, took my hand. "Then don't push. Just trust."

I closed my eyes. "That's harder than it sounds."

"He looks at you like he's choosing you. Every time. But as for you, I don't think you've ever really let someone choose you."

She squeezed my fingers. "You once said you wanted someone who sees you, all of you—the good, the bad, the ugly—and stays anyway."

"I did," I said softly. "I said that."

She squeezed my hand again. "Well, he sees you, honey. We all do, but especially Tucker. He's already staying, Haze. Let him. Tell him. Give him the chance to meet you where you're at."

Tears threatened again, but this time they felt like something else. Not panic. Not guilt. Maybe…release. I swallowed hard and nodded.

From upstairs came a light *thud*. Then another.

The unmistakable sound of a man kicking off his boots.

I forced a smile. "Go." I squeezed her hand back. "Let him see you."

She stared at me for a long beat, pensive, worried.

"I'll tell him," I said. "Now go."

She gave me a slow smile. "If I fall on my face, I'm blaming you."

"Please do. I live for the drama."

With a laugh, she was gone.

Alone in her kitchen, I nodded to myself. I'd tell Tucker, lay out all my cards.

No more secrets.

CHAPTER 31

Tucker

THE PAPERWORK AVALANCHE AT Colburn Restorations had turned into a full-blown landslide. I'd meant to just swing by for the staff meeting and clean out my inbox, maybe tackle a blueprint or two.

Ten very long hours later, I was still at my desk, neck-deep in estimates, design sketches, jobsite reports, and a to-do list so long, it needed its own zip code.

"That's what you get for trying to do two full-time jobs at the same time," Caleb said around a massive bite of his turkey club. "You're burning the candle at both ends, man. You're going to fall asleep on a fire call and end up on their social media accounts for the second time in a week thanks to being a cover model now."

I winced. That damn calendar was haunting my nightmares—and apparently, the town socials, thanks to the station blasting my shirtless, oiled-up calendar centerfold every-fucking-where. "Says the guy who has bags the size of a carry-on under his eyes."

It was low-hanging fruit, but I was too exhausted to win a fight with a fellow Colburn.

"That's because I spent eight hours in bed," Caleb said, "but only six sleeping. The rest was all cardio." He waggled his brows, like a stupid cartoon villain who'd had too much coffee. "Want me to draw you a diagram?"

"Want me to tell Emma you offered?"

He grinned. "Seeing as I'm your favorite sibling, you'd never."

"Maybe Emma's my favorite sibling."

He gave me a pointed look. "Not Hazel?"

I looked up sharply, pulse ticking. "*Nothing* I feel for Hazel is anywhere close to sibling-like. Try again."

He held up his hands in surrender, but his smirk said, *Gotcha.*

I shoved back from the desk, needing out. My brain was fried, my temper low, and my thoughts, unsurprisingly, were back on Hazel.

"Wait," Caleb called. "You still owe me a favor. And I'm cashing it in."

I turned slowly. "For what?"

He shot me that *gotcha* face again. "You crashed Ryder's dirt bike into the irrigation ditch behind the high school, and I used my science project to make it seem like the brakes failed."

"That was over a decade ago."

"No statute of limitations on brotherly blackmail. I don't make the rules." He shoved a small shopping bag at me. "Drop these off at Kiera's when you go pick up Hank."

"What's in the bag?"

"FMPs. Don't ask."

What the—

I peeked into the bag. Strappy black stilettos with a heel thin enough to double as a weapon. Sexy as hell.

Which meant I wasn't sure if I needed a drink, a therapist, or a brain scrub. Possibly all three. "You're telling me Kiera needs to borrow…fuck-me pumps?"

"Told you not to ask."

Half an hour later, I let myself into Kiera's house. The twins were snuggled on the couch with Hank, all three glued to an episode of *Bluey* with the kind of focus usually reserved for playoff games and natural disasters.

No one looked up, so I kept moving, following the scent of sugar and something buttery and the unmistakable scent of an impending meltdown masked in vanilla extract.

My sister baked only when she was spiraling.

Sure enough, her back to me, she had the oven open and was pulling out a tray of soft, puffy chocolate chip cookies with the desperate energy of someone trying to solve all her problems with carbs.

Miguel—*Miguel?*—stood nearby, leaning against the counter like he belonged there. Chill, grounded, his eyes locked on Kiera like she was the one holding the sun on its axis.

My brain hiccuped.

What is he doing here?

And were the FMPs for her to wear for *him*?

"But how am I supposed to keep Hazel's secret from Tucker?" Kiera asked, her voice rising an octave as she jabbed a wooden spoon into Miguel's chest like it was a dagger. "He's my brother. I've never kept a secret from him." She paused. "Okay, maybe once, when I backed his truck into a mailbox and denied any knowledge of the dent."

I stopped in the doorway.

All I'd heard was Hazel had a secret.

From me.

Miguel raised his hands. "Not saying you shouldn't tell him. Just…that maybe if it's not your secret, it's not your call."

"I know it's not, but she's confused. She didn't want to tell me; I tricked her into it with baked goods and emotional blackmail! I shared something first. I told her—" She snapped her mouth shut, looking halfway between panicked and mortified. "Well, never mind what I told her. But then she owed me a secret, so I made her give me one. And it's big, Miguel. It's… *Seattle* big."

I stepped into the room. "What's in Seattle?"

Kiera jumped like she'd been goosed by an electric fence, nearly flinging her spatula. "Jesus, Tucker! You can't just sneak up on people like that! I almost impaled you with this spoon."

"Hazel. Seattle. Talk."

Miguel gave me one look and wisely decided now was the time to overstir something on the stovetop.

Kiera was biting her lower lip. "Okay, look, this is really between you and Haze—"

"Then why do *you* know?"

"I lured it out of her with sugar and nostalgia."

I looked at Miguel. "This is where you back me up."

Miguel hesitated. "You know what? I'm just gonna—" He jabbed a finger to the living room like it was on fire.

Kiera grabbed a fistful of his shirt. "Don't you even think about leaving!"

Miguel brushed a kiss to her temple, a moment that somehow felt private and intimate, even permanent—then dropped another kiss on her mouth, soft and sure, before holding her gaze like she was the only person in the room.

Then he looked over her head at me—protective, unflinching—and disappeared into the next room.

If I hadn't been in the middle of having my heart rearranged by Hazel, I'd have appreciated him standing at my sister's back.

Instead, I muttered, "Did I just walk into *The Bachelor: Drywall Edition?*"

"Don't start." She crossed her arms. "Hazel's scared. She didn't know how to tell anyone, much less you."

"Tell me *what?*"

Kiera studied her bare feet, like maybe they held the answers to the universe.

"*Kiera.*"

"Okay, okay, you don't have to use that annoying alpha voice on me. What's in the bag?"

I tossed it over.

She pulled out the heels and squealed. "They're perfect."

I plucked the bag back, holding it overhead. "Are those for you, or for *Miguel?*"

"Don't ask questions you don't want the answer to." Her expression went serious. Solemn. "Including Hazel's secret."

Something in my chest shifted, uneasy. "I'm going to need you to start talking now."

Kiera sighed, long and heavy. "She got a job offer." Her voice was barely above a whisper. "A big one. A historic-restoration project with a yearlong contract. In Seattle."

My stomach dropped, and the floor seemed to vanish under my boots. The air went tight. My ribs went tighter.

I'd told Hazel things I hadn't even told myself out loud, and she still didn't trust me with this? It wasn't just the Seattle part.

It was what it meant—

That she was planning her future.

And I wasn't even in the outline. "Why didn't she tell me?"

"Probably because I don't think she knows what to do." She stepped forward, wrapping her hand around my forearm. "Does she know how you feel about her? Like *really* know?"

I opened my mouth, then closed it again. Shit.

"I thought so," Kiera said softly and drew a deep breath. "I think it would help." She stepped back. "I shouldn't have told you."

"I'm glad *someone* told me."

"Tucker, she's not trying to hurt you."

"She's not trying to trust me either." Not knowing what to do with myself or the storm raging inside my chest, I headed for the door.

Kiera darted in front of me, planting herself there like a five-foot-four blockade in yoga pants. "What are you going to do?"

I stared at her. "What everyone else seems to be doing lately."

"What, stress bake and gain five pounds?"

I didn't smile. I couldn't. "Whatever the hell they want."

CHAPTER 32

Tucker

GOT HANK BUCKLED into my truck, then slid behind the wheel. Instead of starting the engine, I called Hazel.

She didn't pick up. Probably working.

I'd heard what Kiera said about why Hazel hadn't told me about the job offer, but still, doubts crept in.

Maybe she hadn't told me because she was far less invested in us than I was.

Which sucked.

I dropped my forehead to the steering wheel, barely resisted hitting it a few times.

"Ah?" Hank. Worried.

I sighed. "I'm fine."

"Ah."

Classic Colburn. Calling bullshit with one sound. "Look, this has to do with crap I'm not great at. *Emotions*," I clarified at his confused look. "And that's not exactly your forte either, so don't start."

Something flickered across his face—quick and hard to catch. I wanted it to be regret.

Which was a shitty thing to want, but hey, apparently I was in a mood.

Hank turned his head to look out the window, and I felt like a world-class dick. "I'm sorry. That was uncalled for."

I think he tried to shrug, because his shoulder twitched.

Separating the man in the passenger seat from the one who'd raised me felt a whole lot like recovering from food poisoning— grateful to be up off the bathroom floor, but also? You'd never trust sushi again.

I was glad he'd survived his strokes, glad we could care for him, even glad he seemed to be enjoying his life far more than he ever did pre-strokes. But having him actually showing up emotionally and giving a shit? That was a mind fuck I hadn't finished untangling.

And still… "You happy?"

He blinked, confused.

"I mean, your mobility is limited, you can't talk, and that has to suck, but…" Unable to look into the eyes of the man who'd once been the monster in the closet, I stared out the windshield. "I need to know if you're angry at the world. Or if you've let it all go."

A long beat passed before he looked over and gave me a crooked half smile. Mostly because of the stroke. But his eyes were calm. Maybe even kind.

"Ah," he said.

I didn't know what that meant, but he didn't look bitter, so I took it.

"I wanted to stay mad at you," I admitted out loud, no idea

what he remembered of the past. "But life's too fucking short. I'm leaving it in the rearview. For all of us."

Still watching me, he nodded slowly.

Screw it. If he could try something new, so could I. I reached over and took his hand. "I did something I told myself I wouldn't," I said. "I let myself fall for her again. And I'm pretty sure she's going to stomp on my heart and destroy me."

He nodded again. Like he'd heard every word Kiera and I had traded in the kitchen.

Then he pointed at me.

Like it was on me to fix this.

"I can't fix this. She didn't even tell me about it."

He shook his head. He even tried rolling his eyes, but his face twitched, and his mouth fell open instead.

Apparently, he thought I was spouting bullshit.

Fine. I started the engine and pulled away from the curb. Five minutes later, we pulled down our street.

Hazel's van wasn't out front.

Hank gestured like I should keep driving.

I stared at him. "What?"

"Ah!"

Oh hell. "You want me to go find her."

His satisfied smile said, *Finally caught up, genius.*

"Okay. Do you want me to drop you at Caleb's or Ryder's? Or Bill's?"

Hank clutched the seat belt over his chest like a man refusing to evacuate a flood zone. "Ah."

"Dad, no, you can't come with. I might be out for a while, and it's close to your bedtime—"

"*Ah.*"

Shit. He wasn't going to get out of the truck, and there was no point arguing with a Colburn once they'd dug in. I put the truck back in Drive.

Hazel wasn't at either of the two Colburn jobs she worked on. Not at the tree house. Not with Emma or Penny.

By midnight, I'd gotten Hank to agree to stay with Ryder, and I was officially unraveling. My phone screen had memorized my face. Still no call. No text.

And it wasn't like she owed me anything.

Once again, I cruised slowly through town. Twenty minutes later, I spotted her truck in the park's lot. As I pulled in, my headlights caught a flicker of movement at the far end, thirty feet away.

I couldn't see clearly, but I knew by the way every part of me suddenly felt alive that it was Hazel.

She had a paint roller in one hand, a headlamp on her forehead, and a flashlight clipped to her tool belt. She was mid-stroke over graffiti along the back of the bathroom building—a cartoon squirrel flipping off the mayor's dedication.

"You got a thing against angry woodland creatures with boundary issues?" I asked. "Or—"

She startled, spinning toward me with eyes wide, the roller splashing paint across her boot. "Ohmigod, you scared the hell out of me."

I wasn't even a little bit sorry. She was out here in the middle of the night, alone, her back to the lot. Any-fucking-thing could happen to her. "Wait…" I squinted at the original graffiti. "Is that—"

"My own work from over a decade ago?" She rubbed her face, leaving a streak of paint across her nose as she worked carefully to *not* maintain eye contact. "Yeah. Could do a lot better now, but I think the mayor will appreciate this more."

Scrubbing the sins from her past. One square foot at a time…

My frustration thawed a bit. "Did you know that when you're alive, you answer your phone so people who care about you won't lose their goddamn minds wondering where the hell you are and if you're safe?"

"I dropped my phone into the paint bucket hours ago."

"Oh." Well, okay, that took some of the wind out of my sails. "When were you going to tell me?"

She froze.

I took a step toward her. "*Were* you going to tell me?"

"About…?"

"Seattle."

She blinked in shock. Then bent and set the roller in the paint tray with exaggerated care, like the fate of the world depended on getting it just right. She straightened again and wiped her hands on a rag, the motion too fast, too focused.

"How did you find out?" she asked, like we were making small talk and not standing on a powder keg.

"Does it matter?"

Her expression shifted. "Tucker—"

"You taking the job?" I asked quietly, unable to keep the hurt from my voice.

Carefully, she turned to face me. "It's not as easy for me as it is for you to be here." She waved a hand around us. "You've got your whole life. It's…perfect."

I huffed a bitter laugh. "If you think my life's perfect, you haven't been paying attention."

Again, she looked away. "The Seattle thing…it was a great opportunity."

"Agreed," I said. "But this isn't about Seattle, is it?"

She shook her head.

"It's about what you, Hazel Pierce, do when something real shows up: You don't trust it, so you push it away."

Her gaze jumped to mine, narrowed.

"You think I don't want the best for you, always?" I asked.

"We said no promises. No strings."

I *knew* those words would come back to haunt us. *Me.* "That was way *before* we started acting like this was something." I shook my head. "But if you need that as an excuse to leave and feel less guilty, go for it."

"I didn't plan this," she whispered. "*Any* of this."

"No, but you sure planned your exit strategy."

She folded her arms. "I don't want to do this now."

"You never did."

Her eyes sparked. "Really? We're going to bring up my stupid teenage self again?" She threw up her hands. "I was scared! I didn't know what I wanted."

"Do you know now?"

She stared right at me. "I thought I did."

A gut punch, but at least it was honest. And one I couldn't fault her for. "Look, whatever you decide, I'm happy for you. Proud of you. But it's not just the job, is it? You're deciding on me too. On us."

"You think you know everything, so I don't see why I should bother to answer."

My stomach twisted. "If you wanted out, all you had to do was say so."

Her eyes hardened and she turned away. "This wasn't supposed to feel like forever," she said. "Not this soon. Not like this."

"Then you say that. Say that you need space. Time," I said to her back. "We aren't eighteen anymore, Hazel. If you have a problem, or if this isn't for you, you tell me. We talk about it. And then I back off."

"The job offer was a surprise," she said softly. "I didn't ask for it. And believe it or not, I was going to tell you."

"But you didn't." I shook my head. "I can't decide if you thought I'd hold you back or that I couldn't handle it."

She looked at me then, and her voice cracked. "I didn't think *I* could handle it."

I paused. This hadn't even occurred to me. "Why?"

"Because if you had looked at me like that while I told you I was leaving, I wouldn't be able to go."

My armor splintered.

"And if I stay," she went on, "and this ends like it did before—if you stop showing up, if you change your mind…" Her voice cracked. "I won't survive it, Tucker."

I felt gutted. "I'm not that same guy. You know that'd play out differently now. I'd do whatever it took to stay in your life."

"I know, and I'm not that same girl either."

We stood chest to chest, a million unsaid things in the air.

"This is just a misunderstanding," she whispered.

"It's way more than that. You still don't trust me. Not enough."

She shook her head. "That's not fair."

"Maybe not. But you've said you want to be seen. To be taken seriously. And yet you don't let me see all of you. You hold back pieces. The scared pieces. The messy pieces. Even after I've shown you mine."

Tears welled in her eyes "Don't you get it? It's not *you* I don't trust!"

My chest ached. "I know." And I really did. "Because at the end of the day, you still don't believe in no-holds-barred, unconditional love." I backed up. "And until you do, nothing I say will matter."

Her arms wrapped tight across her stomach, and guilt twisted through me that I'd called her out. But I'd needed to say it. I'd needed her to hear it.

"I just don't want to make the wrong call," she said quietly. "I thought if I gave myself some time—"

"This isn't about the job. And if you have to think about whether you want me in your life…you've already decided."

A tear fell. And it took everything in me not to reach for her.

I would've waited forever if she'd taken just one step for me.

But she didn't.

So I walked away.

And just like that, the woman I loved let me go.

CHAPTER 33

Tucker

WAS HEADING HOME, the last place I wanted to be, when I got a text.

MOST ANNOYING SISTER:

> Why are you driving around at one in the morning?

ME:

> Why are you stalking my dot?

MOST ANNOYING SISTER:

> Because your dot looks sad. If you got a booty call and her name isn't Hazel, you're dead to me.

Okay, fine. That was dramatic. But I'm the one who accidentally spilled the Seattle beans, so I get to check in. You okay? But also, the twins woke me up and now I'm making French toast sticks like a damn hero. Come over. I'll save you some.

I went, but just to kiss the wild wolf pups and grab a plate of French toast sticks. I refused to stay, heading out while dodging Kiera's questions like I was going for gold in avoidance.

Halfway to the fire station, she texted again.

You can run, but you can't hide.

The family motto.

Hazel used to say that too, back when we were kids and she'd ditch school. I'd go after her—we always went after each other. Until one day, we hadn't.

My fault.

My shift didn't start for a few hours, so I took the couch in the main room and closed my eyes. Which was not the same thing as sleeping. There was none of that to be had.

I stared up at the ceiling, pretending not to hear the sounds of the building settling or the way my heart had learned to echo in the spaces Hazel had filled. I could still smell her on my hoodie, something warm and clean—and a dash of sawdust—that made my chest ache.

I'd told myself I was going to be fine.

Liar.

The couch had accepted me as one of its own and dipped beneath me like it always did. I sank into it like I was falling. Not asleep. Just…down.

The thing about loving someone that hard?

When they left, they took gravity with them.

At some point I must've drifted, because I woke to Jayden flipping sausages and eggs like he'd been born a diner short-order cook. Tessa and Harlow were having a push-up competition in front of the couch. And Marcus was singing "Pink Pony Club" like he was onstage in Santa Monica and the headliner had no shame.

I groaned and threw a pillow at him. "Some of us are sleeping, asshole."

"Like you need the beauty sleep," he shot back. "You've got the broody-firefighter look locked down."

"Broody's all I got left."

Marcus just winked and kept singing, purposely off-key and adding his own stripper flair.

The fire alarm went off before I could throw anything else at his face, and we were off and running on what would prove to be a brutal forty-eight-hour shift.

When I finally dragged my sorry ass home two days later, the house was quiet as a stone.

Still.

Hollow.

I walked through each room, my heart sinking more with every step.

Hazel's things were gone.

Her lotions and cosmetics had vanished from the bathroom counter, along with her toothbrush—the one I'd pretended not to notice when it first showed up. Her work boots, always parked just inside the front door, gone. Her clothes, which had somehow ended up in both the guest room and mine, also gone.

And the clincher—my ratty sweatshirt, the one she loved so much, the one that looked sexy as hell falling off her shoulder and hitting her mid-thigh…

Also gone.

Even her pink flamingo coffee mug with BOSS BITCH on it was missing from the sink.

The only thing left of her was the grocery list in her handwriting stuck to the fridge with *marshmallows, duct tape, champagne.*

Somehow this pierced me even more than her missing stuff.

"Mew."

Her Fluffiness trotted up like she'd been waiting for this moment. I crouched to stroke her soft fur, but even the rumble of her purr didn't manage to lift the tight ache in my chest.

That's when I noticed the folded paper tucked into her collar like a message from a secret agent of heartbreak. I was in no way ready to read it, but…

Dear Tucker,

I didn't know how to deliver this apology, so I outsourced it to the only creature in this town more emotionally unavailable than I am.

You asked me why I didn't tell you about the job, and it took me a while to figure it out. It's the same reason I didn't tell you about the pregnancy. Selfishness, plain and simple. I didn't tell you because I believed I was alone—emotionally. I told myself that so many times, my brain took it as fact.

The truth is, you're right, about a lot. A part of me still doesn't believe I deserve to belong: not in this town, not anywhere really, and certainly not with you.

Admitting this is nearly as scary as admitting this one last thing—staying scares me more than leaving ever could.

There. There's my deeply buried, awful, embarrassing truth.

I'm sorry. I never meant to hurt you. You, Tucker Colburn, are the safest place I've ever known.

—Hazel

I stood there, the note trembling in my hand. My vision blurred, just a little, and it took me a second to realize I wasn't blinking.

I sank down to the floor right where I stood, back against the kitchen cabinets. Her Fluffiness crawled into my lap like she knew exactly what I needed and was reserving judgment until I offered snacks.

"Thanks," I muttered, scratching behind her ears. "For being here."

She blinked slowly, then reached over and batted the note with one imperious paw.

I exhaled a shaky laugh. "I've already read it."

She batted it again.

"Fine." I looked down at Hazel's words, reading them again. And again. Like maybe if I memorized every syllable, I could stop my heart from breaking wide open.

But then it hit me.

I'd gotten some hits in of my own.

I should've told her she was safe sooner. That she never had to run again.

That I wasn't going anywhere.

I pressed the paper to my chest and let my head fall back against the cabinet.

For the first time in a long time, I didn't feel numb.

I felt...*everything*.

And I had no idea what to do next. I didn't know if she was gone for good. But if she wasn't—if there was even a sliver of hope—I wasn't done.

If I got another chance, I was going to fight for it.

CHAPTER 34

Hazel

THE PORCH LIGHT WAS on at my dad's. That was my first clue something was off. My dad never left the porch light on, grumbling about the damn electric bill and how if people needed to see in the damn dark, they should just carry a damn flashlight like in the "good old days." And yet there it was, glowing like a beacon calling me home. Like it knew I was raw and rattled enough to actually show up, heartbroken and humiliated and very possibly in stupid, dangerous, soul-rattling love.

I stood there a moment, holding myself upright with sheer willpower and leftover adrenaline. The kind that came from realizing you'd burned down your entire life with one regrettable choice and a hundred smaller cowardly ones.

Two days. That's how long it had been since I'd lit the match.

Almost immediately, I'd gone back to talk to Tucker, but he hadn't been around. He'd gone on shift at the fire station, and I hadn't seen him since. It hurt. We'd been best friends before we'd been anything else, and maybe that was why losing him had felt like losing home.

I worked as much as I could, and when I'd made myself exhausted enough to sleep, I'd crashed in my van.

Not all that long ago, I'd considered it my home.

But after a few weeks at Tucker's—sitting on his kitchen counter while he made me pancakes, watching movies on his couch with me in his lap and Her Fluffiness in mine, making *excellent* use of his big, beautiful bed.

And his shower.

And the beanbag in the tree house….

I sighed at the pleasure the memory brought, then immediately winced, because it was short-lived.

I'd blown all of it to hell.

Now, three days since I'd seen him, after fourteen straight hours at work, I'd gotten into my van, and no matter what radio station I picked, everything that came on was a sad breakup song.

And nothing made me ugly cry faster than a breakup ballad.

The front door opened before I could decide if I was really going in or not. My dad filled the doorway, sleepy-eyed in what looked like a brand-new plaid flannel robe and matching slippers.

He'd never owned a robe or a pair of slippers in his life. This had Sybil written all over it, and I was entirely too wrecked to even crack a smart-ass remark.

Not when he looked so…happy.

His gaze swept over me, taking in the ruined mascara and the trembling hands and the general air of disaster. His brow furrowed. "What's wrong?"

I drew a shaky breath. "I miss Mom." The words broke free like a rip in the hull, immediate and devastating. It made my knees weak, so I collapsed into the porch swing, my shoulders folded inward like I was trying to disappear. "I miss her so much, Dad."

This seemed to crack him wide open. He sat next to me, voice rough. "Oh, Haze. I miss her too. Every day, with every breath."

We sat side by side in silence for a bit, the swing creaking gently in the quiet night.

"You're leaving soon, aren't you?" he eventually said. "It feels like you're thinking about it."

I sniffled. "I would never leave before I know you're going to be okay." I didn't want to leave at all.

What if I let myself believe?

What if I let myself be brave?

What if…what if I told Tucker I loved him?

What if I told him and nothing bad happened?

What if it turned out to be the best thing I'd ever done?

I mean, staying didn't just mean choosing Tucker. It meant choosing *me*. The version of me who didn't flinch, didn't run. The one who faced the fire, literal or otherwise.

Dad had gone still beside me. "You mean…medically?"

I nodded.

"Oh."

There was something in his voice that put me on alert, but I was such a wreck, I couldn't concentrate.

"Something happened, didn't it?" he asked. "Talk to me."

So I did.

I told him everything. About hiding the Seattle job offer. About hurting Tucker with it. How being home still scraped me raw, like I was living inside my own unresolved trauma.

And finally, I told him the big one. "I was pregnant when I left here, Dad. I miscarried."

His face changed, and not just with sorrow. With *recognition*.

"What?" I asked.

He hesitated, then sighed. "I knew about it."

My pulse stumbled. "*How?*"

"Earlier this year, I went looking for scissors. Checked every drawer in the house. I found the sonogram tucked in a book." His face twisted. "I'm not gonna lie. It wrecked me. I mean, I'd kicked you out. I pushed you away from everything you'd ever known. And then I find that…" He drew a deep breath, his eyes suspiciously shiny. "I knew based on our calls and the timeline that you hadn't had a kid, so—" He rubbed at his chest. "Didn't take much deduction."

I stared at him, dread sliding into my heart. "When exactly did you find the sonogram?"

He winced. "Last winter."

"When you had your heart attack?"

His expression gave it away before he could say a word.

My brain emptied of every thought except one. "Dad, tell me you didn't pretend to have a heart attack so I'd come home."

He grimaced. "Would you believe it was a happy coincidence?"

"No. I wouldn't." It felt like the floor gave out under me. Of course, he'd used my love as bait. Of course, he hadn't trusted I might come back on my own. "Did you or did you not have a heart attack?"

"I mean, yes, sort of."

Oh my God. "How do you 'sort of' have a heart attack?"

"It was more like an *impending* myocardial infarction, which they managed to stop with meds and a balloon angioplasty. So I guess, really, it was like a *pre*–heart attack."

"Dad." I stood up, my own heart pounding. "Yes or no only,

please—did you manipulate me into coming home by insinuating your health was on the line?"

He stood too, all pretense dropped. "I was fucking desperate! You wouldn't come, not even to visit. I thought maybe—" He looked away. "Maybe if *you* believed I needed you, you'd come. And maybe you'd…want to stay."

My pulse thumped hard. "You *controlled* me. Just like when I was a kid. Just like you always do."

"That's not what I meant to do. *Fuck.* Why do you always twist everything?" His voice cracked. "I missed you. I wanted you home. Is that a crime?"

"Dad…are you kidding me? You lied to me. You faked a heart attack, you—" I went still, a terrible feeling coming over me. "Wait—did you force the guys to give me those two finish-carpentry contracts? To agree to offer me their future contracts?"

He scoffed. "Have you met a Colburn? No one forces those stubborn bastards into anything."

I was still furious but also so relieved that I nearly sat back down, but…there was something in his eyes. *I missed something.* "You made it happen." I shook my head. "I don't know how, but you got them to fire Ricky so they could hire me."

"Well, it was just sitting right there!" he exclaimed, thrusting out a hand. "It was just too easy. Ricky's a dick and a disaster to boot. He sabotaged himself."

Except…he hadn't. Not this time. "Tell me you didn't steal his trailer and tools."

"I *temporarily* relocated the trailer. And I eventually returned everything."

"Dad! That's not—" I took a step back, stunned. "He got

arrested and was charged with insurance fraud. For attacking me with my own tools!"

His face fell. "I told you him going after you was on me. I should've seen that coming after all that happened."

Chills swept up my arms. He had told me that, the day Ricky had gone after me. I'd chalked it up to emotions from the wild night. But now…

"He's going to do jail time," I whispered. "Again."

Dad's eyes went steely. "He crossed a line when he went after you."

Gutted, I could only stare at him in horror. "You look like a stranger."

"Everything I did was to help you."

"I didn't need help! I was here to help *you*!" I shook my head. "But that was all a lie. Even that day my material drop was wrong—you said that the materials coming were still good stuff, that my craftsmanship would make up the difference. But I never told you what they were replacing. You had no way of knowing— except you did. Because you were the one who changed the order."

He winced. "You did the takeoffs wrong. You chose high-end finishes that would have killed the margin. You're talented, Hazel, but you've still got things to learn."

"If any of that comes out—"

"It won't."

"*If it does*, they'll arrest you."

"For what? Loving my kid?"

"Theft, for starters."

"Well, hopefully you won't rat me out."

I laughed harshly. "Did this all really start with the sonogram?"

"Yes. If you hadn't left, we'd still be a family. I'd be a grandpa."

He shook his head. "I chased you away. You were alone. I could kill Rob for that. I settled for slashing the fancy tires on his precious BMW."

I reeled. "Rob? The neighbor? You think *Rob* got me pregnant?"

He looked confused. "Well, who else?"

"*Not Rob!*"

"Then who?"

Oh, hell no. I wasn't touching that.

He stared at me, realization dawning like a slow-motion freight train. "Hazel. I need you to be straight with me. Was it…a *Colburn*?"

"Dad—"

"Because Caleb and Ryder had left town by then, so that leaves…Tucker." His hands fisted as he bit down on his molars. "I'm going to kill him."

"Dad—"

"I love you, Hazel. I do. But right now I need to be alone." He turned and went into the house.

Maybe that was for the best. I needed to think. I didn't know how to process any of this, but I needed to in order to figure out what to do about it.

My stomach rolled. God. I was going to have to turn in my own dad. The man who'd taught me to build, who still set an extra cup of coffee out even when I wasn't home. My throat burned. But if I didn't stop this now, what was I even doing here?

I'd just gotten to my van when I heard a truck start up. I turned and watched my dad peel out, gravel spinning.

Shit.

So much for processing.

Where would he go? When he was angry, he liked to work, said it calmed him.

The jobsite then.

I hauled ass that way, every nerve in my body buzzing. I was furious. I was gutted. I was all the versions of Hazel I didn't want to be. The one who blew up relationships, who couldn't trust anyone, who *ran*.

Even though I didn't want to be that girl anymore.

I also didn't want to turn my dad in, but I couldn't look the other way on this; I'd never be able to forgive myself. Maybe I could get him to agree to turn himself in. If he was lucky, he might get away with paying restitution instead of jail time.

I could only hope.

Sure enough, his truck was parked out back. I found him in a rear room, staining wood meant for tomorrow's crew. His hands moved in a methodical rhythm—calm on the outside, chaos on the inside.

"I don't want to fight," he said when he saw me.

"Good. Because we don't have time. You broke the law. Ricky got arrested. You have to turn yourself in."

"No one made him attack you."

"Dad."

He met my gaze—really looked—and nodded like he already knew what was coming.

"For what it's worth, I am sorry," he said quietly. "This all got out of control. I was just trying to prove how good you are and build you up. You're so talented, Hazel, but you've never been appreciated in the way you deserve. Do I regret chasing you away all those years ago? Fuck yes. Every single day. Do I regret what I did to get you back here? Not even a little bit. In fact, I'd do it again in a heartbeat."

Had he learned nothing? Heat crawled up the back of my neck. I crossed my arms to keep from flinging a piece of stained oak at his head. "*You'd do it again?*" I repeated, so angry I could hardly come up with the words.

"I was trying to help you—"

I held up a hand. "No. You didn't believe in me. You didn't trust me or my skills, and—" I blew out a breath. "I need more from you if this is ever going to work."

"If what's going to work?"

"Our relationship."

My dad stared at me, stunned. "That's harsh."

"That's truth." I paused. "You do understand, it's not up to you whether it comes out or not, right? The only thing up to you is whether you're going to turn yourself in or force me to do it."

He studied the wood he'd just stained. "If I do…will you stay?"

I looked at the man who'd raised me. Who'd screwed up, sure, but who'd tried—in his own broken, misguided way. Losing my mom had taken a toll, and he'd lost his way.

So had I. But we were still family. I hadn't known it until now, not really. But I truly was done running. I wasn't going anywhere. "I was never going to leave." I just hadn't admitted it yet. I watched the surprise hit him. "I'm staying, Dad. Not just for you. For me. For the version of me who doesn't run. For Tucker too, if he'll still have me—so I'm going to need you to play nice." I paused. "But I'll be here, through whatever comes next."

He swallowed hard. Nodded. "I appreciate that. But if you don't mind, I'd like to be alone now."

I walked out of the job, stopping at my van to take a deep breath and quell the anxiety roiling within me.

This was bad. Really, really bad. But we could survive it.

I reached for the driver's side door—and froze.

I smelled smoke. It was faint, barely there—but sharp enough to make the hair on my arms rise.

CHAPTER 35

Tucker

WAS SLOUCHED AT the island in Kiera's kitchen, nursing a cup of coffee like it had personally betrayed me. The handle dug into my palm, grounding me in the moment even as my thoughts kept trying to escape. I hadn't eaten. I hadn't slept. And clearly I looked like shit, because everyone kept sliding me concerned looks.

Which I ignored.

Kiera's monthly family summit had always been a little chaotic—part therapy session, part tactical command. She lured us here with food, of course, then ambushed us with childcare calendars, birthday assignments, and emotional check-ins disguised as dessert.

Tonight was no exception. Abi and Alex weren't just her responsibility. They were ours too. Her pain was ours. Her joy, ours. Same for the meltdowns. Same for the schedule.

Abi and Alex were currently upstairs sleeping, their sippy cups in formation on the drying rack. The oven smelled like sugar and chocolate. Also, Kiera's kitchen needed to be repainted. These were the inane things I noticed in the silence after we'd finished with business.

It was the kind of silence that thickened like fog—dead still and suffocating. The kind of silence that came when everyone in the room knew you were spiraling and was just waiting for you to bleed out.

My ribs squeezed tighter with every breath.

"Okay," Ryder said into the silence. "I'm just gonna say it—you look like hell."

"Aw, thanks." I added a sarcastic thumbs-up.

"No, I agree," Caleb said, coming around the counter with Kiera's brownies stacked high, all of it so gooey and chocolatey, it probably had a felony record. "You've got that *I'm fine, but my Google search history says otherwise* energy."

I gave him a withering look. "You make that up just for me?"

Caleb opened his mouth, no doubt to say something stupid, but Kiera stepped in front of him, snatched the plate, and pushed it toward me. "Take one. I call them Suck It Up, Buttercup Bars. With double fudge and passive aggression."

"She's got your number," Ryder said, cracking open a soda.

"I've got *all* your numbers," Kiera said sweetly. "And keep it down. Wake the kids, you buy 'em."

Knowing she wasn't kidding, I split one of the bars and gave half to Hank, who sat beside me, munching happily, ignoring the emotional triage around him.

"You ever going to tell us what's going on?" Caleb asked, leaning against the fridge.

"Nope."

"Cool," Ryder said. "Do it anyway."

"He and Hazel got in a…disagreement," Kiera said.

I gave her a sharp look, but this did not shut her up.

She did grimace. "I accidentally spilled one of my secrets. So I made her give me one back." Her voice went quiet. "I didn't mean to then spill her secret, but Tucker showed up and overheard me."

"Overheard what?" Ryder asked.

"She was offered a job in Seattle," I said tightly.

Kiera nodded. "And I wanted her to stay so bad, I didn't stop to think that she needed space to work things out. Or the implications of me telling Tucker before she did."

All three of us stared at her.

"What?" she demanded.

Ryder shook his head. "You're fucking terrifying."

"You're just now noticing?" Kiera sighed. "Look, do I like being bossy and territorial about the people I love? No." She actually looked guilty for a beat. "I'm not proud that I outed Hazel's secret, even if it was accidental. It was a shitty thing for me to do."

I agreed—silently, because I wasn't stupid. Also, because she was already beating herself up.

"So this *disagreement*," Caleb said to me. "Big one?"

Kiera held her hands so far apart, it was like she was describing a shark that ate other sharks for breakfast.

"So just another Tuesday then," Ryder said dryly.

I shot him a glare. "This was different."

"Ah, the old heart-on-the-table, dead-silence-in-return combo. Classic."

That landed way too close to home. The breath I took didn't go all the way in. Over this, I pushed away the plate, shoved Ryder clear of the fridge, and opened it. Pulled out the bottle of vodka

Kiera kept on the top shelf way in the back for emergencies. This seemed to qualify. I took a swig—and choked. "It's water."

"No shit," Kiera said. "You drank all my good stuff last time. I upgraded my deterrent system."

Caleb and Ryder swapped one of their patented Colburn glances—silent, smug, and full of shit.

Caleb said, "You're not going to like this."

"That's literally never stopped you."

He jerked his chin at me. "You and Hazel have been circling each other forever. It's like watching two magnets trying to hump."

"Romantic," Kiera muttered.

"I'm just saying, you're both carrying around enough emotional crap to sink a cruise ship."

Ryder nodded. "And you"—he pointed his brownie at me—"act like showing vulnerability is gonna revoke your man card."

"I do not. And we aren't talking about this."

Too late. He was committed. He leaned in, more serious now. "You never let anyone carry your weight, man. You're the strong one, we get that, but even Atlas had to take a damn knee sometimes."

"And you think that's why she didn't tell me?"

"Maybe she didn't think she could."

I swallowed hard.

Then Kiera chimed in: "Maybe she didn't think she had the room."

All three of us turned to her.

"She didn't tell you about the job offer in Seattle because she was scared. Not of you—of losing something good. Someone good." She paused and met my gaze. "She's used to being the one who's left. Sometimes she leaves first to avoid it happening to her."

My chest tightened. "She believes she isn't worth staying for." Saying it out loud gutted me.

"So maybe this isn't about who's right," Ryder said. "Maybe it's about who's willing to fight for the future instead of the past."

That hit me like a goddamn freight train, and I scrubbed a hand over my face. "I don't know how to fix this."

"Because it's not yours to fix," Kiera said. "But you can show up. You can fight for her. Fight like you're the third monkey on the ramp to Noah's ark and it just started raining."

I huffed a dry laugh.

"You love her," my sister said. "We all know it. But do you show her? Like *really* show her? You're a natural take-charge kind of guy, but not everything needs managing or fixing. Sometimes people just want to be heard."

I was horrified. "I'm not *trying to fix or manage her—*"

Ryder snorted. "Man, you've been managing since you could talk."

"He's not wrong," Caleb said. "One time when you were two, you lined up all our stuffed animals and assigned them chores."

I looked at Hank, who was busy licking chocolate off his fingers, oblivious to the weight pressing down on my chest. Then I looked back at my brothers.

Ryder shrugged. "You risk your life for a living. So why not risk it for love? Or stay the guy who plays it safe."

"I don't play it safe."

"You do with her," he said. "Why not try something new and prove that what you two have is worth staying for?"

In the silence, my phone buzzed loud and urgent. I looked at the message.

"Structure fire. Ridgetop Lane," I read out loud.

My heart stopped. That was the Sonoma project's address. And I had no idea why, but I knew Hazel was there. I called her cell and went straight to voicemail.

I headed to the door. "I think Hazel's there."

Caleb went white. "Go. We'll follow."

I didn't waste my breath answering.

I arrived in hell.

The smoke hit me before I even turned the last bend. Station comms confirmed units were already on the scene. My gear would be there.

Flames clawed at the night sky, swallowing the second floor. Smoke billowed thick and fast, choking out the stars and painting the night in hues of orange and terror. I could already smell it: burning wood, scorched wiring, insulation curling into toxic clouds.

Hazel's van was out front.

So was Bill's truck.

My stomach bottomed out as I ran toward the units already here. "What do we know about who's inside?" I barked at Jayden and yanked on the gear he threw at me.

"Just got here. We saw a female running from the van into the building."

Hazel. *Fuck.* Of course she'd gone back in. She always ran toward the fire, even when she was the one burning.

"There are at least two inside," I said tightly. "Hazel and Bill Pierce."

Cap rounded the side of the truck. "Colburn, you're not on duty."

"Am now."

Jayden backed me up. "This is one of Colburn Restorations' projects. Tucker knows the layout better than anyone here."

Cap, looking like he didn't have time to argue but really wanted to, chose to ignore us. I chose to take that as consent.

"Tessa, Marcus," Cap barked. "Cover the exterior and attic crawl space. Shontz, Harlow—get hoses to the east side. Jayden and Colburn, stay perimeter and prep backup lines."

That was a stall order. I didn't have time for stalls. Once we were clear of Cap, I turned to Jayden. "I'm not waiting on hose backup."

"You're going to get your ass fired."

"I'm going to get her out." I double-checked my SCBA seal, checked Jayden's, and clipped on a second lifeline. "We go in fast but smart."

Jayden gave a grim nod. "Copy that."

We busted through the back door. The heat hit us like a sucker punch. Dry. Choking. Brutal. Visibility was garbage, smoke curling all around us like a living thing, wrapping fingers around our necks, daring us to breathe.

When we hit the stairwell, the building groaned overhead like it was in pain. We used handheld thermal cams and flashlights, their beams cutting through smoke like lightsabers in a burning galaxy.

We didn't find Hazel or Bill on the first floor.

I shoved past a half-collapsed beam. At my back, Jayden

reported in, and the radio crackled in my ear as the others did as well, buying me time.

"Upstairs," I yelled. "Probably third floor."

Jayden looked up the smoke-filled shaft. "You sure?"

On a normal day, I would've found Hazel on the first floor at the back kitchen, where she'd been finishing up the floorboards. She wasn't there, which meant she was most likely with Bill— who'd be on the third floor inspecting the open beams he'd been so intent on busting Hazel's ass over.

"Positive," I said.

Jayden eyed the smoke-laden second-floor stairwell. "Fuck me."

We cleared the stairs, and I led us around a caved-in beam, mentally tracing the blueprints I knew by heart.

We found the third-floor stairwell partially collapsed.

"West staircase is unstable," I heard through the comms.

Cap barked back. "Hold position until roof hoses are in place."

We paused, panting, listening as Tessa yelled into her radio: "Cave-in on west staircase."

We ran for the east side.

"We're at the east staircase," Jayden reported three minutes later. "Advancing to third floor."

"Pull back," Cap said. "The ladder's almost in place; we'll have hoses on the roof in sixty seconds."

All around us we heard the crack and groan of stressed wood, smoke blurring everything.

Jayden looked at me.

I shook my head. "They're up there." I could feel it. "I'm not waiting for that to collapse too."

The radio crackled, and we listened in growing horror at more cave-ins being reported.

"Too unstable," Jayden said, eyeing the fallen beam blocking the stairwell.

"We can move it."

He grabbed my arm. "It could be load bearing—"

"It's not."

Jayden gave me a hard look.

"I know this building," I reminded him. "Inside and out. It's not load bearing, so help me or get out of my way."

"If we don't die," Jayden grumbled, "you owe me big."

Future Tucker's problem.

We braced ourselves, heaving boards aside as smoke belched through the gap. Jayden swore with impressive creativity under his breath but kept going.

Five heart-pounding minutes later, we made it.

And there she was.

Hazel.

Crouched in the far corner, shirt over her filthy and scratched face, wheezing, barely conscious.

"You came," she whispered.

"Always." I dropped to my knees in front of her and cupped her face, tilting it up, needing to see her eyes. Her pupils were blown, her skin pale under soot, but she was here. Alive. "*Always*, Hazel."

"My dad—I tried to get him out." She pointed across what I knew to be a vast room, but visibility was no more than two feet now. "I thought I could do it, but then the beam started to go, and he told me to run…" A sob escaped her, and she sagged into me. "I couldn't get to him."

Jayden was already moving.

"We'll get him." I ran my hands over her, finding a bloody scratch at her hairline and a tremor in her limbs as she wheezed for air. I took a drag off my regulator and gave her my mask. My throat burned like hellfire.

Jayden called out: "Beam pinned him in. He's conscious, but we need more manpower to move the beam."

I wanted to order him to get Hazel out, that I'd work on getting Bill free, but that would've been a wasted breath.

Two firefighters in, two out.

An unbreakable rule.

No exceptions.

We called for backup to get to him ASAP, and I lifted Hazel. This wasn't like her crash into the creek, when she'd been so furious at me, she'd held herself stiff as a board when I'd picked her up. This time she clung to me, fisting my shirt like she never planned to let go again.

Jayden led the way.

Hazel pressed her face into the crook of my neck. "My dad—"

"Another team's on their way, and I'm going back in for him as soon as you're clear."

"No, you don't understand—he didn't mean to start the fire. Not like the other shit he did—" She shifted as if to get down and force me to go back.

I tightened my grip, having no idea what she was talking about, but her words lodged in my chest. Did she mean Bill had accidentally caused this? Or that something bigger was at play? "We'll get him, I promise."

She stared at me. "I'm so sorry, Tucker. About everything. I—"

"Later, Haze." I tucked it away like a match I'd strike later. Right now, there was only getting her out. "We'll have time for all of it later."

"Promise that too."

"I promise."

Behind us, the fire roared louder, swallowing drywall and memories in one greedy gulp. The building grumbled, wood snapping like bones as another crash exploded overhead.

"Run!" Jayden barked, clearing the path.

Our boots thundered over scorched boards, each step a gamble. The hallway pitched sideways beneath us, smoke clawing at our lungs. I held Hazel tighter, imagined I could feel her breath warm and shallow against my throat.

The stairs loomed ahead, steep and sagging, but we didn't hesitate. I hit the first step hard, the next even harder, heart pounding in my ears. Ahead of us, Jayden took them two at a time, clearing a safe path. The banister splintered as I barreled past, heat blasting up from below.

Halfway down, a new spray of water slammed the roof, and steam burst through the cracks in angry hisses. Glowing embers fell around us like furious fireflies, dotting Hazel's hair with ash.

"Almost there," I promised.

The front door was barely hanging on its hinges. Jayden shouldered it open, and we charged outside, smoke trailing us like a ghost with teeth.

The moment our boots hit the wet grass, the roof gave way behind us with a thunderous crack, collapsing in a blaze of sparks that painted the sky orange.

I set Hazel down gently on the grass between the parking lot and the building, gesturing for EMS. Squatting in front of her, I cupped her face again. Her eyes were watery and red, but sharp.

Good.

"Let them look at you," I said. "Get that cut cleaned. I'm going back in for your dad."

Her hand shot out, grabbing my arm with the strength of a superhero as she stared fiercely into my eyes. "Don't you dare not come back. You hear me, Tucker Colburn? You leave me now and I swear I'll haunt your ass."

"You have that backward." I kissed her forehead. "But for future reference, I'll *always* come back for you."

Then I ran like hell, Jayden catching up with me.

"Colburn, Jayden, stand down! That's an order!" Cap's voice cracked over comms. "Colburn—dammit, don't make me write you up posthumously."

But the only thing I could hear was her voice—her pleading voice—and every single time she'd been left behind.

Not this time.

Not by me.

The smoke swallowed us whole, sounding like a future slipping through my fingers if I didn't fight for it.

So I ran with Jayden at my side, boots pounding, smoke howling, carrying Hazel's voice with me like a lifeline.

CHAPTER 36

Hazel

WATCHED TUCKER DISAPPEAR back into the flames as a woman in EMS gear dropped to her knees at my side. I twisted to see past her. Because one second, Tucker had been kissing me through his mask like it was a vow. The next, he was gone, swallowed by smoke and fire and the scream of sirens.

To find my dad…

While I sat here, shaking, covered in soot and crushed under the weight of everything I hadn't said.

The EMT poked and prodded and asked me questions about who I was and how many fingers she was holding. I answered by rote.

When she was certain I didn't seem to be concussed, she pressed gauze to my temple. "Probably feels worse than it actually is, but it wouldn't hurt to go to the hospital—"

"I'm not leaving," I croaked, not taking my eyes off the building—just as two strong arms carefully closed around me from the other side.

Caleb. All heat and muscle, grounding me with the kind of quiet strength only someone who'd known me forever could bring. Then Ryder, who pulled me close with a gentleness that didn't match the fury and concern on his face.

And then a smaller hand slipped into mine—Penny's. Pregnant, radiant, and wearing a face mask to protect her from the polluted air, she looked like a sparkly space alien.

From behind me, another set of arms wrapped around my waist—Emma. I hadn't even heard them arrive, but I was surrounded from all sides.

Held by the people who'd become my family.

The heat from the fire scorched the air, but they anchored the panic clawing up my throat.

"Tucker," I whispered, throat tight. The building was completely engulfed in flames now, shooting high into the night sky. "He went in to find Dad. What if—"

"He knows what he's doing." Ryder tipped my head up to eye the cut on my temple. "Stitches?" he asked the EMT.

"I butterflied it since she refused to go to the hospital."

"Shocking," he muttered, then stood in front of me, eyes fierce. "Haze—"

"I'm not going anywhere. Not until they come out."

Ryder's voice was firm. "He'll come back, Haze. And you know why?"

When I didn't answer, he bent his knees a little to look into my eyes. "Because there's nothing that's going to keep him from you, not this time." He paused. "I know he's got a hard shell, but the way he feels about you—"

My throat burned worse than the smoke. "I know."

"Do you?" he asked almost anxiously. "Do you really?"

I did. For so long, I'd wondered if I was the only one still holding on. If I was the only one who'd never moved on.

But then he'd shown up for me. Over and over. Quietly, constantly.

I could see shadow figures of the firefighters tackling the flames and knew Tucker was inside, putting his life on the line to get my dad out. "Yes," I whispered. "I know. Because I feel the same way."

He let out a long breath and brushed soot from my cheek.

"You can always blame it on the stars," Caleb said.

"Hey." Emma cocked her head at her fiancé. "You saying you only fell for me because of the Legend?"

Caleb grimaced. "No! I didn't mean it like that—"

"Uh-huh."

"Em." He pulled her into him. "I'm so stupid in love with you that I walk around with an even stupider smile on my face, which has nothing to do with the stars and *everything* to do with you. You're it for me."

"Same question for you," Penny said to Ryder.

Ryder, still tense with worry for Tucker, tugged Penny close, giving her a one-armed hug while smoothing his free hand over her belly. "Babe, I fell for you the second I first saw you, way before I saw the stars. And I'll fall again today and tomorrow, and every day after. You're stuck with me for the rest of our lives. And beyond, if I have anything to say about it."

Penny's eyes filled. "Baby hormones," she whispered, fanning her face.

Caleb nudged his shoulder to mine. "You know I was just kidding, right?" he asked seriously. "It's not the stars. It's you. And it's been you ever since you two were teenagers."

Ryder tugged gently on one of my curls. "He's right. Since the moment Tucker realized you were more than just a girl with sawdust in her hair and a wrench in her back pocket, you've been the one."

That hit like a hammer to the chest. I hadn't been just a girl with a wrench in her back pocket. I'd been his. And somewhere along the line, I'd stopped believing I still could be.

Tears stung. "I've made so many mistakes."

"So did this guy," Emma said, hooking a thumb in Caleb's direction. "So did I. So did they." She pointed at Penny and Ryder. "And yet…" She sent Caleb a goofy smile. "I wouldn't trade what I have for anything in the world."

Caleb kissed the top of her head. "The harder you resist, the harder you fall. And when you fall for real, you do really dumb things to protect yourself."

And I had. Over and over. Like leaving without saying goodbye. Like not telling Tucker about the pregnancy. Or the job offer. Like building a thousand defenses around my heart so I could run from love.

But Tucker…he didn't run from anything.

He showed up. Over and over, quietly without fail. He stayed. Even when it hurt him.

I'd spent so much time blaming him for not meeting me that night, for not fighting harder, not realizing he'd been carrying the same shame and hurt that I was.

But he'd never stopped caring. He'd been there for me at my accident. Helped me that night Ricky had come for me. When I was breaking apart and too stubborn to admit it. When I needed a space to breathe, he built it. When I needed air, he gave it. And when I was drowning, he was the one who pulled me out.

When I needed a reason to stay, he was it.

And so much more. Like how he always stood at my side. Letting me work through things on my terms. Staying close but never too close. Holding space without pushing.

And I'd never told him I saw any of that. That I saw *him*.

God, I did see him.

I also loved him.

A shout rang out. I turned, heart stuttering as Tucker and Jayden strode out of the smoke and chaos—carrying my dad between them.

"Dad!"

He waved a hand, coughing. "I'm fine."

Tucker's knees buckled. He sagged forward, and my heart flat-out *snapped*.

I broke from the circle of Caleb's arms and ran to him.

"Tucker." I caught him as he dropped to one knee, my heart falling out of my chest. "*Tucker!*"

"I'm fine," he said hoarsely as EMS swarmed him, pulling off his helmet and gear. I was on my knees beside him, brushing damp hair off his forehead, gripping his gloved hand like it was the only solid thing in the world.

"Probable smoke inhalation," Jayden said, dropping to his knees as well. "He gave his mask to the vic and pulled on his backup, but he was exposed for at least thirty seconds."

Both men were fitted with oxygen masks as I crouched beside Tucker, pressing my forehead to his. "You're okay," I whispered. "You have to be okay."

His eyes locked on mine. Amused. Exhausted. "Are you saying I don't look okay?"

"Hospital now, both of you," Tucker's captain cut in, jogging over. "No arguments. We'll save that for when you're well and I can yell at you both."

"Not arguing," Jayden rasped. "Just breathing."

Tucker looked like he most definitely wanted to argue but had run out of steam. I held on to his hand as long as they let me before they loaded him into the ambulance.

"He'll be okay. It's just protocol," one of the medics assured me.

I nodded and leaned over Tucker. "Don't you dare die, you hear me?"

Definitely amusement in those beautiful hazel eyes, but they were drooping. "Love you, Haze."

I blinked. *Did he really just say—*

I looked up at the EMT, who was grinning. "Maybe he hit his head," she suggested.

I stared down at Tucker, knowing my mouth was agape and I probably had the whites of my eyes showing.

What if, what if, what if…? *What if I let myself believe?*

I gathered all my inner bravery but still closed my eyes to say, "That's convenient, because I love you back. I always have."

At the radio silence, I opened my eyes.

His were closed.

"Tucker?"

They loaded him into the ambulance.

I started to hop in and go with him when a uniformed officer stepped into my path.

He cleared his throat gently, a respectful nod already halfway to a wince. "Ms. Pierce?"

I turned, still dazed. "Yes?"

He looked kind. Tired, but kind. "Your father came to me,

told me about his involvement, and wants to go to the station and make a statement. He's bruised but stable and cooperative, so we're going to take him now. He's asking if you'll come with him."

I stared at him, going from numb to shocked. He'd confessed. The relief nearly buckled me. There'd be restitution. A legal battle. Possibly jail time. But he was alive. And for the first time in a long time, he was willing to face the truth head-on.

I nodded slowly, the weight of the last hour settling onto my shoulders like wet cement.

I turned toward the ambulance. Caleb was climbing in beside Tucker, hand on his foot like he couldn't bear to let go. My chest ached, and a lump formed in my throat.

Tucker had stayed. He'd risked everything. For me.

For us.

And if I was brave enough, maybe, just maybe, I could finally stay too.

But first, this. I nodded to the officer, took a deep breath, and followed him into the night.

CHAPTER 37

Hazel

T WAS THREE IN the morning by the time Dad and I stepped outside the police station into the cold, overlit parking lot. The air was cool and damp, the kind of damp that soaked through your hoodie if you stood still too long.

Dad had answered questions for what seemed like forever, and then possible charges were explained to us: grand theft, false report of a crime, and obstruction and unsafe practices.

All things he was guilty of.

The only thing he hadn't done—on purpose, that is—was start the fire. That was a tragic accident. The oily rags had ignited from the stain, causing a perfect storm of negligence and bad luck.

Dad had offered to pay restitution and do community service. *Even if it takes the rest of my damn life.*

Now, standing in that parking lot, he seemed featherlight, like unburdening had given him back oxygen.

Not me. I felt like I was dragging around a body made of wet sand. I'd planned to go straight to the hospital to sit with Tucker, but scrolling through a myriad of texts from Kiera, I knew he'd been treated and released. "Let's go, Dad. I want to see Tucker—" I turned toward my van and saw him.

Tucker leaned against his truck beneath the harsh glow of a bright light, arms crossed, jaw set. A silent sentinel.

A jolt zipped through me, electric and raw. I stared at him like a starving person at a feast. There was still a smudge of soot on his jaw. A few cuts and bruises. His posture was stiff, like he was trying not to favor one side. Clearly, he'd come straight from the hospital, and my heart gave one solid, painful squeeze. He had to be exhausted. And still, he'd waited for me.

He pushed off the truck and met me halfway, yanking me into his arms. He hadn't just waited for me tonight. He *always* had—through every messy, silent, scared version of me. And now he was here. Again.

He held me tight for a beat, then pulled back and cupped my face, studying the cut on my temple.

"I'm okay," I said, anxiously looking him over. "It's you I'm worried about."

He shook his head. Translation from guy speak to human: *I'm fine.*

He turned to my dad, brows up.

"I'm okay," Dad said, voice scratchy and subdued. His eyes flickered with what felt like shame, and something else—gratitude maybe—flushed his face. I hadn't once thought of the implications as it pertained to his job at Colburn Restorations. Would Ryder fire him?

"You were released," Tucker said.

"Yeah." My dad bobbed his head. "But I could still get jail time."

"He'll have to go before a judge," I said. "But I'm betting with the offer of restitution and community service, he might just get probation."

Dad nodded, and I could see the desperate need to fix this, to make things right, in his gaze.

"Ricky's making a lot of noise," Tucker said. "Even though he has his own legal issues for assault, he could still choose to sue you in civil court—though the attorney thought it was unlikely, since Ricky's on probation and paying restitution to the contractors who sued him in the past."

I was still furious at my dad, but beneath that anger there was love. I didn't want him to go to jail.

Tucker's gaze met mine. "I'll follow you home."

"Did you get in trouble for going back in?" I asked as we reached our vehicles.

Tucker snorted. "Cap said if I ever pull a stunt like that again, he's throwing me into the river. But he was smiling when he said it, so pretty sure he's not going to fire me."

The drive was quiet. Dad didn't say a word as we got out. I heard Tucker park, but he hung back, giving us a moment.

The sky was beginning to soften with the coming dawn, bleeding navy into light blue. Gravel crunched underfoot as we approached the porch.

Dad stopped, turning to me. His face looked older, drawn with regret. "I never meant for anyone to get hurt. Especially you."

"I know. But I'm fine. And still here," I said pointedly.

I knew he wanted to ask how long until I found another reason to go, but he just nodded, then hugged me tight. Fierce. Like he didn't know how to say everything he wanted to say.

When he pulled back, his eyes flicked over my shoulder to where Tucker leaned against his truck, silent. Steady. "Thought you'd blown it with him," he said quietly.

"I did."

"Doesn't look like it took."

"I'm not talking about this to the man who said he'd kill him."

My dad winced and scrubbed a hand down his face. "I overreacted. About a lot of things. Listen…" He sighed. "Tucker's one of the best men I know."

"Whoa. Are you giving me your approval?"

"Like you give a shit about my approval," he said with an eye roll. "But yeah. I am. He just saved both our asses. I'd trust him with my life. And yours."

That's what got me. Of all the things tonight—that. The lump formed fast and thick in my throat. Maybe he'd still have to face a judge, but in that moment, it felt like we were already getting a second chance. "Thanks, Dad."

He hugged me again, warm and solid, and ended it like always with an awkward pat on the back, which made me snort.

Some things never changed. And maybe that was okay.

I waited until Dad let himself in the house before I turned away—and bumped into Tucker, who'd apparently moved like the wind, because I hadn't heard or seen him head toward me.

Without a word, he took me by the hand, steering me away from my van and toward his house.

Around us, the near dawn was quiet except for the distant call of an owl.

And the sheer roar of my thoughts.

Could I make this okay? I didn't know, and that was terrifying.

He opened his front door, and warmth wrapped around me.

The scent of the house was safety and second chances. We walked in, and the floor creaked its greeting.

And I realized the house had changed. I no longer thought of it as our past. We'd made new memories here, painted over the old ones.

"The first shower's yours," Tucker said. "Then get some sleep. We both need rest."

I showered, then went on a hunt for clean clothes as I heard the water running.

Tucker was in the shower, and I absolutely did not picture his miles and miles of lean muscles all wet and soapy.

I found my cookie-covered pajama pants in the dryer, along with yet another of Tucker's massive hoodies. I'd been going for cute and cozy but looked a whole lot more like a lost toddler in Costco.

By now the shower was off, so I headed to Tucker's room.

Early morning light peeked through the window, painting the room in blues and purples.

He wasn't in bed. Nope, he was the tall, quiet, shirtless shadow leaning against the window frame, arms folded, staring out into the predawn like he was trying to find peace in the stars.

"Tucker."

He didn't turn around. He didn't speak.

Heart thudding with nerves, I stepped up behind him. Everything felt a little crooked, a little soft around the edges. Like maybe it wasn't the house that had changed but me.

His window glowed faintly with the purple-pink hue of the morning sky, casting Tucker in silhouette. He stood stone-still, hair damp, wearing a black T-shirt, sleep pants—also black, no cookies—and bare feet.

"You saved me," I whispered.

He didn't turn.

"You said you love me and then almost died."

"I'm too stubborn to die."

A weak laugh escaped me. "You scared me tonight."

"Ditto."

"I love you," I whispered.

He turned slowly to look at me with a stillness that radiated heat.

"And you were right," I went on, swallowing my nerves. "I didn't believe in unconditional love. Not really. But somewhere along the way, it changed. Maybe when you sat beside me in the hospital after my accident. Or when you defended me even when I didn't deserve it. And then you opened up, even after I'd hurt you." I shook my head, marveling. "You haven't stopped believing in me."

He slid a warm palm to my nape, stroking my throat with his thumb. "Never will." His gaze slowly traveled down my body, then stopped at the pajama bottoms, his lips quirking before he met my gaze again, his heated. "You look like an escaped Muppet with a sweet tooth. It's sexy as fuck."

"You have a serious problem."

He smiled. "I know. And her name is Hazel."

I snorted, then went serious. "I never thanked you."

"You don't have—"

"I do," I said. "For going back in. For staying. For not giving up." I had to look away for this. "You didn't give up on me."

"Another thing I'll never do." He set the mug down on the windowsill with a quiet *clink*. "I'd rather cut off a limb." He brushed my hair back from my face, his thumb trailing over my cheekbone. "You're a part of me, Hazel. The best part. I love you more than I thought I ever could love anyone or anything."

His voice was deep and felt like it vibrated into my entire body. Simple, heartfelt words that had my heart cracking wide open and the bones in my knees melting away.

I looked at him, at this man who'd nearly died for me. My voice came out low, barely more than a breath. "Do you regret it? Us?" The question actually escaped before I could catch it. I hadn't even known I was going to ask it.

His expression flickered—pain, maybe—but he closed the distance between us and pulled me into him. I could feel his heat and that steady, undeniable pull I was done fighting.

"I regret every second I wasn't quick enough," he said, finger-tips ghosting over the bandage at my temple.

"The fire wasn't your fault."

He gave a slow shake of his head. "I'm not talking about the fire. I wasn't quick enough all those years ago to make sure you knew what you meant to me. I wasn't quick enough to make sure you knew it this time either—"

"Tucker—"

He put a finger over my lips. "I wanted to go with you that night. I wanted it so bad, it hurt. And yes, I stayed back for Kiera, but I also didn't think I was enough. I didn't think I could be what you needed. I was scared you'd look back in a year and regret me."

I wrapped my arms around his waist and held him close. "I could never regret you."

We sat in the silence for a beat, heavy with everything we hadn't said for over a decade while I worked up the courage to come clean. "I didn't trust you," I said softly. "When I got the

Seattle offer. I didn't tell you because I was afraid you'd step back and let me go without a word."

"Because that's what I did once before."

"That's the past. We were babies." I paused. "Maybe we've grown up enough to get it right this time. To not be scared."

His mouth quirked. "You think so?"

"I do. Because when I watched you run into that fire to save my dad, I knew."

"Knew what?"

Everything inside me shifted. Softened. Realigned. "That I'm not scared anymore."

His hand brushed a loose curl behind my ear. Soft. Intentional. Dangerous in the way only he could be.

The space between us wasn't empty anymore. It was electric.

I'd once waited for him, and he hadn't come. But now…he was the one who waited. Who stayed. Who gave me space not to leave but to choose. "I know you've been the one always holding the line. The protector. But I want to be that for you." I looked deep into his eyes. "I choose you, Tucker Colburn. Every day. Even when you hog the covers and leave your boots in the middle of the room for me to trip over on my way to the bathroom in the middle of the night."

"And you love me," he murmured, sounding marveled.

I smiled through the sting in my eyes. "With every busted piece of me. And you should probably do a full inspection, because there are a lot."

His mouth curved, the storm in his eyes clearing as he stepped into me, brushing a hand down my cheek, his voice thick. "I don't have a history of good things staying good, but this—us—isn't going anywhere. It can't, because my heart beats only if it's holding yours. You're a part of me, Haze, the very *best* part of me, as important and basic as breathing. I feel things for you that I can't even name."

For so long, I'd fortified myself with walls of wit, deflection, and the sharp edges I wielded to protect myself. But those walls crumbled now, coming down piece by piece.

He kissed me, soft and sure, then pulled back, his eyes softening on me as he let his emotions rise to the surface, no longer guarding himself from their weight.

I realized I could do the same. "God, I love you."

"Then it's a good thing I love you too." He kissed me, then nipped at my bottom lip, giving it a little tug. "But you're still banned from flammable materials."

I grinned. "Says the guy who nearly set his turnout pants on fire that time I said I wasn't wearing underwear."

His eyes darkened. "You weren't."

"And whose fault was that?"

He didn't answer. Just backed me to the wall and kissed me like we'd been apart for years.

Which, in a way, we had.

When I could think again, his hands were on my hips, his breath warm at my ear. "Just so we're clear," he whispered, "you're mine now."

"Always have been," I whispered, sliding my hand up his chest. "And you're mine." My heart was full to bursting. "So… what happens next?"

"We stop making this so hard," he said. "You stay here in Star Falls, or you go to Seattle—it doesn't matter, we will make it work."

I paused, thinking of Seattle, of what I'd wanted so badly to outrun. "I want to stay in Star Falls," I said, the truth unfolding as I said it. "I want to work with Colburn Restorations. Get closer to my dad. Be with my friends. Mostly, I want to build something here, with you. I love you. I think I always have."

He kissed me again, and against my lips, he whispered, "We start right now, together. No rearview mirror."

"Yeah?" I asked on a growing smile. "Who's driving?"

He was still laughing when he cupped the back of my neck and kissed me again, slow, reverent, like he was memorizing me cell by cell. We kissed until the hoodie I'd borrowed/stolen was officially optional and sex against the wall became a perfectly reasonable life decision.

Then he pulled back just enough to whisper, "Say it again."

I cupped his stubbly jaw. "I love you."

"Nice," he said, voice husky. "But I meant the part where you're not wearing underwear."

I grinned, and he kissed me again, then pulled back, serious, voice husky. "There's something I didn't get the chance to tell you," he said. "In that fire tonight…" He shook his head. "I realized I no longer wanted to wait."

My heart took off again. "Wait?"

He held my gaze captive. "If I'd known about the pregnancy back then, I would've been there, Hazel. I would've asked you to marry me, and regardless of your answer, I'd have raised our baby with you and never let you feel alone again. I feel the same way now. From the day I met you, my goal was to be yours forever."

He would've stayed. Not out of guilt or duty—but because

he loved me. Even back then, when I hadn't known how to let myself be chosen. He pulled something from his pocket. "I'm not missing another chance." Then he dropped to a knee, that little black box in hand.

I stared at it, then him, my brain short-circuiting. Wait—was he doing what I thought he was doing? "Are you—are you asking me to marry you?"

"Yes."

My breath left my body. Maybe my soul too. "How did you even get a ring so fast?"

"I've had it since that night you left, so it's not going to be all that impressive," he warned. "But say yes, and I'll take you to pick out any ring you want." He flicked the box open, revealing a diamond ring—simple, beautiful, and very me.

I dropped to my knees in front of Tucker, reaching for him with shaking fingers. "I don't need another ring. I just need this one, and you."

"Is that a yes?"

My laugh cracked on a sob as I threw my arms around his neck. "Yes!"

He scooped me up all romantic-like, then tossed me to his bed like I weighed nothing at all. I was still laughing as I bounced, but it caught in my throat when he crawled up my body, looking at me like I was the most important thing in the world to him. And I knew.

We weren't starting over. We were building something from the ashes—something messy and real and ours.

He brushed his mouth over mine, whispering, "Just so we're clear—if you try to run again, I'm bolting myself to your bumper."

I grinned, breath catching. "So…a healthy relationship built on mutual love and mild stalking?"

"Only if it starts right here. Just you and me. And eventually…not even this hoodie."

EPILOGUE

Hazel

STOOD AT THE start of the aisle, heart pounding.

We hadn't sent out invites or booked a venue. We hadn't even told anyone.

The plan was to say our vows quietly, just us, at the riverbank. Right where our whole ridiculous, amazing love story had restarted when I got stung by a wasp, crashed into the river, and fell right back into Tucker Colburn's life.

Full circle. Neat. Simple. Private.

Except nothing in the Colburn orbit stays quiet. Not for long anyway.

Somehow Emma, Penny, and Kiera caught on.

And butted in.

Which meant that within the hour, the entire town had gotten involved. By the time I finished getting ready—simple sundress, hair wrangled into loose waves with a wildflower or three tucked in, thanks to the twins, my bouquet picked from Kiera's garden, also by the twins—the riverbank looked like a low-budget Pinterest wedding planned by a committee of feral woodland creatures.

Folding chairs. Lawn chairs. Coolers. Fairy lights tangled through trees. And one slightly crooked flower arch that looked suspiciously like it'd been liberated from the hardware store's spring display.

Kiera had ordained herself online. The twins clutched handfuls of wildflowers and chucked them like glitter grenades. My dad, at my side, already had tears in his eyes. Hank sat at the front, probably unaware we were getting married but absolutely loving the vibe.

Caleb and Ryder stood behind Tucker beneath the flower arch, which brushed the top of Tucker's head. His hair was still damp—he'd showered and changed at the firehouse locker room not ten minutes ago—and he wore a button-down shirt rolled to the elbows and charcoal pants that fit him like sin.

His expression was calm and steady, like he'd never had a single doubt that we'd end up right here.

And he was all mine.

Emma, Kiera, and Penny walked ahead of me—well, Penny waddled, radiant and due to give birth any second. Abi and Alex hurled petals into the air like they were trying to start a confetti war. Music drifted from someone's Bluetooth speaker—not classical, but Ryder's "Bangers of the Early Aughts" playlist.

The crowd was beaming with excitement. Like they were happy for us, for me. Happy I'd finally stopped running. Happy I'd stayed.

"Ready?" my dad asked, voice thick with emotion.

"So ready." *Happy* didn't begin to describe all I was feeling, but in that moment, all I saw was Tucker. Waiting for me at the other end of the makeshift aisle with that quiet, crooked smile that said I was his favorite part of every day.

Tucker

Music floated from a speaker—Ryder's 2014 playlist, of course. But Hazel was walking toward me, barefoot in the grass with a wild grin that had a grip on my heart. My chest felt too full to hold it all in as she made her way down the aisle on her dad's arm.

And then he was kissing her on the cheek and setting her hand in mine.

We grinned like fools at each other. "You came," I said inanely.

She shrugged. "Heard there'd be cake."

Everyone laughed, and God, I loved her. And I wanted to kiss her. I wanted to do a hell of a lot more than that. I wanted to scoop her up and take her far, far away, where no one could find us for a week.

Make that a month.

Instead, I smiled in marvel that this woman wanted to hitch her life to mine. "You're stunning," I said, voice husky with emotion.

"You too." She went up on her tiptoes to kiss me—

"Don't you dare!" Kiera exclaimed. "I spent all night practicing the right way to do this!" Primly, she opened a little leather notebook. "Dearly beloved," she began, "we are gathered here today to witness what, frankly, most of us have been waiting decades to see. Decades, people."

"So maybe we should get to it," I said, giving her a look.

The ceremony was short and more than a little chaotic, which is to say it was perfect.

"Okay, *now* you may now kiss your bride," Kiera said through tears and a bright smile. "But please don't make it weird. We're all watching."

My brothers looked emotional as well. They wanted this for me, almost as much as I did. We'd all been through so much, and to come out on the other side made me feel grateful beyond words.

We kissed again when the twins demanded an encore.

Hazel was glowing with happiness, somehow still looking like the same girl who'd once talked me into skinny-dipping during a thunderstorm.

I could still hardly believe it, and hell, I didn't deserve it, but I was keeping her all the same. I was so thoroughly hers, I couldn't imagine a life without her.

The music kicked on, and we danced barefoot right there on the grass, wrapped up in each other, with the river whispering behind us and the stars flickering overhead.

Ryder and Penny—her belly like a beach ball between them—danced with us, along with Kiera and Miguel, and Emma and Caleb—whose idea of dancing was swaying his hips with one arm straight up in the air—surrounded by our ridiculous, meddling, wouldn't-change-them-for-the-world people.

Hazel frowned. "Is Caleb having a stroke?"

"That's his idea of dancing."

"More like flailing," Emma said, grinning at Caleb.

"Hey, it's interpretive," Caleb informed us, spinning in a circle, still with that hand in the air like he was swatting bees.

Kiera and Miguel were making out behind a tree, subtlety clearly not part of their skill set.

"Think we could sneak away without anyone noticing?" Hazel asked, waggling her eyebrows.

I kissed her. "Say the word, and I'll follow you anywhere."

"Even into a fire?" she teased, soft against my chest.

"Been there, done that." And thankfully that horrific night was way, way, *way* in our past. Bill had been given leniency, sentenced to community service, though he was still paying restitution, because that would take a while. "*Anywhere,*" I promised, and Hazel now knew I meant that literally.

I scooped her up and threw her over my shoulder, heading up the hill to my truck.

She was squealing with laughter. "*What are you doing?*"

"Guess."

"Hey," Ryder called after us. "That's kidnapping."

"Leave them alone," Penny said, rubbing her belly. "They're in a hurry to get to their private celebration."

"They've been 'celebrating' for months," Caleb said.

"It's true," Penny said, then froze. "Uh-oh."

"Stop," Hazel said. I did.

We both turned to stare at Penny.

"Pen?" Ryder asked, brow furrowed. "You okay—"

"Oh!" She gasped and clutched her belly.

Ryder's eyes bugged out. "Now? It's happening right now?"

Penny straightened and let out a breath. "Sorry, no, it's just heartburn. From the third brownie."

Ryder clasped a hand to his heart. "Okay. Okay. We're okay."

Penny laughed and hugged him. "We're all okay."

"Good," I said. I was still holding Hazel and didn't plan to let go.

"Tucker," she said softly, "I need you to let me down."

"But—"

She made a strangled sort of sound. "Hurry."

Worried at her tone, I immediately complied. "What is it?"

She gripped my arm. "I maybe need to throw up." Letting go of me, she dropped to her knees, pale, so pale that she was almost green.

I crouched before her. "What's wrong? Did you eat three brownies too?"

"No." She inhaled carefully, exhaled even more carefully. "I took a test." She paused. "The kind where you pee on a stick."

Penny, still holding her belly, squealed. "Oh my God! You're pregnant too!"

I…was stunned.

Around me, my brothers whooped, and Penny, Kiera, and Emma—laughing and crying—crowded around me and Hazel, then snatched us into a group hug in the grass.

Hazel is pregnant.

As it sank in, I disentangled my bride from everyone and gently rocked her to me before tilting her face to mine. "We're having a baby?"

"We're having a baby," she whispered, cupping my face. "And yes, I'm just as shocked as you are. I cried for only fifteen minutes and googled it twenty-seven times. I'm not even sure how this happened—" She grinned. "Well, I know how it happened, but I was on the pill—"

"You were also on antibiotics when you caught that nasty cold," Kiera reminded her. "Everyone knows you can't expect your pill to work when you're on antibiotics."

"Not everyone," Hazel said, still staring up at me. "You okay with this?"

I could barely speak. "I'm a whole lot more than okay." I pressed my forehead to hers. "You're astonishing." I smiled. "We're really going to do this."

She grinned. "Yeah, we are."

I kissed her. "I love you, Hazel, so fucking much, it hurts."

"I love you too—"

To our left, Penny gasped and clutched her belly again.

"Okay, no. That's *not* the three brownies," Ryder said, scooping his wife in his arms. "It's labor."

We all raced for our cars to get to the hospital, leaving the town to enjoy our wedding reception without us.

Hazel and I arrived last because I had to stop for Hazel to throw up in a bush.

Twice.

Then, like a miracle, she perked up, got her color back, and grinned at me. "He's already giving us trouble."

I reached over and rubbed her still-flat stomach. "Or she is. We'll arm-wrestle for naming rights." I buckled her in and brushed a kiss to her sweaty temple. "Let's get you checked out while we're there with Penny."

Her gaze softened. "I'm okay." She pressed her hand over mine on her stomach. "We're both okay."

We pulled into the hospital, and I turned to her. "Have I told you that loving you is the easiest thing I've ever done?"

She laughed. "Liar."

I grinned. "Okay, so maybe *easy* isn't quite the right word, but…" I flashed her a smile. "It's the only thing I've ever wanted to do—be with you and have a family."

We'd come so far, and by some miracle, we'd ended up exactly where I'd once been afraid to even hope for.

They say second chances don't come around often.

But maybe they do. Maybe you just have to fight for them.

Love isn't the prize at the end. It's the whole damn story, and we were just getting started. "And if our kid turns out half as stubborn as their mama…" I grinned at her. "We're totally screwed."

ABOUT THE AUTHOR

New York Times and *USA Today* bestselling author Jill Shalvis writes contemporary romance and romantic comedies filled with madcap adventures and shenanigans and sexy times. She's sold over twenty million copies worldwide to date and lives with her family in a small mountain town near Lake Tahoe full of quirky characters. (Any resemblance to the quirky characters in her books is mostly coincidental.)

Website: jillshalvis.com
Facebook: JillShalvis
Instagram: @jillshalvis
TikTok: @jillshalvisbooks

THE COLBURN BROTHERS

Three heart-stopping, sexy romances set in small-town California. The unruly Colburn brothers are getting the one thing they never expected—a happily-ever-after.

From Jill Shalvis, *New York Times* and *USA Today* bestselling author

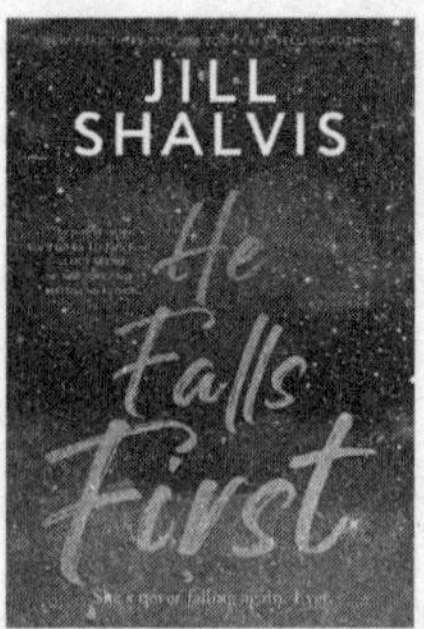

He Falls First

Penelope Rose has had it rough, but she's got a new start, living with her quirky grandmother and tween brother. She has her family, friends, and a good job at a local catering company. Only she doesn't count on enigmatic, sexy local business owner Ryder Colburn, who doesn't want emotional strings either. But something happens every time they encounter each other.

Free Falling

Caleb Colburn and Emma Sumner were fierce college academic rivals. Now they're stuck together and at odds on a renovation project in a remote area of Sonoma County. Each has a lot at stake with this project, and each has sworn off love.

Falling into You

Tucker Colburn and Hazel Pierce are not speaking to each other. Their chemistry? Still sizzling and complicated by a tangled web of secrets, second chances, and unresolved tension. When Hazel is trapped in a fire on her work site, Tucker realizes he can't lose her.

"The perfect escape!"

—Lucy Score, #1 *New York Times* bestselling author

For more info about Sourcebooks's books and authors, visit:

sourcebooks.com